"Josie, I'm thinking that you and I could make a new start together.

"I want to do the very best I can for my family. I want to make up to them for what I've put them through. You're so good with my daughters."

A new start somewhere else? Her mind shot back to those words. "What are you saying?"

"I would be honored if you would marry me and come to Colorado with us," he said.

The night sounds faded into the silent cocoon of her whirling mind and his words took over her thinking. Astonishment stole her breath. Marry him? He'd asked her to marry him?

He was handsome and smart. She'd witnessed his tenderness toward his children, listened to his strong words of love as he preached straight from the Word of God. This imposing and fascinating man sitting on her porch had proposed to her!

Cheryl St.John
and
Elizabeth White

The Preacher's Wife
&
Crescent City Courtship

HARLEQUIN® LOVE INSPIRED®CLASSICS

PIF
Preacher

LOVE INSPIRED BOOKS

Recycling programs
for this product may
not exist in your area.

ISBN-13: 978-1-335-45452-2

The Preacher's Wife & Crescent City Courtship

Copyright © 2019 by Harlequin Books S.A.

The publisher acknowledges the copyright holders
of the individual works as follows:

The Preacher's Wife
Copyright © 2009 by Cheryl Ludwigs

Crescent City Courtship
Copyright © 2009 by Elizabeth White

www.Harlequin.com

Printed in U.S.A.

CONTENTS

THE PREACHER'S WIFE   7
Cheryl St.John

CRESCENT CITY COURTSHIP   249
Elizabeth White

Cheryl St.John's love for reading started as a child. She wrote her own stories, designed covers and stapled them into books. She credits many hours of creating scenarios for her paper dolls and Barbies as the start of her fascination with fictional characters. Cheryl loves hearing from readers. Visit her website at cherylstjohn.net or email her at SaintJohn@aol.com.

Books by Cheryl St.John

Love Inspired Historical

Return to Cowboy Creek

The Rancher Inherits a Family

Cowboy Creek

Want Ad Wedding
Cowboy Creek Christmas
"Mistletoe Reunion"

Irish Brides

The Wedding Journey

The Preacher's Wife
To Be a Mother
"Mountain Rose"
Marrying the Preacher's Daughter
Colorado Courtship
"Winter of Dreams"

Visit the Author Profile page at Harlequin.com.

THE PREACHER'S WIFE

Cheryl St.John

So shall my word be that goeth forth out of my mouth; it shall not return unto me void, but it shall accomplish that which I please, and it shall prosper in the thing whereto I sent it. For ye shall go out with joy, and be led forth with peace: the mountains and the hills shall break forth before you into singing, and all the trees of the field will clap their hands.

—*Isaiah* 55:11–12

With love and appreciation, I dedicate this book
to my mentor, teacher, pastor, prayer partner,
painting buddy and friend, Betty Jo Marples.
Special lady, you give one hundred percent of
yourself to all you do and to everyone who knows
you. Whether I need a listening ear, an advocate or
someone to tell me the straight truth, I can depend on
you. Your example encourages me to look at others
through the eyes of Jesus. You always see the best
in me, believe the best for me and
expect the best from me. Thank you, friend.

Chapter One

Durham, Nebraska, June 1869

Only her husband's physical body lay beneath the lush grass in the fenced-in cemetery behind the tiny white church. His spirit had gone on to be with the Lord, but her mother-in-law insisted that Sunday afternoons were for paying respects to the dead. Josephine Randolph knelt and pulled a fledgling weed from beside the flat piece of granite engraved with her husband's name.

Margaretta slipped a lace-edged hankie from the hidden pocket of her emerald-green dress and dabbed her eyes. "He was too young," she said for the thousandth time. "Too young to lose his life."

Josie nodded. It had been three years, and while she had mourned her husband's death and missed his company, there were no tears left. She had loved him. She had been a good wife. But in his affections she had always taken second place to her mother-in-law. She hastened to remind herself that losing a son or daughter was devastating. Margaretta had lost her only child. Of course the woman was still suffering.

"It would be easier if I could take comfort in the fact that he'd left behind a living legacy."

Knowing and dreading what was coming next, Josie got up and brushed her palms together.

Margaretta sniffed into her hankie. "Your inability to give me a grandchild is almost more than I can bear."

Josie turned her gaze to the countryside, spotted an orange and black butterfly and watched it flutter on the breeze as she steeled herself.

"A child would have been a part of him I could hold on to. If only right now I could be caring for a little boy or girl with Bram's features. I would have so loved to watch him grow. His child would have been such a comfort to me."

Josie wanted to cry, too. She wanted to rail at the woman who made her feel every inch as insignificant as her son had. Didn't Margaretta think a child would have been a comfort to her, as well? Didn't she know that Josie's loneliness was eating her up on the inside? Didn't she think Josie wanted more out of life than... than...*this?*

Momentarily, she closed her eyes against the painfully blue summer sky. She'd never wanted anything more than a family of her own. She'd spent her entire childhood waiting for her circuit-judge father to return home. The times he had, he'd spared her only meager attention before leaving again.

Because Bram Randolph had been a local newspaperman, she'd known he wouldn't be a traveler. She'd married him with the hope of a secure future. Time had proven Bram more concerned with the whims of Margaretta than the needs of his young wife, however. And that was the simple fact.

"You *are* coming to the house for dinner, aren't you?"

And be exposed to yet another opportunity for Margaretta to pursue her weekly harangue about Josie's barrenness? Josie opened her eyes. "I'm fixing a stew for Reverend Martin," she replied matter-of-factly. "I'll stay and keep him company."

"He seems to be recovering well." Margaretta smoothed the fingers of her beaded gloves. "Whatever you're doing must be working."

Josie managed a smile. "God's doing His part, too."

Margaretta gathered the hem of her voluminous skirt and walked across the thick spring grass toward the street.

Josie glanced down and read the headstone again. "Beloved son and husband." Not father. Sometimes she felt so incomplete, so alone. She hadn't given her husband children, and for that glaring inadequacy, Margaretta would never forgive her.

"Have a good afternoon!" she called after the woman.

Margaretta delivered a tepid wave and continued marching toward her home a few blocks away. Josie experienced the same relief she always did when her obligatory mourning session and weekly dressing-down was over. At least she'd had a good reason to forgo lengthening the torment by joining the woman for a meal. Margaretta's house had a cold, depressing atmosphere that matched the woman's attitude.

Josie glanced at the bright blue sky with a longing that was rising up so swift and strong that the ache took her breath away. She'd prayed for contentment, but she needed more than this. When she didn't keep busy enough, she daydreamed of impossible things....

Taking a deep breath, Josie made her way with renewed purpose to the shaded two-story house beside the church. She climbed the back porch steps and let herself in. She'd started a stew earlier, and now checked the savory broth, adding water and salt.

"It's Josie!" she called, removing her bonnet and sweeping along the hallway toward the front of the house.

"Who else would be banging pans in my kitchen?" came the good-natured reply.

She found Reverend Martin in his study, seated where she'd left him, on an overstuffed chair with a plaid wool blanket tucked around his legs. He closed his Bible and removed his spectacles, setting both aside. Last March he'd fallen from the roof of the church while replacing shingles, and had broken several bones, including his collarbone and ribs. A particularly severe break in his leg had become infected, and he'd been bedridden with a fever for weeks. Eventually he'd recovered, and was only now able to move from his bed to the study. The town doctor said it would likely be several more weeks before he'd be strong enough to resume his duties.

She'd always considered him a mentor, but these past weeks had made them friends, as well. "The fire's died down," she said. "I'll get a few logs."

"I can't seem to get warm." He was paler and thinner than before the accident, and the change in such a vital, life-loving man was heartbreaking. The man was probably only in his late thirties, but these past weeks had taken a toll. Josie had dedicated herself to seeing him recover to his former self.

"The stew will warm you from the inside out," she assured him. She took two split logs from the box beside the fireplace and knelt to add them to the fire, then used the poker to adjust the wood until the flames caught and licked up around the sides. The bark snapped in the blaze. Warmth spread from the hearth to where the reverend was sitting.

"That's nice," he said with a grateful smile. "I barely have time to realize a need before you've seen to it."

"It's a privilege to help."

"And a help you are. I don't know what I would do without you."

"God would send someone. But I was available."

He chuckled. "You're a woman of great faith, Josie, but you count yourself a little short."

She seated herself on a nearby ottoman.

"A lot of people are available," he told her. "Few are willing."

She never doubted that God was taking care of the reverend. It was when she thought of her own needs that her confidence got a little shaky. "How about a game of checkers before dinner?" she asked.

He gave her a mock frown and flicked his hand as though shooing away a fly. "Do you think I enjoy your kings chasing my last disk around the board, delaying the inevitable?"

She laughed. "Oh, come now. You win sometimes."

"Only if you feel particularly sorry for me and deliberately pass up chances to jump. We need a new game, one I have a hope of winning."

"Based on chance, rather than skill, Reverend?"

"Didn't I see you and James setting up the board the other evening?"

James, a fatherless lad of about fourteen, came by a few times a week to split wood and perform a few other chores. Josie had quickly sensed that, because his mother worked evenings at the café, James was lonely. She'd offered to teach him the game. "You did. He's fast becoming an apt opponent."

The reverend's enormous calico leaped from its spot on the divan to run through the doorway into the nearest bedroom.

"Must be a caller," the reverend said.

Most everyone knocked at the back door and then walked in, but a rap sounded at the front. Josie and the reverend exchanged a puzzled glance before she got up.

A broad-shouldered man in a brown hat and buckskin jacket stood in the dappled sunlight that filtered through the leaves of the twin maple trees. She had a sudden, swift impression of troubled intensity as his gaze bored into hers.

"Good afternoon, sir," Josie greeted him.

He removed his hat, revealing thick chestnut hair in need of a cut. "Ma'am," he said in greeting. "I'm Samuel Hart. The preacher sent by the First Christian Alliance."

Behind him, three girls of varying ages waited in the street near a dusty team attached to a canvas-covered wagon.

His name registered immediately. "Of course! Come in."

He turned and summoned the girls, the fringe of his jacket swaying as he gestured. The girls she assumed were his daughters were wearing clean but wrinkled clothing, and their hair was neatly tucked beneath stiff-brimmed bonnets.

He handed her his hat, still warm from his head, and she laid it on the hall table before ushering the little troupe into the study. "The interim preacher is here," she said.

Samuel strode forward and shook the elder man's hand. His size and his sun-darkened face and hands made the reverend seem even sicklier in comparison. "Pleased to meet you, sir. These are my daughters. Elisabeth."

Elisabeth was the tallest and oldest, with blue eyes and a full face. Her weary smile was hesitant.

"Abigail." The middle daughter had hair a paler blond than the other two, blue eyes, a narrow face and a prominent chin.

"And Anna." The youngest of the trio possessed wide hazel eyes and a charming smattering of freckles.

A look of confusion wrinkled Reverend Martin's brow. "Josie, didn't the letters say that Samuel was traveling with his wife and family?"

Josie had recalled the same thing. Before she could answer, Samuel Hart said, "My wife died on the way."

The snapping fire was the only sound for a moment.

Anna slipped her hand into Abigail's and the three girls huddled closer, their expressions somber, the pain of their loss evident.

"I'm deeply sorry," Reverend Martin said.

Samuel nodded curtly, the subject apparently closed.

"This is Josephine Randolph." The reverend indicated Josie with a nod. "God sent her to me. She cooks, takes care of the house, does my laundry—she even handled my bills and mail while I was laid up."

"Pleased to make your acquaintance, ma'am."

It was inappropriate that she should notice his well-defined cheekbones or his recently shaved, firm, square chin, but she had. Even his deep, rich voice arrested her attention. But his eyes…she'd never seen so much suffering in a person's eyes, and the sight carved a confusing ache inside her chest.

Samuel turned his gaze to look pointedly at his daughters.

One at a time, they said, "Pleased to meet you."

Glad for the distraction, she said, "You've arrived just in time for dinner. I trust you're hungry. Would you like to help me make biscuits?"

"*I* would," Abigail said with a bright smile.

Watching his daughters' hesitation and discomfort pained Sam. He hoped the pretty young woman's friendly welcome made this day a trifle easier than the rest. The past weeks had been grueling, both physically and emotionally. "All of you will help Mrs. Randolph," he called after them.

Over her shoulder, Anna cast him a wide-eyed glance, her expression so much like his late wife's that it made his breath hitch in his chest.

Reverend Martin indicated the settee. "Have a seat."

Sam brought his attention to their meeting and to the minister for whom he would temporarily be substituting. He was probably about ten years older than Sam.

Taking the offered seat, Sam was glad they'd stopped outside town to wash up and put on clean clothing. The man's home was plain, but tastefully furnished and spotlessly clean.

"I understand you had a setback in your recovery," Sam began.

"I was busted up pretty bad," Henry answered with a nod. "Collarbone was the most painful. Couldn't do anything for myself. My leg was on the mend, but then I got an infection. The doc told me he considered taking it off, but he and Josie came up with a plan for medicine and poultices. The other women took turns staying with her, but she was here day and night through the worst of it. She's a praying woman, that Josie. Has God's ear, too, she does. I can walk on my leg now, but it's almighty weak." He grimaced in exasperation. "Like the rest of me. Kind of lost my gumption."

"That's why the Alliance sent me," Sam assured him. "I'll be here to help you with your duties for the next several weeks."

The First Christian Alliance had offered Sam a church in Colorado. It had always been his dream to travel westward, so he'd leaped at the prospect. At the time, it had seemed like a glorious opportunity. This assignment was a chance he hadn't been willing to miss, so they'd sold their home and packed their belongings.

Meanwhile, they learned of this small congregation in Nebraska that needed someone to fill in while their regular minister recuperated. Sam had set out filled with so much hope and expectancy. He'd embraced the physical challenges of the trip with the enthusiasm of a man running toward his dream. Crossing wide-open country and testing his skills with a wagon and team and rifle was an unparalleled prospect for adventure.

How naive he'd been. He'd walked his unprepared family right into danger, and he'd been unable to protect them.

"I'm sorry about your wife." Henry's tone held sympathy, his kind expression an opening to talk.

Sam hadn't voiced the burden on his heart. He had to be strong and push on. He'd started this, and he couldn't let his children down. He would see this through.

He looked into the other man's eyes and swallowed hard. The weight that had been pressing on Sam's chest sent out a new arrow of pain, and he was weary of holding himself together. "My wife and daughters were thrown from our wagon as we were crossing a river last April. My wife drowned."

My wife drowned. Simple words that didn't begin to explain the ghastly choice he'd been forced to make. It didn't reflect the horror of watching Carrie being washed downstream in a muddy torrent, or of his frantic haste to rescue his daughters and search for his wife.

He couldn't close his eyes at night without remembering the echoing gunfire that had drawn him to where one of the men stood in the shallows. He never woke up without seeing his wife limp and pale, her hair snagged in tree roots. More than anything, he wanted to remember her the way she'd been, but it was her pale, lifeless image that tortured him.

"The wagon righted itself and the team pulled it on across," he said. "Didn't even lose a bag of flour or a wooden bucket." The irony was eating a hole in his gut.

Mrs. Kennedy and another woman had laid out his wife in her finest Sunday dress, a blue one with tiny sprigs of white flowers and lace cuffs. With his heart an aching cavity in his chest, Sam had removed her wedding ring and given it to Elisabeth.

He'd second-guessed himself hundreds of times over the past days and nights, questioned his wisdom in bringing his family west, doubted his choices the day Carrie had died. Elisabeth had been six feet away; Carrie had been twenty or more. He'd shouted for the other men to find Carrie while he rescued his daughters.

What if he'd let the others get the girls and he'd ridden along the bank while he'd still been able to locate her? What if he'd let Abigail cling to that branch until one of the others got to her and had instead taken those precious minutes to find his wife?

The constant examination was pointless. His head told him that regret wouldn't change anything, but the thoughts plagued him all the same. His lofty plans mocked him.

His children were motherless and he was a widower. If he hadn't wanted to come west they would still be living in their comfortable house in Philadelphia. The girls would be in school now and Carrie would be singing as she prepared for their evening meal. He would come home from an ordinary day of planning sermons and kiss her on the cheek. She would smell like fresh-baked bread and lilac water....

The pain was paralyzing. He'd left part of himself behind that day, and he had taken away enough guilt and remorse to sink him the next time he tried to cross a river.

"The next time it rained," he told Henry, "Anna was terrified. Each river we crossed, I had to hold her on the horse with me and wait out her cries, begging me to turn back." His hand trembled visibly as he opened his palm and raked it down his face. "Abigail has nightmares, and she's only ten. Elisabeth is withdrawn. I don't how I'm going to raise them without my wife, and I have no one to blame but myself."

"You didn't kill your wife, Samuel."

He composed himself to say firmly, "It was my choices that took her away from her safe home." His voice shook with anger, and he steadied it by clearing his throat so he could go on. "I've had a lot of time to think back, and I never asked her if she wanted this. She just went along with the move because it was what I wanted. My dream led her to that river and my self-ishness pushed her in. Because of my hasty judgment, she died."

Henry adjusted his weight with a grimace, then asked, "Did you love your wife, Samuel?"

A hoarse declaration burned his throat. "Yes."

"You didn't intentionally put her at risk. Sometimes circumstances are out of our control. You did the best you could. You're answering the call of God on your life, are you not?"

"I thought so. I truly did. But if I am, why did this happen?" Unable to sit, Sam got up, paced to a window and gazed, unseeing. "They dug a hole for her, out there on the prairie. I wrapped her in our wedding quilt. She loved that quilt. And we buried her there, where wagon wheels would roll over and hide the spot."

Henry listened silently.

"We stood there after the others had gone back to their wagons, ready to move on. I was thinking that I hadn't seen it coming. The day had been like any other on the trail. Then Elisabeth looked at me and asked me why God didn't save her mother." He turned to face the reverend. "I didn't have an answer."

"We don't have answers to everything," the other man said.

Sam raised a palm to ask, "But how can I be of use to anyone if I can't help my own daughter? She's thirteen and mature for her age. She needed an answer."

"God doesn't want you to be this hard on yourself," Henry assured him. "You're exhausted and you're grieving. I'm sure First Alliance would understand if you needed some time. You're perfectly welcome to stay here nonetheless."

"No," Sam told him. "I want to work. I need to. I want to plan Sunday sermons and make calls and teach. I need to do it."

If he didn't follow through with his plans, Carrie's death would be for nothing.

Chapter Two

The girls had removed their bonnets, giving Josie an opportunity to admire their neat braids. Elisabeth's hair appeared thick and full; Abigail's was so pale and fine that it shone, while Anna's had darker undertones that complimented her eyes.

"I can't imagine the angels are as pretty as the three of you," she said.

"Father says angels are men," Elisabeth informed her.

"Really? All of them?"

"With names like Michael and Gabriel? Yes, most likely."

"Well, that shoots a hole in all the Christmas pageants, now doesn't it?" Josie replied thoughtfully.

The girls studied her. "What do you mean?" Abigail asked.

"The parts of the angels are always played by little girls," she explained. "'Behold, I bring you good tidings of great joy' and all."

Elisabeth said nothing. Abigail and Anna exchanged a look.

"Why don't you wash your hands at the pump there," Josie suggested, to move past the uncomfortable moment. "You can help me roll and cut the biscuits."

Anna looked up at her through thick lashes.

"And you may be the cutter. I have a tin can that makes perfect circles."

Anna glanced at Elisabeth, who gave her a barely perceptible nod, before taking the can from Josie and watching while she gathered the ingredients.

The simple task was completed quickly, and the biscuits came from the oven uniform and golden-brown. "Let's call your father, shall we? I'll make a tray for Reverend Martin."

After she'd taken the reverend his food, the Harts gathered informally in the roomy kitchen.

"Will you pray over the meal, sir?" she asked Samuel.

He said a brief blessing for their food, thanking God for His provision.

"Help Mrs. Randolph with the dishes," Samuel said after everyone had eaten.

"Please," she said. "Call me Josie. And I can see to the dishes. Let me show you your rooms so you can get settled."

Anna drew a breath in excitement, and she and Abigail looked at each other.

"There's a room for you, Reverend, and one for the girls to share. When we heard you were coming, I set up another narrow bed. Two can sleep on the larger bed and one on the small one."

He glanced at her, and she noticed creases at the corners of his eyes that he'd earned squinting against the sun. "They've been sleeping cramped together on a feather mattress in the wagon. A real bed will be a pleasure we've all nearly forgotten."

She led them upstairs and showed them the two small rooms with sloping ceilings. Anna immediately spread the top half of her body over the larger bed, spreading her arms wide, her cheek pressed against the quilt. She closed her eyes and sighed.

The exhausting effect of their grueling trip couldn't have been plainer. Samuel exuded strength and purpose, but his stance betrayed weariness. The girls' fatigue was evident, as well, and there was an uncertainty in their expressions that saddened her.

She pushed open the wide windows so a breeze could filter through. "The reverend gets chilled easily, so I keep the parlor warm for him. With the shade trees, it cools off quickly up here, if you open the windows on both sides of the house."

"The rooms are nice," Sam assured her. "Thank you."

"This is the parsonage—and the reverend is unmarried, so he doesn't use these rooms. I simply cleaned and aired them out before your arrival. We weren't sure when you'd be here."

"We'll bring in a few of our belongings. Is there a laundry in town?"

"There is, but I'd be glad to take care of it for you."

"You have no idea what you'd be getting yourself into," he replied. "Our clothing hasn't been properly washed since we left Philadelphia. I'd be more comfortable paying someone."

"The laundry is a small building behind the milliner's shop. You can't miss it."

She excused herself and took care of the dishes and the kitchen, then set out kettles, soap and towels. She made sure Reverend Martin had everything he needed for the evening.

"Thank you, Josie," he said as she prepared to leave.

"I'll come make breakfast for our guests in the morning."

"You spend more time here than you do at your own place," he said with an appreciative smile.

"There's not that much for me to do there," she told him. "I'd rather be useful than sit around and do needlepoint."

He shook his head. "You deserve a family, Josie."

"I guess if I was to have one, God would have given one to me by now," she answered matter-of-factly.

She walked the few blocks toward her home, enjoying the setting sun and the pleasant summer scent of freshly cut grass from the lot beside Mrs. Wilbur's property.

The Iverson children, along with a couple other neighborhood youngsters, were playing in the yard beside hers as she passed.

"Gretchen! James! Time to come in!" Alice Iverson called from her front steps. She noticed Josie and waved. "How's the reverend?"

"Doing well," she called back. "And the interim preacher arrived today."

"I'll be looking forward to Sunday." Alice ushered her two up the painted porch stairs, and the neighbor children scampered home.

Josie observed the Iversons' movements through the lace curtains of their well-lit dining room windows for a moment before catching herself staring. She turned away to hurry along her own walk and to climb the wooden stairs to the dark and silent two-story house she had once shared with her husband.

After turning her key in the lock, she paused momentarily before pushing open the door.

You deserve a family, Josie. Reverend Martin's words echoed in her mind like footsteps in a barren house. She'd certainly wanted a family her whole life. She'd thought marrying Bram would fulfill her dream, but it wasn't meant to be.

She entered the waiting silence.

After locking the door behind her, she made her way past the open stairway to the kitchen, where she lit a lamp and put a kettle of water on the stove.

The clock in the parlor chimed the hour and the melodious sound reverberated throughout the rooms. Josie steeped tea and carried a cup with her as she wandered the main floor, ending up in the dining room.

She could probably polish the silver tomorrow. She had invited the ladies to hold their quilting session here later in the week, so she had tablecloths to iron and a luncheon to plan. She stood in the darkened room, sipping from her cup, idly thinking about the menu. Her gaze wandered to the triple windows and the lights on in the house next door.

Her dining room faced the Iversons', and by inching aside the curtain, she could observe the family sitting around the table. Karl Iverson was reading aloud while Alice and the two children sat nearby. Alice held something that looked like an embroidery hoop. Before long, she set down her handiwork, and the four of them bowed their heads.

Josie wished she could hear their prayer. She wondered what their needs were. Perhaps they were all prayers of thanksgiving for their health and family. She let the curtain drop back into place. She had as much to be thankful for as the Iversons. She was healthy. Between inheritances from her father and her late husband, she owned a house, half of a newspaper, and had a generous monthly income. God provided her daily needs plus a whole lot more.

"Thank You, Lord, that You meet all my needs," she said with heartfelt gratitude.

Her thoughts traveled to the Hart family, to those lovely young ladies and the loss and hardships they'd suffered. That day their eyes had spoken of their grief more clearly than any words could have. Reverend Hart possessed a quiet strength. She sensed purpose and dignity in his movements and his words. Something about him kindled suppressed emotions deep inside her. His wife must have been a special person. What a shame those girls wouldn't have their mother as they grew up.

As she rinsed her cup and dried the kettle, she prayed for the Hart family, asking God to comfort them and give them strength and peace.

The house had grown dark, so she lit an oil lamp and carried it to the washroom behind the kitchen, where she bathed and changed into her nightclothes before climbing the stairs to her room.

Since Bram's death, she'd chosen to sleep in a different bedroom than the one she'd shared with him. She'd felt thoroughly alone, and had been compelled to make changes. Margaretta had thrown a conniption when Josie had given all of his belongings to the Lydia Closet at church.

"Bram's barely cold in his grave, and you're erasing him from your life," she'd accused in a hurt tone.

It had been six months after Bram's death, and Josie had been at a place where she needed to do something to move on. She didn't want to grow old and lonely without making an effort to have a fulfilling life. At the time, Josie had known it would be a waste of breath to share her feelings with Margaretta. "I miss him, too, but someone might as well have use of perfectly good clothing," she'd told her.

"You might afford my son the dignity of preserving his memory."

"I've kept his watch and wedding ring and his Bible," she replied. "I have the entire house by which to remember him."

"No doubt you'll change that now, too." The woman had taken several items of clothing from the stacks and turned her back on Josie.

It was *her* house, Josie had thought all along. She could do with it as she pleased. But she liked it fine just the way it was. She'd selected the furnishings and the decor, so of course it suited her.

No, there was only one thing wrong with the house.... Only one thing that she would change if she had the power. It was painfully, glaringly *empty*.

After Sam sorted through the contents of the wagon to find the things his daughters needed for the night, he brought in the copper tub, heated water and sat with

Henry in the parlor while the girls helped each other bathe.

"I'm thinking I need to spend another night with the wagon," he told the other man. "I'm too tired to haul more water for a bath, so I'll get one in town tomorrow."

"You need a solid rest before you push on to Colorado," Henry told him.

Sam agreed with a nod. "I want to hear about your church. About the people. You probably have a list of things you need done. I suppose there are visits to make."

"As one of your first duties, I'd appreciate it if you could call on the Widow Harper. Each spring a few of the men till and plant a garden for her. She's not a sociable woman, doesn't join the other ladies in their activities or come to any gatherings except Sunday-morning service. I think I'm the only one who ever goes to visit her, and it's been a while."

"After my chores in town are accomplished tomorrow, and I've had a bath and haircut, I'll be glad to call on her. Shall I take my daughters with me?"

"You do as you're led," Henry replied. "But if you're concerned they might be underfoot here, don't give it another thought. I won't mind their company. In fact, they might give Josie a break as my companion. She's probably seen enough of this house and my face."

"I'll give them the option," Sam decided. "They have their studies, and I don't want them to have fallen behind in their schooling by the time we reach Colorado."

"They seem like bright young ladies," Henry observed. "I'm sure that won't be a problem."

"Carrie always helped them with their schoolwork." Sam glanced at the dying embers in the fireplace. "I'm seeing now just how much she did." He looked up. "Have you ever lost someone, Reverend?"

"My Rosemary died in childbirth fifteen years ago," Henry replied. "The baby lived only a few hours. A boy, it was. David."

Fifteen years ago, yet sorrow still tinged his voice when he spoke their names. "I'm sorry for your loss."

"Death doesn't take away the impact they made on our lives or their importance to God." Henry waited until Sam met his eyes. "To be gone from here is to be present in glory. It doesn't feel like it now, but I assure you each day will get a little easier. Each week will add more distance from the pain."

Sam trusted the man's wisdom, but he wished there was a more immediate answer. It was up to him to raise three daughters and make up for the loss of their mother.

"I'll see to emptying the tub now and make sure the girls are settled for the night."

Henry got to his feet.

Sam reached out to steady him. "I'll bank the fire. Go on to your bed now."

"You're going to do fine, Sam. Just fine."

Nothing felt as though that would be the case, but Sam had to believe it anyway. Would he always feel as though he was enduring one difficult day after another? He didn't know what to do about it—except pray the reverend was right.

Chapter Three

Josie loved Mondays. On Mondays she had a fresh slate ahead of her, a palette of days that held endless possibilities. A whole new week in which to accomplish as many things as would fit. And this week was even more exciting because there would be tasks aplenty in looking after the interim preacher and his daughters.

She lit the oven, heated water and set full pitchers and towels outside each bedroom door. While coffee boiled, she fried bacon and mixed batter for flapjacks.

When she checked back, Reverend Martin hadn't picked up his water, so she tapped on the door.

"I'm awake, Josie. C'mon in."

He was lying propped on his pillows. "How are you feeling this morning?" she asked.

"Weak as a baby, and tired of it to be sure."

She placed a towel across his lap, prepared his razor and stirred shaving powder into froth with the brush. She handed him the mirror. "I don't mind shaving you."

She'd performed the task many times when he couldn't bear to move.

"I feel like I've taken a step backward."

"Not at all. Your color is good. That wound is healed, and you're eating well. You're just a little tired."

"Hand me the razor, Josie. Your optimism inspires me to push forward."

She handed him the straightedge. "How would you like your eggs?"

"Any way you turn them out will set just fine with me."

"I'll be back for your water. I could send Reverend Hart in to help you dress this morning."

"You're hereby relieved of that task."

As she reached the kitchen, the back door opened, and the man she'd just spoken of entered the house. His clothing was rumpled and dark whiskers shadowed his jaw. He seemed larger than he had the day before, but his direct gaze had the same disturbing effect on her. She stopped in her tracks and pointed to the ceiling. "You— I left water for you upstairs."

"I slept in the wagon. Today I'll store our belongings and bathe in town. I'll sleep upstairs tonight."

"Forgive my rudeness. I was surprised to see you coming in when I hadn't heard you go out."

"You weren't rude, Mrs. Randolph."

She was embarrassed by her reaction at seeing him and spoke too quickly. "Your whereabouts are none of my business, and you certainly don't have to explain yourself."

"May I take water out to the back porch to wash and shave?"

"Certainly. Of course. I wasn't thinking." She lifted a basin from a nail in the pantry and poured warm water into it. "Let me get soap and a towel for you. After you've had your breakfast, would you mind helping Reverend Martin with his clothing?"

"Won't mind a bit." He nodded, took the things she handed him and headed out.

"You certainly made a fool of yourself, Josie," she said in irritation, then turned back to the stove.

A few minutes later, Abigail and Anna arrived wearing clean dresses. Their freshly washed hair was arranged in loose waves down their backs.

"Well, look at the two of you," Josie said, hands on hips and a smile spread across her face. "Aren't you lovely. I've never seen hair so pretty and shiny in all my days." Her own dark hair was wavy and never tended to stay where she pinned it.

Anna beamed.

"Our mama had pretty hair," Abigail told her.

"If you girls take after her, she must have been beautiful."

"She was," Abigail agreed.

"Are you flattering my sisters?" Elisabeth asked.

Josie turned to the oldest Hart sibling now standing in the doorway. "I complimented them. I see you've worn your hair loose today, too. I like the way it shines."

Elisabeth gave Josie an unreadable glance and took a seat at the table.

Josie prepared a tray and carried it in to where Reverend Martin sat propped in bed, clean-shaven.

"Breakfast smells wonderful," he told her.

She rinsed out his shaving supplies in the clean water left in the pitcher, then carried the supplies from the room.

By then, Samuel had returned with the empty enamel basin.

"Looks like there are quite a few towels to launder today," he said, glancing at the basket in the corner. "I can take them when I go into town."

"That's not necessary. I'll do them," she said. "Monday is my usual laundry day. The girls can help."

Elisabeth's eyes widened. "But we're in a town now. You can send them out, can't you?"

"I don't pay for services I can do myself," Josie answered in surprise. Most preachers earned only a modest income. Reverend Martin kept a strict budget. She glanced at Samuel, now regretting she'd spoken so quickly. Perhaps the Harts had family money. She had no business questioning his expenditures.

"My wife took care of the domestic chores," he explained. "But I see no reason why my daughters can't learn a bit of self-sufficiency. They'll need the skills sooner than later." He looked at Elisabeth. "This morning while I'm in town, I want the three of you to take directions from Mrs. Randolph. I'm sure she'll be fair about dividing the duties according to your ages and abilities."

Elisabeth's cheeks darkened and she refused to look up at Josie or her father. "Yes, sir."

"Yes, sir," the other two echoed.

"What can I do, Mrs. Randolph?" Anna asked with bright enthusiasm. "I'm a good helper."

"We'll find you a suitable chore," Josie replied, and then gestured for Samuel to take a seat. "Please."

She served the meal she had prepared, and the reverend said grace before they ate.

Elisabeth didn't speak or raise her gaze the entire time.

"Do any girls or boys live by here?" Anna asked.

"There's a family down two houses," Josie replied. "Susanna Maxwell is probably about your age. How old are you?"

"I'm nine," Anna replied proudly. "Can I see your room?"

Josie glanced up. "I don't live here," she explained. "This is the parsonage. I have my own home a few blocks away."

"Oh." Anna set down her fork. "How come you don't eat with your family?"

Elisabeth finally raised her gaze in interest.

Josie touched her napkin to her lips. "I'm a widow."

Anna glanced from her father to Josie with a puzzled expression. "What does *widow* mean?"

"It means my husband died," Josie replied.

Anna seemed to consider that for a minute. "Are you a widow, Papa?"

He held his mouth in a grim line, but he answered, "'Widower' is the term for a man."

"Why?"

"You've asked enough questions for one meal," he said. "Let Mrs. Randolph finish her breakfast."

"Yes, sir." Anna picked up her fork.

Sam explained that he'd be back that afternoon and what their choices were. "When I return, I'll expect you to have decided whether or not you're coming with me when I go calling."

Anna sat on the edge of her chair and beseeched her

father with eyes open wide. Her eagerness to say something forced Josie to hold back a laugh.

Samuel set down his cup. "What do you want to ask, Anna?"

Her expression showed her relief. "Who's gonna help me with my letters and numbers?"

Elisabeth and Abigail glanced at each other. Apparently their mother had guided their lessons.

"Until we move on to Colorado and get you settled in a school, Elisabeth will help you."

Anna frowned at her older sister. "She doesn't do it the way Mama did."

"Regardless, she will be your helper over the summer. You will answer to me if she reports you've given her any difficulty. Understood?"

His youngest daughter sat back meekly. "Yes, sir."

He strode from the room.

Elisabeth was an efficient yet silent helper. After the meal was cleaned up, Josie got out the washtubs and heated water. She showed the girls how to make proper suds, scrub the towels and sheets on the washboard, then rinse and run them through the wringer. Anna thought the wringer was great fun, though she needed help to turn it as thick material was fed through.

Elisabeth was the tallest as well as the most precise when it came to hanging the laundry to dry, so she helped Josie while Abigail moved the baskets and handed them clothespins. Elisabeth performed the task capably, spacing the garments just so, using the same number of pins for each neatly stretched sheet.

"You do such a perfect job," Josie told her. "I'd never know you hadn't done this a hundred times before."

Without a word, Elisabeth clamped the last wooden pin to the final pillowcase and wiped her hands on the apron Josie had loaned her. Josie knew the girl would have much preferred her father pay to have the task performed, but that wasn't because she was lazy. Her work had proven that.

At noon Josie sliced ham and cheese for sandwiches. Samuel hadn't returned yet, and she invited the girls to eat in the study with the reverend. From the pleased look on his face, their young guests were just the medicine he needed. Several church members had been faithful visitors and he'd even held a Wednesday-evening study at the house the past few weeks, but months of pain and inactivity had grated on the man who was accustomed to being active and independent.

"Maybe there's a skillful checker player in our midst today," Josie suggested.

Reverend Martin's amused gaze shot to hers. "Your implication has been recorded."

Glad to see him in a cheerful mood, she laughed and a discussion of who would play checkers ensued. "Do you like bread pudding?" she finally asked to deter the subject.

"I love it," Abigail replied. "Mama always made lemon sauce."

"I think I'll make a pan. Would you like to help? I'll go home for my cookbook and find a recipe for lemon sauce."

Abigail's face lit up, but her glance edged to her older sister.

"What about going calling with Father?" Elisabeth asked.

"Papa said we could decide," Abigail replied. "I want to stay here and bake."

"Suit yourself. I'm going with Father."

"Can I come to your house with you?" Anna asked.

"I'd love your company," Josie replied. "It's just a short walk."

"Do you have a dog or a cat?"

Josie shook her head.

"I have Daisy," Reverend Martin said. "Silly cat's been hiding since yesterday."

"You have a cat?" Anna asked.

"I'm guessing she's in that bedroom there. She likes to lie on the window seat in the sun. I wouldn't try to catch her. She might scratch you."

A little while later, Anna enjoyed the yards they passed and asked about the neighbors. Once they reached Josie's, she was fascinated by everything in the house, not touching, but commenting and asking questions.

"Did you live here when you were a little girl?" she asked.

"No," Josie answered. "My father traveled a lot, and my mother and I often stayed at my grandmother's."

"How come you don't have any little girls or boys?"

If Josie couldn't answer that for herself, she certainly didn't know how to explain it to a nine-year-old. "I don't know," she replied. "I just don't."

"Do you want a baby?"

Josie appreciated her innocent candor. She stopped in front of the cupboard where she'd gone to find a cook-book and looked down at Anna. "I wanted a baby very much," she said honestly. "But I have friends and tasks to keep me busy, and I think about the good things I do have, rather than what I don't have."

"That's prob'ly good," Anna said convincingly. She watched Josie select a cookbook. "Was it hard to not think about your mama at first? 'Cause I think about my mama a lot, and it makes me sad."

"I still think about her, but now I remember the time we spent together and the things she taught me. I'm still sad that I don't have her, but missing her doesn't hurt like it used to. It's okay to be sad," she assured the child. "We miss the people we love when they're gone."

Anna nodded solemnly.

Josie had the urge to lean down and hug the child, but Anna barely knew her, and Josie didn't want to overstep. "Now let's find a recipe that sounds like your mama's lemon sauce."

Anna smiled, revealing four new front teeth and a side one missing. She was naively honest, charmingly inquisitive and altogether adorable.

After searching and finding what they wanted, they returned to the reverend's with the cookbook. Elisabeth immediately took Anna aside and spoke to her in soft tones Josie couldn't hear.

Elisabeth hadn't warmed to Josie, and it seemed she wasn't comfortable with the fact that Anna had taken to her. Elisabeth got out a slate and chalk and helped Anna with numbers.

Some time later, Josie and Abigail were planning the evening meal when Samuel rode past the house on horseback. He had obviously bathed and shaved, and his neatly trimmed chestnut hair shone in the sunlight.

He wore a new pair of denim trousers, a pale blue shirt and a string tie.

He led the animal into the enclosure and headed toward the house. Josie turned her attention to their list until the pleasing scents of sun-dried clothing and bay rum reached her. Abigail shot across the room to hug him. The holster and revolver still hung at his hip.

He met her gaze, so she asked, "Have you eaten?"

"Haven't had time to think about food, truthfully."

"I'll make you something you can take along."

"That's kind of you. Who's coming with me?"

"Elisabeth," Abigail answered. "I'm going to help Mrs. Randolph make bread pudding. We have a recipe for lemon sauce."

"That's fine." Samuel nodded. "And you'll work on your studies. Run and fetch Elisabeth for me, please. Where's Anna?"

"She found Reverend Martin's cat," Abigail answered on her way toward the hall. "Right now she's watching it sun itself."

One corner of his mouth inched up, and Josie found herself intrigued by the possibility of a smile on his clean-shaven face.

He looked back and found her gaze on him. "Would you prefer I take Anna along, since Elisabeth won't be here to look after her?"

"Anna's no trouble," she replied. "If she wants to stay, I'll keep an eye on her."

"Thank you, Mrs. Randolph."

"Would you mind calling me Josie? When I hear you say Mrs. Randolph I look for my mother-in-law—a fine woman of God," she clarified quickly.

He raised his chin in half a nod.

She sliced bread and made a sandwich that she wrapped and handed to him. "There's a basket of apples just inside the pantry if you'd like to take a couple. You and Elisabeth might get hungry before you return."

He accepted the sandwich and met her gaze. His eyes were the color of glistening sap on a maple tree. The degree of sadness and disillusionment she read in their depths never failed to touch her. She wished she could do something that would remove that look.

"Your kindness is what my daughters need right now, Josie." They were alone in the kitchen, yet he spoke softly as though he didn't want to be overheard. "They've been through a lot." He paused and his throat worked.

His loss was so recent, his pain so fresh. He'd obviously loved his wife very much. Josie didn't presume to know how the man felt, and she knew words wouldn't help right now. She understood and respected his grief.

She found her voice. "They're lovely children, Reverend."

"Every time I look at them, I see how fragile they are. How young and…" Samuel glanced away. "And vulnerable. They're hurting." He drew his gaze back to hers. "Elisabeth is handling it her own way, and I know she's difficult. But…well, thank you for understanding."

"I don't believe in coincidence."

Samuel's eyes showed a spark of interest. "What do you mean?"

Chapter Four

"You're here for a reason," Josie answered. "I'm open to whatever God has planned."

He didn't say anything, but he swallowed hard and nodded.

Elisabeth entered the room, followed by Abigail. Elisabeth paused and glanced from her father to Josie. "I'm going with you." She raised her hem, revealing a pair of trousers under her skirt.

"I figured as much, so I saddled the other horse. Let's grab a couple of apples and head out."

Josie and Abigail followed them onto the back steps and watched as father and daughter mounted their horses.

Abigail waved until they were out of sight. Josie was beginning to wonder if the girl was sorry she hadn't gone along, until Abigail turned wide, eager eyes to her. "Can we start now?"

Josie agreed with a smile and they went back in. Buttering a baking dish, she asked, "Do you like to ride?"

She shook her head. "Not so much. Do you?" Abigail

studied all the ingredients on the table. "What should I do?"

"Tear this bread into little pieces and drop them in the pan," Josie said before answering her other question. "I think I'd like to. I haven't been on a horse since I was small, and my uncle took me."

Abigail picked up the bread. "We only took carriages in Philadelphia. I never rode, till Papa told us we were moving to Colorado. He said we needed to learn, and he taught us."

Josie cracked eggs into a bowl and whipped them with a fork. "I've never been to a city as big as Philadelphia. I've lived here most of my life. What were your favorite things to do back home?"

"I liked school." Abigail layered the bottom of the pan with bits of torn bread. "And parades. And when school was out we took tea in the afternoon, so we still got to see our friends when their mothers brought them or we went to their houses. May I put in the cinnamon?"

"Two teaspoonfuls. That sounds like fun." Josie enjoyed how she and Abigail often held two conversations at once.

"Oh, it was. My Mama has a china tea set with violets painted on the pot and the cups." She paused on the last chunk of bread. "I wonder where it is."

"Your father put your things in storage. I'm sure he was careful to store the tea set where it would be safe."

Abigail dropped in the last piece of bread, measured the cinnamon and then brushed her hands together with a flourish. "Now what?"

"Now we whip the egg mixture, pour it over the top and bake it."

"Was this in the recipe book, too?"

"Actually, no. I just remember how, from seeing my mother do it."

"Maybe we better write it down so I can remember when we get to Colorado. I might wanna make it for my papa."

Josie studied Abigail's serious blue eyes. The afternoon sun streaming through the window caught her pale hair and made it glisten. The girl's foresight touched her. She'd lost her mother, and she needed to cling to familiar things. She needed to feel safe. "That's a very good idea. In fact, I'll make you a little book of all the recipes we use together."

Her expressive face brightened. "You will?"

Josie nodded. Just then, Anna called them to come observe the cat batting at a fly on the windowsill. The child was fascinated by the feline's swift movements, and then grimaced when it caught the insect and ate it. Josie hid her amusement. "I have an idea."

"What is it?" Anna asked.

"I have a tea set. Why don't you and Abigail come home with me for an hour or so, and we'll have tea."

Anna scrambled to her feet. "Do you got any lemon cakes or raisin scones?"

"I don't, but I have some sugar cookies. Those will do, won't they?"

Anna's delighted smile was all the answer required.

The afternoon passed more quickly than any Josie could remember. After they'd had tea and cleaned up, then taken the sheets from the line and folded them, the girls got comfortable on their bed and read while Josie made up the reverend's bed with fresh sheets and put away the towels.

She waited supper until Samuel and Elisabeth arrived. Josie ate in the kitchen with the girls, while Samuel kept Henry company, so they could talk about the calls he'd made. The bread pudding was well received, and Reverend Martin even asked for seconds. She refused offers of help to wash the dishes, and the girls went up to their room to study.

Later, she made coffee and carried a tray to the men and served them.

"Sit with us," Reverend Martin invited. "Unless you have to be going."

She hesitated only momentarily. Evenings were dreadfully long at her house. She jumped at the chance to avoid another one. "I'll get a cup."

Samuel stood until she had poured her coffee and taken a seat. "Your daughters are delightful company," she told him. "I think even Daisy is warming to Anna."

Henry explained how Anna and the feline had held a staring match most of the afternoon. He raised one eyebrow. "Sam said the Widow Harper seemed a trifle standoffish."

Josie knew the woman. Mrs. Harper had been a widow for as long as Josie could remember, though others in town recalled a husband.

"And it seems she's added a chicken to her pets since I was there last," he told her.

"There was a sheep in a pen right beside the front door," Sam said.

"I knew about the lamb," Josie said. "I guess it grew up and was too big for the parlor."

"She's not too keen on people," Henry understated. "Prefers her critters."

"She didn't care much for our visit," Samuel told them. "Feeling was mutual, actually. Elisabeth sat on a footstool with her gaze riveted on that chicken, like it was going to fly up and peck her eyes out at any minute."

Josie fought back a laugh by pursing her lips. Finally, she managed to say, "I would probably have done the same."

Reverend Martin laughed then, a chuckle that started slow and built, until he held his sore ribs and grimaced.

Samuel's cheek creased becomingly in a grin that gradually spread across his face.

Why his crooked smile was of special interest, she couldn't have said, but the sight warmed and lifted Josie's heart.

His laugh, once it erupted, was a deep, resonating sound that Josie felt through the floorboards. She knew instinctively that laughing was something he hadn't done for a long time. She joined their merriment with a burst of laughter.

A shriek came from upstairs, effectively silencing their good humor. The sound came again, followed by a thump on the floor above.

Samuel shot from his chair and Josie followed close behind. He took the stairs two at a time while she gathered her hem and kept a slower pace.

The lamp on the hallway wall led them to the girls' bedroom, and Samuel darted in. Josie found the oil lamp on the bureau and lit it.

She couldn't identify the sobbing, but Abigail's father went unerringly to the larger bed, where the covers were strewn onto the floor and Abigail sat with her arms over her head, white-clad elbows pointed toward the ceiling.

Elisabeth sat up from the narrow bed where she slept alone and blinked sleepily at them.

Anna was on her knees on the mattress beside Abigail, reaching out to stroke her sister's mussed hair.

"It was Mama," Abigail choked out, tears glistening on her cheeks. "Mama was in the water."

Behind her, Anna burst into tears.

Samuel lifted Abigail and she wrapped her arms and legs around his waist and clung to him. He splayed one hand across her back and smoothed her hair with the other, making comforting shushing sounds.

Anna's sobs broke Josie's heart, and the sight of Sam holding Abigail so tenderly stirred feelings from her childhood, reminded her she'd never been held and comforted by her father. She couldn't just stand by and do nothing, so she went to the side of the bed and knelt to touch Anna's arm.

Anna immediately lunged toward her, her weight taking Josie by surprise and nearly toppling her. She regained her balance and sat on the edge of the bed, where Anna nestled right into her lap and tucked her head under her chin. The sweet scent of her hair and her trembling limbs incited all of Josie's nurturing instincts. The girls' heartbreaking sobs brought a lump to her throat and moisture to her eyes. She held Anna securely, rubbing her back and rocking without conscious thought. After a few minutes, Anna's sobs dwindled.

Josie recalled her poignant words about her mother. Her gaze touched on a rag doll lying on the floor, then moved to the narrow bed where Elisabeth had lain back down and was staring at her. Josie stroked Anna's back and gave Elisabeth an encouraging smile. The girl pulled the sheet up around her shoulders and rolled to face the other way.

"It was just a dream, Ab," Samuel said to his daughter. "Just a dream."

"But it was real." Her voice trembled as she explained. "It was just like the day Mama died. I could hear the water...."

At those words, Anna trembled again in Josie's arms. *Oh, Lord, please comfort these children.*

"And I could see her."

"I know," Samuel said. "I know." He lowered her to the bed and perched beside her on the edge opposite where Josie sat holding Anna. In the lantern light, his face was etched with shared suffering. He gathered the bedding and covered Abigail with the sheet. "Dreams do seem very real."

Abigail snuggled into the bedding.

"Remember the psalm we found?" Samuel asked her.

She nodded. "Will you say it, Papa?"

"'When thou liest down, thou shalt not be afraid; yea thou shalt lie down, and thy sleep shall be sweet.'" His voice and those inspired words sent a shiver up Josie's spine.

Sam closed his eyes. "Merciful Lord, give Abigail and Anna and Elisabeth sweet sleep this night."

"Yes, Lord," Abigail said and closed her eyes.

"Yes, Lord," Josie said under her breath.

The remaining tension drained from Anna's frame and she relaxed.

Josie's chest ached with compassion for this man and

his daughters. She admired his love for them, his dedication to their well-being, and was moved by his trust in God to comfort them. They had no idea how blessed they were to have a father who was present in their lives.

Samuel opened his eyes and nodded at Josie. She urged Anna from her lap, and the child slid under the covers to snuggle beside her sister.

"Good night, Mrs. Randolph," Anna whispered. "Thanks for the hugs."

She wanted to cry herself, but instead she gave the child a reassuring smile. "Good night, Anna."

Josie turned out the lamp and followed Samuel into the hallway, where he pulled the door closed and stood in the golden light of the wall lantern. When he met her eyes, she read his anguish.

"I never know what to say," he told her.

"You said exactly the right things," she assured him. "And you're there for them, that's what's important. When they need you, you're there."

"It doesn't seem like enough."

"We're never enough in our own ability," she assured him. "When we acknowledge that is when God works through us. And He worked through you in there."

He turned his face aside, and his voice was thick when he said, "Thank you."

She gathered her hem and moved toward the stairs.

Sam watched her leave, his thoughts a little less confusing than they'd been for some time. He recalled what she'd said about not believing in coincidence. It was no accident that his family was staying in this house. He'd been desperate, thinking he was unable to help his daughters. He'd prayed for guidance, for wisdom, for the weight of the burden to be lifted.

And now, for the first time in months, Sam didn't feel quite so alone.

Josie took the hot iron from the stove and pressed the wrinkles from a pair of plain white pillowcases. The previous evening had been on her mind all morning. A girl as young and sweet as Abigail shouldn't have nightmares. Her terror had stricken fear into Anna, as well. But their anguish was understandable, considering all they'd gone through.

While it was difficult to observe the younger girls' misery, Elisabeth's detachment from the episode was what bothered Josie the most. Elisabeth had watched her sisters until meeting Josie's gaze, and then she'd turned away—as though unwilling to admit any part in it or to show her feelings. Josie folded the pillowcases and glanced over at Abigail, who was sitting at the table reading a book. Anna was probably cat-watching, and unless her father was present, Elisabeth spent most of her time upstairs.

"What are you reading?" Josie asked.

The girl marked her place with an index finger and looked up. "It's a story about a boy growing up on a farm. Farms sound like great fun. Have you ever lived on one?"

"No, but I've visited quite a few. We're in the middle of farm country."

"Maybe we could go see."

"A lot of the members of our congregation are farmers. If you went along with your father when he makes his calls, you'd get to see where they live."

"Really?" Abigail looked excited for a moment, but then her expression changed. "Elisabeth joins Papa when he goes calling. Unless there's school, of course. Do you suppose she saw a farm yesterday?"

Was Abigail feeling unwelcome? "She may have."

Abigail slid a delicate, tatted marker in the shape of a cross between the pages and closed her book. "I'm gonna go ask her." She scampered up the stairs.

A knock sounded on the back door, and Josie set the iron on the stove to see who was calling. Grace Hulbert stood holding what appeared to be a pie covered with a dish towel.

"Come in," Josie greeted her. "The reverend's in the parlor."

"I brought an apple pie for the traveling preacher and his family," Grace told her, peeling back the fabric to reveal a golden-brown crust with a perfectly crimped edge. "Is he here? The preacher man?"

"No, he's out."

"Is it true he's a widower?"

"Sadly so. His wife drowned." Josie took the pie and set it inside the tin-fronted safe.

"They say he wears a holster and a gun about town. Is it so?"

Josie wondered where that question had come from. "I'm certain everyone on their wagon train needed a gun to protect themselves—and to hunt. Is that so unusual?"

"It's unusual for a man of the cloth. Has he shot anyone?"

"I have no idea, Grace. What kind of question is that?"

Grace pinched off her white gloves one finger at a time. "He's the latest bachelor in town, so of course there's speculation."

"Bachelor?" Josie's temperature rose a degree. Grace was a married woman, but she had a daughter who'd been on the shelf since her fiancé ran off six months ago. Josie leveled her gaze on the woman. "Would you like to visit with Reverend Martin? He's in the parlor."

"Oh, no." She had one glove off and stopped removing the other. "I have to run. I just wanted to leave the pie."

"I'll let Reverend Martin know you were here."

Grace headed for the door, but Anna appeared just then. "May I help with the ironing?"

"Is this one of the traveling preacher's daughters?" Grace asked, turning back.

"This is Anna. Anna, Mrs. Hulbert."

"How do you do, Mrs. Hulbert," she said shyly.

"I do quite well, thank you, Anna. It's a pleasure to meet you. You're sure a pretty little thing. Do you take after your father?"

Anna moved to stand beside Josie and seemed disinclined to respond.

"You can sprinkle the sheets to dampen them while I see Mrs. Hulbert out," Josie told her. "Then we'll figure out what to fix for lunch."

Grace didn't give her a chance to move to the door. "I'll be going."

She let herself out and the door clicked shut. Josie stared at it for a moment, absorbing that odd exchange. The women of Durham were looking upon Samuel Hart as a *bachelor?* She tried to shake off the disgust that knowledge made her feel.

Anna was gazing up at her with a curious wrinkle in her brow. "Do I take after my Papa?"

Josie took a sheet from the basket. "Of the three of you, your eyes are most like his. Yours lend themselves to green sometimes, though. Like today, in that pretty green calico dress."

Anna looked down and wrinkled her freckled nose. "This old thing was Abby's."

"You're fortunate to have sisters who wore such nice clothing and took good care of it."

The child cocked her head. "Papa says some little girls don't have nice dresses at all, and they would love to have hand-me-downs."

"Your papa's right."

"He says it's foolish to buy new dresses, when we already have perfectly good ones that fit me soon enough."

Josie understood the practicality of reusing their clothing, but she also knew the pleasure of having a new dress. "Surely you've had a new dress."

"I get one for my birthday every year. And one when school starts. But people saw Abigail wear all these other ones."

"You won't have that problem now, will you?" she asked. "You're meeting all new people, and they won't know someone wore that dress before you."

Anna smiled her charming missing-tooth smile and all was well for the rest of the afternoon.

That evening, Josie prepared their meals and served the reverend and his houseguest in the study. Samuel thanked her, and she met his eyes. Grace Hulbert's brash curiosity came to mind immediately. If Grace could see the pain that Josie read in his eyes, she wouldn't be thinking of him as though he were a prize horse up for sale to the highest bidder.

Josie ate in the kitchen with the girls. They were just finishing when Sam carried in his and the reverend's dishes. "You're an excellent cook, Mrs. Randolph."

She looked over at him with a raised brow.

"I mean Josie. Thank you."

"You're welcome. Mrs. Hulbert brought pie for your family."

He set down the plates. "That was kind. Why don't we have it later this evening? Girls, I'd like you to help Mrs. Randolph with the dishes."

"Shouldn't we work on our studies?" Elisabeth asked.

"Tomorrow's Sunday. Make sure your clothing is ready, and then, after our family time, you may enjoy the evening any way you like."

Elisabeth looked at Josie. "Our Sunday dresses need to be pressed."

"I'll get out the irons for you," Josie answered.

"I don't know how to iron," Elisabeth replied.

"It's not difficult. I'll show you how."

"I know how to sprinkle," Abigail added cheerfully.

Elisabeth cast her father a beseeching look.

"Thank you," he said to Josie. "Elisabeth is a quick learner. And she will help with her sisters' dresses, as well."

Elisabeth's shoulders drooped. "Yes, sir."

"Papa?" Abigail asked. "When you go calling at a farm, can I come with you? Mrs. Randolph said the parishioners are mostly farmers, an' I want to see their animals."

"Of course you may come, Abby."

"Will Elisabeth come that day, too?"

He blinked, but didn't pause in replying, "We'll talk about it. After your dresses are pressed, I'd like the three of you to get your wraps and come for a walk with me."

"At night?" Anna asked.

"Night is when you can see God's heavens most clearly," he replied.

"Yes, sir," they replied one at a time.

Josie kept the stove hot and set two irons on top. Abigail sprinkled their dresses and, using Elisabeth's dress, Josie showed them how to press the collars and sleeves first, then the bodice and lastly the skirts. Elisabeth did an adequate job on her sisters' clothing, and they carried their dresses upstairs and hung them.

The girls came down with capes and bonnets, and the Hart family swept out of doors, leaving the house silent.

Sam held Anna's delicate hand in his, feeling the weighty responsibility of protecting these daughters he loved so well. He'd never felt so inadequate or so incomplete, and he didn't like it. He'd been very careful laying plans for safety and finances, and so far he'd seen most of his puny plans thrown back in his face.

So far, Josie had been the best thing that had happened to them since they'd left home. He didn't want to take advantage of her kindness or overload her with their additional care. Her kindness and selfless generosity was like a healing balm to his conscience, and he hoped her attention would be healing for his daughters, as well.

"While we are guests in the parsonage, I want the

three of you to help as much as you can. Mrs. Randolph already cares for Reverend Martin's needs, and we are an added burden. Your mother and I didn't prepare you for this life. I know that. She took care of you, and things were easy in Philadelphia. I told you it would be an adventure coming west, but I didn't tell you about all the difficulties. On top of everything else, your mother's absence is an exceptional hardship."

"We'll help, Father," Elisabeth assured him.

"We'll do everything we're asked, and make our beds and wash dishes," Abigail agreed.

"I like Mrs. Randolph," Anna said. "She's real nice, and she smells good."

"Mrs. Randolph is a very kind lady," Sam agreed. He appreciated the woman's warm concern and easy affection for his children. Surely the Lord had brought her and his daughters together to ease their way through this life transition.

He considered the possibility that Anna—and perhaps even Abigail—would come to lean on her and then have another heartbreak when they moved on. It could likely happen in the weeks that they would be here.

But an unexplainable assurance convinced him that her attention and warmth were exactly what the girls— all three of them—needed right now. He didn't doubt that God could use Josie to help their family, if she was willing. And she certainly seemed willing.

"I'm going to take care of you," he said with heartfelt conviction. And he would. He was all they had now, and he was going to do everything he could to protect them and see that they had a good life.

Chapter Five

After turning down the reverend's bed, Josie brought him a slice of pie and a cup of coffee. "I guess I'll be going."

"Take your leave if you have something to do, Josie. I'll be fine. Otherwise, sit and have coffee with me."

She didn't need to be asked twice. Josie got herself a cup and settled on a comfortable chair.

"They fill this place with life," Reverend Martin commented, referring to his guests.

Her smile came readily. "That they do."

"That's how I've felt about your being here these last couple of months," he said. "I'd forgotten how nice it is to hear someone in the other room and have conversation at meal time. I've enjoyed having a companion."

"It's been no hardship. I was glad to do it."

"I know you were." He sipped coffee, then set down his cup. "I've been thinking about something, and I just can't get the idea out of my head."

She studied him and waited. He'd lost weight, and the pain had etched a few lines beside his mouth that hadn't been there before. His hair was still dark and his eyes were as kind as ever.

"Maybe this is a poor time to bring this up, but I have to say it. I've enjoyed our time together, Josie. I know taking on another house and caring for me has been a chore for you, but you've never complained. In fact, in most ways, it seems we've gotten along well, even though I'm not at my finest. You've seen the worst of me, and you haven't lit out."

She laughed easily. "You don't have to thank me. Your worst is easily some people's best."

"Well. You've seen who I am. And I've gotten to know you pretty well, too, I think. What I'm trying to say is that…maybe we had this time for a reason."

She studied him curiously.

"I'm not at my best, obviously. But I'm getting there, slowly but surely. I won't be tied down forever. In a few more weeks I'll be back to normal. The Harts will move on, and life will resume as it once was."

Though she didn't want to think of that day, she nodded her agreement. "Yes."

"But we don't have to go back to the way it was. You're a good friend, Josie. I can be a good companion as soon as I can get around. We've both been married before and lost someone, and we can respect that former part of our lives. I wouldn't expect to replace Bram, because I'm not him. But we don't have to be lonely."

Henry Martin's words slowly permeated her thinking, and Josie tried to put them in order in her head. Enjoyable time together. Companionship. Not being lonely. She studied the dancing flames for a moment before casting an incredulous gaze on him. "Are you suggesting what I think you're suggesting?"

"I'm not doing a proper job of it, am I?" He frowned. "When I'm able, I'll get down on one knee   "

"That's not necessary."

"But yes, I'm asking you to marry me. I'm extremely fond of you, Josie. Marry me and come live here with me. Or I'd live in your home if you preferred. As long as we kept each other company…"

Marry him and move him into her house? An image of Margaretta in a disapproving tirade loomed in Josie's mind, and she had to blink away the picture. She gathered her tumbling thoughts. "Reverend—"

"Henry. I'm a few years older than you are, of course, but not that many. Years don't really mean anything."

"I hadn't even thought of that."

"What did you think of?"

"Well…nothing yet. I haven't had time to think."

"Of course you haven't. I just dropped it on you. There's no hurry."

She nodded and rose to stand. She needed to go home.

"Josie."

She looked at him.

He extended a hand.

She took it and held it.

"Think it over," he said softly. "You've been alone for several years. I've been alone for fifteen. We could keep each other company for the rest of our lives and, God willing, that will be a good, long time."

She nodded. "I will. I'll think it over." She released his hand. "Good night. I'll come fix breakfast before church in the morning."

He nodded. "Thank you."

She turned back once to look at him, her thoughts a jumble in her mind. Josie stepped out into the night and walked toward home. It was dark now, and as she passed the Iversons', she could see the family gathered in the parlor. Alice had never bothered closing shades or drapes. Josie's neighbor had nothing to hide.

Marry the reverend? Her thoughts tumbled one over the other.

Alice and Reggie had been married shortly after Josie had married Bram and come to live here. From her next-door vantage point and during occasional visits over the hedge, Josie had witnessed the arrival of Alice's children, seen guests coming and going for family holidays and birthdays and admired the natural flow of their lives. From her viewpoint, it was all quite imposing and foreign.

She'd pretty much resigned herself to being alone, and had found activities to keep her busy. She'd taken on volunteer work to make herself feel useful.

Josie unlocked her door and stepped into the echoing silence of her house. Closing her eyes, she leaned back against the door. No voices here. Nothing of importance for which to set aside chores. No scuffed floors or tangle of sweaters and shoes. No reason not to stay up reading half the night.

Josie didn't feel like stoking and lighting the stove just for a single cup of tea, so the coffee she'd shared with the reverend would suffice.

The reverend. She struggled to think of him as *Henry.* Using his first name seemed disrespectful. Definitely awkward.

If she married him, her motivation wouldn't be for a grand love. She would be striving for companionship. He'd said it as plainly as that, although he had mentioned he'd grown fond of her. Ignoring for a moment the reaction of her mother-in-law, she let herself imagine him living here with her. She would have someone to share her meals and someone to share the fire of an evening. Guests would drop by. Josie pictured ushering them in and pouring them tea and serving cookies and slices of pie.

An uncertain smile curved her lips upward.

Perhaps the reverend would continue to hold his Wednesday-evening Bible studies. She could make an adequate place for the participants in the drawing room.

After lighting the lamp in her room, she undressed and used tepid water to wash before slipping on her nightclothes. It was a warm evening, so Josie opened her bedroom window, welcoming the breeze. She was wide-awake.

Running her fingers over the spines of the books on her bureau, she selected one and made herself comfortable in her padded rocking chair.

She had read the first page at least half a dozen times, without remembering the words, before she closed the book and turned down the wick so the room was thrust into darkness.

Padding to the window, she held aside the curtain and studied the sky. *Lord, help me know the right thing to do,* she prayed. The words to a hymn came to mind, and she sang them softly. *Leave to thy God to order and provide; in every change He faithful will remain.* Her stomach felt funny when she thought of marrying Reverend Martin. Was that a good sign or a bad one? He hadn't been in a rush for her answer, and she was relieved about that.

He was a kind man. Attentive. He engaged her in conversation and was interested in her thoughts and opinions. Perhaps it was irreverent to compare him to her late husband, but she couldn't help the thoughts. Bram had cared more that she was listening to his instructions and plans than for what she had to say. She'd never felt that she was a priority in his life. Well, in all truth, she hadn't been.

But she didn't need all that much attention. Memories of her father surfaced, reminding her of a childhood spent feeling unimportant. He'd traveled during all of her growing-up years, stopping home only briefly every few months, and even at those times he'd caught up on business, entertained friends, scarcely paying her a moment's notice before he was gone again.

And then her marriage expectations had been too high. She'd believed a wife held value and significance, but though Bram was present, he'd closed her out. Especially after she hadn't given him children. A wife who was unable to give a man children held even less value, apparently.

Henry Martin didn't need or want children. He wanted companionship. He enjoyed her company. And she considered him a teacher and a friend. Could a marriage like that be satisfying? She suspected it could. Having someone who listened and valued her presence would be a far cry better than her current situation. Better than nothing and no one. The thought lifted her spirits. Already, the decision didn't seem all that difficult.

* * *

Sam appreciated the tidy little room Josie had assigned him. He woke up a couple of times the first night, thinking he was still sleeping under the wagon. Then the dark and quiet room came into focus, and he remembered where he was.

He'd stayed up late, going over his notes, reading his Bible and praying. He asked God to help him fix his mind on heavenly things and plant his feet on the promises. He didn't doubt God's love or faithfulness. If for a moment he felt that he couldn't preach with heartfelt conviction, he would have resigned then and there. But it wasn't God he doubted; it was himself.

He had to find a way to help his daughters. If he couldn't lead his own sheep, how could he hope to counsel and guide an entire flock? The message he prepared was from First Corinthians, one of his favorite chapters, and he wanted to share what those verses about love meant to him.

On Sunday morning the little church filled to capacity with townspeople and farm families eager to shake his hand and introduce themselves. They'd been without a normal service for months, and this was an occasion to worship and socialize. He took particular comfort in reminding the people of Durham that God is love, and that He's not keeping track of sins or mistakes.

One of the ladies had organized a simple meal afterward, with sliced meat and cheese for sandwiches and a selection of pies and cakes. Sam barely glimpsed the food before members of the congregation sought him out and greeted him, one or two at a time.

He enjoyed meeting all of them, from the youngest

to the oldest. After introducing his girls several times, he quietly suggested they go make their own plates and eat without him. Elisabeth obediently took Anna's hand and led both of her sisters toward the tables.

Glancing away from Mrs. Swanson, who prattled on about her cousin who was coming to visit soon, Sam spotted Josie making a sandwich. She cut a slice of pie and carried the plate toward the parsonage. Reverend Martin was a blessed man to have her looking out for him. Out of nowhere came the question of why she'd never remarried, why no man had snapped her up.

She would make a fine wife. A good companion.

"Max Wilbur," a lanky fellow with a yellowed mustache said by way of introduction. "Fine sermon this mornin'. So you're headed for Colorado."

Sam shook the man's hand. "In a few weeks, yes. I've been assigned a church there."

"Ever seen the Rockies?"

"I have not."

"Wild, beautiful country," Max said, and told Sam about his early prospecting days.

"We're so pleased you're here," a stout, dark-haired woman said, coming up beside Max. She held out a gloved hand. "Grace Hulbert, and this is my daughter, Becka."

In turn, Sam took both the hands offered.

"Becka plays the piano," Grace told him. "And she has a very pleasant singing voice."

The young woman was tall and slender, with a long neck and cinnamon-colored red hair. Without meeting Sam's eyes, she smiled bashfully and blushed a color that nearly matched her hair.

"She's a good seamstress and knows how to put up vegetables and preserves. She made the peach pie. Make sure you try a slice."

"She must be your right hand," Sam said. His stomach growled, and he inched toward the food table. Ladies smiled and served him. Finally holding a full plate, he stabbed a slice of pickled beet and raised his fork.

"There you are, Reverend!"

He turned to greet yet another parishioner.

After taking Reverend Martin his meal, Josie returned to spot a throng of women surrounding Samuel Hart. He held a full plate and nodded with seeming interest as they chattered and boasted of their daughters.

His own three daughters were perched on a bench in the shade of the church, where they'd been enjoying their meal. She prepared herself a plate and joined them. "Looks like everyone wants to talk to your father."

Munching a cookie, Anna swung feet clad in freshly polished black leather shoes. She spared a grin for Josie.

"We're going to a farm later today," Abigail told her.

"Won't that be an adventure?" Josie replied and bit into her chicken leg.

"Want to come?" Abigail asked.

"Mrs. Randolph wasn't invited," Elisabeth pointed out.

"I just did so invite her," Abigail argued.

"By *Father*," the older girl clarified.

"Oh. Well, he won't care," Abigail said.

"I don't need to come along," Josie told them. "But thanks for thinking of me."

The crowd around their father still hadn't thinned.

"I want a lamb," Anna announced.

"We can't have an animal," Elisabeth told her. "We don't even have a home yet. And how would we get it all the way from here to Colorado?"

"It could ride with me."

"Lambs get big and they smell," Elisabeth pointed out. "Father and I saw one at a lady's house, and it was shaggy and dirty."

"My lamb wouldn't smell. I'd give it baffs."

Elisabeth rolled her eyes, picked up her bread and bit into it.

It wasn't long before Josie realized that every mother of a marriage-aged daughter had approached Samuel, and the interruptions were preventing him from eating.

"Do any of you want a slice of pie?" she asked.

"I do," Anna piped up. "Apple, please!"

"I'll be right back." Josie moseyed toward the pie table and placed a slice of pie on a small plate. She interrupted Nettie Boardman as she talked to Samuel about her daughter, the new schoolteacher. "Excuse me, Reverend, but Anna asked for this."

She pushed the plate into Samuel's other hand and pointed toward his daughters.

He blinked in puzzlement, but then his eyes revealed dawning appreciation of her rescue mission. "Thanks, Mrs. Randolph." He turned to Nettie. "Excuse me, ma'am. It's been a pleasure."

Nettie and Josie watched him join his daughters.

"He speaks with such fervor," Nettie said. "His sermon was positively inspired, wasn't it? How long do you suppose he'll be here?"

"Just until Reverend Martin is on his feet again."

"Maybe he'll decide to stay. Maybe he'll meet some-one...you know."

Josie picked up on the woman's interest and tried not to show her irritation. "The man just lost his wife. He's determined to go on to his destination."

"Well, plans change." Nettie waved a hand dismis-sively and turned away.

Josie returned to the Harts, where Sam had seated himself on the grass and dug into his food. He glanced up as she resumed her seat beside Anna. "Thanks."

"You were looking a mite faint there. I thought you needed nourishment."

He grinned. "And air."

Josie returned his smile.

Elisabeth glanced from her father to Josie and back again.

"I think I've met nearly everyone," he said.

She wanted to add "and their daughters," but said, "So it would seem."

Gretchen Iverson ran over to where they sat. "Hello, Mrs. Randolph."

Josie made introductions. "Anna asked me about nearby children. I think you're right between Anna and Abigail's ages."

"Wanna come play?" Gretchen asked.

Anna jumped right up, and Abigail joined her more slowly. After a brief conversation, they ran toward a gathering of young females jumping rope.

Elisabeth watched them go and then turned her gaze on her father.

"This is what they need," he said. "It's good for them to resume normal activities and be with other children."

Josie wondered if being around people and using his gifts was something he needed, as well. She'd appreciated his heartfelt words that morning. He had a resonating voice and a sincerity that one couldn't help but recognize. God's wisdom was evident in calling this man to the ministry.

At the sound of stiff skirts swishing through the grass, they turned their attention to Margaretta's approach.

Chapter Six

She wore a black gabardine dress and a pinched expression.

"Reverend Hart, this is my mother-in-law, Margaretta Randolph."

Sam stood and brushed crumbs from his trousers. "Mrs. Randolph. It's a pleasure to meet you."

"Likewise," she replied without much fervor.

"This is Sam's oldest daughter, Elisabeth," Josie added.

The woman raised her eyebrows at the introduction, but barely nodded. "Are you ready to visit my son?"

"I'll walk back there with you." Josie spoke to Sam then. "We visit the cemetery on Sunday afternoons."

Sam nodded politely, and she followed Margaretta. Seeing the woman reminded her of the decision she had to make regarding Reverend Martin's proposal.

As strongly as the woman felt about giving away Bram's clothing and visiting his grave, Josie sensed that an announcement of a new marriage wouldn't be received well. She couldn't let disapproval make up her mind for her, but she wished she had someone with whom to discuss the possibilities.

They entered the well-tended cemetery through the white picket gate in the fence and crossed the lush cropped grass, picking their way around small headstones.

Margaretta stopped at Bram's grave and pulled her hankie from her pocket. Cue the tears, Josie thought.

"Margaretta, I'd like to talk to you."

The woman sniffled. How could she still call up tears after all this time? "Bram left you plenty of money," she said.

Josie stiffened with hurt. "So did my father. It's not about money."

"What do you want?"

"When have I ever asked you for anything? You're the closest thing I have to family. I thought we could talk." She glanced away. The afternoon was stretching out clear and fair. Back by the church, people were packing up and heading home. "I'm still a young woman," she began. "I'm lonely."

"We all have our crosses to bear," Margaretta replied.

Josie lowered her attention to study the familiar words on the headstone. *Beloved son and husband.* Even in death, her mother-in-law came before her. Josie's gaze drifted beyond the cemetery to the fluffy white clouds in the sky and the tops of the leafy oak trees along the stream. The sounds of children's laughter rang out.

"Don't do anything to embarrass me in this town."

Margaretta spoke the words like a warning, effectively pointing out Josie's foolishness in thinking the woman would suddenly feel a measure of compassion toward her son's widow. Why was Margaretta compelled to issue such an admonition? What did she imagine Josie would do to embarrass her?

Josie tucked away her longings and refused to take offense. "I'd better go help clean up."

She started toward the gate.

"Is that all you had to say?" Margaretta asked. "You're lonely?"

"No, I'm fine, actually." Josie held her skirt with the hem above her shoes so she could walk through the grass quickly. "I've never been better."

Escaping, she calmed herself with a few deep breaths and a silent prayer for peace in her heart.

Darting through the long grasses, Anna scurried across her path with a wave and ran down the hill to join her friends. Anna must have mentioned inviting Josie along to her father, because Sam found Josie as soon as she returned. "You're welcome to come with us this afternoon."

"Thank you," she replied, prepared to decline the offer. But something made her turn and look at the woman still at the cemetery. An afternoon spent with the children would be an extraordinary distraction from her usual depressing routine. "The change of scenery will do me good. Where are you heading?"

"Henry asked me to visit the Dunlops. Seems the mister hasn't been to church for a while."

"That would be Ned. Eva and the children come pretty regularly."

The girls changed from their Sunday dresses while Josie went home and did the same. Sam simply removed his jacket, but wore his white shirt and tie. He settled a dun-colored hat on his head.

Josie hadn't been for a carriage ride in a long time. She sat on the front seat, with Anna between her and the preacher. Her straw hat shaded her eyes from the glare of the sun. Birds flew up from the brush. Deer mice and ground squirrels scampered across their path. Sam pointed out a pair of mule deer standing motionless on a ridge, as the land sloped downward and they approached a bridge.

For a moment, she had the illusion of what it might feel like to be part of a family, to have a kind and caring man as a husband. It was the kind of unrealistic daydream she tried not to entertain.

Anna grabbed her father's arm and spoke in a breathless panic, "Go back, Papa!"

Puzzled at the girl's sudden alarm, Josie shot her a glance.

"We've a lot more bridges to cross before we reach Colorado," Samuel replied. He set his mouth in a grim line.

"Please!" Anna begged and burst into tears. "Please go back! I want down now. Let me down!" She attempted to stand, but he restrained her with the back of his arm across her chest. She plopped back onto the seat, her distress real and her expression one of panic.

Confused, Josie looked from Anna to her father. He had his eyes on the road and the bridge ahead. "What's wrong, Anna?"

"Tell Papa to turn back! I don't want to go anymore." She burst into tears.

The sound of water running over stones reached Josie

then, revealing the reason for Anna's distress. The water. Her mother had drowned crossing a river. The poor child was terrified.

"Come here," she said calmly, and wrapped her arm around Anna's quaking shoulders. "The bridge is perfectly safe. Half a dozen families crossed it on their way to church and home again just today."

Sobbing, Anna buried her face against Josie, and Josie held her as tightly as she could, covering her ears. A glance over her shoulder told her the other girls were white-lipped and distressed, as well, whether from the sound of the water or their sister's wailing, she couldn't be sure.

Anna's delicate body trembled, and her vulnerability sent empathy and concern spiraling straight to Josie's heart. Hot tears burned her eyes. "It's going to be all right now," she promised her. "We're almost there."

The carriage rattled the weathered boards as they crossed the river, and Anna trembled so violently, her teeth chattered. Josie cast a glance at Samuel. He was as tight-lipped as his daughters, though he wore determination like a shield.

Josie blinked away stinging tears. Anna's fear and the whole family's grief were so real to her at that moment that she felt their sorrow and anguish all the way to her bones.

The rattling stopped as they reached the ground on the other side. Josie loosened her tight hold and rubbed Anna's shoulder comfortingly. Eventually, the rushing sound of water faded into the distance and the only noise was the jingle of traces, the plodding of the horses and Anna's occasional sniff.

The child lowered her head to Josie's lap and lay with her eyes closed. Josie smoothed her hair away from her clammy face.

Josie wished she knew what to say to comfort this family. Finding no words, she silently prayed for the Lord to do it with His infinite love and mercy. The Harts deserved peace.

A few miles later, Josie broke the silence. "Oh, my goodness. I do believe those are real, live milk cows."

"Where?" Anna sat up and searched the landscape, spotting the brown and white cattle in a pasture. "I see 'em!"

The Dunlops' fields stretched on either side of the road, row after row of young corn and flourishing hay meadows. Chickens squawked and ran in a dozen directions when Sam pulled the carriage into the dooryard.

"Look at all them chickens," Anna cried, pointing.

"*Those* chickens," her father corrected.

He climbed down and assisted Anna, followed by her sisters, while on the other side, Josie used the step and hopped to the ground without help.

When he looked at her, Sam's expression conveyed his frustration and helplessness. She accepted his silent nod as approval for comforting his daughter. Josie gave him a hesitant smile.

Eva Dunlop came out of the small, square house, wiping her hands on her plain white apron.

"Mrs. Randolph, what a pleasure," she said with a warm smile. "Reverend Hart, I'm honored that you've called today. I can make fresh coffee."

"No call for that, ma'am. I was hoping to speak with your husband."

"He's in the barn."

Sam touched the brim of his hat with a courteous nod.

Elisabeth stepped up behind her father, but he stopped and turned to her. "Join the ladies this time."

She watched him walk away, her expression unreadable.

"Come on in," Eva said, gesturing to Josie and the girls. The Hart daughters followed the two women into the house.

The kitchen was tiny, with a well-worn table and four chairs. Rachel, who was about Elisabeth's age, turned from where she'd been kneading bread and studied the visitors. The girls stood waiting.

"Let's sit out of doors," Josie suggested. "It's too nice a day to waste inside, and you have a fine shade tree out there."

Sam introduced himself to Ned Dunlop. "I'm the interim preacher."

The man squinted through the rivulet of sweat that trickled into his eye as he leaned over a wagon wheel suspended on two sawhorses. "Preacher, huh?"

"Yes, sir."

Ned tugged a kerchief from the rear pocket of his denim pants and wiped sweat from his eyes. "You do anything besides preach?"

"Quite a lot of things actually. But the ministry is my calling and profession."

"Well, make yourself useful and sand that spoke there."

Sam rolled up his shirtsleeves. Picking up a spoke freshly crafted out of hard ash, he applied the sandpaper while Ned sawed another to the proper length. "Figured I'd replace all the old ones before they give out."

Once the spokes were all sanded, Sam helped him fit them into place around the hub.

Ned had propped the axle on a length of aged tree stump to hold up the wagon and remove the wheel. "That must've been quite a task alone. I'll help you get this back on."

"I keep that hunk of tree just for this," Ned told him. "Perfect height. Gotta grease the axle first." Had his tone made the task a challenge?

Sam spotted the pail of black grease with a foot-long paddle stuck in it. He stirred the muck to get a good amount and carried it to the axle.

Ned watched him smear it on the wood. Once Ned thought the job had been sufficiently accomplished, they set to working the wheel onto the axle and removing the stump at the same time.

Several grunts and a good deal of sweat later, they stood and wiped their faces on their sleeves.

Ned eyed Sam. "You been here over an hour, and you haven't said nigh a word about your Jesus."

Sam returned the look. "I showed you my Jesus."

"Y' think puttin' your back into my wagon will get me to church?"

Sam shrugged. "It's not my call to get you to church. I came to see what I could do for you."

Ned cast him a puzzled glance before turning toward the open doorway. "Gonna hitch up a team so I can take hay to the cows. This wagon's been out of commission for two days."

"It was a pleasure to meet you," Sam called after him.

Ned paused. "The missus will give you a cold drink before you head out." He met Sam's gaze briefly. "Appreciate the hand."

"Glad to be of help." Sam left the barn and approached the shade tree where the women sat on a blanket.

"There's a cake of lye soap and a pail of water on the porch, Reverend," Mrs. Dunlop called.

Josie looked up with surprise. A lock of Sam's dark hair had fallen over his brow, and he had grease streaked up both corded forearms. She suspected his damp white shirt would require special treatment at the laundry, but he looked more relaxed than she'd seen him since he'd arrived.

He washed, and Eva got him a jar of lemonade, which he drank thirstily before they said their good-byes and headed out.

"How did your visit go?"

"Ned's a hardworking fellow. Didn't want to hinder his work, so I gave him a hand."

"Was he surprised?"

"Are you?"

His question caught her off guard. She didn't know why, but she had been surprised. "I guess I shouldn't have been."

His aware gaze edged to Anna seated between them. Josie suspected what he was thinking. Hoping to distract the child, she suggested, "Why don't we sing?"

Abigail joined her enthusiastically, and even Sam caught on and sang hymns in his deep baritone.

Not tricked, Anna watched the road with dread, seeing the bridge before she heard the water this time. Josie wrapped her arm around the child and tucked her tightly into her embrace, covering Anna's ears and continuing the song.

Anna cried and trembled, but she didn't beg her father to turn back. Perhaps she understood the bridge was the only way back to where they were staying. When the river was behind them, Josie loosened her hold and used her hem to wipe Anna's tears.

Sam's face had lost some of its healthy color, and Josie thought she noticed his hand tremble on the reins. Though he adjusted the brim of his hat and glanced across the waving prairie grass as though unaffected, she knew better.

Josie silently reminded the Lord about her prayers for the Hart family's comfort and strength and thanked Him for His love.

His daughter's distress ate a hole in his gut. Sam hated feeling helpless. It was because of him that his wife was gone and his children were miserable. Elisabeth's question haunted him every waking hour. Why hadn't God saved Carrie?

He'd prayed for their safety every morning and every night. He didn't believe God slept or turned a blind eye on His children. Sam should have been able to answer his daughter. He was a man of God. But there was no good reason, no answer for why he'd left his wife lying in a barren patch of prairie he'd never see again. Her burial place had blended into the countryside as though she'd never existed. Carrie was lost to him forever.

He felt sick at the fact that she wasn't buried near her parents, or even in a decent place, with shade trees and a marker; but then he forced himself to remember she had gone on to be with Jesus and was walking on streets of gold right at that moment.

His lofty plans mocked him. Life had to go on without her. Now that his children were motherless and he was a widower, he second-guessed his choices. If he hadn't wanted to come west...

Anna's sobs took him back to the hoarse convulsive sounds she'd made the day they'd stood over Carrie's grave. Her wet braids had thumped against her back with each burst of tears. Elisabeth had trembled so violently, her teeth had chattered. Abigail had grasped Anna and held her tightly, even though shock was plain on her red-blotched face.

Only the previous night, he and Carrie had sat beside the fire and talked about their new home. That morning had been like every other on the trail—no sense of impending disaster, no forewarning of the tragedy that was about to devastate their family.

Regret and misery had squeezed Sam's chest until he didn't know how his heart could still beat.

Why didn't God save her? Elisabeth's heartbroken question had sliced through Sam's cocoon of shock.

And now Anna's ragged breaths reminded him of all the suffering and loss he was helpless to change.

"Would you girls like to come to my house in the morning?" Josie asked. "I'll be preparing for the ladies to come quilting on Tuesday. I would enjoy your company and your help."

Her lighthearted question brought Sam out of his reverie and into the present. For a brief moment he almost resented that it was her sitting on the other side of Anna on the wagon seat and not his wife, but he corrected himself. Josie was exactly what all of them needed right now.

"I want to come!" Anna responded immediately.

"What do you need help doing?" Abigail asked.

"A little sweeping and dusting," Josie answered, and then grinned. "Oh, and I almost forgot. There are cookies and teacakes to make."

Abigail squealed. "Yes! I love to bake!"

Sam met Josie's gaze and read the pleasure in those amber depths. She truly enjoyed his daughters. The knowledge eased the ache in his chest. *Thank You, Lord.*

Josie glanced back at Elisabeth, but Sam's oldest daughter said nothing.

"What about you, Elisabeth?" he asked.

"I have reading to do."

Josie looked away, but not before Sam detected hurt. Elisabeth needed more time. And he had to believe that time would be a healer for all of them.

Chapter Seven

On Monday morning, Abigail and Anna left Elisabeth studying and walked to Josie's.

"We'll write these recipes in your journal," Josie told Abigail as they measured butter and cut it into sugar to make dough for wafer cookies. "Then you can make them yourselves when you get to Colorado."

Abigail paused with her hand on the wooden spoon. Josie glanced over to catch a flicker of pain crossing her expression.

She lifted Abigail's chin on floury fingers and looked into her eyes. "Your life is going to be different than planned, isn't it?"

The girl nodded.

Josie released her chin, but Abigail continued to look at her, as though waiting for help or encouragement. Though she felt inadequate, Josie was compelled to offer what she could.

"Sometimes it feels like we can't get through things. Like it's too hard to go on. But we keep going because people depend on us. And we grow stronger than we ever thought we could be."

Abigail nodded. "Papa says the joy of the Lord is our strength."

"Your papa's a wise man. And he loves you very much."

Anna hopped down from where she'd been stirring eggs at the table and stood beside her sister. Her wide hazel eyes were filled with concern. "I don't think there's enough joy to make me not scared of the river."

Josie didn't know what to say that would help a nine-year-old conquer a fear like that. She and her sisters had been swept away by a swift current, and that had been terrifying. And the river had taken her mother's life. "What does your papa say about that?"

"He doesn't say anything about it. I think he's kinda scared, too."

Josie doubted he was as afraid of water as he was of how he was going to raise three daughters without a mother. "When I don't have an answer," Josie told her, "and I don't know what to do, I ask God to show me the way."

"And does He?"

"He promised never to leave us or forsake us," she replied. "And He said we could always trust Him. So I do." Josie placed her cutting board on the table and instructed Anna to sprinkle flour on it. "Now we work the dough until it's smooth, and then let it stand."

"Elisabeth is missing all the good times," Abigail said softly.

It was obvious that Elisabeth resented Josie and every attempt she made to befriend the girls. Josie was only happy to help make their lives more pleasant. They'd been through so much and had lived in trying conditions along the trail. They'd be back at it soon enough, and she only hoped to ease their burdens during the time they were here.

"Can we be here when your friends come tomorrow?" Anna asked.

"It's not polite to invite your own self," Abigail scolded.

"I was going to invite you," Josie said kindly. "I just didn't know if you'd want to spend the morning with a bunch of chatty ladies, while they sew and drink tea."

"Oh, I do!" Anna assured her.

Josie looked at Abigail, who nodded with a hopeful smile.

"Of course you're welcome. We'll ask Elisabeth to join us, too. The ladies will enjoy your company. Have any of you ever quilted?"

They shook their heads.

"But we liked tea parties in Philadelphia," Abigail assured her.

"Well, I'll make some practice squares for you, and you can watch how it's done and try your hand with the needle and thread."

"And eat cookies!" Anna said emphatically.

They turned their attention to their task.

That evening at supper, the two younger girls chattered about their day and anticipated the following morning's event.

With assistance, Reverend Martin had made it to the dining room to sit at the table with them.

"Elisabeth, I'd like it very much if you joined us in the morning," Josie told her.

Elisabeth glanced at Samuel. "What will you be doing in the morning, Father?"

"I'm counseling the young couple I'll be marrying next weekend. You go and enjoy yourself with the ladies and your sisters."

"Thank you, Mrs. Randolph. I accept your invitation." Her tone didn't reflect much joy.

Samuel smiled at her approvingly.

Elisabeth's desire to please her father was evident in all she said and did. Josie recognized her need for approval, and she appreciated Sam's attention to his daughters.

There was a rap at the back door. Josie dabbed her lips with her napkin and went to answer it.

"Brought a load of wood," James told her. He stood holding am armful of neatly chopped limbs.

She stepped back. "We're just eating supper. Will you join us?"

"Yes'm." He arranged the pieces of wood so they fit in the bin beside the stove, then hung his cap on a hook.

She handed him a stack of dessert plates and picked up the pie. "James," she said once they'd reached the other room. "These are the Harts. This is our friend, James Lester," she told them. "He's my checker chum, aren't you, James?"

The fourteen-year-old glanced at the sisters. Without a reply, he ducked his head and took a seat on the chair that Josie scooted closer for him.

She dished slices of dried apple pie onto the plates and Elisabeth stood to pass one to each person.

James thanked her without meeting her eyes.

Anna, never at a loss for words or questions, spoke

up. "Do you live close? Do you go to school here? Are there lots of girls in your class? Is your teacher nice?"

"Me and my ma live on top o' the barbershop," he answered.

"I never heard of anyone living on top of a barbershop," Anna said. "Is it a long way up?"

"Anna, let James eat his pie," Samuel said, with an apologetic glance at the boy.

"Why don't you stay this evening?" Josie suggested. She looked at the sisters. "We never learned if any of you are checker players."

"Father and I used to play in the evening when we lived in Philadelphia," Elisabeth answered.

"We'll take turns, then," Josie said.

"I wanna learn!" Anna piped up.

"I have a board and disks at my house in a closet," Josie told her.

Josie and her chattering little friend took a walk in the cool of the early evening, pausing to wave to Alice Iverson, who sat on her front porch with her children. Josie felt a sense of purpose this evening. The melancholy feeling she normally experienced when she saw Alice and her youngsters remained blissfully at bay.

When they returned, Reverend Martin gave Josie a tender smile, reminding her he was still waiting for her reply.

"Can I bring you anything?" she asked.

"Not until my coffee later," he answered. "I'll be glad when I'm able to do something for you, for a change. You deserve the return of kindness."

Uncharacteristic warmth climbed her cheeks, the

thought that she was blushing embarrassing her all the more. But no one seemed to notice, and she showed Anna how to set up the pieces on the checkerboard.

Josie and James played at a small table, while Elisabeth and her father shared a game on the ottoman. Anna bobbed back and forth between both games, asking questions.

"She'll catch on quickly once she plays," Josie predicted.

Elisabeth captured Sam's last king, and they waited while Josie and James finished their game. Josie moved down to oppose Anna, and Elisabeth seated herself at the table with James.

Abigail sat beside her father on the sofa, and he wrapped an arm around her. Josie caught herself watching them, instead of making suggestions for Anna's moves. Abigail looked at him with such adoration, and he absently rubbed the back of her hand. Josie thought of all the evenings she'd sat alone, waiting for her father to return, only to have him breeze past on his way to the next place.

She shook off her discontentment. Her father had been an important man who helped a lot of people acquire justice. He'd loved her and provided for her, leaving her well off after his death. She had much to be grateful for.

Reverend Martin had to remind her when it was her turn to move.

The evening wore on and Anna got tired, yawning behind her hand. Samuel took her up to bed, allowing the other two girls another game if they wanted one. James and Elisabeth played again, while Reverend

Martin took on Abigail by sliding the ottoman close to the chair where he sat. Josie watched contentedly. She couldn't remember a time when her days had been so full and she'd felt such accomplishment at the end of the evening.

Samuel returned, taking a seat. His interested gaze rested on Elisabeth and James. Earlier, they'd behaved awkwardly with each other, avoiding eye contact and speaking rarely. Now Elisabeth's shy smiles and the nervous bouncing of James's knee under the table hinted of age-old boy-meets-girl chemistry.

They seemed so young to Josie, and they were. She barely remembered being Elisabeth's age.

Much later, after James had gone home and the girls had scampered up to bed, Sam assured her he would see to the reverend's needs. The two men planned to talk a while longer.

"Good evening, then." Josie checked the stove before heading home.

A movement on the other side of the street surprised her, and a slender figure stepped out of the shadows into the moonlight. "Hello, Mrs. Randolph."

"James! What are you doing out so late?"

"My mother isn't off work yet, so I was walkin' until it's time to get her. I like to walk her home."

"That's nice of you. I'm sure she appreciates it, but maybe you should stay a little closer to the café."

"It's all right. I can walk you home if you want."

"Okay."

"Elisabeth is smart. She beat me at checkers twice."

"You didn't let her win?"

"Maybe once."

Josie laughed. They paused in front of her house. "Why don't you come for supper tomorrow evening?"

"Thanks, Mrs. Randolph!" James grinned and spun to leave.

Smiling, she climbed the stairs to her home.

Josie couldn't have put her feelings into words the following morning as she and Abigail draped her dining room table with a heavy lace cloth. With her tongue poking out of the corner of her mouth in concentration, Anna carried trays of cookies and tea cakes into the room.

As Josie took the last one from her, Elisabeth joined them. "I've arranged the chairs in a big circle, as you asked."

Josie loved having the girls in her home, enjoyed hearing their chatter. Planning this day and carrying it out was an experience like none she had known. Their mother must have felt so blessed and been so proud. What did it feel like to have brought fresh new lives into the world? To nurture and love them and watch them grow into sweet children and pretty young ladies?

She'd never wanted anything more than to know how that felt. But her dreams of family and children had slowly and painfully faded—dying altogether with Bram.

She shook off her gloomy thoughts, opting to make the most of every minute with the girls. "I've never been prepared this early."

The sisters had dressed in their Sunday frocks, Elisabeth's a bright blue that brought out the vivid color of her eyes, Abigail's a deep violet that set off her shining, pale hair and Anna's a lemony yellow that made her hazel eyes appear darker.

"These were our last new dresses," Abigail said, glancing at Elisabeth's hem, which was already a trifle short.

"I might be able to let that down for you," Josie told the eldest sister.

"Most likely, Father will take us to the seamstress when we reach Colorado," Elisabeth answered.

"Papa said we'd be making the best of our clothing," Abigail reminded her. "You should let Josie take down the hem."

"I could do it myself."

"I think you can," Josie agreed. "I could show you how to hem it evenly, if you like." She understood that Elisabeth had taken over the mothering position for her sisters. Apparently, their fondness for Josie—and Josie's help—threatened her in some way. Her prickliness over Josie's involvement stemmed from losing her mother.

Josie didn't want to be pushy, so she let the subject drop.

Always curious, Anna asked, "How did your dad—I mean—um—how did your Mr. Randolph die?"

"My *husband*," Josie supplied, "ran the newspaper office. He set all those tiny letters that make up the print into trays." She arranged her silver forks in a shiny, cascading row as she spoke. "He started having bad headaches, so painful that he often came home and went to bed. Light hurt his eyes, so I had to make the room dark with heavy draperies." Those had been difficult times, and the memories weren't pleasant. "After a few months, he lost his vision—"

"Did you help him find it?" Anna asked.

"That means he couldn't see," Abigail told her.

"That's right." Josie nodded. "It wasn't long until he died. The doctor believed he had a growth in his head. I'm afraid we'll never know for sure."

"Who puts the tiny letters into the trays now?" Anna asked.

"Well, I inherited the newspaper," Josie told her. "But I have no idea how to run it, nor do I want to learn, so I took a partner. A man by the name of Carlisle bought half. I don't know if he does the typesetting himself, or if he hired a helper."

"I'm sad for you," Anna told her with sympathy in her expression.

"Don't be sad for me," Josie answered. "I have lots of friends, and I stay very busy."

"I think you should get a new dad," Anna stated.

"Husband," Elisabeth corrected.

"I might just do that one of these days," Josie said with a smile. The bell on the door grated, effectively ending their conversation. "Here we go!"

Grace and Becka Hulbert were the first to arrive, followed by several others. The quilting ladies were pleased to have the Hart girls join them. Grace asked the sisters numerous questions about themselves and their father. Josie had already experienced the woman's interest in the newly widowed preacher as a prospect for her daughter, and the other ladies picked up on it right away.

"Grace, let the children work on their practice squares," Mrs. Wilbur admonished her in a deliberately good-natured tone, and then launched into a commentary on the marigolds she'd planted around the edge of her tomato garden. "They're going to keep the rabbits away."

Nettie laughed. "You're going to need more than marigolds, Pauline."

Josie helped the girls with their squares, showing them the embroidery stitches. As with everything, Elisabeth displayed skill and precision with hers. Abigail chose variegating colors and Anna liked red. Even the leaves on her rose were red. Elisabeth pointed out that they should have been green, but Josie and Abigail assured Anna that any color she liked was beautiful and just right for her square.

"Maybe we can make a quilt for Papa's bed," Abigail suggested.

All three girls fell silent.

Josie glanced from one to the other. None of them met her gaze. "Is something wrong?"

Elisabeth shook her head. Anna got tears in her eyes.

"What is it?" Josie asked, kneeling in front of the youngest child and placing her hand over Anna's.

"Our mama was wrapped up in the wedding quilt when we—when she—when we left her behind," Anna said.

Behind Josie, the ladies became uncomfortably silent.

Chapter Eight

By the looks on the ladies' faces, Josie was certain their hearts went out to these girls just as hers did.

Seeing the children's pain, Josie wanted to cry, too. But she squeezed Anna's hand. She knew the grief of losing a mother.

The ladies murmured, more than one sniffed, and their quilting resumed. Josie assured the girls that they could work on quilt squares as often as they liked, and she would even help them if they wanted to take on the project of making a quilt for their father.

Together they served refreshments, and after the ladies went home, the sisters helped Josie clean up. These girls needed a woman in their lives. She prayed that once they reached their destination and settled into their new church, that time would heal the wounds and they would welcome a new wife for their father. Of course, it wouldn't be the same as having their own mother, but any woman would be blessed to marry into their family.

At the thought of Samuel caring enough for a woman to marry again—and the idea of the girls lending their affections to that wife—Josie's heart skipped an erratic beat. She had become involved. She cared about them. Her life was going to be unbearably quiet and empty when they left.

Josie's chest ached at the prospect, so she cast her thoughts aside, to be concerned with only today. They'd come into her lives for a season, and she was determined to enjoy it.

At supper that evening, Sam appreciated the animation with which Anna and Abigail spoke about their afternoon. Even Elisabeth smiled once or twice, adding a remark to the conversation. Their talk of embroidering and eating ginger cookies held more normalcy than anything had in the past months.

He had Josie to thank for that.

The girls didn't have to be reminded to help clear the table. Reverend Martin talked about a tornado that had passed through a few years previous, and Sam listened with interest.

After finishing his coffee, he picked up his cup and the reverend's to carry them into the kitchen.

Josie was speaking softly, and he heard his wife mentioned, so he paused just outside the doorway and peered in.

All three girls and Josie were seated at one end of the kitchen table, as though Josie had gathered them there.

Josie held Anna's hand and looked directly into her eyes. "It's a good thing to remember your mama," she told her, and then included the other two with her warm gaze. "We keep people alive in our hearts by remembering the good times and the love we shared when we were together."

A shard of pain pierced Sam's heart, quickly followed by a flash of anger. Who was this woman to address such a difficult subject? His children didn't need their wounds reopened.

"I missed my mother terribly for a long time. But now when I think of her, I think of all the ways she made me laugh. I remember our evenings together by the fire."

Sam strained to see his daughter's expressions. Anna's face had lit up and she listened intently.

"What's the best time you can remember having with your mother?" Josie turned her gaze. "Abigail?"

Unbelievably, Abigail's eyes brightened. "We went to the theater and watched a ballet before Christmas."

Sam's surprise was so great he had to focus on not dropping the cups he held.

"On the way home," Abigail continued, "we stopped for hot chocolate. It was snowing, and Mama was so pretty in her black wool coat and fur muff."

Similar images sabotaged Sam's mind. Carrie had been so young and lovely.

"That's a wonderful memory." He tore his attention back to the scene before him. Josie turned to Elisabeth, and Sam's heart nearly exploded. "What about you, sweetie? Do you recall a good time with your mother?"

Sam didn't believe his oldest daughter would answer, but she studied her sisters' faces and replied, "Sitting in church every Sunday morning. Mother was so proud of Father."

Sam could hardly breathe.

"She watched him with a special look on her face," Elisabeth added. "And she was the prettiest lady there."

Abigail and Anna nodded.

Those were the times and the days he'd robbed them of. Those were the things they'd never get back.

"That's awfully nice, Elisabeth." Josie turned to Anna. "What about you?"

Sam's heart melted as he waited for his youngest child to share something about her mother.

"Mama used to give me a baff and wash my hair, and then we'd sit by the stove and she'd brush it dry. She told me about when she was a little girl and Grandmama dried her hair by the fire." Anna paused for a thoughtful moment. "Elisabeth helps me wash my hair now."

"Elisabeth's a good sister." Josie smiled and released Anna's hands. "Thank you for sharing your good memories."

They were silent a moment, but then Abigail said, "Talking about her made me sad, but it was a different kind of sad. I miss her, but if I remember the good times it's not so hard."

"It's good to talk about her," Josie assured them. "It's good to think of her and remember how much she loved you. You are blessed to share those memories with each other. You'll always have them in common."

The girls glanced at one another with hesitant smiles.

"I'm gonna draw a picture of Mama," Anna announced.

Josie stood. "Why don't you all run along now and enjoy your evening reading…or drawing. I'll finish up here."

Advising them to think of pleasant times should have

come from him, but how could he lead anyone somewhere he'd never gone? Realizing he would be discovered eavesdropping if he didn't move, Sam collected
himself and stepped into the kitchen.

Anna spotted him and ran over to hug him around
the waist. "I'm gonna draw a picture of Mama."

Josie hurried toward him and took the cups, so his
hands were free.

"I'll be up in a little while, and we'll read together."

With a clamber of shoes and a whirl of skirts, they
were gone, leaving him to face the woman he'd had unkind thoughts about only moments ago. Guilt engulfed
him at his quick leap to anger when he'd heard her mention his wife. *Forgive me, Lord.*

Her intentions were pure and kind. His daughters had
opened up to her with stories of their mother in a surprisingly forthcoming manner. What did he know about
little girls? What did he know about losing a mother?
Josie Randolph apparently knew about both and cared
enough to counsel them. He studied her as she checked
the steaming teakettle. He'd noticed that she was a lovely
woman, of course, but he hadn't looked at her as anything other than Henry's helper.

He appreciated that she'd been a blessing to his dis-
traught family, but he took a moment now to appreciate
her dark, shiny hair and the curve of her ivory cheek.
She'd lost someone just as he had, and for the first time
he wondered about her grief and loneliness.

He reached for a stack of dishes. "Let me help."

"I can do this." She waved her free hand. "You go
read with the girls."

"Actually, I wanted a moment alone with you."

"Oh?" The squeaky syllable showed her surprise. As did the way she quickly and efficiently shaved soap into the enamel dishpan. "What can I do for you, Reverend?"

How like her to ask. He shook his head. "You've done so much already. I want you to know I recognize your care and concern. I appreciate everything. More than you can know."

Obviously uncomfortable with his praise, she lowered her lashes and absently skimmed the edge of the table with her index finger. "They're lovely young ladies. So different from one another."

She raised her caramel-brown gaze to his. Surely the affection he thought he felt for her at that moment was only appreciation. He didn't have it in him to feel more. He didn't want to feel more.

He had so much turmoil on his heart that he couldn't sort through it to find adequate words. Perhaps there simply weren't any. "Their mother doted on them. Took care of everything."

She picked up a towel. "The loss must be difficult for all of you."

"I guess," he said, pausing to study her, "that you know about loss yourself. You lost your husband."

She nodded and answered simply, "Yes."

"How did you do it?" he asked. "Go on with your life after that? How did you bear the days and nights without him?"

A flicker of pain creased her brow.

"I'm sorry. That was too forward of me."

"No, it wasn't, Sam. It's an honest concern. I just don't know if I have a helpful answer. I didn't do anything particularly brave or wise. I just got up and made every day count somehow. I didn't want to lose myself." Her rich caramel-colored eyes beseeched him to understand.

And he did—because he had lost something of himself.

Overwhelmed with confusion, he nodded. He wanted so much for them. He'd had a vision for his family that had never taken this daunting possibility into consideration. He felt sorely inadequate for the task laid out before him. "I understand," he said softly.

"You're fortunate to have your children," she told him. "To still have a family."

"I am blessed," he replied.

"And you recognize your blessing. With all you have to do, you make time for your daughters," she said almost reverently. "They know you love them and they can tell that they're important to you. You make them feel safe."

Sam stared blindly at the dishes on the table for a moment. How could she think that? Anna's terror nearly tore his heart out. Abigail's nightmares were most likely the same horrifying images he dreamed. And Elisabeth didn't even seem like herself anymore. He shook his head.

Josie had the feeling she'd said too much. Using the towel to protect her hands, she poured hot water from the teakettle and set it back on the stove. After adding cooler water, she lowered a stack of plates into the suds. There were things she'd observed that she wasn't comfortable mentioning. Abigail's beseeching looks when Elisabeth accompanied her father, for one. But Josie wasn't a part of their family, and she had no business meddling.

Samuel's presence had become disconcerting. More often than not when he was near, she found herself thinking about the wave in his near-black hair or the clean, solid line of his jaw. He was a tall, broad-shouldered man, but he moved with a fluid agility and masculine grace she couldn't help but appreciate. She reminded herself that he was a widower, a father and a preacher. Besides those facts, she was considering marrying Reverend Martin.

"I just meant to say thank you," he said, finally looking up.

"I'm just making every day count," she replied.

"Don't minimize your importance or my gratitude."

"All right. You're welcome."

One corner of his mouth turned up and the atmosphere between them changed. She would probably float if he turned on a full-fledged smile. She was unaccustomed to the buoyant sensation—but she liked it.

With that, he turned and left the room. Josie let her hands fall still in the dishwater as she pictured him going upstairs, Abigail sitting close to him, and Anna squirming onto his lap. The empty feeling that image created forced her to turn her thoughts in a new direction.

She was supposed to be giving thought to Reverend Mar—*Henry's* proposal. Why was it she had to work to focus on the issue, to even consider the possibility? Henry was a kind man who served the Lord with all his heart. He would make a good companion, and she needed companionship.

Give me wisdom, Lord. "I want to make the right choice," she prayed softly. "I don't want to be alone, but I want to fulfill Your purpose for my life, so please show me what You would have me do."

Josie finished the dishes. Her talk with the girls had brought back memories of her childhood and the time she'd spent with her mother. Her mother must have missed her husband. Josie realized that she had probably been a comfort to her mother during those long days and nights while her father traveled. At least, she hoped so. A child would have been a blessing to *her,* had she been able to have one.

Somehow, her thoughts had come full circle. Josie wiped the last plate and turned down the wall lamps. She found Henry in his study with his Bible open on his lap. He sat with his chin resting on his knuckles, his elbow on the arm on the chair. His smile greeted her.

She stood for a moment, clasping her hands in front of her. She should have something more to say to him. She felt bad for not having a ready answer. The prospect of becoming his wife had changed the once-easy rapport they'd shared.

"Is everything all right?" he asked.

She nodded. "Fine. I'm tired. I'll see you in the morning."

She shouldn't have been relieved to go home. Normally, she stayed until it grew late. Closing the door behind her, she strolled out onto the brick walkway and turned to look up at the light in the bedroom window. A few words of the hymn she so often thought of came to her lips.

"Be still, my soul: thy God doth undertake
to guide the future as He has the past.
Thy hope, thy confidence let nothing shake;

and now mysterious shall be bright at last."

God was in control of her future, and in that she could place her trust and confidence. She prayed to be sensitive to His leading and to hear clearly when He guided her decision.

"I'm listening, Lord. I'm listening."

In a clear voice, Elisabeth read a particularly exciting chapter of *Alice's Adventures in Wonderland*. Carrie had purchased the novel the year it was published, and they'd read it through a half dozen times since. This was only Anna's second time to hear the story.

Elisabeth sat on the end of the bed, her slender bare feet dangling above the wood floor, her long, thick hair cascading over her shoulders.

Sam sat in a comfortable chair only a few feet away, with Abigail at his feet and Anna perched on his lap. His concentration wavered as the image of the three of them gathered at the kitchen table sharing memories of their mother sharpened his already overworked conscience.

The overwhelming need to fix what he'd done to them never went away. He had their futures to think of, a life to build for them, and now a secondary plan had to come from scratch.

He held so much self-recrimination and doubt inside that he didn't have the ability to draw his children out the way Josie had tonight. He should have been the one helping them remember their mother. He should have been the one assuring his girls that their grief was a normal thing. But he hadn't been. Instead, he continued to let them down.

Hearing their conversation, seeing their faces and

Josie's genuine concern had been hard to accept at first. But now, after he'd had time to absorb it, he saw that she could do for them what he couldn't.

They needed someone to guide them, someone to nurture and care for them. Only a woman understood feminine mysteries and only a woman could fill that place in their lives.

Maybe in the back of his mind, he'd imagined that once they were settled in Colorado and had a home, he might find them a mother. But he hadn't truly allowed a complete thought to form, because that would have been disloyal to Carrie.

His daughters needed a woman to teach them things like embroidery and cooking. A woman could help them develop into proper young women.

His mind raced. At first his thoughts were so shocking, he didn't want to entertain them, but once he gave himself over to the possibility, the idea seemed perfect.

He needed a helpmate. His children needed a mother. Josie was levelheaded and lovely, the picture of an ideal woman. She was a pleasant companion and a strong woman of God. Granted, he hadn't known her long, but he'd never heard a cross word from her, and had seen only her kindness and generosity.

Josie was a widow. She had no children of her own. She was everything the girls needed, and she already cared about them.

She was the perfect answer.

Chapter Nine

He had the answer.

Sam couldn't change the past, nor could he replace Carrie, but he could fix things by securing this perfect woman to take care of his children.

A weight in his chest gave him pause. What would Carrie think? Would she approve?

Sam had asked God to help him through this time. He prayed continually for direction and wisdom and strength. At that moment, he understood that Josie was the answer to his prayers. Carrie would approve.

Anna yawned as Elisabeth ended the chapter.

He kissed the top of Anna's head. "Get yourselves into bed now."

Elisabeth made herself comfortable on the narrow cot, and the other two snuggled into the bigger bed. Sam kissed each of them. "I love you," he said with emotion making his words thick in his throat.

"I love you," they echoed.

His feet barely touched the stairs. Henry had already

taken himself off to bed, so Sam checked the fireplace and stove and let himself out of doors.

Anna had shown him which street Josie lived on, and he hurried, seeking the house she'd described. In the dark, he wasn't sure if he'd be able to find it. This probably hadn't been a good idea, but he'd been eager to set things in motion. He reached the end of the block and started back toward the parsonage.

"Good evening, Reverend," a male voice called out.

Sam stopped before a two-story home with a wide porch.

A form separated from the shadows.

He recognized Reggie Iverson and stretched out a hand in greeting. "The missus and I are real pleased that you're here. It's good to have church again."

"I'm enjoying the people of Durham," Sam told him honestly. "And there are a lot of excellent cooks among the wives."

They chatted a few minutes longer. Sam had pretty much given up on finding Josie's house that night.

"Josie lets us pick apples from her backyard." Reggie turned aside and gestured. "Alice makes apple dumplings that melt in your mouth. If you're here for the season, she'll cook some up for you."

Sam's attention had once again been captured. "Mrs. Randolph has apple trees?"

"A whole row of fine ones," Reggie replied. "Lives right there, she does. Shame Bram died so young and left her on her own. He must be gone…oh, three or four years now. Ran the newspaper, her husband did."

"I'll look forward to those dumplings."

The man turned and walked toward his house and

let himself inside. Sam observed as the door blocked out the light, then he studied Josie's house in the dark.

A solitary light shone from an upstairs window.

He loped across the lawn without bothering to take the walkway and leaped the stairs three at a time to reach her door. He groped and found a metal knob to twist, hoping the grating noise didn't alert the neighbors.

Sam ran his palms along his thighs and waited.

Finally, the door opened. A light behind Josie outlined her loose hair and her slender form in a wrapper. "Reverend Hart?" Quickly, she stepped out onto the porch. "What's wrong? Is it Henry?"

"No, no. Henry's fine." Anticipating her next question, he added, "The girls are fine. I—need to speak with you."

Her pause was barely discernible. "All right." She glanced at the doorway. "Do you want to come in?"

"We can talk out here."

She pulled the door closed and stood in front of him.

Sam glanced around and spotted wicker chairs at the other end of the porch. "Let's sit."

She padded in front of him and took a seat. Sam lowered himself to the chair opposite.

Here, the moonlight was bright enough to see her smooth features and the sheen of her dark hair. She waited expectantly. It was highly unusual for him to call at this hour of the evening—or to call at all. "Did I get you out of bed?"

"No. I've been sewing upstairs and had just changed my clothes."

A silent moment passed. Beyond the Iversons' hedge, a cat yowled. She must be wondering what in creation brought him here, and already he wasn't doing a very good job of this.

"Please don't think me presumptuous," he began. "Is there anything…any*one* tethering you to this place? To Nebraska?"

She changed her position on the chair. "Durham has always been my home. But I don't have any family, if that's what you mean. Except, of course, my husband's mother." She glanced aside. "I have this house."

"Would you ever consider leaving?"

She shrugged. "I don't know. I've never thought about it. There's never been any reason."

"What about starting over? Would that be a good reason?"

Josie studied what she could see of Samuel Hart's face in the shadows of the porch. His questions were puzzling, though she was trying to make sense of them and follow his train of thought. Starting over where? "I-I'm not sure."

"Josie, I'm thinking that you and I could make a new start together."

He had her interest now!

"I want to do the very best I can for my family. I want to make up to them for what I've put them through. You're so good with my daughters."

A new start somewhere else? Her mind shot back to those words. "What are you saying?"

"I would be honored if you would marry me and come to Colorado with us," he said.

The night sounds faded into the silent cocoon of her whirling mind, and his words took over her thinking.

Astonishment stole her breath. Marry him? He'd asked her to marry him?

He was handsome and smart. She'd witnessed his tenderness toward his children, listened to his strong words of love as he preached straight from the Word of God. This imposing and fascinating man sitting on her porch had proposed to her!

Her heart raced against her ribs.

Josie pressed her hand to her chest and let her thoughts settle. *I would be honored if you would marry me and come to Colorado with us.*

She thought of her earlier prayer for wisdom in making choices. God knew she didn't want to be alone, but she'd hesitated over Henry's proposal. Perhaps this was why she'd been unable to make that commitment.

The irony struck her, and she couldn't hold back a chuckle. "Oh, Lord, You do work in mysterious ways."

"What are you thinking?" Sam asked.

She was thinking that she'd been unable to give Reverend Martin an answer because God had something else planned. He was offering her more than a companion.

Sam had suggested a new beginning together. And God was providing the family she'd so desperately yearned for. Emotion welled within her and hot tears flooded her eyes. "I'm thinking I would love to marry you and move to Colorado to start over."

Sam released a pent-up breath and leaned out of his chair to engulf her in a hearty hug.

Startled, Josie returned the embrace, enjoying the warmth, breathing in his scent, a combination of clean clothing and bay rum. God had deemed to give her an affectionate husband after all. And children, as well! Her heart brimmed to overflowing. God's mercy and kindness knew no bounds.

Sam released her to stand and take a step back as though realizing the impropriety of hugging her on her porch.

He reached for her hand, and she took his.

"Father," he said, his voice low and reverent. "Thank You for Your grace and mercy. Thank You for setting my feet on the path of righteousness and pointing me in the direction You'd have me take. I've made mistakes in the past, but I only want to hear Your voice. I know if I trust in You, You will bless this family we are creating to serve You."

His earnestly spoken words touched Josie so deeply she could scarcely breathe. She appreciated the way he spoke to God, as though he was having a conversation, and that thanking God had been the first thing on his mind.

"Help me be the man You want me to be, and give Josie all the strength and love she's going to need for the weeks and months ahead. I ask in Jesus' name. Amen."

"Amen," Josie said around the emotion thickening her voice. *Thank You for this man,* she wanted to add, but her voice wouldn't work.

He backed to the stairs. "You'll have things to take care of to get ready. I'll help you in any way I can."

"I-I'll have to sell my house." And her share of the newspaper. And tell Henry her decision. And Margaretta. She pressed both palms to her hot cheeks. "Oh, my."

"Is selling your house a problem?"

She got up and followed him to the stairs. "Not at all. I'm just feeling a bit overwhelmed."

"We'll have a ceremony before we leave for Colorado," he continued.

She nodded. She would have to decide what to do with all of her belongings. "I need time to tell a few people."

"Of course. We'll wait long enough for that, and then we'll tell the girls together. This is a good plan," he said.

Josie didn't think "good" was descriptive enough for the new surge of hope that swelled in her heart. "It's a lot to think about right now, but with God's blessing, what more could we ask?"

Sam glanced aside and then at her. He descended a couple of steps. "I'd—ah—I'd better go. Good night." He turned and jogged down the rest of the stairs.

She strained to watch him until his tall form blended with the night and he was gone. Wrapping her arms around herself, she returned to sink onto the chair in a state of awe.

She was going to be Samuel Hart's wife!

Her head filled with images of the new life they would build, of the beautiful mountain country she'd never dreamed to see. She would prepare their home and fill it with loving touches. She would be a loving and devoted wife, and she wouldn't expect too much from her husband. He was a busy man who put God first and had his ministry and his daughters to concern himself with.

Josie imagined helping Abigail and Anna with their homework and their hair. She could buy patterns and make them new dresses. Elisabeth would warm to her. Josie would never replace their mother, of course, but she could fill a place of need and become an important thread in their lives.

She would be part of the Hart family. Josie Hart. When they arrived in Colorado, she would be at Sam's side as they met the new congregation.

She barely slept that night, exhilarating thoughts of her new life swirling through her mind, and eventually in her dreams.

The next morning reality barely dimmed her fantasies. She hummed as she prepared breakfast. The girls looked prettier than ever, and when Sam entered the kitchen in his black trousers and white shirt, the sight took her breath away and joy rose in her heart. She gave him a secret smile and turned away before one of his daughters noticed.

"Good morning," he said from behind her. "Did you sleep well?"

She'd barely slept a wink. "Yes, thanks. And you?"

"I slept better than I have since we arrived here."

She turned back with a plate of fried potatoes. "Have you checked on Reverend Martin?"

"He shaved and dressed himself."

"He's getting stronger every day. I think your family has been good for him. And you've taken away the burden he felt about letting down his flock."

The man they'd been discussing appeared in the doorway. "What's that I smell? Is it bacon?"

"And corn-bread muffins," Josie replied.

"What's the special occasion?" Henry asked, stiffly seating himself at the head of the table.

Josie quickly turned back to the stove. The thought

of disappointing him stabbed her with dismay. The last thing she wanted was to let him down or—even worse—hurt him.

"Where are you going today?" Elisabeth asked her father.

"I have a telegram to send, and I need to make a visit to the bank and the farrier. Then I'll be studying in the church."

"May I go on your errands with you?" his oldest daughter asked.

"Why don't all of you come with me for the morning? We'll leave Mrs. Randolph to her tasks, and Reverend Martin can listen to the silence."

Henry laughed. "I have plenty of quiet time. Don't worry about me."

Everyone was in a good mood while they ate. Josie declined help for the dishes, and Sam and his daughters left.

Sometime later, Josie took another cup of coffee to the reverend's study, but he wasn't there. Surprised, she walked through the house. Glancing out the front window, she spotted him on the porch.

He thanked her for the coffee and took a sip. "For a while there, I wasn't sure I'd be seeing the sun again."

She perched on the porch rail, facing him. A falling sensation in her stomach betrayed her nervousness, but she couldn't hesitate.

He set down his cup.

"Henry," she began, still uncomfortable with his given name. "I've made a decision."

Henry studied her with uncertainty.

"I care for you very much, as you know. I respect and honor you. You're a fine man."

His expression didn't change.

"I'm sorry to disappoint you."

Henry quirked his mouth to the side before saying, "But you don't want to marry me."

"It's become a little more complicated than that."

"How so?"

"I truly considered marriage to you, and I didn't find it an unpleasant idea at all. But something just didn't feel quite right about the decision, and I dragged my feet about giving you my answer."

"What happened?"

"I think I know why I didn't say yes." She took a deep breath. "Reverend Hart has asked me to marry him and join his family in Colorado."

Henry's face showed his genuine surprise. He glanced away as if gathering his thoughts and emotions. Without looking back at her, he asked, "You said yes?"

"I said yes."

"And your decision felt right?"

"It did."

He looked at her then, and his gaze was still warm and affectionate. "Of course it did. He's a young man with a bright future. You need someone to look after, and those children couldn't do better than you."

His words brought tears of acute relief to her eyes.

"You and Sam will be making a brand-new start. That's what God does best, you know? Gives second chances."

"Thank you for understanding."

"I told you that you deserved a husband and a family, didn't I? This is it."

Blinking away the moisture in her eyes, Josie knelt at his knees and took his hand. "You're happy for me. You're a good friend."

"You're a good friend, too, Josie. I'm going to miss you."

"You and James will keep each other on your toes."

A smile creased his cheek. He covered the back of her hand with his other one. "I will pray for you without ceasing. And I'll look for letters telling me of the good things you're accomplishing in your new home."

"Thank you. I'm looking forward to a new start. But I have someone else to tell, and to be honest, I'm dreading it."

"Your mother-in-law?"

She nodded. Margaretta would not take the news as graciously as Reverend Martin had. Josie could almost hear the accusations now.

"She *is* quite devoted to your late husband's memory. Margaretta may not understand your need to move on with your life. She's one of those people who lets the past hold them back. She has dwelt on memories of her husband and son until she's probably blown them up into something far greater and better than they truly ever were."

"I feel as though I need to put on my battle armor."

"You're never without it," he answered. "Rest assured the helmet of truth and breastplate of righteousness protect you from those slinging arrows."

"You do know her."

"You might have to accept that she won't give you

her blessing. You're not seeking her approval, though, so don't let her discourage you when you know what you're doing is right."

She appreciated his wisdom. "I believe I'm doing what God wants me to."

"God tells us in the book of Jeremiah that he has good plans for our well-being and peace. When you're listening for His direction, you can plan with confidence."

She released his hands and stood. "I'll remember that."

Josie rang the bell on the front door of the house where Bram had grown up. A minute later it opened.

"Josie?" Margaretta blinked with surprise. Josie had never come uninvited. "Well, come in. I'll make tea."

Josie conceded to let her get out her china and make a big fuss out of steeping her imported tea leaves. When eventually they seated themselves on Margaretta's brocade settee, Josie sipped the sweetened brew.

"Do you need something?" Bram's mother asked.

Josie was acutely aware of the woman's intolerance. She'd always been the outsider. But she was leaving, and Margaretta would never influence her life again. The knowledge gave her more confidence. "I've never needed anything but acceptance and perhaps a measure of understanding," she replied. Without giving Margaretta time to form an insult, she pushed on with what she'd come here for. "I'm going to be married again."

The woman gasped. Her face drained of color, and the cup and saucer she held slipped from her hand with a clatter. It landed on the rug without breaking. Tea seeped into the wool fibers.

Josie got up and used her napkin to quickly soak up the liquid.

Ignoring the spill, Margaretta stood. "Of all the ungrateful and mean-spirited things I've ever heard! I guess I could have expected nothing better of you. You'll never be satisfied. Which wealthy man have you dug your claws into this time?"

Sitting back on her heels and looking up, Josie refused to allow the stinging words any credence. "You don't know me at all, if you can think of me like that."

"I know you, and I know your kind. My son's memory means nothing to you."

Josie closed her eyes. She had expected the worst, but Margaretta was the closest thing she had to family, and it didn't feel right to make decisions without letting her know. She couldn't have let her find out from someone else.

"Who is it?" Margaretta asked.

Josie shook her head. "Never mind. I shouldn't have said anything to upset you."

"Of course I'm upset. My only son is dead. I have no grandchildren, only an unappreciative daughter-in-law who can't wait to marry another unsuspecting man."

"Unsuspecting of what?"

"You can be sure that I'll warn this new husband of yours that you're of no use to him in procuring children. If he wants heirs, he'd best look elsewhere. Of course, that suits you, doesn't it? All the money goes into your bank account."

Finding a chink in her armor, those words cut deep into Josie's insecurities and stirred up painful feelings of inadequacy. She released the napkin and cup and stood slowly.

She looked at Bram's mother, unable to comprehend her bitter ire. "He's not rich and he doesn't need children. Reverend Hart actually appreciates me."

"Reverend Hart!" Margaretta shrieked and threw her hands in the air. "You've been with that man every day, likely spending unsupervised hours in his company. I should have suspected you had a plan to ensnare the poor, unsuspecting widower."

Josie shook her head at the hateful accusation. "I had no idea he was even thinking such a thing until last night."

"Last night! And already you've jumped at the chance. How convenient that Reverend Martin is back on his feet to pronounce you married before the Hart fellow can get away."

Angry now, Josie picked up her reticule where it lay on a side table. "Well, thank you." She gathered the hem of her skirts in preparation to go. "I'm so glad I came for this little chat. You've been so helpful. I can always count on you when I need a friendly ear or a shoulder to lean on."

She made it as far as the door and turned back. "Your son was *exactly* the same way, God rest his soul."

Margaretta's chest puffed out with indignation, and her face turned beet-red. "How *dare* you speak to me that way?"

With her head held high, Josie spun and kept walking through the foyer, out the front door, down the steps. She would never, *never* have another word to say to that woman as long as she lived. Margaretta may be lonely and bereaved, but she'd been just plain mean to start with.

"Josie!" Margaretta called. "Don't you dare turn your back on me!"

Josie wasn't accountable to Bram's mother for anything. Reverend Martin had counseled her not to seek the woman's approval, and Josie hadn't expected it. She had endured all she intended to. That chapter of her life was behind her.

"Josie!"

And getting farther behind all the time.

She actually smiled and slowed her walk to a stroll.

That evening was Reverend Martin's Bible study, in which Josie and the Harts participated, and the following day was full for Sam, so it wasn't until Thursday that he was able to gather Josie and the three girls for their meeting.

He asked all of them to join him for a midday picnic.

Abigail and Anna thought it was great fun. They gathered purple clover and made chains for their hair and to wear as necklaces. Anna made one for Josie and hung it around her neck. Elisabeth had brought along a book, and she sat cross-legged under a tree, reading.

Josie had packed sandwiches and apples, along with pint jars of lemonade. After they ate, Sam called the girls and asked them to gather on the faded blanket in the shade.

"Josie and I have something to share with you," he said.

"We're getting a lamb!" Anna squealed.

"We can't take a lamb all the way to Colorado with us," Sam explained.

Elisabeth gave her youngest sister an I-told-you-so look and turned her attention back to her father.

Sam didn't beat around the bush or preface the news. "Josie and I are going to be married."

Chapter Ten

Sam's daughters stared at him.

"She's coming with us the rest of the way, and she'll live with us in our new home."

"Mrs. Randolph is going to be your wife now?" Anna asked.

"You'll have to get used to calling me Josie."

"But what about Mama?" Elisabeth asked, her voice revealing her shock and concern.

"What about her, Elisabeth?" Sam asked.

"How can you just forget about her and marry Mrs. Randolph?"

"I haven't forgotten your mother," Sam answered. "I'll never forget her. I loved her very much."

Elisabeth's chin quivered. "But you're getting married again."

"That doesn't mean I didn't love your mother. It only means we're making a new family."

"I *like* Josie," Anna said. "I'm glad she's coming with us."

Abigail gave Josie a shy smile, but glanced at Elisabeth and said nothing.

"Josie wanted a baby," Anna blurted out, "but she didn't get one. Can we give her a baby? Can it be our brother?"

Her question hung in the air for an uncomfortable moment.

Afraid of what Sam's expression would reveal, Josie couldn't look at him, so she didn't see his initial reaction. Her heart raced in the silence.

Apparently, he finally gathered his wits. "We'll just wait and see what God has in store for us."

A sinking sensation dropped in Josie's belly. She'd been so caught up in the anticipation that this particular reality hadn't entered her head. She couldn't have children. What if Sam wanted more? She would have to tell him. He might change his mind!

Enthusiasm drained from her spirit in a downward rush. What had she been thinking? Announcing an impending marriage might have been for naught.

Elisabeth's blue eyes held a cold accusation. The girl touched the bodice of her dress where Josie knew she wore her mother's wedding ring on a slender cord. Josie understood. Elisabeth obviously felt her father was betraying her mother's memory.

She regretted the parallel she drew to Margaretta's narrow-mindedness. This was nothing like that. Elisabeth's was a fresh loss, and she probably saw Josie as a threat to her importance with her father.

Sam spoke of the trip they'd soon be taking and the preparations necessary.

"How many rivers are there, Papa?" Anna asked.

"The only big one is the Platte." The fact that he knew and answered immediately proved it was a serious issue he'd already considered. We'll cross at Ogallala, where a ferry will take us across."

Josie didn't know about the exact location of their destination, but Union Pacific had completed laying rail across Nebraska two years ago. She would ask Sam about that when they were alone. Perhaps a train wouldn't be as terrifying to the girls as their wagon.

After more discussion, Abigail and Anna chased a butterfly across the grass and Elisabeth went back to her book. The fact that she didn't look at Josie again plainly told of her distress.

Josie gathered her courage. "There's something I didn't mention. It might make a difference."

Sam plucked a long blade of grass and held it between his teeth. "What is it?"

"You know I was married for several years."

"Yes."

"I never had any children. I'm barren."

Sam blinked and took the grass from his mouth. "I'm sorry, Josie."

She didn't want to hear his answer, but, steeling herself, she asked anyway. "Does that make a difference? I'll understand if you change your mind."

Her heart raced as she waited.

"Of course it doesn't change my mind. I already have children. I don't need any more. When I said I was sorry, I meant I felt badly for you if you were disappointed."

Relief flooded over her in a wave. Tears prickled behind her lids, but she blinked them back and looked away with a single nod. "Good. Good, then."

"You'll have your hands full with the girls," he assured her.

"I will at that." She remembered the other subject. "Sam. I'm not questioning your wisdom or decisions when I ask out of curiosity why you haven't considered taking the train to Colorado. The railroad would be much quicker, and perhaps safer."

"It would also be far costlier," he explained. "We have a wagon load of belongings, plus our passage. Carrie and I made the decision to take our belongings, even though the trip was more difficult. It meant a lot to her to have her things." A muscle in his jaw worked. "Another poor choice, since it ended up costing her life."

"You had no way of knowing. You did what you believed was the right thing. We could all torture ourselves with regrets if we didn't move past them. What about now? From here to Colorado?"

"I'd have to sell everything left for the tickets. I don't know if the girls could cope with that. They need something of their former life when we get there."

"I intend to ship my things," she said. "Not everything, of course, but some of my furniture and of course the clothing I don't pack for travel. It couldn't be that much more to add your things to mine."

He studied her. "You're willing to suffer the cost of shipping your belongings?"

"I'm selling my house. I can afford it."

"You don't owe anything for your home?"

"Bram paid for it when we were married. And as his widow, everything that was his became mine."

"I think you're underestimating the cost of including our things."

"I don't mind. I want to do it to make the journey easier. And safer."

His rusty brown gaze turned to the countryside while he thought. "*You* would feel safer?"

"Much. And it would be so much easier on the girls."

He turned his gaze back to her. "I could sell the wagon and then buy another to finish the last leg of the trip. There are no rails leading to Jackson Springs."

She agreed with a smile.

"But if the cost is extreme you'll let me know, so I can figure out a way to help."

"It won't be. Can we tell them?"

"Let's tell them."

The news of their engagement buzzed through Durham faster than a swarm of bees. Josie was elated by the greetings and congratulations she heard at church and in the mercantile that week. It did her heart good to know that Margaretta's narrow-minded opinion was hers alone, and that Josie's friends and acquaintances were happy for her.

For the next few weeks, Margaretta didn't speak to her at church, nor did she request Josie's presence when she made her trek to the graveyard.

On the Sunday before the week of their wedding, Sam noticed Margaretta standing alone inside the picket fence. "I understand people's reluctance to let their loved ones go. It's a blessing she has a place to come to, to remember her son, but she's perhaps too zealous in clinging to the past."

Josie hadn't told him how rude the woman had been to her. She simply nodded.

"She came to see me, you know."

Josie glanced up at him in surprise. Margaretta had threatened she would warn him about her. "I doubt that was pleasant for you."

"I don't think I was able to set her mind at ease."

"I doubt anyone could."

"According to her, you're the devil incarnate."

"Something like that."

"She believes you're using me for your own selfish purposes."

Josie got a sinking feeling in her stomach. It was one thing for Bram's mother to have such a distorted opinion of her, but pressing those beliefs onto others carried the venom too far. Had she put questions in Sam's head? Doubts?

Sam looked at Josie directly. "I told her if you wanted a wealthy man, you'd made a poor choice."

Of course one bitter woman's prattling hadn't changed his mind. He was a man of wisdom and integrity. She smiled in relief. "Is that why your sermon this morning was about not setting up our treasures here on earth?"

"It's a good reminder for everyone." He glanced toward the front of the church, where Reverend Martin sat on a white bench, greeting parishioners. This was his first Sunday to make the trek from the parsonage and attend the morning service.

"He looks tired," Sam said.

"He can rest after we eat. I'd best go see to the meal, while you help him back to the house."

Their last Sunday dinner in Durham was pleasant. James came by and ate with them. Reverend Martin brought up the approaching wedding. Ever since Josie had actually realized he would be performing the nuptials, she had appreciated him all the more. He was truly happy for her. The man was a living example of unselfish love.

James and Elisabeth played checkers afterward, and then moved out of doors, where they sat on the grass in the shade.

"I don't want her to grow up," Sam said from where he stood at the window in Henry's study.

"She's only thirteen," Josie reminded him.

"She's mature for her age."

"She has a level head."

"She's always been serious and thoughtful," he said.

"Has she always wanted to go everywhere with you?"

Sam seemed thoughtful for a moment. Josie knew that Elisabeth was most often the one who traveled with him, and she always questioned him about his visits. "She has."

"She wants your approval. She works hard to please you."

"She's the oldest, so that's natural."

Josie considered her next words. "Abigail wants to go places with you, too, but if Elisabeth is going, she holds her tongue."

He turned to look at her. "Abigail has never expressed an interest in accompanying me."

Josie suspected Abigail's hesitation might be because she feared being looked over for her sister. "She may not want to compete for your attention or affection."

"My relationship with each of my daughters is different."

Josie agreed with a nod. It wasn't her place to question how he handled things with his children. She changed the subject. "Only a few more days, and we'll be married and leaving," she said. "The time has passed quickly."

"The time we've been here has been well-spent," he said. "Henry thinks I was here to help him, but it was the other way around."

"I have no doubt that God brought you to Durham for a reason," she replied. "Because He loves us, and He's watching out for us. When we put our trust in Him, He can do things we never thought possible."

"Like moving away from your home?" Sam asked.

"Moving away isn't all that difficult."

"I pray you'll still be able to say that in a few weeks, when you're faced with a new city and the responsibility of three daughters."

She was tired of sitting on the edge of life, watching other people have families. She was grabbing on to this opportunity for all she was worth. "Just hearing you say I'll have three daughters makes me happy, Sam."

He'd said nothing of the fact that she would also have a new husband. Josie couldn't help studying him at the window and thinking of all that would entail.

She wouldn't be alone any longer.

Sometimes, when she heard the way Anna or Abigail spoke of their mother, and saw the look on Sam's face, she remembered she wasn't his first choice, or the woman he loved with all his heart. He'd lost that woman, and Josie didn't hope to replace her. Nor would she try.

But she longed for the comfort and intimacy of a family. She would see to their needs and make herself indispensable. She would make Samuel Hart a good wife. Doing her very best and earning his approval would be enough for her.

Anticipation hummed through the congregation seated in the small wooden church. Josie held the bouquet of daisies James had thoughtfully picked for her, and tried not to crush the stems and stain her white gloves.

"Are you ready for this?" Henry asked her with a smile.

They stood at the front of the church. The noon sunlight shone through the tall, narrow windows, creating long arrows of light across the worn oak floors.

"I'm ready," she answered confidently.

Josie hadn't seen Reverend Martin in his suit for months. He'd lost weight, so the black coat didn't quite fit his frame the way it once had.

A couple of years ago she'd given away the satin dress she'd worn to marry Bram. This time she'd chosen a pastel yellow confection from the dressmaker and had lace inserted around the collar and cuffs.

She wore a strand of pearls and matching earbobs that had belonged to her mother and had donned the wispy hat the girls helped her make, with tiny paper roses and Battenburg lace—not a veil, because that would have been inappropriate for her second wedding.

She was more than ready for this day and everything it brought.

Sam entered the church from the side door and caught sight of Josie. She turned, and a jolt of surprise shot through him. She was beautiful! Sunlight illuminated her pale yellow dress. A tiny lace hat showed off her lustrous dark hair. Thick lashes fringed her lovely eyes, and her smile was as warm and welcoming as the woman herself.

He'd made this arrangement for purely practical reasons, but he was taking a lovely young woman as his wife. He glanced to where Elisabeth, Abigail and Anna sat on the front bench in their best Sunday dresses, their shining pale hair braided. Anna beamed from ear to ear. Abigail gave him a hesitant smile. Elisabeth refused to look up and meet his eyes.

She would come around.

Sam felt good about marrying Josie. Even the day and the weather were perfect. This marriage was the best choice he'd made in a long time. He looked at Henry and nodded.

Reverend Martin performed the ceremony, reading from the book of Corinthians and encouraging them to keep God at the center of their marriage.

"And now, by the power given to me by God and the state of Nebraska, I pronounce you Mr. and Mrs. Samuel Hart."

Josie had anticipated the words, but they still gave her a tingle of pleasure. Sam's hand was large and warm as it enveloped hers.

"You may kiss the bride."

She looked up. Sam's expression didn't reveal his thoughts. He had never kissed her. Without hesitation, he leaned forward and pressed a kiss to the corner of her lips—sort of a half kiss, half peck on the cheek that, however unsatisfactory, sealed their vows.

They were man and wife. Her new life had begun.

She smiled hesitantly and together they turned to face the approving congregation. Anna, a vision in the pale dress that nearly matched the color of Josie's, ran forward to hug her father around the waist. She released him and gave Josie an affectionate hug, pressing her head into Josie's midriff and squeezing her tightly.

Josie touched Anna's hair and thanked God for the child's loving, accepting nature.

Ten minutes later Sam held a signed certificate. The women of the church had prepared cake, punch and coffee, and now served them in the shaded side yard. Josie glanced at the simple gold band on her finger. She'd had so many dreams and expectations of her first husband and their marriage, and most of them had been unrealistic. She wouldn't make the same mistake this time. She would be satisfied and therefore not disappointed.

She accepted the hugs and well-wishes of her friends and neighbors. Margaretta was conspicuously absent, and Pauline Wilber mentioned the fact, as a small gathering crowded around Josie.

"She should have married again herself," Nettie said. "Maybe she wouldn't be so miserable if she had."

"You're so good for putting up with her all these years," Laura Caldwell added. "You deserve this new start."

Josie thanked them and changed the subject.

She had asked the invited guests not to bring gifts. Most of her belongings had already been sold, donated or shipped to Colorado, along with Sam's furniture and trunks. Anything extra would make their trip more difficult.

To her delight, a couple that had just added a new

baby to their family bought Josie's house. Josie had spent the last two nights with Nettie Boardman.

In winding up her life here, she had signed an agreement with Frank Carlisle. He would be sending her a payment every month to pay for the other half of the newspaper. She looked forward to that as an additional income that would help the family.

There were a few gifts, so they opened embroidered dish towels and monogrammed handkerchiefs and thanked the givers.

Tomorrow morning they would set out for their new home.

Sam and the girls delivered her to Nettie's, so she could change and collect her things. They returned to the parsonage, where they spent their evening as usual.

Once it grew late, Sam tucked the girls into bed.

Josie packed the gifts and readied their satchels for morning. After changing, she brushed out her hair and glanced around the room. She didn't know what to expect from now on. Sam had kissed her, only when pressed in front of their wedding guests. He didn't have those kinds of feelings for her. But it was okay.

Josie put her hairbrush back in her satchel and removed her Bible. She had a lifetime ahead. She was well pleased with her new life.

Chapter Eleven

Their travel through Nebraska was fairly quick, as the train chugged across open stretches of prairie. Anna and Abigail were fascinated with every aspect of the trip, from the passengers who accompanied them to the scenery.

Josie, who had traveled before and knew the hardships, had purchased tickets for six seats, even though there were only five of them. The additional seat gave them two poorly padded benches that faced each other and a little room for wiggle. They took turns using the extra seat for uncomfortable naps, during which Sam filled the space between benches opposite each other with a crate.

Toward evening the first day, a man ahead of them spotted a herd of bison and alerted the passengers. The Hart family watched with fascination as the beasts grazed beneath the orange sphere of the sun.

Travel became slower as they reached Colorado, with its winding curves and steady inclines. The train stopped at every station to take on water and coal. The travelers were afforded anywhere from thirty to sixty minutes to use the primitive facilities and, if they were fortunate, buy a meal and a drink.

The inside of the railcar was hot and stuffy. Even though dust and smoke blew in the open windows, the ventilation was necessary.

A young woman traveling alone with an infant occupied a seat behind them. The child fussed and cried, much to the dismay of the poor girl and the disapproval of the other passengers.

"I haven't seen her eat," Sam said quietly to Josie, late the second morning of their journey.

Uncertain of his meaning, she glanced from Elisabeth, who was reading, to Anna and Abigail, working on quilt squares. They'd all had breakfast that morning. "Who?"

"The girl behind us. I'm thinking she has no money."

The child's fussing again drew scowls from nearby passengers. "What can we do?" Josie asked.

"Invite her to join us when we stop next."

"All right."

Deborah Bowers declined Josie's first offer to join them, so Josie offered to hold the child while the girl used the facility. Upon her return, Deborah thought better of her answer and accompanied them into the rustic dining hall attached to the station.

Josie held the tired little boy throughout their meal. She fed Jack a few bites of bread she soaked in milk, and he ate them happily.

"He's a good little fellow," Deborah told them. "He's not used to being held so much. My husband has a place ready for us in Fort Collins. We've already been traveling for a week."

"We're going as far as Fort Collins," Sam told her. "Why don't you let my wife and I help you with him?"

Hearing Sam call her his wife pleased Josie so much she got tears in her eyes.

"You're so kind," Deborah said with heartfelt gratitude. "Everyone else is giving me dirty looks."

"If you think he'd sleep for a while, we have an extra seat for that purpose," Josie offered. "We can cushion the crate with his blankets and let him nap."

Deborah tried to pay for her meal, but Sam used his own coins. They boarded the train and he temporarily took Deborah's seat so she could get Jack to sleep and sit beside him.

"Your husband is a kind man," Deborah said to Josie later. The girls were all napping while sitting up and Jack was sound asleep.

"Yes," Josie replied with a smile. "He is."

"I hope my husband still looks at me the way your husband looks at you after we've been married as long as you have."

Deborah's statement took Josie by surprise. How did Sam look at her? As she ruminated that question, Deborah's misconception became clear. "We've only just been married actually. I'm the girls' stepmother."

"That makes their blond hair clear to me," Deborah said with a nod. "And the fact that you're newlyweds explains those admiring glances."

Josie's cheeks grew warm, and it had nothing to do with the heat inside the car.

When the two returned to their own seats later, Josie

tried to catch Sam looking at her, but she didn't notice anything out of the ordinary.

"How much longer?" Abigail asked after a supper of tough steaks and nearly burnt corn bread.

"This is the last night we'll spend on the train," Sam assured her. "Tomorrow we'll reach Fort Collins and buy a wagon and horses for the rest of the trip."

"And then we'll take the wagon to our new house and unpack our stuff," Anna supplied.

"Wait till you see Mama's teapot and cups," Abigail told Josie. "They have violets painted on them."

"I'm sure they're lovely," Josie answered.

"We won't have everything all at once," Sam told them. "Josie shipped a lot of things ahead by rail. We'll bring some of them from Fort Collins to Jackson Springs, but the rest will be delivered in due time."

"What about beds?" Abigail asked. "Will we have beds?"

"We brought one with us," Sam reminded her.

"I had one shipped," Josie added. "We'll buy another when we get in our home."

"Perhaps not right away," Sam told her. "The girls can make do with pallets or sleep together."

Any bed sounded good to Josie right about then. She was exhausted. Her back and hips hurt from the uncomfortable seats and lack of exercise. The girls fell silent and eventually nodded off to sleep, with Anna on the makeshift portion. Josie shifted to find the least torturous position and closed her eyes.

She had drifted off when behind her Jack fussed. Josie got up, reached across a snoring lady to reach Deborah and took Jack. She settled with him on her lap and gave him the brass compact from her reticule to hold. He chewed on the side and looked up at her in the semidarkness.

Sam studied Josie from beneath the lowered brim of his hat. She was as hot and uncomfortable as everyone else, but she made the best of every situation and didn't complain. Her face had been flushed a becoming shade of pink nearly the entire journey, and the dampness and humidity had coaxed wispy corkscrew curls to frame her cheeks and temples.

He couldn't forget the sight of her in her lemony-colored wedding dress, nor could he ignore the anticipation that had coursed through him when Reverend Martin and instructed him to kiss her, and he'd done so.

He hadn't married her for his own gain or pleasure. He'd married her for his daughters, and he believed Carrie would have approved. But what would Carrie have thought of his reaction to that kiss? He'd immediately been ashamed that he could so easily have abandoned thoughts of his wife and entertained the promise of new possibilities.

Lord, thank You for strength and wisdom, he prayed.

Josie was so good with the girls. And apparently she would have been excellent at comforting and mothering an infant. Sam never questioned God about why things were the way they were, but he did believe it was a shame that Josie had been unable to have her own babies.

But God knew everything that was and would be, so He'd known in advance that Sam's children would need the perfect mother at just this place in time.

Soon they'd be in their new home. Living together as man and wife. *Lord, thank You for strength and wisdom.*

Sam closed his eyes and slept.

This time his dreams were not about his wife's death.

He dreamed of a woman with dark, wavy hair that escaped the pins and curled about her face. He admired her caramel eyes and dewy pink skin. In his dream he kissed her.

And he wasn't sorry.

"Four days of dust and heat without a bed or a bath makes me admire trail drivers and soldiers all the more." Josie brushed at her hopelessly wrinkled skirt, then shook the hem.

Sam loaded the last of the foodstuffs into the back of their wagon and tied them down on top of the heavy items. "We sometimes went weeks without a bath on our way from Philadelphia."

She wrinkled her nose. She had purchased supplies for the trip while he secured a wagon and team, and they now stood in the street outside the mercantile, ready to travel.

"How many days will we travel in the wagon, Father?" Elisabeth asked from her position beside the rear wheel.

"Three or four, depending on the team and how often we stop." He fastened the canvas over the back opening to keep out as much dust as possible.

Abigail remained on the boardwalk in the shade. Her bonnet had lost its starch in the heat and humidity, and the brim sagged over one eye. "It will be scary without other wagons."

"It's a well-traveled route, Ab," her father assured her.

"We'll likely see other travelers coming and going. And there's a stage, so we'll pass a way station."

"And no rivers, Papa."

"No rivers," he assured Anna.

She gave him a nod, and her eyes widened with enthusiasm for her next subject. "Did you see the big kitty beside the barrel?"

"I did," Sam answered. He reached for her on the boardwalk, lifted her to kiss her cheek and effortlessly swooped her up to the front of the wagon.

"He rubbed hisself on my boots an' let me pet him," she said. "He's more friendlier than Reverend Martin's kitty."

"Cats are rather like people in that regard," he answered. "Some are friendly, others are not."

Sam found an empty crate and positioned it so Abigail and Elisabeth could climb up. They ducked inside the wagon, seating themselves on the interior bench.

Anna remained standing so she could ask, "Are lambs friendly?"

"Some are," he answered, looking at Josie and raising his eyebrows as if to say, *She isn't letting that go, is she?* Instead, he asked, "Ready?"

Josie walked to the front and used the crate, then the spokes of the front wheel as a ladder. Sam helped her the rest of the way.

Anna scurried to the seat just inside the cover of the canvas, and Josie situated herself on the hard seat.

Sam tucked the crate between them on the floor, but instead of sitting, he reached for Josie's hand. At the touch, she glanced up in surprise. He urged her to stand and turn, then led her under the canvas arch. Crouching in the space before his daughters, he took Elisabeth's hand with his free one.

Anna and Abigail clutched hands and Abigail reached for Josie so they formed a circle. Josie's heart fluttered at being part of this family. Sam's hand was large and strong and Abigail's small and soft.

"Thank You, Lord, for a prosperous journey by Your will. We commit our way to You," he prayed, and emotion welled inside Josie.

"Father, I pray for the people of Jackson Springs, that their spirits are open to whatever gift and whatever Word it is You'd have me impart to them. Lord, make me an encourager for them. Open doors for Elisabeth and Abigail and Anna, so that they will have friends and teachers to bless them. Father, as my wife, I thank You that Josie is taking her own special gift to your children there. Bless the labor of her hands and the desires of her heart, as she prepares our home and opens it to the people.

"Now keep us safe in all our ways as we travel, and we praise You in the mighty name of Jesus."

"Amen," Josie and the girls chorused.

As Sam seated himself, picked up the reins and clucked to the horses, Josie was filled to overflowing with gratitude for this good, upright man God had brought into her life.

If she'd set out to search a hundred cities and a thousand places, she would never have found a man seeking God's heart as determinedly as this one beside her now.

And he had chosen to marry her.

Thank You, thank You, thank You.

* * *

Sam, Elisabeth and Abigail were familiar with setting up a camp, gathering firewood and finding water, if need be, but everything was new to Josie. She burned the first night's biscuits and undercooked them the second night. On the third evening, Sam took over and made the biscuits over the fire, while Josie used another skillet to fry the two whitefish he and Elisabeth had caught in a nearby stream.

At least she'd been assured that this was their last night before reaching Jackson Springs. Each night, she and the girls had slept on top of the furniture and supplies lying in the bed of the wagon, padded with blankets, while Sam slept on the ground underneath.

"The evenings are so much cooler than the days here," she said. "I'm going to like that for sleeping."

"I'm keeping a journal of all the trees and flowers and animals," Abigail told them. "I don't know what all of them are called, but my teacher might be able to help me."

"I found a pretty stone while I was gathering sticks," Elisabeth said.

She didn't often add to the conversation, so Josie stopped eating to ask about her discovery. Even though the conditions were less than ideal, their trip had been a good experience. The close confines had given them opportunities to talk.

"There's a secluded spot just beyond those cottonwoods," Sam told them, indicating the area. "It's a perfect opportunity to bathe and wash any clothes you might want freshened."

No one wanted to miss the luxury of being clean

when they arrived in town the next day, so the females took turns bathing. They gathered around the campfire, drying their hair while Sam bathed and tended the horses.

He tucked his daughters into the wagon for the night and returned. "The church has a parsonage for us," Sam told her. She had washed the plates in the stream and packed away all but the coffeepot. They would eat the remaining biscuits in the morning. "The council mentioned that there was an allowance if we prefer different housing, but I'm sure it will be sufficient."

Josie imagined a home as comfortable as Reverend Martin's and nodded. She poured each of them a cup of coffee and sat on an empty crate near Sam. "I'm sorry I haven't been more of a help out here."

"You haven't complained a bit, and for that I'm thankful."

"I'm having an adventure," she said. "I've never seen the mountains, and as they become bigger and bigger on the horizon, the sight takes my breath away. Everything is green and lush, and there are so many trees."

"The countryside is beautiful," Sam agreed, but he was looking at her where she sat, with her hair loose over her shoulders.

Josie glanced aside. Was that the look Deborah had mentioned? "I'd better get ready for bed."

She stood and made her way into the brush that surrounded their campsite. On her return, something rubbed against the hem of her skirts, nearly tripping her. A startled shriek escaped before she could tell herself it was probably only one of the muskrats or martens Sam had told them about.

With her heart racing, she shot toward the safety of the fire. Sam dashed forward to meet her halfway. "What is it?"

"Something in the brush surprised me, is all." She felt foolish, but she was glad for the arm he wrapped around her, and she tucked into his embrace with a rush of relief.

They stood that way, out of the circle of firelight, with the moon bathing them in its glow.

Sam smelled of the soap he'd used, along with the same touch of wood smoke that clung to all of them. He was warm and solid, and a sense of security and well-being infused her. Josie hadn't been held this way for a long time.

"I feel safe here," she said softly.

She felt his hand in her hair, threading through the length like a caress, coming to rest on her shoulder.

Her heart beat faster than it had when she'd been startled moments ago. After a second's hesitation, she looked up.

Sam met her gaze in the darkness. She couldn't see his eyes. Could he see the moon reflected in hers?

He moved his hand from her shoulder to cup her jaw with his palm. His thumb moved along her cheekbone in a gentle caress. The night sounds closed around them, cushioning them in the mysterious cocoon of the night.

Chapter Twelve

Without conscious thought or effort, she found herself locked in his embrace. He lowered his head and she met his kiss with eager anticipation.

The rightness of the moment took over.

He was a mystery, this husband, strong and tender at the same time. She'd been more than ready to cast aside loneliness and entrust herself to him and the future she believed waited for them. The future seemed painted with exquisite possibilities.

He represented everything that was good and perfect about fathers and husbands. Strange, unfamiliar feelings made her light-headed. She couldn't help the little sigh that escaped her.

Josie had no idea there were kisses like this.

Kissing him was everything she'd ever imagined it could be, and she wanted to cry with the rightness of the moment.

Sam ended the kiss and rested his forehead on hers. She recognized her keen disappointment that the moment had ended.

He threaded his fingers into her hair. She reached up to skim his jaw with her fingertips.

Sam reacted to her touch with a start, releasing her. Though he kept a hand on her elbow to steady her, he took a step back, putting distance between them. "It's late," was all he said.

Josie tried to make sense of his rapid change and his obvious discomfort. "Yes, of course."

She thought she'd replied, but wasn't sure the words had actually passed her lips.

He removed his hand from her arm and turned toward the fire.

Josie followed at a slower pace.

He regretted kissing her.

A debilitating ache knotted in her chest and swelled to crowd the newfound joy from her heart.

Had he been reminded of his beloved Carrie? Undoubtedly. Their evening around the fire most likely stirred up memories of their trip to Nebraska. Maybe kissing Josie was a disappointment.

She got angry with herself then. She'd vowed a hundred times that she wouldn't allow her expectations to swell out of proportion. Idealism only set her up for a fall, as she well knew.

While he banked the fire, she climbed the wagon wheel and silently made her way to where the girls slept soundly. After removing her outer clothing, she found her spot. The space was crowded with four of them, but the squeeze was better than lying out of doors and most likely encountering insects and scurrying creatures.

I am content, she told God silently. *You provide all my needs, and my soul is satisfied.* Her distress was childish, and she refused to let foolish emotions control her and steal her joy. She was delighted to be here, grateful to be starting a new life.

If she gave herself over to the growing urge to cry, she would wake the girls, so she closed her eyes against the dark and prayed.

The following morning, Sam led the horses to their positions and fastened the tongue to their harnesses. By the time he had them ready, Josie had coffee made and now divided the biscuits. She handed each of them an apple, avoiding Sam's eyes and careful not to graze his hand with her fingers. He found himself studying her for a reaction to his presence.

Last night he'd lain awake far too long for a man who needed to be alert for the day's travel. His feelings toward this woman were confusing, and he didn't like his weakness one bit. His obligation was to his family's safety, and he had no business allowing an attraction to Josie to distract him.

He was responsible for all of them. A woman's influence never aided a logical decision, and he needed to make choices for their safety. He'd married her to take care of the girls. He hadn't expected to be so absorbed with thoughts of her…and he hadn't expected to think about the curve of her cheek or the way she smiled.

"Do you want to sit beside your father this morning?" Josie asked Anna.

"Oh yes, thank you!" the child replied.

"We'll take turns today, so you can each see your new home a little better."

Was Josie avoiding him? The thought and the possibility disturbed him more than they should have.

Eventually, the road took them past sprawling ranches with horses and cattle on the hillsides and houses tucked into the valleys. When the sun was high overhead, he led the team across a field to the shade of a stand of willows, with drooping branches and crooked, reddish trunks.

While Josie got out the makings for sliced ham and bread, he dipped water from their barrel and made several trips to the horses. The mundane task allowed him to watch her from beneath the brim of his hat. Everything she did was graceful; her voice, when she spoke to the girls, was gentle, her words kind. He'd made a good decision.

After they ate, Anna inspected a thicket of chokecherries and brought a handful to show Josie. "Can we eat 'em?"

Josie nodded. "While we're here, let's fill a pail and we'll make jelly when we get to our new house."

A little over an hour later, from her seat beside her father, Abigail spotted the town. "There it is! Is that it, Papa?"

"That's it."

Josie, Elisabeth and Anna crowded behind the front seat to get their first glimpse of Jackson Springs. Josie's initial reaction was to marvel at the way the various-colored buildings stood on slopes of uneven heights. She was used to the flat plains of the prairie, not the wooded inclines or ore-stained escarpments that sectioned this town into levels.

"It's charming!" she said with delight.

"There's the church!" Abigail cried, pointing toward

a white steeple rising against the startlingly blue, cloudless sky.

"Thank You for safe travel and for blessing us with all we need for our new life," Sam said in a husky voice.

Tears blurred Josie's vision.

He chose that moment to glance over his shoulder, and directly into her eyes. They shared a silent moment of expectation and excitement. The side of his mouth turned up in an uncustomary grin.

She blinked away tears and turned her attention back to the town.

"Let's go see the church." Sam clucked to the horses and shook the reins.

Main Street had most likely been the very center of town at one time, but homes and businesses now sprawled along inclines to the west and south. The buildings on the thoroughfare were all the same height and constructed of brick, though their facades were trimmed with bright blues and reds, and the top of each made a unique silhouette against the sky.

The general store bore a shingled porch roof, and two gingerbread-trimmed windows with canvas awnings that looked like lidded eyes in the upper story. A portly fellow in a white apron paused his sweeping to raise a hand.

"Welcome to Jackson Springs!"

"Who-oa," Sam called and tugged the team to a halt. "Afternoon, sir."

"What's your business?" the man asked.

"I'm Reverend Hart," Sam replied. "This is my wife, Josie, and these are my daughters."

Two women who'd come out of a nearby building

stepped to the edge of the boardwalk. "We've been expectin' you," the lady in a blue calico dress said with a smile.

"The parsonage is the white house beside the church," the other woman told them. "The ladies have stocked the pantry with enough to see you through a few days while you settle in. And now that we know you're here, we'll bring supper tonight."

"That's exceptionally kind of you," Sam replied and Josie nodded.

After a few more pleasantries, Sam guided the horses and turned onto Birch Street, where the church sat.

The wagon rolled to a stop before the only house right beside the handsome house of worship.

Josie stared. Had there been some mistake? Hadn't they been expecting a *family?*

Sam collected himself and looped the reins around the cleat. In the next instant, he hopped down from the seat to the ground, then turned and helped the girls, one after the other. When Josie stood above him, he reached for her.

Their eyes met and she recalled his prayer, giving thanks for all he needed to start over. Did his thanks include her?

His strong hands were warm at her waist, and she covered them with her own. The moment seemed to stretch out until they were absorbed in each other's eyes. She was his wife now. They'd arrived at their new home, and this was a fresh beginning for all of them.

She hopped down, and he settled her lightly on the ground. As though he didn't want to release her, one hand remained at the small of her back while he turned and studied the arrangement of the church and parsonage on the same parcel of land. There was probably only ten yards between the two structures.

The little house had been given a fresh coat of paint, and it was unembellished, without a shutter or a flower or even a porch. She stepped ahead of him finally, to climb the four steps leading to the door. The portal opened directly into a tiny little room with a braided rug. Josie's bright mood dimmed.

Another door opened into a bedroom that would hold one bed and little else.

The kitchen sat beside the first room. It held a narrow stove and a cupboard. Right beside the kitchen was the only other bedroom, marginally bigger than the first, though the extra feet were in length, not width.

"There's no closet," Elisabeth pointed out.

"And no dining room," Abigail added.

"Will all three of us sleep in this room?" Elisabeth asked, her eyes wide with dismay.

And probably in the same bed, Josie figured. There wasn't room for two.

"We've done just fine till now," Sam said. "How much room do we need? As soon as we're settled, you'll be at school all day long. I can work at the church during the day. It looks plenty big enough to have an extra room for my desk and books."

The girls said nothing, but the excitement that they'd all shared at seeing the town and anticipating their new home had drained away.

Josie had never seen such a tiny house.

Chapter Thirteen

"Where do we bathe?" Elisabeth asked.

Through the window, Josie spotted a structure that obviously wasn't the outhouse because it had a chimney. She opened the back door, and the others followed her out.

A stack of firewood had been neatly piled within a wooden lean-to. The little building, no bigger than a shed, but sided and roofed just like the house, held laundry tubs, buckets, a copper bathing tub and an ancient cast-iron stove.

"Here you go," Sam told them. "A place for canning, cooking, laundry and bathing."

Elisabeth cast a skeptical glance around the room. "Doesn't it get awfully cold in the mountains in the winter?"

"I'm assured it does," he replied.

Josie silently agreed it would be inconvenient to run between the two buildings to bathe, but it was a small hardship.

"Paul wrote the book of Philippians while he was in

jail," Sam reminded them. "In a dungeon. And what did he talk about? Joy, that's what. 'Rejoice in the Lord always, and again I say rejoice.' He had joy in spite of his circumstances, and his circumstances were a lot worse than these."

He headed for the door. "After I have a look at the church, I'll bring in as much as I can unload on my own. The bureau and bed will have to wait for more hands."

"I'll help, Papa!" Anna called, running after him.

The three females stood in the silence of the little outbuilding. Elisabeth and Abigail looked at each other and then at Josie. "It's dreadful, don't you agree?" Elisabeth asked.

Josie chose her words carefully. Their father had hidden his own disappointment well and had been adamant about being joyful. "I am quite surprised at how small it is, yes. Perhaps the last preacher was unmarried or his children were grown and gone."

She headed back toward the house and the girls trailed behind her.

In her mind, she was picturing all the furniture and belongings that would be arriving soon. Would they have to sell everything after all? Would they have to find storage?

All her dreams for making a grand, comfortable home, and entertaining the parishioners, and holding Bible studies and quilting circles were perched to fly out the window.

The five of them would be hard-pressed to sit comfortably in that small parlor—or in this kitchen, for that matter.

She opened the single cupboard to find canned meat

and vegetables, flour, sugar and coffee. "That was nice of them."

"I wish we'd never left Philadelphia," Elisabeth said from behind her.

Josie turned and caught the disappointment and frustration in her expression.

"If we'd stayed there, none of this would be happening. Mama would still be alive, and we'd still have our rooms and our beds and our friends. This is a dreadful house in a dreadful town, and I don't want to be here."

She turned and ran out the back door.

Josie knew better than to imagine she could comfort her. She stared at the open doorway. She understood Elisabeth's disillusionment.

"Everything looks quite clean," she said to Abigail. "Let's go ahead and bring in a few things."

Two young men arrived to help Sam carry in the trunks and pieces of furniture. Once their belongings were inside, the space shrunk all the more.

Elisabeth remained in the backyard, where she spread a blanket and sat with a book.

"Do you want her to help you?" Sam asked sometime later.

Josie had been bumping into someone everywhere she turned. "No. Let's leave her be for now."

Two ladies who introduced themselves as Ruby Adamson and Vanessa Powell brought savory beef stew and warm corn bread, along with a jug of fresh milk, a pint of cream and butter.

After they ate, Sam put the bed together in the room beside the kitchen. "We'll sleep on pallets until another bed arrives," he told her.

She nodded in agreement. "I'm happy for the girls to have the bed."

Their trunks lined each wall of the parlor. Feeling overwhelmed, Josie was studying the chaos when Sam said, "I'm going to take a few things over to the church."

He hadn't asked her to join him, so she nodded and watched him go.

"May we take baths?" Anna asked.

Josie agreed that bathing sounded like a marvelous idea, and went in search of the water source.

Having bathed with warm water and dressed in their nightclothes for the first time in a week, the girls snuggled together in the only bed that had made the trip with them, the walnut four-poster they'd brought from Philadelphia. The bureau wouldn't fit in the room, so it sat outside their door in the kitchen.

Josie left a lantern burning on the kitchen wall, so if one of them awoke in the strange place, they wouldn't be frightened.

She warmed milk and poured herself a glass. Carrying it out of doors, she sat on the top step.

The evening was already cool. She would need to unpack her shawls. Light illuminated one of the arched windows at the church, and she surmised the room beyond was a study.

She felt as discouraged as she had the night before, so she told herself she'd known what she was doing by accompanying Sam. She was here for the girls. She'd gone along with that.

Standing and walking away from the house, she turned and looked up at the dark, pine-covered mountain. They could do some exploring soon. She liked the crisp, clean scent in the air and the way the heavens seemed so close. The stars twinkled overhead like a thousand diamonds, the moon a pale globe in their midst.

An hour or so later, the sound of the front door opening and closing woke her. She'd been fast asleep on a thick padding of quilts and blankets, and she rose on one elbow. Sam eased open the door with a creak. "Didn't mean to wake you."

"It's all right."

Easing off his boots, he set them against the wall. He blew out the lantern she'd placed on a crate in the corner, and his clothing rustled.

"Is the church nice?" she asked.

"It's more adequate than the house."

Those quiet words assured her he wasn't as unaffected as he'd behaved in front of the girls.

"I'm sorry, Josie," he said. "I'm sure you were expecting more. You're used to much nicer accommodations. As soon as I've had time to settle into my position and make some headway, I'll see what I can do."

"Don't worry about the house, Sam. You've got more important things to focus on right now."

"Thanks for understanding."

She was feeling disconnected…and left out. She should have gone with him to the church, rather than hanging back, but she'd felt awkward about joining him uninvited. "The girls are going to do just fine," she told him. "They've been through a lot. Now they'll have time to get comfortable with the town and turn their thoughts forward. Once we're all settled, we'll get them in school."

"Thank you, Josie."

"Please don't thank me. I want to be here, and I want to be a real part of their lives. Yours, too, if you'll let me."

He recognized how hard Josie was trying. He hadn't realized how much Carrie had handled, or the extent of the sacrifices she'd made until she was gone. He didn't intend to make the same mistake over again.

Sam's emotions conflicted so often that, admittedly, he hadn't been handling things well. Josie was doing her best to fulfill her part of their arrangement. He hadn't made any wild promises to her or expressed his devotion—it was still too soon—but he had entered into a holy commitment. And already he cared deeply for this woman.

In order for this to work, their marriage must be a marriage in more than name only. He had every intention of honoring all the aspects that their commitment entailed.

By the end of the week it was apparent that the house was woefully inadequate. While Sam was busy meeting with the town council, overseeing a newly formed advisory board and studying for his first sermon, Josie instructed the girls to help each other iron their dresses and prepare for an outing.

Eager for any opportunity to escape the confines of the little house, they joined her outside.

"Where are we going?" Anna asked.

"Your father is extremely busy and has important

things on his mind," she told them. "There are things we can do to make his duties and all of our lives easier. We'll take care of things on our own and not bother him with domestic details." That was, after all, why he'd needed her. "I need all of you to help me."

"Are we going shopping?" Abigail asked.

"That we are," Josie replied. "We're shopping for a house."

Elisabeth's eyes lit up, delighting Josie no end. "A *bigger* house?"

"Definitely a bigger house. I know the good people of this town intended to do well by us, but a home needs to be a place of comfort and safety, as well as a place to invite friends and the community."

Delighted, the sisters shared hugs and pleased smiles. Anna grasped Josie's hand and led them toward Main Street. "Where do we find a house?"

Sam had spoken to the girls about being content, and he was doing his best to set an example.

She wanted to make things easier for him at home, so they would have more time together as a couple and as a family. If he had time to devote to a search and if he wasn't concerned about money, he would have done this himself. She was grateful that a large-enough house was something she could do for all of them. Josie led them to a building with a real estate sign hanging from its porch. The door was open, so they entered.

A woman sweeping the floor glanced up in surprise. "Well, good morning! What can I do for you?"

"We need to buy a home," Josie told her.

She propped the broom against a wall. "You need to

speak with my husband," she answered. "I'll get him straightaway."

An hour later they had seen four homes, and none of them had impressed Josie as being what they needed. The one that came closest was too far from the church.

"There's only one house near the church," Thomas Payne told her as they sat in his canopied buggy. "And it belonged to a man who owned the mill. His wife had family money."

"May we see it?" Josie asked.

"I'm afraid it's not really a preacher's house." His tone was apologetic.

"Why not? It can always be redecorated if it doesn't suit our tastes."

"Oh, no, ma'am, it looks fine. It's just that—well, it has a pretty hefty price tag."

"Oh. How much?"

He told her, but she wasn't deterred. "All right. Show us, please."

Mr. Payne's eyebrows shot up. He lifted the reins to set the horse in motion. He led them past the church and their crowded bungalow, then turned the corner onto a tree-lined street that slowly inclined. At the top of the hill was a house set back from the street, the lot edged by shrubbery and mature trees.

When Josie spotted the colorfully asymmetrical house, anticipation had her leaning forward and taking in every elaborate detail. The gabled house presented an interesting arrangement of bay windows, balconies, stained glass, turrets, porches, brackets and ornamental masonry.

The structure was two-storied, except for a third

story at the top of one pointed turret. Someone had painted the ornate trim a garish pink and black, but the wood siding was a cream color, the shingles on the gables a soft bluish green. The steeply pitched, uneven roof was a pale gray.

The fanciful structure stood silhouetted against the lush green pines on the hillside behind. Even though the house sat above most of the town, it was protected by the shadow of the mountain behind.

Josie loved the place the moment she saw it.

Anna squealed and leaped from the buggy to run toward the gate. Abigail and Elisabeth followed, their skirts flying.

Mr. Payne opened the gate, and the sisters dashed up stairs made of huge slabs of stone to wait impatiently on the shaded front porch.

The man held out his brass key ring and fumbled until he found the correct key. Anna's boots clattered in the foyer as she ran forward and came to a stop. With a rising surge of hope, Josie took in the large foyer.

The first floor comprised a drawing room with a stone fireplace, a spacious dining room, a roomy kitchen with a pump and sink and a front parlor that sat in a three-sided bay.

Five bedrooms and a sunroom were on the second floor, and the third-floor room could only be reached by dropping down a trapdoor with a ladder. It was a charming but odd-shaped room, with two windows on each of four sides. Two walls sloped, the others were gabled dormers.

"Can this be my room?" Anna asked with excitement lacing her voice.

"If we were to buy this house, I believe the three of you should sleep on the floor below," Josie replied. "This could be your playing and reading and thinking room."

She looked out the windows that faced the mountain, charmed to see deer on the shaded slopes. "Look!"

When they were finished ogling the countryside in all directions, Josie turned back to find Mr. Payne with a pleased smile on his face.

"It's a ghastly shade of pink," she said to make certain he knew she didn't intend to pay the full price he'd quoted.

"Remedied easily enough," he replied. "Did you note the beautiful floors?"

She had. The previous owners had worn nary a layer from the perfect walnut planks or their varnished sheen. "There is a lot of overgrown shrubbery that needs to be cut away from the foundation," she told him. "And not a flower in sight."

"Your daughters will certainly enjoy that bathing chamber," he assured her.

She didn't doubt that for a moment. "I imagine the previous owner took his stove with him. We would have to invest in a good one."

"Victor Larken, over at the general store, has a couple of the latest models in his back room. And he can order anything that strikes your fancy."

"I imagine that would cost a pretty penny."

The girls followed them down the ladderlike stairs and into the hall below. "Why don't you admire the scenery while Mr. Payne and I have a talk?" she said to Elisabeth.

Elisabeth nodded and ushered her sisters into one of the bedrooms.

Downstairs again, Josie pointed out wallpaper she didn't care for in the drawing room, and found the door leading to the pantry had no brass knob to match the plate.

After learning she intended to pay with cashier's checks and didn't need a loan, Thomas Payne lowered the price. He cheerfully took them to the bank where she made arrangements and then on to the telegraph office. Later she signed a couple of papers before she and the girls headed for the general store.

"Papa's sure gonna be surprised, isn't he?" Anna asked.

"I expect he will," she answered with a smile.

Elisabeth paused on the boardwalk in front of the store with a question. "Will we each have our own room?"

Josie nodded.

"We don't have curtains for all those windows," she said with a frown.

"We can make curtains," Josie assured her. "But I don't believe that room in the tower needs any, do you?"

"When are we moving in?" Abigail asked.

"I have a little more business to take care of first," Josie told her. "Banking and signing papers."

"Does Papa have to sign the papers?"

"I'll buy it and put his name on it," she explained. "We won't have to trouble him with the details."

"When are we going to tell him?" Elisabeth asked.

"When do you want to tell him?"

Elisabeth appeared thoughtful. "I suppose we could wait until all the business is done."

Abigail and Elisabeth glanced at each other. "Let's surprise him when it's ready," Abigail suggested. "We can move in the furniture and everything first. It will be a grand surprise that way."

"I'll hire the men who are delivering our things from the train station to take them to the new house," Josie agreed with a joyful grin.

Elisabeth turned to look down at Anna. "Can you keep this absolutely secret?"

"Oh, yes! Papa will love our surprise!"

With all of them in agreement, they entered the store. It was the first time Josie had seen all three of them looking so pleased and hopeful. At last she'd been able to do something that made a difference.

Chapter Fourteen

On Sunday, Sam preached his first sermon to the people of Jackson Springs. The pews were filled to capacity, as all the church members and other curious citizens showed up to meet the Harts.

Josie couldn't have been prouder than to be introduced as Sam's wife. Even Elisabeth put on a smile and greeted parishioners cordially.

After the service, the men arranged makeshift tables in the lot behind the church. The ladies served food and drinks, chatting all the while. The men set up a croquet game, and then stood watching the children.

Josie recognized that people and traditions were pretty much the same, wherever a person traveled, with men and women dividing into separate groups, and the children frolicking in the grass.

She studied the hillside, where she still hadn't had time to explore.

"What are you thinking?" Sam had come up beside her.

"Oh!" She gave him a warm smile. "I was thinking

about walking through the trees up there. You can see deer from—"

She caught herself before she gave away too much. "From here if you squint."

He squinted. "You have excellent eyes. I don't see any deer."

"Well, maybe it was just the wind moving in the pines."

She glanced at him, and their eyes met.

He gave her a warm smile.

Now that they were here and he had the position he'd been called to, things were less strained between them. She didn't expect flowery expressions of devotion or demonstrative gestures. They were living together as man and wife. They shared a marriage bed. He came home every evening, and they spent family time together. He was kind and considerate. It was more than she'd ever had.

It was more than she'd hoped to have.

Josie wanted to capture every precious moment and enjoy it for all it was worth. At last she had a family to care for and to love. Loneliness was a thing of the past, and she had no regrets about making this choice.

She often wondered how Reverend Martin was doing, and she had written him twice already, to let him know they'd arrived safely. When she thought of her former life and of Margaretta, she felt sadness for the woman who had made her son her whole life. She had excluded others to such an extreme that, once Bram was gone, she had nothing.

"What are you thinking?" Sam asked from beside her.

"I was thinking how blessed I am that God brought you to Reverend Martin's door."

Then he did something altogether unexpected. He reached to take her hand, lacing his fingers through hers and said, "We are the ones who were blessed."

She remembered how the mothers and daughters had flocked around him in Durham. "You could have had your choice of young women, once you got here."

"But once again, God saw the bigger picture and pointed out the wisdom of asking you."

She had asked God to take away her desire for a family, but the acute desire had never diminished. Now she knew why. Sam didn't know he was the answer to her prayers.

Josie enjoyed the knowledge that she was able to give something to Sam in return. She imagined his reaction to the house, and prayed he would love it as much as she and the girls did. He'd done a good job of covering up his disappointment over the parsonage.

Enjoying the strength and warmth of his hand holding hers, she looked up into his blue eyes.

"Do you miss Nebraska?" he asked.

"I think about the reverend from time to time, but no. There's no comparison to being here and having a full life with a family."

His gaze dropped to her lips, and her heart lifted with the anticipation of a kiss. She glanced to the side, noting that they stood in full view of their new neighbors and parishioners.

"Hold that thought," he said, surprising her, and the corner of his mouth tilted upward.

"How do you know what I'm thinking?"

"You're blushing."

"Perhaps it's the sun."

"Perhaps."

Their eyes met and locked. His were surprisingly warm.

"I expect some other man would have claimed you for his wife if I hadn't asked first."

Not wanting to draw unwanted attention, she turned and faced the children playing croquet. "Actually, you didn't ask first."

Sam's fingers tightened around hers. "What? What do you mean?"

"Someone else asked me before you did."

Sam didn't let her view the crowd, but tugged her hand until she faced him. "Who? Did I meet him?"

"You met him. It was Reverend Martin."

"Henry?" he asked, his eyebrows climbing his forehead. "But you refused him?"

"Not at first. I was thinking strongly about accepting."

"Why didn't you?"

"Because before I could, you asked me."

His expression revealed he was plainly disconcerted. He looked aside, but she could tell he wasn't actually seeing anything. He was thinking over what she'd just revealed.

"I told him the truth."

His wordless gaze shot to hers.

"That I couldn't marry him because you had asked me, and I'd accepted."

"You chose us over him? Over staying in your hometown and with your friends."

"As you'll recall, it didn't take me long to make a decision."

Indeed, Sam recalled her acceptance. At the time, he'd been so focused on the mission that he hadn't stopped to analyze or imagine her reasoning. She'd agreed to come, and he'd been relieved.

Now he was grateful, and perhaps a little ashamed for plowing ahead with his plans and not stopping to look at her needs or her desires.

He'd done the same thing with Carrie, uprooting her and moving her from her safe, comfortable home, into the dangerous land that had taken her life. Sam determined in his heart that he would not take Josie for granted, nor would he make her regret her decision to marry him and start over in a new land.

He would do everything in his power to take care of her the way she was taking care of his daughters.

The following week passed rapidly. Sam did most of his calling during the day hours, but he was trying to meet everyone in the first couple of weeks, so he traveled each evening.

Josie recognized that his daughters missed him when he went calling, and understood what that was like. She took special care to fill those hours with activities and studies. She reminded them often that their father loved them and would be home for their bedtime.

They used two of those evenings to scamper to the new house, where they swept and washed and dusted in preparation for the arrival of their trunks and furniture.

During the day, they sewed new curtains and worked on the quilt Josie had begun. Elisabeth preferred the curtains to the quilt work, and her stitches were straight and even, so Josie merely supervised.

She hired a painter and selected a color for the outside trim, but the man and his son would be unable to come until the following week.

On the day their belongings were due to arrive, Josie spotted two wagons in front of the tiny parsonage.

She ran out and glanced toward the church, hoping Sam wasn't near a window. "Those aren't to be delivered here," she told the dusty man driving the first wagon.

"Man at the station told me to find you here," he replied.

"Yes, he was right about that. But everything goes to a different house. If you turn the wagons around and head up that last street you passed, the house is at the top of the hill. You can't miss it. It's trimmed in pink. I'll be right behind you."

"Pink?" he asked.

"Let me get my girls and I'll meet you there."

Laughing and giggling, the Hart sisters accompanied her up the hill.

"I hope your father didn't see us leave," Josie said.

"He's gone this morning," Elisabeth assured her. "He asked if I wanted to come along, but I knew today was the day, so I said no."

The two fellows were tired and thirsty, so Josie sent Elisabeth back to the house for supplies to make lemonade in the new kitchen.

It became clear to Josie that the two men weren't able to work fast enough to have all the furniture unloaded and settled in the appropriate rooms by supper, so she hurried into town and located a couple of young men to accompany her back and join the hauling process.

It was a warm afternoon, and there wasn't a person there who didn't show the exertion of their tasks. Josie didn't have time to stop for a breath.

So that she could get back and fix supper, she instructed the men to leave the last several items in the middle of the drawing room and asked the young fellows to come back the next day.

She paid each one what he was due and they hurried home.

Supper was a feast of quickly sliced ham and fried eggs.

"Ab, your hair looks as though you tangled with a mountain lion today," Sam said jokingly.

"Oh, yes." Abigail reached up in a useless attempt to smooth her braid. "I must have forgotten to brush it."

"You all look a little red-faced this evening."

Josie tried to remember if she'd checked her appearance in the mirror after she'd changed into fresh clothing. None of the females met each other's eyes or Sam's. No one said a word. If pressed, the girls would not lie.

"The sun must have been hot today," he commented. "Were you outdoors?"

"We did go out," Josie replied for all of them. "And the sun was quite warm."

"I've been gone several evenings," he began.

"If you have someone to call on, Father, you go right ahead," Elisabeth told him. "We don't mind a bit. We understand you're introducing yourself to all the new people."

He was still for a moment. "I'd invite them here if I could."

"It's okay, Papa," Abigail seconded. "Josie keeps us busy while you're away."

"We got a whole *lotta* work to do," Anna said with a nod.

Josie stood quickly. "Mrs. Powell brought us a jar of her applesauce. Why don't we have some for dessert?"

She unwrapped oatmeal cookies they'd baked the day before and served them with the applesauce.

Sam excused himself to the outbuilding to wash and shave before he went calling.

"You almost *told*," Abigail chastised her little sister.

"No, I did not," Anna argued.

"Come, let's do the dishes so we can hurry up the hill as soon as he leaves." Josie stacked their plates.

The mood was quite conspiratorial as they whisked the dishes from the sudsy water through the rinse pan, Elisabeth drying and putting them away.

When Sam returned, dressed in a fresh white shirt and a black tie, wearing black trousers, the handsome sight took Josie's breath away.

His daughters, preoccupied and used to seeing him dressed so, gave him dismissive hugs and kisses.

After they'd scampered back to their tasks, he paused and studied Josie with uncertainty. He was clearly uncomfortable and questioning how to handle the moment.

Sparing him a decision, she stepped toward him just as each of his daughters had done and pressed her cheek to his. He smelled of shaving soap and starch, and the scent gave her strangely contradictory feelings of longing and satisfaction. His cheek was smooth and warm, and he turned his face to press a kiss against her temple.

"Have a nice evening," he said against her ear.

A tingle of appreciation passed along her nerve endings. "And you, as well."

He stepped back, his gaze roaming her hair, coming back to her eyes, but settling on her lips. He kissed her then, in the middle of the kitchen, with the girls only a few feet behind him. They fell uncharacteristically silent. He released her slowly, holding her hands in his large warm ones, and looking at her as though he'd just noticed something.

"Is something wrong?" she asked.

He smiled and ran his thumb along her jaw, framed her face and kissed her again, this time with so much feeling that her head felt faint when he released her. "Everything's right," he whispered.

Joyful tears stung behind her eyelids, but she smiled.

Sam turned and left the kitchen.

Josie stood with her heart pounding. Sam's kisses set her heart aflutter and left her wondering what he was thinking.

Anna came to stand beside Josie, curling her fingers into hers. Abigail trailed after her father and returned a minute later. "He's gone."

Elisabeth continued to observe Josie with a reserved expression. Josie met her eyes and gave her a hesitant smile. It must be difficult for her to see Josie in the position that had once been her mother's.

Elisabeth looked away.

Josie removed her apron. "Let's go!"

They shot into action, gathering the items they'd

stashed to take with them, and left the little house to climb the hill.

"I still can't believe this is our house," Abigail said with a giggle, dancing ahead through the gate and up the stone steps.

"Do we have room for a lamb now?" Anna asked with all seriousness.

"You are going to have to take that up with your papa," Josie answered.

The foyer was cluttered with crates and cartons and odds and ends that had been dropped in their hurry, but it looked wonderful to her. She loved the high-ceilinged entry, the magnificent sweeping staircase with its curving banister and the ornate lamp that hung a good six feet above them.

"How do you light that?" Abigail asked.

"I have no idea," Josie answered. She turned and surveyed the mess, then the girls. "All right." She gathered her thoughts. "Let's work on putting away as much as we can in the kitchen and the dining room. Tomorrow, when our helpers come to get the rest of our things up the stairs for us, we'll do the bedrooms."

The men had situated her china hutch and sideboard in the dining room. Kneeling, Josie opened crates to inspect her dishes.

"We brought china, too." Elisabeth stood to the side, her fingers laced in front of her. "There's a set that were Mother and Father's wedding gift."

Josie paused to look from Elisabeth to the other girls, taking note of their concern. The things they'd brought with them from Pennsylvania were all they had left of their mother and their former life. "Why don't we put those in this cabinet so you can see them?" Josie said. "Mine aren't particularly special. I can keep them in the kitchen, for everyday dishes."

Though Elisabeth had been careful with her expression, Josie took note of the way she relaxed her posture and nodded. Had she thought Josie wouldn't want her mother's things in sight?

"What about Mama's tea set?" Anna came and leaned against Josie, where she knelt beside the crate.

Quite naturally, Josie put her arm around the child and pulled her close in an easy embrace, while she glanced about. "I have the perfect place. How about right smack dab in the center of the sideboard there? The sun will hit the china as it comes through the windows."

She settled the lid back on the crate and stood to look around. "Which trunk do you supposed holds your mama's china and tea set?"

"These two are ours," Abigail told her, pointing.

They opened the trunk and found dishes carefully packed between clothing items and baby clothes.

"Those were ours," Anna told her. "There's a dress and bonnet that each of us wore. Mama said she would keep them forever."

Josie held up the miniature white dresses, meticulously stitched and embroidered. She imagined Sam's wife tenderly touching them as she packed, reminiscing about the sweet babies she'd borne and nursed and rocked. "I'll bet you were the most beautiful babies in Philadelphia." She laid them out, pressing the wrinkles with a reverent touch. "I'll iron them and we can put them safely away in the trunk. Do you know whose is whose?"

Abigail frowned. "They all look alike."

"Maybe Father will know," Elisabeth suggested.

"Yes, maybe," Josie agreed.

She placed the dinnerware in the cabinet, relieved that all the pieces had made the journey safely. "Your mama did a good job packing these."

When all the pieces had been unpacked and put away, they stood back to admire their handiwork. The girls grew silent.

"Remember, it's good to talk about your mother if you want to," Josie told them.

"I remember washing these dishes with Mama," Abigail said.

"They will be our Sunday dishes," Josie assured her.

After pushing the trunks against the wall, they took a last look and moved into the kitchen.

Josie didn't want any of them to think she was trying to replace their mother or that she felt her place was any more important than Carrie's had been. Carrie was their mother, and it would always be that way. She hoped her actions showed that she valued their feelings.

Exhausted, they spent the following evening at home, not finishing until the day after and finalizing their plans to surprise Sam.

"It has to be during the day that we bring him," Elisabeth said. "So he can see the mountain from the turret."

Josie agreed wholeheartedly.

On Thursday morning, Josie and the girls exchanged conspiratorial looks at breakfast. Josie poured Sam a cup of coffee and nodded at Elisabeth.

"We have a surprise for you," she told her father.

"I love surprises." He sipped his coffee and studied Elisabeth over the rim of the cup. "What is it?"

Chapter Fifteen

"We have to show you," Abigail said, grinning from ear to ear.

"Well, I'm ready." He set down his cup. "Shall I close my eyes? Have you sewn another quilt square?"

Anna giggled. "No-o," she said, drawing the word out in mischief. "It's a lot bigger than that."

"If you're finished eating, we'll show you," Josie said.

Sam followed, hesitating every so often, as though he expected them to pull something out from behind them.

"It's not *here*," Abigail said. "We have to take you to it."

Out of doors, the pine-scented mountain breeze lifted all their hair as it rustled the sleeves of Sam's white shirt.

Abigail and Anna each took one of his hands and practically pulled him up the hill.

"Are we going to climb that whole mountain?" he asked in mock concern.

"Just a little farther," Anna told him.

Josie enjoyed the look of anticipation on Elisabeth's face.

Sam recognized the animation and pleasure with which his daughters were orchestrating this outing. He couldn't imagine what they were planning, but they'd been quite preoccupied most of the week. It pleased him to see their lighthearted behavior. He'd been so busy that he had only Josie to thank for the mood she'd created.

He glanced over his shoulder to see she wore a similar expression of expectation. So often when he looked at her, his reaction surprised him. This time he hadn't expected to appreciate the color on her cheeks or notice the sun on her lustrous, dark, wavy hair. When she gazed up at him, something hard and hurting inside him softened a little more.

Her optimism and her outlook made him believe they were going to do all right here in Colorado. She had infinite patience with Anna's never-ending questions and encouragement for Abigail's moments of sadness and loss. She handled Elisabeth's resentment with kindness and understanding.

She met his eyes and something warm and undeniably affectionate passed between them. Something he wasn't expecting, and it made him look forward to time alone with her.

"A little farther!" Anna called out.

Sam turned his attention to the street. "What have you females cooked up?"

The homes they passed were as nice as any he'd seen in the affluent neighborhoods back east, most with flower gardens and some with carriage houses.

As they reached the crest of the hill, they came to a halt before a large house with garish pink trim. He stared at the house, then turned to his daughters and

Josie. They glanced from the sight before them to his face with expectancy.

Sam couldn't have been more confused. "Do we know someone who lives here?"

Anna and Abigail giggled. "Yes!" they chorused.

Elisabeth opened the gate, and they towed him up the thick stone stairs bordered by foliage. "Who?" he asked.

They urged him toward the porch and Anna released his hand to dance around him.

Still puzzled, he climbed the stairs. "Who lives here?"

Adding to his surprise, Josie produced a key and proceeded to insert it into the lock and turn it. The door opened, and the younger girls rushed forward into the interior.

Confused, Sam looked at Elisabeth, who simply gestured for him to enter.

"Who lives here?" he asked again.

"We do!" they shouted together, and their voices echoed in the foyer.

Sam glanced around the entryway, feeling decidedly off-kilter. Nothing looked familiar, but neither was there any home owner rushing to discover who had entered his house. "Would someone mind explaining?"

"It's *our* house, Papa!" Anna told him.

"We bought it and brought all our stuff here," Abigail explained. "Wait 'til you see!"

Sam looked to Josie for confirmation, and she nodded with a smile. "It's ours."

"Come look!" Anna took his hand and pulled him along the hallway, past a room full of unfamiliar furniture to a dining room with more unfamiliar furniture.

The girls had rushed in ahead, but now they parted, giving him a view of a cabinet filled with dishes.

He recognized the plates and bowls as being the same set they'd had at home. His gaze traveled until it lit upon the dainty, violet-sprigged tea set arranged before the window, and the facts fell together. Carrie's teapot and cups.

He looked beyond the room to the one beside it, and a rocking chair immediately caught his attention. He walked toward it, into a small room with a few trunks still stacked against a wall.

He reached out and gently set the familiar rocker into motion. Carrie had rocked every one of their daughters in this chair and had insisted it come west with them for future generations of Harts. These were their things.

"Show him the rest of the house," Josie suggested.

They gave him a tour of the spacious kitchen, with a brand-new cast-iron stove, the bathing chamber and the drawing room.

Upstairs, the rooms were not completely furnished. When they showed him the largest bedroom, he recognized that the bureau and wardrobe held his own clothing, which had been in one of the trunks they'd brought with them.

The shock had him thinking too slowly. "Where did all of this other furniture come from?"

Josie clasped her hands together. "I had most of it shipped, you'll remember. We picked out a few ready-made pieces at a furniture maker's in town. Of course, if there's anything you don't like, we can exchange it."

"I knew you shipped your belongings, but I had no idea there was…so much."

They now stood in the wide upstairs hallway.

"I hope you don't mind that I kept nearly everything." She gestured to a narrow table against a wall. "That was from my father's study."

"Everything is quite...*nice*."

"Not *too* much?" she asked, a wrinkle of concern creasing her forehead. "Don't you like it?"

"It's not that I don't like it," he said, bringing one hand up to his jaw in thought.

"Look at the room above," Elisabeth suggested.

They took him up ladderlike stairs to a room with a breathtaking view of the mountainside. Anna pointed out deer trails. He couldn't imagine how they'd gotten the few chairs up here. The girls' books were stored neatly in two small crates turned on their sides and an oil lamp sat atop the stack.

She'd bought a house. A very nice, very *expensive* house.

When the girls disappeared down the stairs, he turned to her and asked in a low voice, "Did the bank give us a loan?"

She shook her head. "The house is paid for. It's in your name." She raised a hand to her throat in a nervous gesture. "I have the deed for you."

"You paid for it?"

"Yes. I assure you there's no debt."

"And the stove and the new furnishings?"

"Paid for, as well. Cash."

Surprised, he called down, "Give us a moment, please."

Josie's caramel-brown eyes widened as she studied him. "How did you afford it?"

"I had accounts transferred to the local bank. The local banker was quite accommodating."

Of course he was. "I know how funds are transferred," he said, keeping his voice calm. "What I don't know is how you happened to have so much of it to throw around."

"I told you I sold my house in Durham."

Granted, he'd only seen the outside of that house, and it was fine indeed, but this one surpassed that. "You told me you spent that money on shipping our things."

"Not all of it. And I had more, besides. I sold the newspaper. I got a modest down payment, and I'll be getting a payment each month. It will be plenty to live on, if you're concerned about the upkeep of the house. And remember that the board will pay us a housing allowance."

He shook his head, absorbing the information.

"I have other accounts that are still untouched," she added matter-of-factly.

Other accounts? He leveled a gaze on her.

"My father left me an inheritance," she explained with a shrug. "As did my first husband."

Sam felt as though he'd been sucker punched. He opened his mouth, but couldn't breathe for several seconds. Finally he drew in a breath and released it. "You're—rich."

She blinked at him. "I've always been blessed with more than I need, it's true. But I'm not foolish, nor do I value earthly things above treasures in heaven. Whatever I have became yours when we married. We have enough to live comfortably."

"And you never bothered to mention this?"

"It never came up. It wasn't important."

"Well, it's pretty important to me."

She clasped her hands. "I'm sorry. I didn't deliberately keep the money a secret."

"It seems as though you did all this without telling me because you knew I wouldn't approve."

Her expression showed surprise at his words. "That's not why we didn't tell you. You have important matters to handle. We didn't want to distract you with trivial details." Her eyes filled with tears. "Sam, you don't approve?"

He rubbed his forehead and tried to think without letting her tears affect him. She always spoke so rationally, and she never failed to consider decisions with a spiritual perspective. The irony of that wasn't lost on him—him, the man of God. "You heard what I told my daughters when they complained about that little house."

"Yes," she whispered. "I thought you were making the best of the situation. I didn't think you wouldn't want another house, if it were possible. I never dreamed you would disapprove." She shrugged in a self-deprecating manner. "I guess that was foolish."

"It's not that I don't approve of you or even the house," he began. How could he have missed the fact that she had a lot more money? He'd known about her house and remembered something about her husband working at the newspaper. Inheritances were news. But then he'd never thought to ask.

"Papa?" Anna called from downstairs. "Are you ready to see the outside in the back?"

"I should be the one providing for you and for my

daughters," he told her, feeling as though he'd failed them. He could never have done all this on his salary.

"I didn't stop to think of it like that," she said. "God is our Provider, Sam. We wouldn't have any of this if He hadn't seen fit to give it to me. I consider it a blessing, and I never thought you'd see it any other way."

Well, yes, there it was, her straightforward reliance on God, with nary a glance to the left or the right. There was no way he could argue with her reasoning, and he'd be a fool to try. Of course she looked to God as her Provider, and of course His wisdom was greater than theirs. "I should have been in on a decision of such magnitude."

"Yes, of course."

The question crept into his head about the reaction of the townspeople. Would they question such extravagance or wonder at its source? It would be his own fault for overlooking these details and being in such a hurry to marry Josie and get her here that he hadn't cared to learn more.

"Go ahead." He gestured to the stairs. She gathered her skirts and descended ahead of him.

All the joy she'd taken in seeing the girls' pleasure and planning the surprise was gone, leaving Josie feeling she'd disappointed her husband.

Elisabeth appeared concerned over her father's lack of enthusiasm, but the other girls hadn't seemed to notice.

Abigail led the way through the kitchen and out of doors. Sam lifted his gaze to the verdant hillside and stood studying the landscape.

"Can we bring our bed and sleep here tonight?" Anna asked.

Josie said nothing.

Elisabeth looked at her, then at her father.

"I want to know why this house is significant," Sam said at last. He turned to Anna first. "Why is this particular house so important to you?"

Anna scrunched her nose for a minute as she thought, then said, "'Cause we got all our own stuff and our own rooms and a big, big yard. See how big this yard is, Papa?"

"I see that," he answered. "Ab?"

Abigail seemed a trifle caught off guard by the question. "This house is important because...we can have all of Mama's things here, and we can all sit at the table in the dining room on Sundays."

Sam nodded and turned to his oldest daughter.

"We thought you would be pleased," she said, obviously taking a more defensive tone. "We don't have enough room in that little house, and this one is nice. It's big enough for all of us. You were busy, so we did all this ourselves."

That last bit could have been interpreted as accusatory, but Sam didn't comment. He turned his gaze on Josie. "What does this house mean to you?"

Chapter Sixteen

It wasn't just the house. This move and this family meant everything to her. "I know the church board meant well by providing the other house. No doubt it was the best they could do, and we're grateful. But here you can hold Bible studies and invite neighbors to dinner. It's a stunning example of just how much God loves us that we can live here and welcome our new friends. I hoped it wouldn't be just a house or a thing. I hoped it would be our *home*." She looked into his eyes and spoke earnestly. "But I would live in a cave if you thought it was best for all of us."

His expression softened, and he shook his head. "A cave won't be necessary." He turned and peered up at the back of the house. "I do recognize how much this means to each of you. I simply don't want any of us to be ungrateful or unappreciative. We have to learn to be content wherever God leads us."

"I don't think God led us to that little house," Abigail said in all seriousness. "I think He had this one waiting. We just didn't know it, and the church people didn't know it."

"Hmm. Do you think God is fond of pink?" Sam asked, still studying the architecture and details.

The girls were quiet for a few seconds, and then Abigail giggled. "God made pink flowers."

"And I saw a bunny with pink eyes once," Anna added.

Josie relaxed marginally. His daughters' comfort and peace of mind meant everything to Sam. She prayed he recognized that she hadn't been thinking selfishly when she'd come up with this idea.

"Painters are coming next week to change the color," she assured him.

He took a step back and shaded his eyes with a hand for a better look. "I could do that myself and save the cost."

Josie's heart leaped into her throat at the thought of Sam on top of the house. She'd spent months taking care of Reverend Martin after a fall from a roof not as high as this one. "Some things are better left to professionals," she said quietly.

He turned and raised an eyebrow.

"Reverend Martin was nearly killed falling from the church roof."

"We'll talk about it."

"Yes, of course."

"We'll talk about a lot of things, so that I don't have any more surprises." His voice was kind as he asked, "What do you have planned for today?"

"I hoped to move the bed and the rest of our things from the other house."

"I'll help."

The girls crowded around him, exclaiming.

"I need to do *something* to help." His gaze touched each of them, but returned to Josie. "You've been working so hard."

"I just know how busy you are," she said.

When the girls hurried back into the house, they followed more slowly. Sam stopped her with a hand on her arm. "Things that concern the family aren't less worthy of my time than church matters," he told her.

"I know that," she said. "I hope you don't think I was attempting to go around your authority. I simply hoped to make things easier for you."

He tilted his head. "I vow to be more approachable."

But he hadn't actually said he approved of the house or that he was pleased with it. Josie had the feeling that his reluctant acceptance of their move had come about because the girls would have been devastated otherwise. They'd been through too much for him to deliberately disappoint them again.

Josie wished she had the confidence to throw herself into his embrace and find the assurance she craved in his arms. She yearned to do just that. "Our helpers are bringing their wagon," she told him. "I already had it arranged."

"No one will ever call you a helpless female," he said with a grin. "Come on."

Sam took the bed apart and carried the pieces outdoors, in time to greet the two young men who had pulled a wagon up in front of the parsonage.

"Gilbert Stelling, sir." The tallest one extended a hand.

"Will York," said the other.

As Gilbert explained, the two were cousins who worked on a ranch, but they were in town for a holiday. They'd been in the general store the day Josie had been looking for help, and earning a few extra dollars appealed to them.

Will looked to be about fourteen, and Sam noticed that every time Elisabeth carried something out of the house, he took it from her arms.

There really hadn't been that much in the house, and every time Sam ran into a doorjamb or couldn't get out of a room because someone was already standing in the cramped space, he recognized just how tiny the parsonage was and how foolish his recommendation that they make the most of it. He understood why the girls had been so upset. He hadn't wanted to admit the house was too small, because there'd been nothing he could do about it.

Later that afternoon, he watched Josie pay the two young fellows. They climbed onto their wagon seat and rode down the hill.

The Harts ate a cold supper in the new kitchen. Afterward, Josie made coffee and they lingered around the table.

"We can take baths inside this winter," Elisabeth pointed out.

"That is a very good reason to like this house," he admitted.

"Can we get a lamb now?" Anna asked. She'd likely been waiting several days to ask that question, and her restraint in waiting until now impressed him.

"Lambs grow into sheep very quickly," he told her.

"We don't have a barn—or a pasture. A sheep wouldn't be very happy here. Remember Elisabeth telling you about the lady back in Durham who kept a sheep tied up by her door? The poor animal can't be happy living like that."

"I remember," Anna replied in a dejected tone.

"Tomorrow morning we will all go to the schoolhouse to meet your teacher," he said.

Josie got out papers and charcoal sticks and suggested Anna draw pictures. The subject was once again sidetracked.

Sometime later, as they sat in the drawing room together, Anna complained of a stomachache. A look of worry crossed Sam's face, and he turned to Josie. "Do you know what to do for her?"

Josie set down her sewing and stood. "My mama used to have something to fix that right up. Get her ready for bed and I'll be up."

She went into the kitchen and boiled a few peppermint leaves, then added a sprinkling of ginger root. While the liquid was cooling, she found a sock, filled it with dry rice and heated it in the oven.

Anna sipped the warm, fragrant brew from one of Josie's plain stoneware mugs. "Now we'll lie this on your tummy and it will help you feel all better."

Sam turned to where Elisabeth and Abigail perched at the foot of the bed. "Will one of you sleep with Anna tonight?"

"I will," Abigail offered quickly. "I didn't want to sleep alone this first night, anyway."

"I'll stay with them, too," Elisabeth offered.

So that night, the three of them ended up sharing a bed after all.

"Anna might be nervous about attending an unfamiliar classroom," Josie mentioned when she and Sam were alone. "And I wonder how much of her ailment was the thought of sleeping by herself for the first time."

He looked at her dubiously. "Do you really think so?"

"New surroundings can be frightening."

It was such a relief to have someone with whom to share these responsibilities, and especially nice that she was capable and exceedingly kind. "Thank you for knowing what to do. They've never been sick. Not a day I can think of."

Now that she thought about it, her stomach was a little on the queasy side, as well, and she wasn't worried about sleeping alone. Josie made herself the same concoction, sipped it and prayed the family would be spared from sickness.

Late that night, Josie crept silently into the room where Anna lay sleeping with her sisters. They were so beautiful, each of them in their own unique way. She touched Anna's forehead, finding her skin cool. Reassured, she nonetheless knelt at the foot of their bed and prayed.

Sam awakened to find Josie's place beside him empty. Concerned, he rose and pulled on his trousers. Perhaps she'd gone to the kitchen, or maybe he'd missed hearing one of the girls cry out.

His first thought was to look in Abigail's new room, and then he remembered she hadn't slept there. He crossed to Anna's.

In the moonlight, he made out his daughters' silvery

pale hair upon their pillows as they lay still and peaceful. Near the foot of the bed knelt another figure, this one with dark hair streaming across a pale white nightgown.

At the sight, emotion swelled within him. He'd done the same thing many times, praying over the children he loved so dearly. Since Carrie's death, he'd never hoped to know another person who loved them so deeply, who was so concerned with their well-being that she would share his devotion.

Yet here she was, this woman God had sent to him. He didn't feel as lost or as lonely as he once had. Humbled, he thanked God for the reminder and the correction. Whenever he overlooked the obvious, whenever he let pride get in the way of what was best, God graciously pointed his foolishness out to him.

A dark and private place inside his heart had begun to open itself to the light. The opening hurt as much as it gave him pleasure, because while this was a beginning, it was also an end. An end to life the way he'd known it—but the start of something rich and beautiful.

"Thank You for waking me up and showing me this," he whispered.

If he looked back over the past weeks, over his days and nights with Josie, he could mark each of the moments that had awakened him to this beginning. Her riding beside him on the wagon seat, the sunlight glistening from her eyelashes. Holding her outside the circle of their campfire, feeling her heart beating against his chest, breathing in the delicate scent of her hair. Josie turning from the sink to greet him, suds dripping from her fingers and a smile curving her rosy lips.

Sam still had a lot of sorting out to do, but he wasn't

foolish enough to deny what he was beginning to feel for his wife. He didn't want to miss out on any of the blessings God had in store for him.

Anna was fine the next morning, though Josie continued to sip peppermint tea, and ate only a few bites of the oatmeal she'd prepared.

Miss DeSmet greeted them when they entered the white schoolhouse. "You must be the Harts!" she said with a broad smile. "I've been expecting you."

The thin woman wore a plain gray skirt and a calico shirtwaist. She had bright red hair pinned in a knot at her nape, and her eyes were a vivid green.

Sam introduced each of them. "The girls will be starting next Monday. We're nearly settled into our home."

"I understand you're living in the big house up behind Church Street."

"Indeed we are," Sam replied.

"The Collins family lives at the foot of the hill. I'll speak with the children today. You can all walk to school together."

"That will be nice, once they get into a routine," Sam told her.

Miss DeSmet showed them which desks they would be using, and explained the curriculum for their age groups.

By the time they left, Josie thought the girls had a good picture of their new school.

A few evenings later, Anna brought up her favorite topic again. They sat in the drawing room where Elisabeth was reading, and Abigail was working on a quilt square.

Anna looked up from her wooden horse figures to ask, "Is a bunny small enough to be happy at our house?"

"Rabbits are wild creatures, Anna," Sam told her.

"What about a brother? Can we have a brother?"

Josie's hands fell still on the hem she was stitching into a curtain.

"We got those little clothes Mama saved."

Sam met Josie's eyes briefly, and his look was apologetic. "Three daughters are a handful. We don't need any more children."

"Some families got lots of brothers and sisters," she persisted.

"Some families do indeed," he agreed. "But this family is big enough just the way it is. Babies take a lot of work, and Josie has her hands full taking care of you."

Josie was relieved at his reply as well as his certainty that he didn't want more children. She would have struggled, had she known she was disappointing him.

"We received an invitation for tea at a neighbor's next Saturday," she told the girls. "All of our names were included, so we have an outing to plan."

Abigail set her sewing aside. "What will I wear?"

"One of your church dresses will suit the occasion," Josie told her, already knowing Abigail would dearly love to wear dresses that hadn't belonged to her older sister. "We'll come up with something."

The following morning, Josie suggested they go into town and shop for fabric and patterns. They may not have new dresses in time for the tea if they had to order from a catalog, but they could work on them for future events. "We need to think about clothing for school, as well," she reminded them.

"We didn't make our own clothes at home," Elisabeth told her.

"Well, you can learn now," she replied.

"I want to sew," Abigail said brightly.

The general store carried only a small selection of serviceable fabrics, and very few patterns. Victor Larken suggested they visit the dressmaker across the street, who had a room of fabric, scrap and trim in her shop.

Opal Zimmerman was a tiny little lady with a surprisingly booming voice that caught Josie off guard. She hadn't met her in church, but there was another denomination where a portion of the townspeople worshipped, so it was possible she attended there.

"We're going to make dresses ourselves, and Mr. Larken suggested you might have suitable fabric we'd be interested in."

Opal ushered them into her side room. "He doesn't have much of a selection, does he? Once I discovered that, I started ordering and keeping pretty fabric in stock. Some seasons, I can't keep up." She opened the front shutters. "I keep these closed so the material doesn't fade. There's a selection of patterns in those drawers back there. They've all been used. If you have any to trade, I'll trade or give you credit."

Josie found several patterns she thought she could alter to make them more fashionable, and she let the girls select their own colors and trim.

"We will work on one dress at a time," Josie told them as they left the shop.

"Abigail may have her dress first," Elisabeth offered.

Abigail squealed and danced around them. "Maybe it will be ready in time for the tea!"

They stopped so Josie could make a purchase at the butcher's, and then they hurried home.

Sam arrived to the delectable scent of savory beef cooking. The women had turned the dining room into a dressmaking shop. Spools of thread, scissors and bolts of colorful fabric covered the length of the table. His first thought was that they could never have managed this at the little house, but his next reaction was to consider the source of all the material on display.

"We went shopping today!" Abigail told him. "Look! I'm getting a new dress for the tea! It's blue like my eyes, and it has these tiny little pink roses in the stripes. Isn't it going to be beautiful?"

"Indeed," he replied. "Didn't we talk about your dresses lasting another season?"

"But Josie's teaching us how to sew our own," Abigail explained. "She said it's not nearly as expensive as having a dressmaker do it."

"Do you *need* these dresses, or are they something you wanted because they're pretty and new?"

"Oh, we needed them, Papa," Abigail assured him. "We go to school on Monday, and we have a tea to attend. I won't have to wear all of Elisabeth's old dresses now. And Elisabeth's dresses are getting too short on her."

Sam glanced at Elisabeth where she stood beside the table. Her ankles were indeed showing under the hem of her dress.

"Did you open an account?" he asked Josie.

She took straight pins from her mouth to reply. "Oh no, I paid for the supplies we got today."

She was wearing a soft, rose-colored shirtwaist with ruffles down the front, and a deep brown skirt. She always dressed impeccably and often wore clothing he'd never seen. Plenty of her trunks must have contained clothing.

She'd been a pretty young widow, with enough money to keep her living comfortably for the rest of her life when she'd accepted his proposal. Sometimes he wondered why she'd said yes to him rather than Reverend Martin. She was used to more than he had to offer, but that didn't really matter, since she could take care of herself.

And his daughters.

Seeing their pleasure with the house and their rooms and this clothing assured him they had what they needed. He'd done the best for them that he'd known how, though his desire for them had been Josie's nurturing, not her money.

And she was nurturing. Kindhearted, loving—all the things a mother should be. If her only flaw was spoiling them, he could overlook that.

He wondered why the thought of her being able to provide all this bothered him, and again he scoffed at how he hadn't noticed the fact that she had so much money before she bought the house.

Maybe he hadn't wanted to know. Sam had never inquired about financial details. *He hadn't been paying attention.* If he'd paid as much attention to her as she did to him and the girls, he would have known.

As he considered his neglect, he supposed he wouldn't have proposed to her if he'd known how truly well off she was—or that Henry had asked her first. He would've felt foolish for offering her a life with far less than she was accustomed to.

Maybe she hadn't settled.

Maybe it was best he hadn't known of her wealth.

The image of her kneeling at the foot of Anna's bed came to him then, forcing him to compare his feelings of inadequacy to her unselfish devotion.

He'd known she was perfect for his daughters because of her kindness and her faith. The fact that his new wife had come with a lot of money was taking some adjustment. He'd been confident about her suitability, partly because of her generosity, so it only stood to reason that she'd be openhanded with her money.

As surely as he knew his own name, he knew the obstacle standing in his way was pride.

The fact that she could provide the means to make their lives better and easier wouldn't bother him, if it weren't for his stubborn male pride. "'A man's pride shall bring him low, but honor shall uphold the humble in spirit,'" he quoted aloud to remind himself.

He loved the book of Proverbs for its straightforward wisdom. Sometimes he could even laugh at the irony of the analogies Solomon had made. This had been the first verse that popped into his head, but he wasn't laughing now.

"What does that mean, Papa?" Anna asked.

"It means a man's pride will drag him down."

"But you're proud of us, aren't you?"

"That's a good kind of pride. I'm proud to be a child of the living God. I'm proud to be your father. The pride that we shouldn't allow in our hearts is the kind that puffs us up, or that stands in the way of our being humble."

"I don't understand," she said with a frown.

"That's okay. You don't need to think on it."

But *he* did. He needed to think on it a lot.

Chapter Seventeen

Constance Graham entertained half a dozen women and as many of their daughters on her shaded front porch. She was a rancher's daughter who had married a banker and moved to Jackson Springs several years ago.

"I have two sons," she told Josie. "They're rowdy and loud, and I couldn't invite you here if they weren't off working. I have to keep my tea things under lock and key so they aren't trampled in the daily stampede."

Previously, Josie had met Ruby Adamson and Vanessa Powell, but now she was introduced to Melissa Larken.

"Like Mr. Larken at the general store?" Josie asked.

Melissa's eyes were bright and her complexion glowing. She was expecting a baby very soon. "He's my father-in-law. My husband is the deputy sheriff."

Arlene Stelling introduced herself. "Over there are my daughters, Libby and Patience."

The two young ladies she indicated were conversing with Elisabeth and Abigail. The group of girls slowly moved to form a gathering on the lawn.

"You've met my son," Arlene told Josie.

"I have?"

"Yes, Gilbert and my brother's boy, Will, helped unload the wagons into your new home."

"Oh!" Josie smiled and touched Arlene's arm. "What a nice young man. He's such a hard worker. He was so patient with us when we couldn't make up our minds where everything went. And both of them even came back a second day."

"They were pleased with the work," Arlene told her. "Gilbert is saving for a horse he wants to buy."

Constance served tea, and Josie accepted a cup.

"We're delighted that you've come to Jackson Springs," Constance told her. "Our last minister was quite elderly. We all loved him dearly, but for the last year or so he just wasn't up to the job. He's gone to live with a younger sister in Denver now."

"Sam has had only good things to say about the people he's meeting. And apparently he has big shoes to fill."

"Your husband's sermons seem so heartfelt," Vanessa said. "He always has something to say that makes me look at my own situation and try to see how I can apply the teaching. His examples from the Bible give me a perspective I didn't have before."

Josie nodded. "He does have a way of making the Scriptures come to life, doesn't he? He talks about Paul and Peter and so many, as though they lived only yesterday. And Sam strives to use their examples of faith and courage for his own life. I admire that."

Ruby leaned toward Melissa to say, "I always feel

better about a preacher man when his wife admires his character."

"It sounds like love to me," Melissa replied with a smile.

Josie's cheeks warmed in an uncomfortable blush.

Constance waved a censoring hand at the ladies. "Josie is our guest of honor and you've embarrassed her. Shush now."

"We're aware that you're newlyweds," Ruby said with a laugh. "Don't be embarrassed."

"Melissa's still a newlywed, too," Vanessa said. "We often hear about Deputy Dan's sterling qualities."

"Likely we'll be sewing little nappies for Josie soon," Melissa said.

"Indeed," Ruby answered. "There's just something about this mountain air."

The ladies giggled.

Josie quickly disguised her feelings of inadequacy and smiled. She couldn't bring herself to deny their suppositions. After enough time had passed, they would stop bringing up the subject in her presence, just the way it had been in her past experience.

Josie had been looking forward to participating in ladies' events and making new friends and being part of this community. No longer was she seen as a widow, nor was she living under a shadow of disapproval. She should have been satisfied, but the women's talk made her feel even more strongly that something was still missing. What was that mysterious extra that these women seemed to have that she could never quite seem to possess?

Josie reined in her thoughts. As many times as she'd

read the story of the Israelites and their mumbling and grumbling, and wondered how they could be so ungrateful, she was doing nearly the same thing. Sam had taken her from Margaretta's oppression into the promised land, and she wasn't going to get caught up in being unsatisfied.

The girls had so much fun with their new friends that Arlene invited them to come spend the afternoon at her house. After learning the location and promising to come for them at four, Josie walked home.

It was the first time she'd been by herself in the new house—the first time she'd been alone for many weeks. She ambled through the rooms, touching surfaces, admiring how well the relocation had all come together.

There was so much of Sam's first wife here, from the quilts on the girls' beds to the dishes—and the Bible that lay on Sam's bureau.

Josie didn't mind. She wanted the girls to have those things around them so they could remember their mother. Carrie Hart's belongings were no threat to Josie.

But Carrie's memory—that all-encompassing part of her that remained in their hearts—sometimes Josie wondered if there would ever truly be room for her.

Sam was kind to her. It was his nature. He was even-tempered and generous. And she had more. So much more than she'd ever known with her father or her first husband.

She was grateful to be in Sam's life and to be entrusted with his precious children. This was what she'd always wanted. So why the uneasiness? Maybe she was trying too hard. She was doing her best to be content, so she didn't like feeling that something was still missing.

Josie stood in the towering turret and gazed out at the mountainside. Though she hadn't had an opportunity to do any exploring, the mountain beckoned her. She went downstairs to change her shoes, found her Bible and carried it out the back door. Picking her way here and there, she located a path in the foliage and followed it upward.

The woods tucked their pine-scented silence around her, until the only sounds were the sticks that broke beneath her boots and the occasional scurrying of a wild creature.

After several minutes, she had to stop to catch her breath. She spotted a bird's nest and a patch of mushrooms.

Pushing on, she followed a deer trail. It came out along an open area that overlooked the hillside and a panoramic vista of trees and rocks, with a purple mountain range in the distance and the town sprawled below. The sight took her breath away.

Stopping on a flat ledge of rock, she sat and studied the scenery. After several minutes the birds picked up their singing. A yellow and black butterfly drifted on the breeze and landed on a coneflower, where its wings beat in a steady rhythm.

Josie opened her Bible to the psalms, flipped a few pages and read one of her favorites. She often tried to imagine how the psalms had sounded when David had sung them. This one was particularly lyrical, and the words so filled with awe and reverence. It was exactly how she felt at this very moment.

"'Because Thy loving kindness is better than life, my lips shall praise Thee. Thus will I bless Thee while I live. I will lift up my hands in Thy name.'" She tried out the words as a lilting melody and imagined a harp accompanying her.

"'When I remember Thee upon my bed, and meditate on Thee in the night watches. Because Thou hast been my help, therefore in the shadow of Thy wings will I rejoice. My soul follows after Thee. Thy right hand upholds me.'"

God loved her just the way she was. He didn't need anything from her except her love and her faith in Him. "Thank you for giving me a family," she prayed. "Thank You for being concerned about how lonely I was feeling. Help me be the best wife and the best mother I can be. And help me not expect more of my husband than he has to give. I do so want to be pleasing to him. You are so generous, and I'm content, Lord."

Josie sang the song again, just to try it out and hopefully so she would remember the tune for the future.

She had forgotten to bring a timepiece, and she didn't want to be late to get the girls, so she made her way down the hillside and back to the house. Turning at the back door, she looked up, but couldn't spot the ledge where she'd perched.

She would find it again.

Each day she rose early to prepare breakfast, make lunches and send her family off to school and church. The days and weeks passed quickly. In the evenings, she and the girls stitched dress after dress while Sam studied by the fire or read to them. She gradually took over helping them with their studies, though Elisabeth refused her help and sought her father instead.

They had settled into a comfortable routine by the

time Josie confided to Sam that she'd come down with something that kept her running to the privy. That week Sam cooked and saw to the girls while she rested on the front porch or napped upstairs.

On Wednesday, he climbed the painted wood stairs after leaving the girls at school. "I was the only father there," he said sheepishly. "Am I being overprotective by taking them every day? They do have the Collinses to walk with."

Josie smoothed the coverlet over her lap. "They love having you take them." Frustrated, she glanced around. "I feel so useless just sitting here." The past two mornings, when she'd insisted on getting dressed and out of bed, he had guided her to a comfortable place and handled the household.

It was probably for the best that she wasn't around the girls right now. No need to spread this any further. But she didn't like the inactivity.

"It's all right to take a few days to recuperate," he assured her. "You've been working awfully hard, and you need the rest. The Grahams have some sort of sickness at their house, too." He headed for the door. "I'll make your peppermint tea. That helps, doesn't it?"

"That will be nice, thanks."

He brought her a cup of tea. "I noticed you prefer the plain cups over the fancy set."

It pleased her that he'd paid attention to something so trivial. She took a sip.

He pulled a chair nearer to her and sat. "I admit I've prayed harder over you than for my sermon this week."

She looked at him in surprise. "I'm fine, Sam. Don't concern yourself about me."

"You are my concern, Josie."

Just as it would be for any member of his flock, she thought. He took his shepherding responsibilities seriously.

"I think we should have the doctor come have a look at you."

"Oh, Sam, I don't think that's necessary. I'm not all that sick. I'm sure I'll feel better in a day or so. Anna's upset stomach only lasted a day."

"Well, this has gone on longer than that. I want to be safe, so humor me."

She gave in with a shrug. "Have you met the doctor?"

He nodded. "Yes." He said nothing more.

"What?" she asked.

"A rancher's young boy was thrown from his horse. I was called to come pray for him, but he'd died by the time I got there. That's where I met Dr. Barnes."

"How awful. Is there anything we can do for the family?"

"I invited them to church. I thought maybe seeing friends would be helpful, but the father isn't happy with God and doesn't want anything to do with the church."

Her heart went out to the hurting family. "I've seen people get mad and blame God when something bad happens in their life. It's very sad."

He agreed.

"You never did that, did you? You didn't blame God for what happened to Carrie?"

He shook his head. "It wasn't God's stupidity that tried to float a wagon loaded with furniture across a river. I bear the full responsibility." He had donned a pair of Levi's that morning, and he sat rubbing his thumbnail along the denim covering his knee. "I was the one all fired up to come west. She would have been perfectly happy staying back east."

How Josie had missed this particular burden he'd taken upon himself, she wasn't sure. His words and expression fell into place, and a deep sadness rested on her heart.

He blamed himself for his wife's death and for the fact that his daughters had lost their mother. He carried the guilt like a cross. "You blame yourself for Carrie's death," she said softly.

Leaning forward, Sam leaned his elbows on his knees and steepled his fingers under his chin. Still, he didn't meet her eyes. "I am responsible."

She sat forward to circle his wrist with her fingers. "You were answering a call from God, Sam. You didn't just set out on a fanciful trip for the sake of adventure."

"Didn't I?" He looked her in the eye then. "How can you know that? The whole idea of traveling west sounded like a grand adventure calling to me. Maybe I did take a fancy and drag them into danger."

She reached beside her for her Bible and opened to pages worn from turning so many times. "Listen to the words of this psalm," she said. "'Trust in the Lord and do good; dwell in the land and enjoy safe pasture. Delight yourself in the Lord and He will give you the desires of your heart.'

"God doesn't just give us any old selfish thing we want," she pointed out. "But when we're trusting Him for direction and doing good, He give us desires that please Him. If you weren't trusting Him for direction, He wouldn't have given you the aspiration to come live and work here. It wasn't a bad or a selfish wish. He called you for a purpose, according to the plan He has for your life. For *our* lives, now."

"But Carrie died on the way. You can't tell me that worked into His plan. Elisabeth stood over Carrie's grave and asked me why God didn't save her mother. I didn't have an answer for that. I still don't."

They sat in silence for a few minutes, the breeze rustling the cottonwood leaves on the trees that bordered the property. A bird called from the woods.

"I haven't told you the worst," he said at last.

Josie couldn't imagine anything worse than what he'd just shared.

"When Carrie was swept away, the girls were screaming and crying out for help. In a split second I made a decision. I had a hold on Anna. I shouted for riders to head downstream and I grabbed Ab and took the two to shore, then went back for Elisabeth where she was clinging to a branch. In that time Carrie drowned."

Josie was at a loss for helpful words. She was grateful to know the cause of the pain Sam had been in all this time.

"I understand your frustration," she said at last. "By your very nature, you're a man who seeks to have all the answers, a man who wants to be able to meet the needs of everyone who turns to you. When you don't have an answer, you feel as though you've let them down."

"I did let her down. I let all of them down."

"No, you didn't. You kept on going. You kept trusting God to put one foot in front of the other, and you continued on."

"There was no choice."

"There *was* a choice," she disagreed. "But you would never consider other options, because of who you are. That man who lost his son had the choice, too, but when something bad happened, he chose to blame God. You chose to trust Him. You've done everything in your power to give your girls the best life you can and to serve the people of this town at the same time."

He studied the tips of his boots for a minute before turning his arm so he could take her hand. "I'm going to go find the doctor. I'm not taking any risks with you."

The tender way he looked at her assured her she hadn't said anything that offended him. In fact, she could almost interpret the tender look in his blue eyes as appreciative.

Chapter Eighteen

Matthew Barnes was a little older than Sam, evidenced by the silver gracing his dark hair at the temples. A handsome fellow, with a ready smile and a startlingly deep voice, he wore a closely trimmed beard and mustache.

"The fact that you get out of breath is most certainly due to the change of altitude," he told her. "You're probably noticing that breathing is a little easier each week, and it will continue to be."

"The altitude never occurred to me."

Sam had seen the doctor to their room, and then left Josie alone with him. "You and Anna may have shared a germ that brought on your upset stomach," he said. "Hard to say, but your continued nausea is easily explained."

"It is?"

"When did you last have your menses?"

"My…" She blushed at the straightforward question spoken by a man, and then reminded herself he was a physician who knew about such things. She directed her thoughts to answering his question. "I don't know for certain. It's been several weeks at the very least." She frowned. "Do you think there's something wrong with me?"

He chuckled and closed his bag. "I believe you're in perfect health. And I think your baby is just fine, too."

"My…" Josie blinked in confusion. "Dr. Barnes, I don't have a baby."

"You will have," he assured her. "In about six more months. Congratulations."

His meaning sunk in. "But that's *impossible,*" she told him. "I can't have children. I'm…well, I'm barren."

"Mrs. Hart, you are definitely not barren. You have a baby growing inside you." He ticked off all the signs, and she had to concur she had the symptoms.

"But I was married for several years before my first husband died," she told him. "And we never had a child."

"Then the fault was his, not yours. You, my dear, are expecting a baby."

Josie's head spun with the revelation. Her heart thudded at a galloping pace. "How can this be?" she asked, but it wasn't really a question, and it hadn't been directed at the doctor. "How can this possibly be?"

Josie clamped one hand over her stomach and the other over her mouth, so she wouldn't gasp and cry and fall apart. A gasp escaped her regardless. "Oh, my. Oh! Oh, Lord," she whispered. "A baby. I'm going to have a baby." She grabbed Dr. Barnes's sleeve. "*We're* going to have a baby!"

"Yes," he said with a nod.

"You're certain? There's no mistake?"

"Quite certain."

Visions of a sweet-faced infant made her arms ache to hold her baby right then and there. *Thank You, Lord.* "Thank You!"

A dozen thoughts tumbled through her head at once. Anna's delight. The years of disgrace and criticism from her former mother-in-law. The nursery she'd never dreamed to create, the tiny clothes and nappies. Sam.

Sam.

Other images faded when she focused on her husband.

Sam didn't want more children.

He'd been insistent about the fact that he had plenty to handle with his daughters. She tried to recall his exact words. *This family is big enough the way it is. Babies take a lot of work, and Josie has her hands full taking care of you.*

Anna would be happy, but Josie feared Sam, and most likely Elisabeth, wouldn't share that joy.

Her initial excitement faded into concern. She had told Sam she couldn't have children. If he truly didn't want any more, he had taken her at her word.

She had disappointed one husband by not having babies, and now she stood to disappoint another by having one.

"Don't tell my husband," she said to Dr. Barnes. "I mean, I want to tell him, so please don't let on yet. Will you do that for me?"

"Of course." Grinning, he carried his bag to the door. "I'll mention the altitude and that you probably just need a little rest. You can surprise him later."

The doctor disappeared through the doorway. Josie

washed her face and hands with tepid water left over from that morning and put on a fresh shirtwaist.

A knock on the open door startled her.

She turned to find Sam standing inside the bedroom. "Dr. Barnes said you're fine."

She raised her chin. "Yes."

"He thought you might need a little time to adjust to the climate."

She nodded.

Sam took several steps farther into the room until he stood beside her. "I'm relieved."

She watched their reflection in the mirror as he moved to stand behind her. He wrapped his left arm across her chest to rest his hand on her right shoulder and lowered his head to settle his chin beside her ear.

She watched as he turned his face into her hair, then heard him inhale. He released a warm breath against her neck. "You smell good."

"Sam?"

"Yes."

Her heart beat too rapidly. She ran the words through her mind, and they made her stomach dip with nerves. It was beautiful news. A child was a blessing.

He already had three. He'd married her to take care of them. He'd been confident that Josie couldn't have any. She'd been so sure.

She'd been so ignorant.

"Thank you for getting the doctor," she said.

"Do you want to rest?"

"Yes, I think I will."

"I'll go to the church, so you have quiet the rest of the morning. Unless you want me to stay."

"I'll be fine. You go on about your day."

"I want you to know I'm taking in everything that you said earlier," he told her. "Don't give up on me because I'm hard-headed, and don't stop talking to me when you know I need to hear something."

Straightening, he turned her to face him and raised her chin on one knuckle. His other palm flattened against the small of her back so he could pull her closer. She readily folded into his welcome warmth and strength, where she felt safe. Josie had no reason to deny either of them the simple pleasure of this closeness.

Sam's gaze grazed her lips, his blue eyes sparking fire before he lowered his head and covered her mouth with his. She liked the way he took control of the kiss and framed her face with gentle hands. Josie craved this affection, reveled in the way he focused his attention on her during their moments alone. The yearning inside made her want to believe this meant he cared for her, but her hesitant, protective side called that presumptuous.

His kiss was tender, yet asked a measure more than any in the past ever had. As he held her this way, while she felt alive and special, her feelings came into distinct focus. She loved him. She was deeply and passionately in love with Samuel Hart. And it was a feeling like none she'd ever known.

Sam ended the kiss and stepped back to offer her a smile.

I love you, she thought, the newfound discovery bursting inside her.

He touched her cheek, as though he regretted leaving her. "Have a restful day."

He left the room and a few minutes later the front

door closed. She watched him through the parted curtains on the multipaned window as he took the stairs at a brisk pace and let himself out the gate. Her hand went unconsciously to her belly.

He was doing his best to make them a family and to show her affection. If not consulting with him about the house had been a problem, springing a baby and knocking him off course was a worrisome prospect. Expecting more than he was able to give had never been her plan.

As soon as she could no longer see him, she picked up her Bible and headed for the mountainside. No use worrying, when she could be talking to God.

Sam had finally laid it all out. His guilt. His lack of confidence in himself. Josie was a good listener.

As he sat in the study at the church that afternoon, he couldn't stop thinking about their conversations, about the way he wanted to share everything with her, and how much better he felt afterward.

In those moments, he realized that he'd never placed all those concerns before God. Of course God knew what he'd been going through, but He couldn't do anything until Sam laid down the burden and stopped carrying it himself.

With the afternoon sun creating splashes of color across the floorboards, Sam knelt and poured out his heart. He admitted his feelings of guilt and uprooted all his inadequacies and helplessness from their long-buried places.

"I regret that I didn't allow Carrie a say in the move," he said. "She went along with my dream and sacrificed everything—even her life. I don't want her death to be for nothing, Lord. I don't want to live my life enduring one difficult day at a time."

God didn't speak to him in a booming voice, nor did a wind carry a dove through the open window, but Sam felt God's presence all the same. Josie's words came to him, words of encouragement and hope. *You've done everything in your power to give your girls the best life you can.*

As he got to his feet, he realized that while his daughters sewed and studied and played of an evening, they talked about their mother in natural conversation. They remembered her alive, and those memories eased their grief.

While listening to them, he'd remembered her alive, as well. He'd thought of days when the girls were small, of the good times they'd shared. And it had been weeks since he'd dreamed of Carrie's death. The images that had been seared in his mind were fading—and being replaced.

Those images were no longer the first thing he thought of in the morning.

Thank You, Lord.

Sam was looking forward to spending more time at home with his family...with his wife. From the beginning, he'd counted on how perfect Josie was for the girls. It had taken him this long to admit—to open his eyes and see—she was perfect for him, as well.

"We got a letter from Reverend Martin," Josie told Sam after dinner a few evenings later. "I picked up the mail this afternoon."

The girls had helped her with the dishes, and he'd carried in wood. "What does he say?"

"I haven't opened it. Go ahead."

Abigail pumped water into the teakettle and set it on the stove. "I'll make tea."

"Tea sounds wonderful, darling," Josie told her.

Sam slit the envelope with a table knife and unfolded the ivory parchment. "Henry's been preaching on Sundays, and is even able to do chores."

Josie smiled. "That is good news."

"Ned Dunlop attended church with his family."

Josie let her hands fall still on the dish towel and turned to Sam. "Ned? Why, that's wonderful!"

"I'll bet his wife is happy about that."

"I'll bet *God* is happy about that," Josie replied, and they laughed together. "I've been thinking about something. What would you think of hosting a party soon?"

"What kind of party?" he asked as they moved to the drawing room.

"Just a friendly get-together. I'd like to open up our home to the community so they can get to know us and feel comfortable here."

"Are you up to it?"

"Oh, goodness, yes. I'm perfectly fine."

"Well, if you don't think it would be too much."

"It's why we have this great big house. For just such occasions."

"It's a fine idea," he assured her.

She smiled and skirted a chair to gather her sewing basket. He stopped her by taking hold of her hand and tugging until she knelt in front of the fire beside him.

"There's something I need to say."

She smoothed her skirts with her free hand, but grasped his hand with her other. "What is it?"

"I never said this outright, and I need to. I trust your motivations and I appreciate how kindhearted and generous you are."

She blushed in the firelight. "You don't need to say that."

"Yes, I do. And I need to explain that I let pride get in my way of appreciating this house. I thought I should be the one providing everything for the family. The fact that you could do so much more financially threatened my pride. I'm aware that God providing the means through you is just another way for Him to bless us. I like the house a lot. You've made it a home."

He was surprised when her eyes glistened with tears. Had he been that insensitive to her efforts and her feelings? How many other things had he missed?

There was more, too, things he couldn't put into words, but concerns all the same. He'd been able to share so much because Josie was strong in her faith, and steadfast in her belief that God was taking care of them. He didn't need to spare her by keeping problems to himself. He had sheltered Carrie from difficulties, and now he saw that in doing so he'd done his first wife an injustice. He had no words to explain those feelings.

Footsteps sounded on the floor, and he turned as Abigail carried a tray toward them.

"I only carried the cups, 'cause I didn't want the tray to be too heavy," she explained.

Sam released Josie's hand and took her elbow as she got to her feet.

Josie settled on a comfortable chair. "The three of you are quick learners."

"Did Reverend Martin mention Daisy?" Anna asked.

Sam handed her the letter. "No mention of the cat."

Elisabeth carried in the pot of tea on a second tray.

Josie smiled and poured steaming liquid into each of the five cups. They had just taken their first sips when the front bell rang. Sam stood and strode into the foyer to pull open the door.

"Hello, Reverend," said a tall, dark-haired fellow with a beard. He stuck out a hand. "Karl Stone. Sorry to be interruptin' your evening, but my mother is bad sick. I sent for the doctor, but she thinks she's dyin'—and she wants a minister."

"I'll get my coat and my Bible and join you," Sam told him. "Is it far?"

"It's a spell outside town, but I'll take you and bring you back home in my wagon."

Sam let his family know, and then kissed each of the girls in turn, lastly giving Josie a brief hug with the girls looking on.

"I could come with you, Father," Elisabeth suggested.

He glanced at the clock, noting it was barely after seven. "Gather a wrap and come, then."

Chapter Nineteen

Elisabeth's bright smile assured him he'd done the right thing.

Mr. Stone drove the team away from town, and the night folded them in its inky darkness.

"My mother hasn't been herself in a month of Sundays," Mr. Stone told him. "She loses her balance and forgets things and has terrible headaches."

"That sounds like how Josie described her husband before he died," Elisabeth whispered to her father.

They arrived at a square two-story house with light shining from all the windows. As they approached the door, they heard the sound of glass breaking.

"Mother Stone, lie back on your bed now," a woman demanded in a pleading tone.

"Where is the parson? I'm dying!"

"Karl is bringing him."

They followed Karl along a hallway and into a drawing room. A harried-looking woman with a red scarf tied around her hair was attempting to get an elderly woman to lie back on a fainting couch covered with blankets and pillows. The old woman fought the restraint and jumped to her feet, where she swayed.

Sam handed Elisabeth his Bible and gestured for her to take a seat before he approached the two women. "How do," he said. "I'm Reverend Hart."

"It's about time!" the old woman shouted. "I'm going to meet my Maker, and I want a God-fearin' man to pray over my departing soul."

"I'll start praying right now, if it comforts you," he assured her.

There was a loud knock and a man's voice called out, "Hello? It's Dr. Barnes. You folks down here?"

"We're in here, Doc," Karl called.

Matthew Barnes entered the room.

"Too late for that!" Mildred lunged up and pushed past her daughter-in-law. She bumped into the edge of the tea table, stumbled and grabbed it for support, toppling herself and the other woman both to the floor.

"There's no help to be had!" she cried, flailing arms and legs and trying to roll to her hands and knees so she could stand. "I'm going now!"

"For heaven's sake, lie still!" the younger woman pleaded. She disentangled herself and leaped away to stand. She crossed her arms over herself and shook her head. Promptly, she burst into tears.

Poor Karl obviously didn't know whether to console his wife or go pick up his mother, but since Mildred was attempting to stand and could at any moment topple again, he went to her aid.

Sam joined him, and together they steadied her and got her back on the couch. She lay back and draped an arm over her face. "Just let me die now. I'm miserable here."

Dr. Barnes inserted himself between the others and set down his bag. "You're not going to die until I say so. Let's have a look at you."

Mildred raised her head to peer at him with bleary eyes. "Last time you were here, you told me to rub liniment into my joints to feel better. Now look at me. I can't even walk."

Dr. Barnes turned to her son and daughter-in-law. "Is it possible she's eaten something poisonous?"

"She hasn't been out of the house, and I feed her well," the younger Mrs. Stone said.

"She gets a delivery from the apothecary a couple of times a week," Karl added. "Her liniment, I reckon."

"Impossible to go through that much liniment," the doctor said. He turned back. "What does the apothecary deliver to you, Mildred?"

"Just my prickly ash bitters."

"Where is it now?"

The old woman waved a hand. "In my room."

"Go get it," the doc said.

Karl hurried upstairs. Sam joined the doctor beside Mildred.

"Damnedest thing to get this old," she said, looking Sam square in the eye. "Don't get old."

Within a few minutes, Karl returned with a lumpy pillowcase. He turned it upside down on the carpet and two dozen or more empty brown bottles clanked into a pile.

"What are those?" the younger woman asked.

Dr. Barnes picked up a bottle and looked at the label.

"Her elixir for joint pain." After unscrewing the cap, he sniffed. He jerked his head back and opened his eyes wide. "Seems she's been feeling no pain of any sort for weeks now."

"What is it?" Karl asked.

Dr. Barnes held the bottle toward the other man.

Karl sniffed and drew back with a grimace.

"I'd say ninety percent alcohol," Dr. Barnes replied.

"She's drunk!" Karl turned to his mother. "Ma, you're drunk."

"Bring some of that over here," Mildred said, flicking her fingers.

"Make her some coffee and put her to bed. She'll have a nasty hangover, but she'll come around in a few days." The doctor picked up his bag. "Oh, and make sure you cancel her standing order at the apothecary."

Karl's wife looked mad enough to bite nails. "All this time, I've been treating her like a naughty, sick child, trying to get her to eat, cleaning up after her…"

Sam gestured for Elisabeth and they followed the doctor toward the door.

"And she's been *drunk!*" she cried behind them.

They stood on the porch. "Can you give us a ride home?" Sam asked the doc.

None of them laughed until they reached the edge of the property.

Abigail was glum that evening, finishing her reading without looking up from her book, and spelling her list of words for Josie without her usual enthusiasm.

"Is something wrong?" Josie asked.

Abigail shook her head and refused to meet her eyes.

Sam and Elisabeth came home smiling, a fresh out-of-doors scent clinging to their hair and clothing. Abigail immediately excused herself and went upstairs.

"Is it time for bed?" Anna asked.

"You have a few more minutes," Josie replied.

Sam seated himself on his overstuffed chair, and Anna hopped into his lap. He looked at her slate. "You're learning your numbers quickly."

Josie carried in glasses of milk and slices of the apple pie for him and Elisabeth. The rest of them had enjoyed an evening dessert earlier. Once he'd finished eating, Sam ushered the girls upstairs and Josie joined them.

While Elisabeth readied for bed and Josie helped Anna, he rapped on Abigail's door. His voice carried across the hall as he asked her a few questions. Josie couldn't hear Abigail's replies.

After Anna was tucked in, Josie got a sweater and sat on the front porch steps, enjoying the crisp mountain air and the expanse of twinkling stars scattered across the heavens.

Only time and gentle love would heal Elisabeth's heart. Josie understood her need for her father's approval and her desire to be with him. But Abigail's lack of assurance and silent yearning for attention and affection were painfully close to Josie's own lack of confidence. Watching Abigail struggle with her feelings of inadequacy broke her heart.

Josie stood and strolled along the walk. As she'd done constantly, she thought of the baby she was carrying and placed her hands on her midsection. Surely, Sam would love this child, even though he hadn't wanted another.

Surely, there was enough fatherly affection and attention to go around.

Gazing up at the broad expanse of sky, she appreciated God's limitless love for all of His children.

The door opened and closed, alerting her to Sam's presence. His boots scuffed along the path, and she turned.

"I was looking forward to an evening at home." His words sounded like an apology.

"You make a lot of sacrifices," she replied.

He told her about the woman who'd been dosing herself with liquor, and she smothered a laugh.

"Dr. Barnes and I chuckled, too," he said. "But not in hearing distance of that poor Stone woman who's been caring for her for all these weeks."

Josie's stomach felt as though it were full of butterflies as she formed her next words, but her conscience wouldn't allow her to stay silent. "Sam. I need to say something."

"You may say anything you like," he assured her.

"You're a wonderful father. You're caring and affectionate and…and *present*. My father was a good man. I loved him dearly, but I never had what your daughters have."

"Your father was a kind man, wasn't he?" he asked.

"I'm sure he was. But he was never home. And when he was, he never had time for me. I have to wonder if my mother felt the same way."

Sam simply listened.

"I learned not to expect much, so that I wouldn't be disappointed. So that I wouldn't feel rejected. It didn't help."

She tucked her sweater around her more tightly.

"I can feel the same hesitation coming from Abigail. She hangs back and doesn't seek time with you the way Elisabeth and Anna do. Elisabeth goes after what she wants and she gets it. Anna confidently climbs into your lap without a doubt of her welcome.

"But Abigail...well, she's reluctant to make the effort, for fear of rejection. And it's not that you're not loving toward her or that you don't include her...it's just that she's less confident of her position. But she's yearning, Sam. I feel it. I recognize it. She needs to be..."

Tears sprang to Josie's eyes and burned her throat. The desire was so real to her—so achingly intense. "She needs to feel *special,*" she finished.

And she wasn't speaking only for Abigail. The yearning was Josie's buried insecurity pouring out.

Sam was silent for a moment. "You feel very strongly about this."

"Very," she managed.

"You said something similar back in Nebraska."

She nodded.

"If this is true, if I never saw this, then I've let her down."

"She hides it well."

"*You* saw it."

She felt it more than saw it. Identified. "Thank you for hearing me out. I know I'm not...well..." She didn't finish.

"Not what?"

"I'm new to the family, is all."

Sam surprised her by taking her hand. "New doesn't mean you're not important or that your observations aren't valid. Every day, the fact that I made the right choice in asking you to come with us is reinforced. I need you for this kind of thing. Thank you."

Relieved, she relaxed her posture. "You're welcome."

She was glad he had considered her concerns valid, but hearing that he only needed her for this stung. She was still the same foolish girl yearning for attention.

There were still unresolved issues. A baby wasn't something she could hide. Nor did she want to. She would have to tell him soon.

During the week that followed, Sam asked Abigail to accompany him on one of his calls. At first she seemed hesitant to accept, looking to Elisabeth for her cue on how to react.

Sam had obviously explained things to Elisabeth beforehand, because she nodded and encouraged her sister to go. After they left, the older girl stood in the dining room longer than necessary.

Josie studied her as she held her book to her chest and raised her chin. "You're a good sister," she told her.

Elisabeth swung her attention to Josie. Without a reply, she left the room.

Abigail grew in confidence after that day. She was more open with her father, more certain of her place in his affections. Sam learned that she was good with people. She asked questions, listened when they shared with her, and she paid special attention to the elderly men and women they visited.

Sam was grateful to Josie for bringing about a change that made all their lives better. He hadn't been used to anyone questioning him, but he needed a different perspective, and he appreciated Josie's perceptiveness. She had felt so strongly about Abigail's hurt, had understood it so perfectly.

Another window into his wife's character opened. She had identified with Abigail, and it made sense, given the times she had mentioned her own father's lack of attention.

Sam noticed something else, too. It became painfully clear to him that Josie was open and affectionate with Anna and Abigail, while she held back with Elisabeth, who was openly resistant to her attention.

And she hesitated with Sam, as well. Sometimes he saw in her eyes…in the way she held herself—that she wanted to touch him…or kiss him, perhaps. But she always waited for him to approach her.

She carried insecurities from her childhood, from her first marriage…. It was up to Sam to make her feel secure. And apparently, he hadn't done that yet.

But he thought on it day and night.

Something inside him, something that had been cold and dead, was slowly, steadily coming to life, unfurling, warming, questioning. What was it his wife needed most? What was it he had to offer her?

As another week passed, Abigail and Josie finished the book of recipes they'd been working on, and Abigail said she'd keep it and add to it always. Sometimes she carried both the recipe book and her drawing journal. Comforted by a growing sense of security and at ease in the new house, Abigail's nightmares became a thing of the past.

As the aspens turned to yellows and oranges, and

dried leaves were tossed across their lawn, the Harts put the finishing touches to the house and opened the doors to their community for a harvest party.

"I found this long brass candle lighter in the pantry," Josie told Sam. He lit the wick in the fireplace and then used the flame to light the gas lamps in the chandelier.

"So that's how you do it!" Abigail clapped for her father. "Josie and I were puzzled over that, weren't we?"

"That we were. Oh, look! Our guests are arriving!"

More people had accepted the invitation than had ever been in church at the same time. Parishioners and neighbors were curious about the preacher man, his wife and daughters, and everyone wanted a glimpse at the family who'd bought the big house on the hill.

"I've admired the new colors every time I've looked up the mountain," Vanessa Powell told Sam as he took her coat. She gazed up at the chandelier and then steered toward the drawing room. "I've always wondered what the inside of this house looked like."

"I'll show you around," Josie offered.

Sam turned to greet the Larkens—Victor and Nadine, who ran the general store, and their son, Dan, the local deputy, and his wife, Melissa, who held their new baby wrapped in blankets.

Elisabeth carried coats to the back porch where Josie had strung rope and placed a rod between two tall cabinets.

The girls' teacher, Miss DeSmet, arrived, and Sam learned her name was Kathryn. She was immediately followed by the Paynes, the Collinses and the Stellings.

Abigail and Anna greeted Libby and Patience Stelling, and the girls disappeared into the kitchen.

A few of the guests brought small gifts, so, after refreshments had been served and people had warmed to the occasion, Sam and Josie opened packages containing fresh canned goods and practical household items.

"I have a gift for the family, too," Dr. Barnes announced. "I had to check with Samuel on this one, and he said it was all right. I'll be back."

Josie glanced at Sam. He grinned and a lighthearted wink caught her by surprise. She laughed and observed the girls who were waiting with interest.

The doctor returned with a crate, covered by a remnant of an old blanket. He set the container down on the floor and stepped away. The blanket rippled.

Anna and Abigail knelt beside the crate.

Hesitantly, Anna reached for the blanket, but a movement startled her and she drew her hand back.

Without further hesitation, Abigail grabbed the corner and pulled away the blanket.

A white spaniel puppy with brown spots and ears and a ring around one eye looked up and sniffed the air curiously.

"A dog!" Anna squealed. "You got us our very own dog?"

Murmurs rippled through the bystanders, and several chuckled at Anna's supreme excitement.

"Can I pick it up?"

"Sure," Dr. Barnes answered. "Your ma will tell you where he can sleep and the like."

Anna and Abigail didn't even notice his reference to Josie, but Elisabeth deliberately avoided looking up.

Anna picked up the wiggling puppy, and Abigail petted his head. "What's his name?" Abigail asked.

"He's your dog now," the doctor replied. "You'll need to name him."

"Let's call him Daisy, like Reverend Martin's cat," Anna suggested.

"You can't call a boy dog Daisy," Elisabeth objected.

"Is it a boy?" Abigail asked.

"That he is," the doc replied.

Libby and Patience joined them, and even Gilbert and his cousin, Will, offered names for the new pet.

Josie and Sam thanked all of the guests for their kind gestures, and conversation resumed among the adults.

Sam sipped a cup of rich black coffee and watched Josie as she spoke with Melissa Larken. His wife looked particularly lovely in her violet-sprigged dress and beaded collar. She had curled tendrils of hair that hung becomingly against her slender neck. He knew exactly how good her hair smelled and how soft the skin under her ear was.

"When are you and your lovely wife going to make your announcement?" Ruby Adamson asked from beside him.

He redirected his attention. "What do you mean?"

She gave him a sly smile. "I've already figured out why you've gathered everyone together."

"We wanted to let the people of Jackson Springs know they're welcome," Sam explained to her. "Josie feels very strongly about opening our home to people."

"Well, then it's simply a convenience that you have an important announcement to make."

"I'm afraid I don't know what you're talking about, Mrs. Adamson."

"Why, I'm talking about your new family member,

of course. Some of us guessed weeks ago. Women know these things, Reverend. Why, look at Josie! She's positively glowing."

Sam did look, and yes, Josie was glowing as she held Melissa Larken's baby against her heart and smiled down at him. His wife was lovely, with her eyes sparkling and her ivory skin aglow.

"It's a blessing that you've been given a child of your very own together," Ruby told him. "Your wife must be beside herself with happiness."

Sam studied Josie again, watched as she handed the baby back to his grandmother, and then raised one graceful hand to her hair in a feminine gesture.

Questions and images shifted through his mind in a haze. Mornings resting on the porch. Subtle physical changes… She hadn't been ill during those days she'd rested and frightened him with her paleness! She was as healthy as could be. And she certainly wasn't barren.

Josie was carrying a child.

At the realization, his knees grew weak.

"Reverend?" Ruby asked. "Are you all right?"

He tore his gaze from his wife to look at the woman. "Yes. Yes, I'm fine."

He didn't know what to think. Why hadn't Josie told him? Didn't she know? Of course she knew. Dr. Barnes had called on her. The fact that she was keeping something so important to herself concerned him. No, it hurt him.

Josie turned and arranged a few plates on the food table. She rested her hand on Abigail's shoulder, and Abigail and Libby carried plates toward the kitchen. Josie turned and spoke to Constance Graham.

His lovely wife was in her element in situations like this. Efficient, industrious, capable. It was when she spoke to him—and sometimes when she looked at him—that he saw the doubt in her eyes. Doubt he'd allowed to take root.

Ruby moved on to visit with a friend and Roy Stelling sauntered up beside Sam. "Looks like all of our young'uns have made each other's acquaintance."

"The girls told me about your daughters after attending a tea party," Sam answered.

"Those females," Roy said, shaking his head. "If it isn't their ma confusin' me, it's the daughters."

Sam grinned. "They tend to have their own language, don't they?"

Roy chuckled and swung his gaze in another direction. "And look over yonder."

Sam followed his direction, to see Elisabeth and young Gilbert engaged in an awkward-looking yet seemingly friendly conversation near the table that held the punch.

"I reckon my boy could do worse than a preacher's daughter," Roy said in a teasing tone.

Sam couldn't think that far ahead. He was contemplating diapers at the moment, not wedding bells. Josie was going to have a baby—*their* baby. He'd been through this before, so it shouldn't have been as stunning, or have affected him as deeply as it had. Was everything all right?

He thought back over the house situation. He'd taken responsibility for not learning more about her and for not giving her the opportunity to discuss her finances with him. What else had he neglected? Was she afraid to tell him? Worried that he wouldn't be happy? He tried to recall what he might have said or not said.

Sam did his best to set aside his concerns and converse with the guests. After what seemed like an eternity—but was actually only a few more hours—he gathered wraps as neighbors prepared to leave. After the last couple left, he found the brass hook and turned off the gas chandelier.

"I'll clean up here if you want to see the girls to bed," Josie told him.

"Where's Gideon going to sleep?" Anna asked, still holding the puppy.

"So that's the name you've chosen. I like it. First we'll take him outdoors and then we'll make him a bed on the back porch," Sam told her. "There's a screen door, so he'll be safe."

He helped her take the spaniel out of doors, and then they found an old coverlet and made him a place to lie within the safety of the built-on porch.

Anna ran to Josie and hugged her around the waist.

Josie stopped her task to kneel before the beaming child.

"Thank you for letting us have Gideon," Anna said breathlessly.

"That was entirely your father's doing," Josie told her.

"But you didn't make him sleep outdoors. And you like him."

"Sure I like him. He's cute."

Anna hugged her again and ran up the stairs ahead of her father. "Night!"

Josie enjoyed the tranquility of the quiet, empty

kitchen. She hummed the notes of the tune she'd created for her favorite psalm and sang the words softly.

Arlene and Constance had done a lot of the dishes, so she arranged them in their proper places, took tablecloths out to shake and rubbed a bar of solvent onto the stains, then rolled them for laundering later.

She filled a bucket and had washed a corner of the dining room floor when Sam's heels sounded on the wood. "What are you doing?"

"I'm nearly finished, Sam."

"No, you're *finished,* Josie. Upstairs with you."

At his stern request, she stood, though his admonishing tone puzzled her.

He took the bucket and rag and waited for her to turn away.

"I'm going." She headed for the stairs.

A knock beckoned Sam to the front door. "Miss DeSmet?" he greeted the schoolteacher.

"I apologize, Reverend, but our horse has gone lame. Can you provide us with a ride home? My mother is too old and frail to walk far."

"Just let me tell my wife," he said, and ran upstairs to tell Josie he would return shortly.

Sometime later, Josie had checked on the sleeping girls and was about to prepare for bed, when she heard the sound of a horse on the street below. She glanced out the window, and sure enough, a buggy pulled to a stop in front of the house.

She hurried down the stairs.

"I need the Reverend."

Josie peered out at the man on her porch.

"Frank Evans, ma'am. My wife is asking for your husband to come pray for our boy, Zeb. He done mowed into a nest o' yellerjackets yesterday, and today he's so swollen, his skin's about to pop."

"My husband's not here right now, but he'll be back shortly. Has the doctor been out?"

"Yes'm. Hannah don't want Zeb to die without bein' prayed over proper."

Josie glanced up the stairs. She would tell Elisabeth where she was going and accompany Mr. Evans to his son's bedside. "I can come with you, if it will comfort your wife, Mr. Evans."

"You'll have to do, I reckon."

Josie ran up the stairs and opened Elisabeth's door. "Elisabeth?"

"What?"

"I'll be right back. I'm going to the Evanses' to pray for their boy. Listen for your sisters, should they wake. I'll leave your door open. Your father will be home soon."

"He'll be back shortly," Elisabeth replied.

Josie grabbed her sweater and her Bible and joined Mr. Evans.

Chapter Twenty

Sam returned half an hour later to find the front door unlocked, but the house dark and silent. He removed his boots and silently climbed the stairs.

Their bedroom door stood open, so he stepped inside. Josie must have fallen asleep quickly, though he couldn't see her outline in the bed. He'd wanted to talk to her. He had so much to say, and some things to make up for. He hadn't wanted to wait any longer.

As his eyes adjusted to the darkness, he noticed that the moonlight spilling across the bed didn't reveal a form there. "Josie?"

Surely, she hadn't gone back downstairs to clean up. The house had been dark, though he hadn't looked in the kitchen.

He groped for matches and lit the oil lamp on his bureau. The bed was still neat and unwrinkled. She hadn't come to bed at all. He grabbed the lamp.

The lower floor was deserted, the pail of water standing where she'd left it earlier. Sam went back out, thinking he might have somehow missed her on the porch, where she liked to sit—but there was no one.

After a search of the house, he checked the girls' rooms and their beds. Abigail hadn't had nightmares recently, but she may have cried out and Josie might have comforted her with her presence.

Finally, he set the lamp beside Elisabeth's bed and touched her shoulder. "Elisabeth."

"What?"

"Have you seen Josie?"

"Mama made that sweater for me. Put it back in the drawer."

"Elisabeth, wake up."

"I haven't any coins for your licorice."

"Elisabeth, wake up!"

She rolled to her back at that, blinked against the light and sat. "What is it?"

"Do you know where Josie is?"

His daughter blinked in sleepy confusion. "She isn't in your room?"

"No. I took Miss DeSmet and her mother home, and when I came back, Josie was gone."

Elisabeth shook her head. "I don't know."

"Go back to sleep, then."

She pushed the covers aside. "No, I'll help you look for her."

"I've already searched the house and the yard. I'm sure there's a reasonable explanation."

She accompanied him down the stairs. He lit lamps and stoked the fire in the drawing room.

"There wasn't a note?" she asked.

He shook his head.

An hour passed. Sam felt as though he had a ball of lead in his belly. His unease grew heavier with each tick of the clock.

"She's a capable woman," he said more to himself than to Elisabeth. "But she should have let me know where she would be."

Elisabeth had been watching him pace, stare out the window and then sit and try to relax, as though he wasn't concerned.

"She wouldn't have done anything foolish," he said. "Like going near the mountainside in the dark."

"It's not safe," Elisabeth said, her eyes wide.

"And she knows that," he assured them both.

Another half hour passed, and Elisabeth's chin trembled. "I haven't been kind to Josie."

"What do you mean?" Sam asked.

"I've been rude to her, and I even told Abigail that she was being unfaithful to Mama by letting Josie take her place in our family." A tear trickled down her cheek. "She didn't deserve my meanness. She's always been kind...to all of us."

"Did you really feel that way?" Sam's voice was husky with emotion. "That you would be unfaithful to your mother if you let yourself love Josie?"

Elisabeth nodded.

A stick popped in the blazing hearth, the distraction drawing their gazes to the fire. "I felt that way, too," Sam told her softly.

"You did? But you asked her to marry you and come with us. I thought you had already forgotten Mama."

"I'm not going to forget your mother," he said to her. He got up and moved to perch beside her on the divan.

With his thumb, he brushed away her tears. "I loved her. I cherish her memory. I felt like I let her down, let all of you down by bringing you here. By not preventing her death."

"What happened wasn't your fault," Elisabeth said softly.

"I'm learning that. It's eaten me up inside that I didn't have an answer for you that day, Elisabeth. When you asked me why God didn't save her."

"I was so sad," she admitted.

"I know. And I've learned that I don't have all the answers. I'm not the savior of the world. I'm just one man doing his best to share God's love with as many people as I can."

"You're doing a pretty good job," she told him.

He kissed her forehead. "Thank you. I've been doing some thinking about all this, and I thought about what I would have wanted for your mother if things had been the other way around. If I had died, I would have wanted her to be happy. To love someone again."

"Mama would like Josie." She gave him a tremulous smile. "Anna loved Josie right off."

"I expect you're right." He smiled at her. "You know how the Bible says we should all be like little children?"

Elisabeth nodded.

"Children love easily," he said.

"I guess we don't have to stop loving Mama in order to love Josie, do we?" she asked.

"We sure don't. That's the good thing about the way God made us. Our love can just keep growing and growing."

The sound of the front door closing had them on their feet and running toward the foyer.

"Josie!" Sam called.

Sam engulfed her in a bear hug that lifted her off her feet. "Sam!" she managed against his shoulder. "What is this all about?"

"We didn't know what had happened to you," Elisabeth said.

Sam released her, and she steadied herself against his arm. "What do you mean?"

"Why didn't you leave a note?" Sam asked. "Are you all right?"

"I'm fine. I told Elisabeth I was going to the Evanses'. Their boy Zeb was stung by yellow jackets and Hannah was afraid for his life. I prayed for him. I thought you'd want me to, since you weren't here."

"Will he be all right?" Sam asked.

"I think so. Hannah said he hadn't been able to drink before, and we got him to take some broth."

"I'll go out there tomorrow," Sam said. "So you went up and spoke to Elisabeth?"

Josie nodded. "She didn't tell you?"

Sam shook his head. "She often responds while she's sleeping, but then she doesn't remember a thing in the morning."

"I had no idea."

"I'm sorry," Elisabeth added.

"It's not your fault," Josie told her. "I should have taken time to write a note."

"I'm sorry about how mean I've been to you." Her lower lip quivered. "I just missed my mother, and I didn't want my father to forget about her."

The girl's painful admission touched her deeply.

"It's okay," Josie told her. "I understand."

"I was afraid to stop loving her and to forget about her."

"We won't let that happen," Josie assured her.

"We didn't think you would go on the mountain at night, but I was pretty worried when I thought about the animals that might be out there." Elisabeth lowered her gaze to the floor for a moment, and then raised it to look right at Josie. "I love you, Josie. Thank you for coming with us and for loving our family."

Tears rose in Josie's eyes and emotion swelled in her chest. "Thank you, Elisabeth. I love you, too."

Josie took the first step, but Elisabeth threw herself forward, pressing her face against the folds of Josie's sweater and hugging her tightly. The girl's slender body trembled in her embrace.

Looking up, Josie caught Sam's tender expression. He offered her an encouraging smile.

Watching them, love for his daughter and his wife rose up swift and strong. Sam had held himself as much in reserve as Elisabeth had. He had failed to make Josie feel secure within their family. He had made her feel like…a second thought.

He had never told her he loved her.

He did love her.

"I'm proud of you for being so grown up," Sam told Elisabeth. "Come give me a hug before you run on to bed."

His daughter gave him a hug. "Good night," she said. "To both of you. I'm glad you're safe, Josie."

"Thank you, dear. Good night."

Once she was gone, Josie turned to Sam. "We'd better get to bed. It's awfully late."

"We have a little more talking to do," Sam told her.

At those words and his serious expression, she focused her attention on him. "What is it?"

He gestured for her to lead the way into the drawing room, and pointed to the chair in front of the fire. "Have a seat."

Removing her sweater, she draped it over the ottoman and sank onto the seat cushion.

"We have something important to talk about, don't we?"

Josie's heart fluttered with nerves. She didn't want him to be disappointed. She didn't want him to regret any part of what they had together—or his decision in asking her to marry him.

"There's something you haven't told me."

Her gaze shot directly to his. His penetrating blue eyes stared right through her. "Th-there is?"

He nodded. "And I'm pretty sure I know why you haven't told me."

"Why?"

Sam sat on the ottoman at her knees. "Because you didn't trust me."

She didn't know what to say. She held her silence, but her heart raced and the slim thread of safety she'd been clinging to snapped.

"I haven't given you reason to trust me. I haven't made you feel secure."

He was confusing her now.

"You're pregnant, aren't you?"

She thought her heart would stop, but it kept going—

chug-chug-chugging away, like a train going up the side of a mountain. She hadn't wanted to let him down.

"Aren't you?" he asked.

How could she have been so naive? She nodded.

"Why didn't you tell me?"

She had to speak around the lump that she could've sworn was her heart, right there in her throat. "I—I was afraid to tell you."

"Afraid of my reaction?"

"Yes," she whispered.

"I remember you telling me not that long ago that when we trust God for direction, He gives us desires that please Him. Do you remember that conversation?"

"Of course."

"And you desired a family, didn't you?"

She nodded again.

"What about a baby of your own? Was that your desire, too?"

"It was once, Sam. But not for many years."

"You aren't pleased to be carrying our baby?"

"Of course I am, but you—"

"What about me?"

"You told me you had enough children. You said I would have all I could handle taking care of the girls." Her voice broke. "You don't want more children."

"Yes, I said that," he told her with a sigh of regret. "But remember I believed, just as you did, that we would be unable to have children together. And that would have been all right, Josie. I was prepared to be content with our family the way it was. But at that time I had no idea there would be more."

She stared at him. "What are you saying?"

"I'm sorry that you didn't have confidence enough to tell me something so important. It's a shortcoming on my part."

"No, Sam—"

"Josie, if you had felt confident about your place in our family—if you had felt secure and trusted me—then you would have been glad to tell me."

"I trust you."

"No. Trust must be earned. Trust comes from being confident in someone's love for you. You never even questioned the fact that not having a baby wasn't your fault, did you? Remember, I met your mother-in-law, Josie. You've never spoken ill of your husband, but I can guess how you were made to feel."

"I assumed it was me."

"I was willing to be satisfied, but at the time, I had no idea we would create a child together." He smiled. "This baby is no surprise to God. He's not up there saying, 'Oh, no! Now what?'" Sam smiled. "God knew all along."

"I was content with you and your daughters, Sam. Truly I was."

He took both of her hands. "I know you were. But God's plans are always bigger and better than ours. I had no idea I was going to fall in love with you."

Josie worked to absorb those last few words. He'd had no idea.... "You fell in love with me?"

"Think of it, Josie. The Scripture says He knew us before we were formed in our mother's wombs. God knew our child and gave him to us."

"Sam...you're in love with me?"

His blue eyes held concern and devotion, and, yes,

they shone with love as he studied her. "I've said all the wrong things, I know. But I took all the right steps, even though my motives weren't clear to me at the time.

"I needed you to help me with the girls. I thought God led me to you for them. And He did, but that's not all. God hasn't just provided for the girls. He knew I needed you before I admitted it."

"*Have* you admitted it?"

He blinked. "I think—the problem is that you humble me, Josie. There's a peace about you, and you have a steadfast trust in God that I admire…that I aspire to, actually."

"Sam," she admonished softly, wishing he hadn't said those things. Wishing he would just come out and say what she needed to hear.

"It's true," he said. "I've expended all my efforts on trying to fix things for my daughters, while *you* " he gestured to her "—you've taught them to do things for themselves and you've set an example."

"Our positions are quite different. You carry all the responsibility for them and for the church. You've done a good job at all of it," Josie explained, her voice trembling.

"Everything except assuring you of your place and of my feelings for you."

"If you keep me waiting one more moment, I'll—I will…"

"I love you." He released her hands so he could frame her face. "I love you, Josie, and I'm thankful we're going to have a baby together. I never want you to be afraid to tell me anything again. I don't want you to have a single doubt about how important you are to me.

"I want you as my wife. I want our child. I need you because you're *you*—not because you are good with the girls or because of any reason except that you are the woman I love."

Sam folded her into his embrace and she rested her cheek against the place where his heart beat.

"Thank You for this wife You gave me to love, Lord," he said. "And thank You for our child."

With her heart full to bursting, tears stung her eyes and a sob caught in her throat. Around it she managed to tell him, "I love you, Sam."

He drew back and held her face where he could look into her eyes. "Say it now."

"I love you," she whispered.

With the fire snapping, he kissed her more tenderly than she could ever remember being kissed. He kissed her the way a man kisses the woman that he loves.

"We'd better get some sleep," he told her finally. "We have some exciting news to share in the morning."

"Do you think we can top the puppy?"

"I'm confident we can."

After banking the fire, he took her hand and led her up the stairs. The answers to her prayers had been realized. For the first time, she truly felt loved and accepted.

Never again would she hold herself back. Never again would she be on the outside looking in, because now and forever, she held her place at the very heart of a family.

* * * * *

As a teenager growing up in north Mississippi, **Elizabeth White** often relieved the tedium of history and science classes by losing herself in a romance novel hidden behind a textbook. Inevitably she began to write stories of her own. Torn between her two loves—music and literature—she chose to pursue a career as a piano and voice teacher.

Along the way Beth married her own Prince Charming and followed him through seminary into church ministry. During a season of staying home with two babies, she rediscovered her love for writing romantic stories with a Christian worldview.

Beth now lives on the Alabama Gulf Coast with her family. She plays flute and pennywhistle in church orchestra, teaches second-grade Sunday school, paints portraits in chalk pastel and—of course—reads everything she can get her hands on. Creating stories of faith, where two people fall in love with each other and Jesus, is her passion and source of personal spiritual growth. For more about Beth, visit her website at bethwhite.net.

Books by Elizabeth White

Love Inspired Historical

Crescent City Courtship
Redeeming Gabriel

Love Inspired Suspense

The Texas Gatekeepers

Under Cover of Darkness
Sounds of Silence
On Wings of Deliverance

Visit the Author Profile page at Harlequin.com.

CRESCENT CITY COURTSHIP

Elizabeth White

While Jesus was having dinner at Levi's house, many tax collectors and sinners were eating with him and his disciples, for there were many who followed him. When the teachers of the law who were Pharisees saw him eating with the sinners and tax collectors, they asked his disciples: "Why does he eat with tax collectors and sinners?" On hearing this, Jesus said to them, "It is not the healthy who need a doctor, but the sick. I have not come to call the righteous, but sinners."
—*Mark 2:15–17*

Chapter One

New Orleans, November 1879

Gasping for breath, Abigail Neal pounded on Charity Hospital's enormous oak front door, bruising her fist and driving a splinter into the heel of her hand. She'd covered the six blocks from the District at a flat-out run, but no one had offered to pick her up and take her to her destination. Not that she'd expected it.

"Come on, come on," she muttered. "Someone answer the door." She pounded again, this time with the flat of both hands. The sound echoed off the tall columns and wooden floor of the porch and reverberated through the hallway inside.

Where was everyone? Yanking the splinter out of her hand and sucking away a welling drop of blood, she peered through the little pane of glass in the door. Why lock the door of a hospital? To defend against marauding sick people?

Tess wasn't going to make it if a doctor didn't come soon.

Abigail was about to bang again when a pair of filmy, protruding eyes met hers on the other side of the window. The latch scraped back and the door opened, revealing a short, barrel-chested man with a pockmarked face. "You'll have to go to the back door," he said, squinting up at her. "Nurses are all in evening prayers."

"I don't need a nurse. I want a doctor." Abigail forced herself to stand still, clutching her fingers together to keep from wringing her hands. People often wouldn't help a person who seemed desperate.

The man scratched his head, disturbing the few wisps of gray hair clinging to his shining scalp. "Ain't no doctors here to the front. That's why I says go to the back and wait—that's where the clinic is." He looked her up and down. "You don't look sick, no ways."

"I'm not sick," Abigail said, striving for patience. "I want you to fetch a doctor so that I can take him back to the—I want him to come with me."

"Ain't none here right now," the guard repeated stubbornly. "Doc Laniere's teaching a surgery lesson—"

"Doctor Laniere?" Abigail grabbed the man's arm. "He's the one I want. Someone told me he's very kind and he's the best doctor in the city."

"He's the best all right. But he's busy, and—"

"Take me to him immediately." Abigail straightened, well aware of the intimidating effect of her full height. "What is your name?"

"They call me Crutch." The man glanced uneasily over his shoulder. "Mayhap I could see if Nurse Charlemagne—"

"I told you I don't want a nurse. I want the doctor." Abigail found herself on the verge of frustrated tears.

Every moment of delay endangered not only Tess's life but that of the baby. Pride hadn't done a bit of good so far. "Please, Mr. Crutch. My friend is having her baby—she's been laboring all day and most of last night. She's getting weak, I don't have a way to get her here and I don't know what to do."

An enormous sigh was followed by a clicking of tongue against teeth. "He's gonna squash me like a mosquito," Crutch muttered, then to Abigail's relief, disappeared through a white pedimented doorway beyond the staircase.

Even though Crutch left the door standing wide, allowing an unobstructed view of the unadorned entryway, Abigail remained on the enormous two-story porch, unwilling to risk expulsion. She stood watching horse-drawn carriages rattle down Common Street. Some turned on Baronne before reaching the hospital, some continued to Philippa, where they rounded the corner of the beautiful green sward of grass which gave Common Street its name, then disappeared beyond tall rows of businesses. The scene was infinitely refined and orderly.

And she was going to bring the great doctor back with her to a tenement in the District. Well, he would just have to take her and Tess as he found them. She sat down on the broad top step of the porch and linked her fingers across her knees.

An interminable time later, Abigail heard the clatter of footsteps on the stairs behind her. She jumped to her feet and turned, expecting to see Crutch returning with the doctor. Instead she found a young man striding toward her with a black leather case in one hand and a fine felt hat in the other.

"I'm John Braddock," he said with curt nod. "I understand you need a doctor."

"Yes, but—" Wide-eyed, she stared at him. That name. What an odd coincidence. She blinked. "Mr. Crutch went for Dr. Laniere. He should be right back."

"I sent him to bring the mule cart around for us."

"But—I wanted the house surgeon. Where is he?"

Braddock frowned. "Dr. Laniere is conducting a surgery. Do you or do you not need a doctor?"

"I do, but—"

"Then we'd best hurry. Here's Crutch with the cart." He ran down the steps to the drive path, where the messenger was alighting from a small wagon pulled by a lop-eared mule.

Abigail picked up her skirts and followed. "But are you a doctor?" He was very young, perhaps in his mid-twenties.

Braddock vaulted onto the seat of the cart and took the reins from Crutch. "This is a medical college," he said, reaching a hand down to Abigail. "I'm a second-year student, top of my class. Professor Laniere wouldn't have sent me if he didn't think I could deliver a baby. Come on, get in."

Abigail stared up at him. A *student?* But Dr. Laniere was in surgery and Tess needed help now. She allowed young Braddock to pull her up onto the narrow seat, settling as far away from him as she dared without pitching herself onto the pavement.

"Where is the patient?" he asked, glancing at her.

"Tchapitoulas Street."

"That's a long street. Which part?"

"The District," she managed, burning with humiliation. "We're next to the saloon on the corner of Poydras."

"I might have known." He flapped the reins to set the cart into motion.

Abigail refused to look at him again, although the jostling of the cart forced her elbow to brush his again and again. She gritted her teeth. By the time they traversed the short distance to the tenement room she shared with Tess, her nerves were a raw jangle of anxiety, fear and resentment.

The young doctor spoke not another word to her until he stopped the cart in front of the saloon and lightly jumped down to tie the mule to a hitching post. He reached for his bag, then offered a hand to Abigail. "Perhaps you could tell me what the trouble is and who I'm to treat."

Disdaining his hand, Abigail got down from the cart on her own. "My friend Tess has been laboring to deliver her baby all day and most of last night. She was so weak and frightened... I didn't know what to do."

"When did contractions start?"

Abigail hurried for the door of the tenement. "About this time yesterday."

Braddock grabbed her arm. "She's been in labor for twenty-four hours and you're just now asking for help?"

"I've delivered babies before." She jerked away from him. "It's just that I've never encountered this difficulty." Not for the first time she wished she'd had the opportunity for training this rich boy had. Then she'd have known what to do without incurring his disdain.

"Never mind. Which room?" They were in the tiny

ground-floor entryway. Narrow unpainted doors opened to the right and left and the treads of a rickety staircase wobbled straight ahead.

"This way." Abigail turned to the door on the right and lifted the door latch. There was no key because there was no lock. "Tess?" She entered the dark, shabby little room, frightened by the silence. She could sense the silent young doctor behind her.

A soft moan came from the shadows where Tess's pallet lay against the wall.

Relieved, Abigail hurried over. "Tess, I've brought a doctor. He's going to help us bring the baby out."

"I can't… I'm too tired, Abby." Tess's voice was a thread.

Abigail fell to her knees and laid a gentle hand on Tess's distended belly. "Yes, you can. Dr. Braddock is going to help you." She looked over her shoulder to find him setting his bag on the table.

He looked up. "We'll need all the extra linens you have. You've a way to boil water?"

Abigail swallowed. "Of course."

"Abigail? Abby?" Tess's voice sounded terrified. "It's starting again. The pain—" A scream interrupted her words, ripping from the center of her being.

Torn between compassion and the practical need to attend to the doctor's wishes, Abigail hurried to find the pile of clean rags she'd been collecting against Tess's lying-in. As she mended the fire she'd left burning low in the tiny cookstove that squatted against the only exterior wall of the room, she was conscious of Tess's inhuman, wailing accompaniment to Braddock's rather jerky movements.

He laid out a collection of shining instruments on one of the rags, arranging them with fastidious neatness. He seemed slow, reluctant.

She watched him with resentment. *She* should be the doctor, not him.

By the time she had a tin pot of water boiling to her satisfaction on the stovetop, Tess's screams had subsided to whimpers. Abigail gestured for Braddock's attention. "Now what?"

He got to his feet. "We need to let the water cool a few minutes. I want to wash my hands and instruments. Do you have lye soap?"

She frowned. "We need to hurry. She's not going to be able to stand another contraction like that."

Braddock scowled. "I'll remind you that you came to me for help. Professor always washes everything."

Abigail stared at him. If she argued with him, he would stand there until Kingdom Come, and Tess would die. Tight-lipped, she found him the soap, then knelt beside Tess to bathe her head with a cool cloth. "Hold on," she murmured. "Just a few more minutes."

Behind her John Braddock doused his instruments one by one in the boiling water, then returned them to the clean cloth. After removing the pot from the stove, he stood waiting for it to cool, hands in the pockets of his trousers, staring at nothing.

Abigail watched him. His body was tall and strongly built inside those fashionable clothes. He'd laid the beautiful hat on the shaky pine table, revealing a headful of wavy golden brown hair. She supposed one could call him good-looking, although her perspective on handsome men was admittedly skewed. She had yet to see him smile, but his nose was firmly arched, with fine nostrils, and the eyes wide-set and intelligent.

His brain was the most important part of his body as far as she was concerned.

Finally, just as Tess started screaming again, he decided the water was cool enough to the touch and proceeded to thoroughly soap and rinse his hands. Catching Abigail staring as he dried them, he gave her a mocking bow.

"Now, your ladyship, I'm ready."

Chapter Two

John knelt beside his moaning patient and stared at the baby in his hands. For the first time in his life he uttered the name of God in prayer. He'd never lost a life before—at least not on his own.

He laid the stillborn infant on a ragged towel, then turned to the woman who had been quietly hovering behind him for the past two hours. He held out a shaking hand. "Give me that needle and suture."

She handed him the implements he required, watching his every movement with vigilant, protective eyes.

He began the job of sewing up the woman's torn body. "Here, hold this sponge."

His provisional nurse knelt and followed his gestured instructions. "What about the baby?"

"You can bury it later. It's more important to take care of your friend."

Abigail gasped, dropping the sponge. "The baby's dead? How could you let it die?" She picked up the infant and cradled it against her bodice. Her face twisted and silent sobs began to shake her thin body.

John swallowed against a surge of sympathy but kept stitching. Crying wasn't going to bring the baby back to life. He finished the sutures, efficiently mopped the wound and sat back on his heels. He studied his patient's chalky face. At least she was still breathing, harsh painful gasps between bloodless lips. Her eyes squeezed shut as he drew her dress down over her knees. She would live.

"Where's her husband?" He got up to rinse his hands in a bowl of sterilized water, wiped them on the last clean towel, then opened his bag to stow his instruments.

"I'm not married." The gritty whisper came from his patient. Grunting, she tried to sit up. "Abigail, let me see the baby."

"Here, lie down or you'll start the bleeding again." John knelt to put a hand to her shoulder, which was almost as thin as the skeleton that sat in a spare chair in his boarding house bedroom.

The patient speared him with pain-clouded eyes. "I have to see him."

"It's—it was a girl," John stammered. "She didn't make it."

"A girl. Please, let me hold her just a minute."

John met Abigail's eyes for an agonized moment. She looked away.

"Give it to her," he managed.

His patient took the infant's naked, messy little body against her own, cuddling it as if it were alive and ready to suckle.

What was a fellow supposed to do? He was no minister capable of dealing with these depths of grief. Inarticulate anger seized him as he took a deliberate look around. The tiny, shabby tenement room was scrupulously clean—apparently the lye soap had been put to use—but the odor of mildew and age infused every breath he took. This was no place for two young women to live alone, no matter what their morals.

Dr. Laniere would have known exactly how to deal with the situation. But back at the hospital, Crutch had interrupted the professor demonstrating the amputation of an infected finger for a ring of medical students. The professor had sent John, assuring him he was perfectly capable of delivering a baby.

Eagerly he'd accepted the assignment. John had always assumed he could do anything he set his mind to. But his confidence had diminished as he realized the breech presentation had left the baby in the birth canal too long.

Capable. A crack of despairing laughter escaped him. Lesson learned.

Unfortunately, there was nothing more he could do here. Snapping the latch of his bag, he turned toward the door.

He'd taken no more than a couple of steps when he found himself deluged from behind by lukewarm water. It streamed down the back of his neck, plastered his hair to his forehead and nearly strangled him as he took a startled breath.

With a choked exclamation, he turned to find Abigail glaring at him, the cracked pottery bowl held in her hands like a battle mace.

"Where do you think you're going?" she demanded, looking as if she might fling the bowl at his head, too.

Speechless, John dropped his bag and swiped water

out of his eyes with his sleeve. Intent on getting to the patient, he hadn't properly looked at the woman who had summoned him. For the first time it dawned on him that the woman's few words had been spoken in cultured tones, rather than the typical Creole waterfront accent. And although she was dressed in a ratty brown skirt and blouse, she had the tall, sturdy build of a warrior princess. Nobody would call this woman beautiful, but it was a face a man couldn't forget once he'd seen it.

A furious face. Light green eyes glittered with the flame of peridots set in gold.

John found his voice. "How dare you."

It wasn't a question. It was his equivalent of a bowl of water dumped over the head, uttered in a drawl cultured by a lifetime spent in the elite drawing rooms of New Orleans.

"How dare I?" She bared a set of lovely white teeth, but it was not a smile. She clonked the bowl down on the table and stalked up to him. He was a tall man and her eyes were on a level with his lips. "I'll tell you how I dare. I prayed for you. Not for Tess and the baby, but for *you!* I could tell you were scared spitless, you stuck-up beast." She sucked in a breath. "You *laughed.*"

Stung to the heart, John sucked in a breath. Of course he hadn't been laughing at her or Tess, but at the irony of his own impotence.

"What do you want me to do?" he said through stiff lips. He could hardly let her see his humiliation, but perhaps he could redeem himself somewhat.

The girl studied him, taken aback, as though she'd expected him to either hit her or leave without a word. "You could at least help me bury the baby."

"I'm a doctor, not a grave digger."

"You're not much of a doctor, either."

John flinched at this brutal truth. "Is there a...grave-yard nearby?"

The girl shook her head. "We're nearly underwater here. The charity burial grounds is on the north side of the city."

Tess began to cry, clutching the child closer.

John didn't know what to do with this slide into help-lessness. Despite her derisive words, Abigail looked at him as if she expected him to do something heroic. Clearly he had a maudlin trollop, a corpse and an angry Amazon to deal with before he could go home and go to bed. And he'd been up since before dawn.

With a sigh he walked toward a rusty sink in the corner of the room and activated the pump. He stuck his head under the anemic stream of murky water, rubbed hard, and came up dripping. His coat was ruined, but that was the least of his worries at the moment. Slicking his hair back with both hands, he turned. "Abigail, wash the baby and wrap her in a blanket. We'll take Tess to Dr. Laniere. Then I'll send someone from the hospital to take care of the burial."

Abigail nodded, a rather contemptuous jerk of her severely coifed brown head, but moved to obey.

John knelt beside his patient. "Where are your clean clothes?" He touched her shoulder again, aware of the awkwardness of the gesture.

Her anxious dark eyes followed Abigail's ministrations to the child. She shook her head. "I don't have any."

John sat back on his heels and looked around. Other than the cookstove, a shaky three-legged table shoved next to the far wall and the two straw-filled cots, there wasn't a stick of furniture in the room.

His sister, Lisette, had two armoires stuffed with more dresses than she could wear in a year. Her shoes lined a dressing room shelf that ran the entire length of her bedroom.

The abject poverty of these women filled him with guilt. Releasing a breath, he gathered Tess up in his arms, ignoring the blood on her skirt that soaked through his sleeve and the shabby shoes tied to her feet by bits of rope. He concentrated on rising without disturbing her sutures.

The girl let out a gasp of pain and clutched his neck.

"It's all right, you're all right," he muttered.

"Be careful!" Abigail turned, clutching the blanket-wrapped bundle close. "Should I go look for help?"

The last of John's patience fled. "Just open the door," he said through his teeth.

Those light eyes narrowed. She gave John a mocking curtsy as he passed with Tess in his arms. "Your lordship."

He was grateful to find the cart still tied in front of the building. Equipages had been known to disappear during calls in this part of the city, especially after dark. Thank God he had decided at the last minute to bring it. Riding would have been faster, but one never knew when a patient would have to be hauled to hospital.

Hitching her skirt nearly to mid-calf, Abigail climbed into the back of the cart with a lithe motion that gave John an unobstructed view of trim ankles and a pair of down-at-the-heels black-buttoned boots. She sank cross-legged onto the clean straw and opened her arms. "Here, lay her head in my lap."

Swallowing a time-wasting retort, John complied. Later he would impress upon her who was in charge.

Abigail stroked Tess's damp reddish hair off her forehead, a tender gesture at odds with her brisk, no-nonsense manner. She looked up at John, brows raised. "Let's go."

Scowling at her presumption, John climbed onto the narrow bench at the front of the cart and flapped the reins. With a snort the mule jerked into motion. As the cart bumped over the uneven bricks of Tchapitoulas Street, John could hear an occasional groan from his patient, accompanied by hisses of sympathy from Abigail.

"Can't you be more careful?" she shouted over the clop of the mule's hooves and the rattle of the cart.

He stopped, letting another wagon and several pedestrians pass, and stared at her over his shoulder. "Would you care to drive, Miss—?"

"Neal." Darkness had nearly overtaken the waterfront, but John detected a hint of amusement in her tone. "My papa often asked my mother the same thing when I was a little girl." All traces of levity vanished as she sighed. "Forgive me. I know we have to hurry."

"Yes. We do." Surprised by the apology and puzzled by an occasional odd, sing-song lilt in the girl's cultured voice, John stared a moment longer, then turned and clicked his tongue at the mule. He would question Abigail later—after the baby was buried.

A grueling ten minutes later, the cart turned a corner onto St. Joseph Street, leaving behind the waterfront's crowded rail depots, dilapidated shanties, cotton presses and towering warehouses. Inside the business district, two-and three-story brick buildings hovered on either side of the narrow street like overprotective mammies. Streams of green-slimed water, the result of a recent rain, rushed in the open gutters beside the undulating sidewalks. Businessmen intent on getting home after the day's work hurried along, ignoring the stench of decayed vegetation, sewage and shellfish that permeated everything.

John frowned, unable to overlook the city squalor. He had tried to convince his father that a platform of sanitation reform would solidify his mayoral campaign. The senior Braddock preferred more socially palatable topics of debate. If all went well, John's father would be elected in November.

If all did not go well, the pressure would be on John to quit medical school, go into the family shipping business and try for political office himself. Phillip Braddock often opined that power was a tool for good; he meant to grab as much as possible, even if it had to come through his son.

Because John had no intention of becoming anyone's puppet, he was concentrating on getting his medical diploma and staying out of the old man's way. As much as John admired him, his father had a great deal in common with the new steam-powered road rollers.

As he guided the cart onto Rue Baronne, he wondered what his father would have to say about these two passengers. Probably shake his leonine head and expound at length on the wages of sin.

He glanced over his shoulder again. Abigail had rested her elbow on the side of the cart and propped her head against her hand. She seemed, incredibly, to be asleep, with Tess dozing in her lap.

What set of circumstances had brought the two of them to such a pass? He saw women like them often, when he and his friends did rounds in the waterfront, but he'd never before had such a personal confrontation with a patient. Or a patient's caregiver.

"You just passed the hospital," Abigail said suddenly.

"I thought you were asleep." Annoyed to have been caught daydreaming, John flipped the reins to make the mule pick up his pace. "We're not stopping at the hospital. Dr. Laniere has a clinic and a few beds at his home. Tess will be better cared for there."

"I see." Abigail was quiet for the remainder of the trip.

The professor's residence on Rue Gironde was a lovely three-story brick Greek revival, with soaring columns supporting a balcony and flanking a grand front entrance at the head of a flight of six broad, shallow brick steps. Wrought iron graced the balcony and the steps, lending a charming whimsy to the formal design of the house.

John bypassed the curve of the drive circling in front of the house and took a narrower path that passed alongside and led around to the back entrance into the kitchen and clinic. The house and grounds were as familiar to him as the home he'd grown up in. The Braddocks and the Lanieres had maintained social ties since John was a boy, despite the fact that the Lanieres' loyalties to the Confederacy during the "late upheaval" had been in serious doubt. It was even rumored that Gabriel Laniere had been a Union spy and had fled prosecution as a traitor,

leaving Mobile with his wife and a couple of body servants in tow. Phillip Braddock chose to discount such
nonsense; ten years ago he had been appointed to the
board of directors of the medical college, and remained
one of its main financial contributors and fund-raisers.

John drew up under a white-painted portico designed
more for function than elegance, which opened into a
tiny waiting room off the clinic. He got out and tied the
mule, then went around to reach for Tess and the baby.
As he slid his arms under her back and knees, Abigail
stopped him with a hand on his shoulder. An oil lantern
hanging beside the door illuminated a surprising sprinkle of freckles across her formidable nose.

"Thank you for bringing us here," she said. "You
didn't have to."

And why had he? John studied the anxious pucker
between her level brows. He frowned and straightened.
"Hope Willie's still here," he muttered to himself. "We'll
need to send the baby to the hospital for burial preparation while we get Tess settled." He shifted his burden
and stepped back. "She needs a clean gown and I want
to check her sutures after that ride."

Abigail struggled to her feet, apparently numb from
having sat in one position so long. "Who's Willie?"

"House servant. Butler, coachman, a bit of everything." John moved aside as Abigail swung over the
side of the cart to the ground. When she appeared to be
steady on her feet, he jerked his chin at the door. "Ring
the bell and somebody will let us in."

Abigail pulled the tasseled bell cord and moments
later the door opened with a jerk.

"Winona." For the hundredth time John shook his

head at the waste of such exotic loveliness cooped up in a kitchen and doctor's clinic. "Is there an empty bed in the ward?"

The Lanieres' young housekeeper's smooth dark brow folded in instant lines of concern. "Mr. John! What you doin' here so late?" Clucking her tongue, Winona moved back to let him enter with his slight burden. "Of course there's a bed. Nobody else here, in fact. Who's this poor lady?"

She led the way out of the waiting room into the well-stocked dispensary, then into a third room. She lit a gas lamp on a plain side table. Bathed as it was in quiet shadows and antiseptic odors, the room looked inviting enough. John was glad he'd elected to come here, rather than the hospital.

"A maternity call I made late this afternoon. Breech delivery." As Winona turned down one of the four beds with movements unhurried but efficient, John kept an eye on Abigail. She stood just inside the room, hands clenched in the folds of her skirt. She looked more than out of place. She kept looking out the window as if expecting to be followed. "This is Abigail Neal," he said.

Winona, in her unassuming way, exchanged nods with the other woman.

"We lost the baby," John said as he laid his burden on the smooth, clean sheet.

"Bless her heart," Winona breathed, touching Tess's wan face and pulling up the top sheet.

"She'll be fine, but we need to arrange a burial in the morning." John took the baby out of Tess's arms. "Where's Dr. Laniere?"

"Gone to deliver another baby."

John winced. "Gone how long?"

"Maybe an hour. He'd just come back from the hospital and sat down to supper. Miss Camilla's upstairs puttin' the children to bed."

"All right. I'll stay until he comes back." John glanced at Abigail, who looked like she might topple over, if not for the wall behind her. "Winona, could you fix Miss Neal a cup of tea and a biscuit or two? Maybe find her a clean dress and a nightgown for the patient?"

Winona nodded. "Was just goin' to suggest that. Be back in a bit." She paused in the kitchen doorway and gave Abigail a kind glance over her shoulder. "Ma'am, there's a chair over there in the corner if you want to sit down."

"Thank you—" But Winona had already disappeared. "What a lovely young woman." Abigail moved the wooden straight chair close to the bed.

"Yes, and she's a wonderful cook, too." John had been moving about the room, but when the silence became prolonged, he looked around to find Abigail, head bent, folding pleats in her ugly skirt. "What's the matter?"

"Nothing."

John shrugged and moved to the window, where he stared at his reflection in the dark window. He hoped the professor would be back soon.

Chapter Three

Abigail straightened the lye-scented sheet across Tess's shoulders and brushed the lank hair away from her face. The chair beside the cot had become most uncomfortable in the last hour, despite the pleasure of the tea and biscuits Winona had provided.

Tess, now clothed in a plain white nightgown Winona pulled from a supply closet, was finally asleep. Abigail herself had been given a faded dark blue cotton dress with elegant jet buttons marching up the front and ending at a neat white stand-up collar. She couldn't remember ever having worn such a lovely garment.

She looked up at John Braddock. He had ceased prowling the room and now towered at the foot of the bed, holding Tess's nameless little one close to his sharp-planed face. He had not put the baby down once since he'd picked her up. Expression somber, he brushed the waxen cheek with his knuckle, then examined her minute fingers one by one.

Abigail wondered what drove the emotions that crossed his expressive face. Was it remorse for the loss of his little patient? Did he regret his earlier conde-scension?

She could hardly believe some of the things she'd done and said to him in the past few hours. Up to this point, her anger at him and fear for Tess had given Abigail strength beyond herself, but something about the young doctor's tearless grief flayed her emotions. She bent to lay her forehead beside Tess's shoulder and let hot tears soak the sheet. She was empty. She didn't know what to do, where to turn.

"Birth and death, all at once."

Abigail turned her head. "What?"

"I never realized how closely tied they are. Some of us get a lot of time and some get none at all." John lifted his gaze from the baby's face and Abigail saw stark confusion in the heavy-lidded hazel eyes. "Do you think it's all predetermined? Am I wasting my time?"

"I don't know." She sat up and scrubbed away her tears with both hands. "The baby might have been dead before you got there." It was hard to admit that. "Tess would've died, too, if you hadn't come. I was thinking— I'm not sure I could've carried on if she had."

John's face was a study in consternation. "Is she your sister?"

"No." Abigail adjusted the sheet again and checked to make sure Tess's breathing was still regular. "Six months ago I arrived in New Orleans with nowhere to go, no family and no friends. Tess took me in and helped me find a job."

He stared at her and she felt her face heat. What must she look like to this educated, expensively dressed young high-brow? Even in stained and wrinkled clothing, with his thick hair falling into his eyes from a deep widow's peak, he looked like he belonged in somebody's parlor.

"Where did you come from?" His elegantly marked brows drew together. "You don't look like the usual fare from the District."

Abigail came out of her chair. "Give me that baby right now—" she tugged at the infant corpse—"and get out of here." When he resisted, looking down at her as if she were crazy, she glared up into his multicolored eyes. "If you don't like the way I look, go put on your smoking jacket and settle down for a beer with the fellows. Then you can laugh over us slum wenches to your heart's content and not think about us one more second."

The fellow refused to behave in any predictable way. He hooked his free arm around Abigail's shoulders and yanked her close, the baby between them. "Abigail, I'm sorry." His voice was husky, almost inaudible.

Abigail stood with her face buried in the fine, still-damp wool of John's coat, the soft, bulky shell of a baby pressing against her bosom. Her world shifted.

How long? How long since she'd been held in the hard strength of a man's embrace? Not since she was a small girl, before her mother left and her father became the Voice of God.

She ought to pull away from this improper embrace. Humiliating to need it so much. No more crying, though. She stood stiff, wondering what he was thinking.

"Braddock, what's going on here?" The deep, resonant voice came from the doorway.

John Braddock let Abigail go and stepped back. "S-Sir! I'm so sorry, but I didn't know what else to do."

"Looked to me like you knew exactly what you were doing."

Abigail turned, straightening her hair and smoothing her skirt in the presence of the tall, distinguished man who strode into the clinic carrying a black medical bag. His thick black hair, gray-shot on the sides, and the lines fanning out from intelligent black eyes put his age somewhere in the mid-forties, but the trim, athletic figure would have rivaled many a younger man.

Abigail glanced at John, waiting for an introduction. The younger doctor seemed to be struck dumb with mortification. She dropped a curtsy toward the professor, whose mouth had quirked with disarming humor. "Thank you for coming, Dr. Laniere. I'm Abigail Neal. I'm the one who came for you on behalf of my friend Tess."

"Ah, yes." Dr. Laniere's expression sobered. "The difficult labor." He approached Tess and bent to lay a gentle hand against her forehead, then lifted her wrist to check her pulse.

Abigail met John's gaze. She started to speak, but he shook his head once, hard, his lips clamped together. "Prof, the baby didn't make it." At the professor's inquiring look John continued doggedly. "Breech presentation kept the baby too long without oxygen. The mother was losing blood quickly, so I made the decision to save her." His tone was firm, almost clinical, but Abigail heard the note of distress in the elegant drawl.

The young doctor's contained anguish inexplicably drew Abigail's sympathy. She had a crazy urge to comfort him.

Dr. Laniere steepled his fingers together, propping

his forehead against their tips. For a moment the only sound in the room was Tess's harsh breathing, then the professor dropped his hands and looked up with a sigh. He approached John to clasp his shoulder. "We'll talk about your procedures later, Braddock." He laid his other hand on the baby's head, as if in benediction. "Why did you bring him here?"

Although he'd missed his guess at the swaddled infant's sex, Abigail noted with gratitude that he didn't call the baby "it."

"They wanted a burial and didn't have any place to go," said John. "I told them you'd help us find a minister and a gravesite."

"Did you?" Dr. Laniere sounded amused.

"Please, sir," Abigail intervened before John's defensiveness could spoil their advantage. "We'd be grateful if you could help us. All we can afford is the charity catacombs and I just can't see that poor little one abandoned there."

Dr. Laniere stood with his hand resting on Braddock's shoulder, but he fixed Abigail with a look so full of compassion that she nearly broke down in tears again. "I understand your distress. But you know the baby is in the arms of the Father now." He smiled slightly. "Perhaps, of all of us, the *least* abandoned."

Abigail wished she could believe that.

Hope lifted the discouraged droop of John Braddock's mouth. "That's so, isn't it, sir?"

"As I live and breathe in Christ." Dr. Laniere squeezed his student's shoulder. "Now let's see what we can do to make your patient more comfortable and take care of the baby's resting place."

* * *

"You will not give her that beastly powder." Abigail stood in the kitchen doorway, effectively preventing John's entrance into the clinic. The professor had gone to take care of the burial arrangements, leaving the two of them to watch over Tess. "I've known women who never rid themselves of the craving, once they taste it."

John showed her the harmless-looking brown bottle of morphine. "But it would ease her pain and help her sleep."

"Yes, but if you slow her heart enough, she may not wake up at all."

"What do you know about it?" John stiffened. "We'll ask Dr. Laniere."

She'd studied on her own, but hadn't known enough to help her mother. "I know what I've seen—"

"John, at the risk of sounding uncivil, what are you doing here so late?"

Abigail turned.

A pretty, curly-haired young matron entered the clinic with a baby of about six months propped on her hip. She tipped her head to smile at Abigail around John's shoulder. "I'm Camilla Laniere. Meggins, say 'How do you do.'" She picked up the baby's hand to wave.

John looked guilty. "I'm sorry if we disturbed you."

"Nonsense. I was just surprised to see anyone here, that's all."

When the baby stuck her chubby fist in her mouth, Abigail smiled. "How do *you* do, young lady?"

"Afflicted by swollen gums, I'm afraid," said Mrs. Laniere, brushing her knuckles gently across the baby's flushed cheek. "We came down for a sliver of ice." She paused, a question in her soft voice. "I didn't know we had a patient in the clinic."

Abigail brushed past John. "I'm not the patient, ma'am. My name is Abigail Neal, and my friend Tess is in the ward here. Your husband sent Mr. Braddock to us. He brought us here when—" She faltered. "Tess is very ill. She lost her baby."

"I'm so very sorry." Mrs. Laniere reached to clasp Abigail's hand. She glanced at John, heading off his clear intention to continue the opium debate. "You did well to bring them here, John. What have you done with my husband?"

John blinked, reverting to some instinctive standard of manners. "He's taking care of laying out the—the body. He sent Willie to find a couple of grave diggers."

"Ah. Then I assume we'll have the burial in the morning."

"Yes, ma'am, before church." He hesitated. "Because the professor will be back soon, I believe I'll leave the patient in his hands. She's resting fairly comfortably now. I've a pharmacy test to study for." He pressed the vial of morphine into Abigail's hand. "You can trust Dr. Laniere to do the right thing."

"I'm sure I can." Pocketing the opiate, Abigail gave him a dismissive nod. "Good evening, Mr. Braddock."

"Good evening, Miss Neal."

When he closed the door behind him with a distinct thump, Meg flinched and snuggled her face into her mother's neck.

Shaking her head, Mrs. Laniere hugged the baby. "Please overlook John's abruptness. He's...a bit tense these days."

"I suppose I should have thanked him." Abigail leaned against the table, rubbing her aching temple. "Does he think he knows *everything?*"

"I'm afraid it's rather characteristic of the *genus homo.*" Mrs. Laniere smiled. "But John in particular, being considered brilliant in his field, tends to be a bit... insistent in expressing his opinions."

Abigail laughed. "That's one way to put it."

"You must be worried about your friend." Mrs. Laniere hesitated, swaying with the baby. "My dear, would you care to sit down with me for a cup of tea?"

"I couldn't impose. Tess—"

"—is resting. We'll be near enough to hear her if she calls. And I'd like a bit of intelligent female conversation while I nurse the baby."

Abigail studied Camilla Laniere's frank, friendly face. There seemed to be no ulterior motive. She smiled faintly. "I'd adore a cup of tea, Mrs. Laniere."

"Please. Camilla. I'm not *that* much older than you."

The doctor's wife led the way into the kitchen, then unceremoniously handed the baby over to Abigail and began tea preparations. Despite her itchy gums, Meg seemed remarkably placid. Giving a contented sigh, she popped her thumb in her mouth and laid her head on Abigail's shoulder.

After a startled downward glance, Abigail smiled and patted her charge's cushioned bottom. Leaning against the dough box, she watched Camilla's familiar movements around the roomy, well-equipped kitchen. "Where did the servants go?"

"Winona and Willie are our only house servants." Camilla measured tea into a lovely floral china teapot.

"They both go home on Saturday evenings to be with their families on the Lord's Day."

"I suppose we interrupted your family time tonight, but I was so grateful when your husband arrived—"

"My dear, you mustn't apologize." Camilla set the kettle on the stove to boil and smiled over her shoulder. "Gabriel is always glad to be of service. I would have been down here myself if I hadn't been putting the children to bed."

As Abigail stared into Camilla's golden-brown eyes, something flashed between them—an intuition of friendship, an offer of human connection. Abigail looked away, hardly able to bear this sudden kindness.

After a moment Camilla quietly took the baby, leaving Abigail empty-handed and feeling foolish. "I think you need a place to stay tonight. To be with your friend." She laughed as Abigail shook her head. "I'm being utterly selfish, you know. Winona and Willie won't be back until tomorrow evening. If our patient needs something, you'd be here for her."

"All right." Abigail returned the smile. "I'll stay. And of course you must call me Abigail. 'Miss Neal' ran away many years ago and hasn't been heard from since." Touching the baby's pink foot, she looked up from under her lashes. "Besides, I have to make sure the Barbarian doesn't try to feed opium to Tess."

Feeling a soft little hand patting her cheek, Abigail struggled out of deep sleep into utter darkness.

"Winona! Winona, wake up, I'm thirsty!" lisped the small, invisible person behind the hand. "It's hot and Mama's rocking the baby and I can't sleep."

Abigail suddenly remembered where she was. Winona's little room off the clinic, just a few steps from Tess's bed in the ward. This must be one of the Laniere children.

She sat up. "I'm not Winona, I'm Abigail. But I'll get you a drink of water—just a minute, let me light a candle."

"Ooh! Just like Goldilocks! What're you doing in Winona's bed?"

Abigail laughed. "Winona will be back tomorrow." Swinging her legs off the side of the bed, she lit the candle and held it up so she could see the wide, bespectacled eyes of a little boy who looked like his mother—probably around seven years old, judging by the missing front teeth. His hair curled in every direction but down and his nightgown was buttoned two buttons off, so that the hem hitched crookedly around his knees.

He poked his spectacles up on his button nose with one finger. "You ain't Goldilocks. Your hair's brown."

Abigail tugged the braid hanging over her shoulder, wishing for a proper nightcap. "It is indeed. What's your name?"

"Diron. Are you gonna get me a drink or not?"

Since Camilla had thoughtfully provided a pitcher of clean water and a cup for her guest before retiring, Abigail smiled and poured a drink for the boy. Diron downed it quickly and held out the cup for more. It was then that she noted the small red blister on the child's forehead.

"Just a minute." She reached out to push back the bright curls. His forehead was warm.

Enduring her touch with a long-suffering frown, Diron scratched his stomach.

"How long have you been itching?" she asked.

"I dunno. I must've got a bunch of mosquito bites. Can I *please* have some more water?"

"Certainly. But I want to see your tummy."

She poured the water, then while he drank it, matter-of-factly unbuttoned his nightgown. His chest and upper abdomen were covered with the tiny red blisters. Chicken pox.

No wonder the poor child was so hot and thirsty. Camilla was busy with the baby, but she would want to know.

When Diron finished his water, Abigail took him by the hand and led him into the clinic and through the kitchen. The sound of both of their bare feet slapping against the wooden floors tickled her sense of humor and she enjoyed the feel of his small warm hand in hers. He was a trusting little fellow.

In the carpeted hallway she saw the stairs to the upper floors. It was a large, airy house, bigger than anything Abigail had been inside before, with lots of screened windows and light, gauzy curtains stirred by a cool nighttime breeze.

On the first landing she felt Diron tug her hand. "Miss Lady. I'm tired." He gave an enormous yawn.

"Would you like a piggy-back ride?" He nodded and she walked down a few steps to let him climb on. "Goodness, you're a big boy." She grunted as he clutched her around the neck and waist. "Hold tight now."

As Abigail trudged up the remaining steps to the

first floor, Diron leaned around. "Where'd you get that funny accent?"

"China," she replied without thinking.

"Oh, pooh. I didn't believe you was Goldilocks, neither."

Chapter Four

A chill had sneaked across the river during the night, sending fog drifting across the graveyard, twining through Abigail's hair and muting her and Dr. Laniere's footsteps. The ground was soft, even on this elevated patch a mile or so away from the river, and she had to step over puddles of water in the shallow hollows of sunken graves.

Abigail carried the baby, dressed in a tiny white gown worn by Meg just a few months ago. Camilla would have attended the funeral service, but she'd had to remain with the feverish and itchy Diron. Tess was induced to remain in bed only by Abigail's promise of writing down exactly what was said at her baby's interment.

They were to call her Caroline.

"Here we are," said Dr. Laniere, halting beside a tiny fresh grave, barely three feet long and a couple of feet wide. He opened the lid of the small wooden casket he'd carried from the house and looked across the top of it at Abigail. "It's time to put her in the casket." His deep-set dark eyes were somber, filled with sympathy. "Remember—"

"I know. She's with the Father." Abigail closed her mind against the instinct to pray. She'd been brought up to talk to God at every turn and the habit kicked in at moments of stress. But it was difficult to believe God was really interested in either her or this small wasted life.

Placing the baby in the box, she arranged the lacy white skirts in graceful folds. She was glad Tess couldn't see this. She could remember Caroline cuddled in her arms like a white-capped doll.

Dr. Laniere placed the lid on the box and was about to lower it into the grave when pounding footsteps approached.

"Wait!" John Braddock ran out of the mist, panting. In one hand he carried his black medical bag. "Professor, I want to see her again before you bury her."

Dr. Laniere straightened.

Abigail hadn't expected the young doctor to actually come for the burial. She was even more surprised that he'd apparently already been on a medical call. "What are you doing here?" she blurted, sounding perhaps more defensive than she'd intended.

"I've a right to be here," he said breathlessly. "I delivered this baby, and—" He swallowed. "Let me see her, please."

When the professor opened the box, Braddock removed his hat, clutching it as he stared at the baby. "I'm so sorry," he muttered. "I promise I'll learn to do better."

Abigail's throat closed. She didn't want to like this

privileged rich boy. Pressing her lips together, she looked away.

She heard the lid go back on the box and then the gritty sound of wood landing on sand and clay. The two men picked up the shovels left by the grave diggers and began to fill in the small hole in the ground.

The job took less than a minute. She made herself look at the mound of fresh dirt, the only visible trace of Tess's baby—except the scars on her friend's body. She thought of her father's pontifications on Scripture. Ashes to ashes, dust to dust. The Lord cherishing the death of his beloved.

She couldn't find anything particularly precious about this stark moment.

"Oh, God, we know you're here." Dr. Laniere lifted his resonant voice. "We know you give and you take away and you are sovereign. We pray you'll remind us of your presence even in the darkness of grief. We pray you'll be ever near to Tess as she recovers. Please champion these young women and help them find real help as they seek you. Please use Camilla and the children and me to meet their needs. And I pray you'll hear and meet young Braddock's desire to be a healer, even as you heal his heart."

What about my *desire to be a healer?* Abigail thought as the professor paused. *What about* my *wounded heart?* She opened her eyes and looked up just as a ray of sunshine broke through the patchy fog. An enormous rainbow soared from one end of the graveyard to the other. She caught her breath.

"In the name of our Lord, who takes our ashes and turns them to joy… Amen."

The professor and John replaced their hats. Abigail, shivering in the cool morning dampness, hurried toward the cemetery entrance. She wanted to get back to Tess, to write down the words of the service before she forgot them. *Ashes to joy...*

"Wait, Abigail." Shifting his medical bag to the other hand, John caught up with her, took her hand and pulled it through his elbow. "I thought you should know I went back to the District last night."

"Did you?" Stumbling on the soggy, uneven ground, she reluctantly accepted the support of his arm. "Needed a bit of alcoholic sustenance?"

"No, I—" He gave her an exasperated look. "Must you assume the worst?"

She shrugged. "I don't know many men who lead me to expect anything else."

"Well, in this case you're wrong. I went back there because I'd heard a child coughing in the apartment next to yours. The walls are so thin—"

"Yes, they are." She didn't need to be reminded. "That would be the McLachlin baby. He has chronic croup. I've tried to get Rose to move him out of that mildewy apartment, but she can't afford anything better."

"Well, I went back to see about him. Stupid woman wouldn't let me in, even though I *told* her I was a doctor."

Abigail looked up at him. "To the contrary. For once she was using her head, not letting a strange man into her apartment."

There was a brief silence. "I see your point." John opened the graveyard gate and held it as Abigail passed through. "Then perhaps you'd agree to return with me this afternoon and persuade her of my good intentions. I'd like to look at the baby to see if anything can be done about that cough."

Abigail hesitated. "She can't afford to pay you."

"I know that." He let out an exasperated sigh. "Prof encourages us to see charity cases when we have time. It's good practice."

"Oh, well, then. For the sake of your education, I suppose I'd best come with you."

He stiffened. "Miss Neal—"

"Mr. Braddock." She squeezed his elbow. "I was only tweaking you."

He looked at her for a moment before a slow grin curled his mouth. "Were you, indeed? Then for the sake of *your* education, I'll allow you to observe a man who practices medicine for more than money. Perhaps you might learn something."

His eyes held hers. Something shifted between them. Abigail looked over her shoulder to find the professor's reassuring presence several paces back.

John followed her gaze. "Prof, I'm going back to Tchapitoulas Street with Miss Neal to look after a sick little boy."

"Fine. Just bring her back before noon and you may stay for dinner, too." Dr. Laniere waved them on and turned off toward Daubigny Street, where his family attended church.

For the next couple of blocks, Abigail maintained a tense silence. In the distance church bells began to ring. "Are you a church-going man, Mr. Braddock? Perhaps your family will wonder where you are."

"My family would be quite astonished to see me at

all on Sunday before late afternoon," he said easily. "I don't live at home."

"Oh." When he didn't elaborate, she looked at him. "Then a wife or—or sweetheart?"

"I assure you I am quite unattached at the moment. Are you trying to get rid of me?"

"Of course not." Abigail looked away, blushing, as they turned the corner at the saloon. "I agreed to come with you to check on the baby." Her relief that he was unattached was absurd. There was nothing personal whatsoever in his escort.

"Yes, you did. And here we are." He stood back as Abigail opened the outer front door and knocked on the door across the entryway from her old apartment with Tess.

She could hear the baby crying inside, Rose's anxious voice, the other two children giggling and shrieking. "Rose?" She knocked again. "It's Abigail."

The door jerked open and Rose appeared with the baby on her hip. A little girl and a little boy of about four and five clung to her skirts, one on each side. "Abigail—what are you doing here? Is something wrong?"

Abigail glanced at John over her shoulder. "I brought Dr. Braddock with me. He wants to look at Paddy."

Rose's big blue eyes widened. "Paddy's fine."

Abigail laid a hand on the baby's back and felt the rattle of his lungs as he breathed. He'd tucked his face into Rose's shoulder, but Abigail could just see the curve of a feverish cheek. "Rose. Please let us in. Denying trouble never made it go away."

Rose stared at John, one hand clasping the baby, the other protectively on her daughter's head. Abigail knew she must be thinking of the drunken husband who had brought her and the children over from Ireland and abandoned them two months ago. As she'd told John earlier, Abigail herself had little reason to rely on any man's trustworthiness. But some tiny part of her insisted on giving this one a chance to prove himself.

John seemed to realize he was here on sufferance. "Mrs. McLachlin, I think I know what's causing Paddy's cough. If you'll just let me look at him for a minute, I can give him some medicine and he'll feel much better tonight." His tone was, if not exactly humble, moderate enough to reassure.

Baby Paddy suddenly erupted in one of his fits of croupy coughing. Rose took a flustered step back. "All right. Come in, both of you, but don't look at the mess. The children have been playing all morning."

Abigail would not have increased Rose's embarrassment for the world, but she couldn't help marveling that the young Irishwoman had survived this long on a laundress's wage with three small children. Clearly she was in dire straights. Except for two dolls made from bits of yarn and a pile of rusty tin cans the children had been playing with in the center of the room, there was little difference between this apartment and the one Abigail had shared with Tess. Poverty had a way of leveling the ground.

To her surprise, as she and Rose seated themselves on the two wooden chairs, John took off his hat, sat down cross-legged on the floor and opened his bag. He produced a couple of splinters of peppermint candy wrapped in waxed paper and smiled at the two older children, who stared at him from behind Rose's chair.

"Look what I've got here, widgets. I'll give it to you, but you have to open your mouths wide and let me see if there's room for it to go in."

The little girl, Stella, glanced at her brother. "It's candy," she whispered.

"I want it," he whispered back. The first to conquer his shyness, he edged toward John, who held the candy just out of reach. Apparently seduced by the twinkle in John's eyes, he dropped his jaw and stuck out his tongue. "'ee? 'ere's 'oom."

John laughed and deftly plied a tongue depressor as he peered down the little boy's throat. "There is, indeed. Here you go." He laid the candy on the boy's tongue. "What's your name?"

"Sean." The boy danced backward, eliminating any chance of the candy being snatched away. His eyes closed in ecstasy. "Marmee, I like this."

"Me! Me!" Stella gaped wide as she crowded close to John, gagging slightly as he depressed her tongue. But she patiently held still to let him look at her throat. When she received her candy, she sucked on it furiously, gazing at John with adoration. "Can Paddy have some too?"

John shook his head. "Paddy's too little. But maybe he'd let me look at his throat anyway?"

By this time, Rose was thoroughly disarmed and handed over the baby without further protest. John took him with a gentle competence that reminded Abigail of the way he'd held poor little Caroline that morning. Her throat closed as Paddy blinked up at the doctor's handsome young face.

John examined the baby thoroughly, laying his ear against Paddy's chest and back to listen, gently moving his arms and legs, palpating the glands beneath the soft little chin. He tracked the movement of Paddy's eyes by moving his finger back and forth, grinning when the baby grabbed it and tried to suck on it. "No, no, boo. Dirty." He looked at Rose as he lifted Paddy onto his shoulder and patted his back. "Definitely teething, which causes fever. But the cough worries me. It means there's mucus draining into his stomach, maybe collecting fluid in his lungs. You'll need to suction out as much of it as you can, keep him at a comfortable temperature, wash everything that goes in his mouth. Keep him fed—which means taking care of yourself." His eyes softened as he looked around at the bare room. "Do you get enough to eat?"

Distress took over Rose's worn young face. "I do the best I can, but there aren't many vegetables available this time of year, and meat…" She swallowed. "I can't afford—"

"Fish," Abigail blurted. "Tess and I used to go to the docks early in the morning and ask for whatever wasn't quite good enough to send to the market. You can make stews and gumbo, rich in good stuff."

Rose blinked back tears. "Maybe I could ask Tess to bring back extra…in return for laundry service."

Abigail exchanged a smile with John. "I'm sure she'd be happy to when she's back on her feet."

John handed the baby back to his mother and began to repack his bag. "Yes, that's a good idea. And meantime, wrapping the baby up and taking him outside for cool night air will ease his breathing and help him sleep. Just be sure he doesn't get too cold."

Rose stood up and swayed with Paddy clasped to her

bosom. "Dr. Braddock, thank you for coming back. I shouldn't have been rude to you last night." She hesitated as John rose and dusted the seat of his trousers. "I'm sorry I can't... I don't have the money to pay you for your trouble."

He stared at her, a hint of the old arrogance drawing his brows together. Or perhaps, Abigail thought, it was simple embarrassment. "I don't need your money," he said.

"Then perhaps you'd care to bring your laundry by." Rose's soft chin went up. "I'm considered the best in the neighborhood."

Catching Abigail's warning look, John shrugged. "I've no doubt you are. We'll see. But I promised to return Miss Neal to the clinic before noon, so we'd best hurry. I or one of the other fellows will stop by here tomorrow to check on Paddy. I'll send some bleach to wipe down the floors and ceiling. Some say that keeps down the spread of croup." He gave Rose a quick nod and offered his hand to little Sean. "Help your marmee out by playing quietly when the baby's asleep, won't you, old man?"

Sean nudged his sister. "Would you bring more candy when you come back?"

John winked. "I'll see what I can do."

"Goodbye, Rose." Abigail smiled at her neighbor as she followed John out to the entryway. "Don't forget about the fish."

"Thank you, Abigail." Rose's expression was considerably less troubled than when they'd first arrived. "I don't know what else to—just thank you." She shut the door hurriedly.

As they began the long walk back to the Lanieres', Abigail took John's proffered arm and sighed. "She'll listen to you, I think." She glanced at him. "You were very sweet to the children."

She knew she'd used the wrong word when his fine eyes narrowed. "Perhaps you'd expected me to growl at them."

Smiling, she shrugged. "You did surprise me a bit. I confess your motivations confuse me, John. People like Rose—and Tess and me, for that matter—cannot pay you in coin, and you seem to have a rather contemptuous attitude toward our entire class. Why do you want to be a doctor? Is it simple scientific hunger?"

He didn't immediately answer. "Imperfections bother me," he said slowly. "I suppose that could be considered a character flaw. But I see no reason for those little ones to suffer from hunger and disease if there's anything I can do about it." He glanced at her, cheeks reddened, she thought not entirely from the wind whipping off the river. "I don't mean to be arrogant."

An inappropriate urge to giggle made Abigail look down, pretending to watch her step. "Because imperfections annoy me as well, I'll take it upon myself to correct you as needed." She gave him a mischievous glance from under her lashes.

To his credit, John laughed. "Magnanimous of you, Miss Abigail. You'll give me lessons in social intercourse, and I'll keep your considerable predisposition for interference well occupied. We should get along famously."

Almost lightheaded with the unexpected pleasure of intelligent repartee with an attractive—if slightly prickly—male, Abigail turned the conversation to his background with the Laniere family. John Braddock was like no man she'd met in her admittedly abnormal life. Perhaps she had more to learn than she'd thought.

"It's got to be here somewhere," John muttered to himself that evening as he skimmed through the last of six pharmaceutical books he'd borrowed from Marcus Girard. He sat on his unmade bed, his back propped against the wall, a cup of stout Creole coffee wobbling atop the tomes stacked at his elbow.

The cramped and exceedingly messy fifteen-by-fifteen-foot room on the second level of Mrs. Hanley's Boarding House for Gentlemen was one of John's greatest sources of personal satisfaction. It hadn't been easy to endure his mother's tearful accusations of ingratitude nor his father's blustering threats of disinheritance. But in the end, John's determination to live on his own had worn them both down. Two years ago, on his twenty-third birthday, he had packed his clothes and books into four sturdy trunks and had them carted to the boarding house. He then rode his black mare, Belladonna, to the livery stable around the corner on Rue St. John—another serendipitous circumstance which afforded him no end of amusement.

Mrs. Clementine Hanley insisted on absolute moral purity in her lodgers—the enforcing of which she took quite seriously and personally. She also set a fine table and could be counted upon to provide fresh linens daily.

Unfortunately, she was not so dependable in the matter of functioning locks.

John looked up in irritation when the doorknob rattled. The key worked its way loose and hit the floor with a clank. "Girard, if you come in here again, I'm going to souse every pair of drawers you own in kerosene and set them on fire."

The door opened anyway and Marcus's ingenuous, square-cut face insinuated itself in the opening.

John glared. "Go away!"

Marcus leaned over to pick up the fallen key and tossed it at John. The key plunked into the half-full coffee cup. "Oops." He gave John an unrepentant grin. "A little iron supplement for your diet, old man."

Snarling under his breath, John used his pillow case to mop up the sloshed coffee. "You'd better have a good reason for interrupting me again." He fished the key out of his cup.

Marcus swaggered into the room with his usual banty-rooster strut, hands thrust into the enormous pockets of a peacock-blue satin dressing gown. He paused in front of the skeleton spraddled in a straight chair under the room's tiny, solitary window.

"Hank, old bean." Marcus bowed, sketching a salute. "I trust this evening finds you hale and hearty."

John resisted the urge to laugh. Encouraged, Marcus could go on for hours in that oily false-British accent. He closed the book on his finger. "What do you want, Girard?"

"Stuck-up rotter, ain't you?" Giving the skeleton a thump on the cranium, Marcus hopped onto the window sill and folded his arms across his barrel chest. "Came to rescue you."

"Rescue me? The only way you can rescue me is to find me another pharmacy book."

"Braddock, I've lifted every book m'father has on the subject. If what you're looking for ain't there, it just— ain't there. Come on, I know you've memorized the lists for the test. Let's toddle over to the District and slum a little."

The notorious red light district was located a few blocks from the medical college and Mrs. Hanley's Boarding House. It also happened to be where John had encountered Tess and Abigail. Yesterday's experience had destroyed whatever appeal the District once had. And going back with Abigail this morning to visit the McLachlin family had turned it rather into a source of conscience.

John opened the book again. "I'm busy. And if you had even half as many brains as Hank, you'd take one of these books down to your room and have a look yourself."

Marcus gave John a puzzled look. "What's got into you today? You didn't go to church this morning, did you?"

John gave a bark of laughter. "Not exactly. I attended a funeral."

Marcus sat up straight, his thin, sandy hair all but on end. "I'm sorry, Braddock! Who died?"

"Nobody you know." John had no intention of exposing the life-changing experiences of the last two days to Marcus's inanities. "I'm just—not in the mood. *Comprendez-vous?*"

Marcus pursed his lips. It was common knowledge that John's family ties took him in directions that less well-connected students could only dream of. "Certainly. I understand. Death and all that." He slid off the window seat and sidled toward the door. "You were my first choice of companion, but I guess I'll head down to Weichmann's room to see if he'd care to get his head out of the books for a bit." He paused with his hand on the doorknob. "If Clem asks, tell her we've gone on a call."

Mrs. Hanley would certainly ask, should John be so foolish as to stick his nose outside the room. He gave Marcus an absent wave as the brilliantly hued dressing gown disappeared into the hallway. There had better be no emergency calls tonight.

He took a sip of the stone-cold coffee, then propped the cup on his chest, dropping the book onto the floor. He'd been studying the composition and medicinal uses of opium for hours and there was still no conclusive evidence that Abigail Neal was wrong. It was true that opium and all its derivatives—including morphine and laudanum—could be addictive when consumed even once. Certainly the substance was effective as a pain-killer, but were the side effects worth it?

John didn't know. He was discovering there were a lot of things he didn't know. The more he studied medicine, the more he realized its practice was largely in the realm of guesswork, intuition and trial and error. Frequently even mysticism. Even Dr. Laniere, his favorite professor and mentor, sometimes made fatal judgments. He had as good a record of success as any physician John had yet to meet, but...people did die under his care.

Why didn't God just tell people how to go on? Why did they get ill and injured in the first place? If he could heal at all, why didn't he heal everybody?

Irritated at the intrusion of such unscientific thoughts, John slung his coffee cup onto the bedside table and got up off the bed. He took a deep breath and bent to touch his toes a few times.

He'd been entertaining a lot of God-related meanderings ever since the delivery of that stillborn baby. All day he'd had a sense of someone looking into his mind, prodding his thoughts and feelings. One of the main reasons he'd taken Abigail back to visit that croupy baby was to escape the strong urge to go to church.

Just a bit spooked, he turned a full circle, taking in his familiar surroundings. Nothing out of order. The narrow, tumbled bed with the coffee stain on the pillow. The square table holding a pile of anatomy textbooks and the Tiffany lamp his mother had given him on his twenty-first birthday. Sepia-toned photographs of his parents and her sister Lisette on the mantel above the tiny fireplace. Hank holding court in the chair under the window. The plain mahogany chifforobe with its mirror reflecting his confusion back at him.

John thrust both hands through his hair and stared at his own reddened eyes. Not enough sleep lately. That was all it was.

Then he looked at his hands. They shook. The nails were immaculate, the signet ring on his left little finger dull gold with a garnet set into the family crest. Rich man's hands? Healer's hands?

He hurried to the window, leaned out and sucked in a draft of thick, clammy, November air. He'd lived in New Orleans all his life and the humidity had never bothered him before, but he found himself struggling for a breath. No wonder little Paddy McLachlin was so sick.

John looked down, watching passersby fading in and out of the pools of gaslight spotting the sidewalks. When had it gotten dark out? Maybe he should try to catch up to Girard and Weichmann after all.

He pulled his head back inside the room, banged down the window sash and yanked the curtain closed. He sat down to tug on his boots, decided against a coat and tore out of the room, slamming the door behind him. He pounded down the stairs, shoving the useless key into his pocket.

God couldn't influence his thoughts if he wasn't there.

Chapter Five

The next morning John slumped at a table in a nearly empty classroom, listening to the heavy marching of the clock on the wall behind him. Traffic clamored from the street outside the open window to his left.

He stared at the test in front of him and wondered which of the medicines he'd just listed would be the quickest remedy for acute hangover. Maybe he should go straight for the arsenic. Quelling a strong desire to hang his head out the window and heave, he contemplated the top of Dr. Girard's bald head, visible behind the Monday morning *Daily Picayune*.

Marcus's father was a cold-hearted old goat, a brilliant lecturer whose written tests had been known to reduce grown men to tears. He sat at the front of the lecture hall, behind a bare table which exposed his short legs, stretched out and crossed at the ankle. His scarlet-and-lemon-striped waistcoat, half-inch-thick watch chain and green paisley ascot revealed the source of Marcus's love for sartorial splendor.

John wished the professor had his son's amiable temperament.

He was one of only two students left in the room. Everyone else, including Marcus himself, had either completed the test or given up in despair. He glanced across the room at Tanner Weichmann. Weichmann had not indulged in spirits last night, but had come along more or less to keep Marcus out of trouble. In fact, it had been he who put both Marcus and John to bed, after paying for a hack home and supporting the two of them up the narrow stairs. Good thing Clem slept like the dead or they might all have been out on the street tonight.

John supposed he should be grateful not to have awoken in a gutter somewhere, robbed of his clothes and money. Weichmann was a serious pain, but he was dependable. Perhaps not as gifted a scientist as John, not nearly as much fun as Marcus, but methodical to the point of insanity. John was certain he'd finished the test long ago, but Weichmann would check his answers to make sure every word was spelled correctly and all sentences complete.

Weichmann suddenly looked up, his dark eyes probing John's. He wiggled heavy black brows and elaborately pulled out his watch.

John couldn't resist looking over his shoulder at the clock. Nearly noon. Time was almost up. He suppressed a groan, bent over his paper again and dredged up the therapeutic and alterative uses of mercury. By the time he finished his answer, Dr. Girard had folded his paper in a neat square and waited, stubby fingers linked and his brow creased in impatient lines. John looked around. Weichmann had disappeared.

"Braddock, you seem determined to make me miss my noon meal," growled Dr. Girard. "Are you quite finished?"

"Yes, sir. Sorry, sir." John rose and clattered down the steps of the amphitheater, sticking his pencil stub behind his ear. He reluctantly handed over his paper. "When will you have them graded?" If he failed this test he would have to repeat the course. Pharmaceuticals tended to be his downfall because of the spellings.

Without looking at him, the professor stuffed John's test into a leather portfolio. "You'll know soon enough." He rolled out of the room without a backward glance.

John ran a hand around the back of his neck, popping the joints to relieve tension. At least it was over. Pass or fail, there was nothing he could do about it now. He needed to go lie down.

He headed for the door and nearly jumped out of his skin when someone grabbed his arm as he passed into the hallway.

"How did you do, Braddock?"

John wheeled. "Careful, Weichmann, or you'll be cleaning your shoes. I'm still a bit unsteady this morning."

Weichmann gave an evil chuckle. "Speaking of morning, you missed rounds. Prof wasn't happy."

Dr. Laniere wasn't the only professor, of course, but every med student distinguished him with the title. No one wanted to disappoint Professor Laniere.

John lifted a shoulder and continued down the hall toward the stairs. "Couldn't be helped. What did you tell him?"

"Told him you had a previous engagement."

"You did not."

"No. But I should have. Braddock, you never drink. What's gotten into you, old man?"

Since the words were almost a direct quote of Marcus's the day before, John hurried down the marble stairs without replying. He wasn't going to admit that a prostitute's dead baby had resulted in his hearing from God.

Weichmann's long, skinny legs had no trouble keeping up. "There's a few minutes for lunch before anatomy lab. Want to go for a beignet and coffee?"

John's stomach revolted. "No!"

"Oh, sorry... Didn't think."

John sat down and planted his elbows on his knees, laying his pounding head in his palms. He could feel Weichmann hovering behind him on the stairs, his breath wheezing and whistling. It took little to get the young Jew's asthma kicked up.

"No, *I'm* sorry. I don't know what's wrong with me." John stared at the gray squiggles in the white marble between his feet. "Weichmann, has God ever communicated with you? You know, like Moses and the burning bush?"

Weichmann didn't answer for a long moment. John could hear the clatter of students changing classes down in the east wing and, through the open windows, the rattle of carriages passing in the street. The heavy odors of mildew and chalk and the stench of the dissection lab drifted from two floors up. He looked over his shoulder and found Weichmann staring at him as if he'd lost his mind.

"Maybe you'd better go home and go to bed," suggested Weichmann.

John's head fell back against the wrought-iron spindles of the stair rail. "I was planning to." He got to his feet and descended the remainder of the stairs. At the bottom, he turned to Weichmann, who followed tsking like an agitated squirrel. "Don't tell anyone I asked that, would you?"

Weichmann shook his curly head. "Nobody would believe me if I did."

The haunting strains of a hymn sung in a rich, throbbing contralto drifted through the kitchen and clinic/dispensary to the ward, where Abigail was feeding Tess her evening meal of barley soup. In the daylight, Abigail had discovered the ward to be a large, airy room with doors opening into the kitchen on one side and the clinic on the other. The three long, curtainless windows of the third wall looked out on the garden, where even in late fall birds sang in tall flowering shrubs and fruit trees gave off an intoxicating scent. Lined up on the interior wall of the room were four narrow cots, each with its own bedside table holding a small basin-and-pitcher set, with a chamber pot underneath the bed.

"I know not what the future hath of marvel or surprise," sang the unseen singer, "assured alone that life and death His mercy underlies."

Sighing, Abigail spooned soup into Tess's mouth. The song brought to mind a vivid image of her mother, singing over her fine embroidery, dressed in the traditional Chinese wide-sleeved, knee-length cotton overshirt and loose trousers. Darling, vulnerable Mama, trying to fit in despite her "devilish" blue eyes, red hair, and normal-sized feet. Papa had thought to have Abigail's feet bound, but Mama managed to convince him that, at the age of five, too much growth had already taken place.

The Chinese women had been repelled by such foreign females. Abigail, always tall for her age, got into the habit of slumping. Only since returning to America had she trained herself to stand upright.

The words of the hymn seemed a symbol of all Abigail had run away from, a mockery of the dire circumstances of her life.

Tess had awakened off and on all day, slowly gaining strength. Still, Abigail couldn't help worrying. She had been much safer in the relative anonymity of the District. Besides, if she and Tess didn't report for work tomorrow, they might return to find that they had been replaced. Their miserable jobs in the sail loft were all that stood between them and starvation—or prostitution. The Lanieres seemed to be kindhearted folk, but there was a limit to most people's charity, as she knew only too well.

"Who is that singing?" whispered Tess, pushing away the spoon. "Thank you, but I don't want any more."

Abigail set the bowl on the floor, leaning over to lay her head on the sheet beside Tess. She was so tired. She'd been up until dawn this morning, giving cornstarch baths to Diron and his ten-year-old sister Lythie, also discovered to be stricken with chicken pox. Camilla had been occupied with the fussy and equally poxy baby Meg. After Abigail snatched a few hours of sleep, Tess had wakened and called for her. She'd sat trying to stay awake in this uncomfortable wooden chair all day.

Winona came back yesterday afternoon to take over

the household duties, but Abigail had seen little of her, other than at mealtimes.

Abigail yawned. "Sounds like an opera singer. Do you suppose the Lanieres hired someone to entertain us?"

Tess giggled, gladdening Abigail's heart. It had been a long time since Tess had anything to laugh about. "Go and see, Abby. I want to meet her."

"All right." With mental reservations that any guest of the Lanieres would care to meet two women from the District, be they ever so inwardly genteel, Abigail picked up the half-empty bowl and pushed to her feet.

She found Winona straining cooked pears into an enormous pot on the kitchen stove. All Abigail could see of her was the mane of inky curls cascading down her slender back, a pair of café-au-lait-colored arms, bare beneath the rolled-up sleeves of a coarsely woven blue-and-white-checked blouse, and a plain brown gathered skirt.

But the voice. Abigail marveled as it poured from the woman's tiny body like the throaty eulogy of a dove: "I know not where his islands lift their fronded palms in air; I only know I cannot drift beyond his love and care."

Abigail wanted to weep at the beauty and hope of the words and melody.

Winona turned around to dump the pear pulp into a bowl next to her elbow. When she saw Abigail, a smile lit her face, turning the dark eyes to black gemstones. Her features had an exotic sort of elegance, more interesting than any pale perfection. "Ooh, you startled me!" She laughed, giving the sieve a good shake with competent, blunt-fingered hands, then set it down to wipe her fingers on a towel tucked into the waistband of her apron.

"I heard you singing." Odd to hear such a glorious sound from a servant. On the other hand, who was she to look down her nose at anyone?

"Pshhh, I'm sorry. Miss Camilla said not to disturb you, if you and the lady patient was asleep." Winona gave a rueful shrug. "I get carried away."

"Oh, no, it was lovely." Abigail smiled. "We—Tess and I—thought it was an opera singer."

Winona went off into gales of throaty laughter. "Me? Oh, help us, that's a good one!"

Abigail found herself joining in. "Your voice is finer than a woman I know who once sang on the stage in Paris." Amusement died as Abigail pictured poor Delphine's perpetual drug-induced stupor. These days her voice was rarely lifted in anything other than black despair.

"I wish I could learn from a real teacher." Winona turned as an insistent knock sounded at the kitchen door. "That would be Mr. John. He's the only one of Dr. Gabriel's students who comes direct to the kitchen. Can't nobody talk him into coming to the front door." She went to open the door.

Abigail found her heart clanging around in her chest like the Vespers bell in the tower of St. Stephen's. She'd wondered when Braddock would deign to bestow his presence upon them again.

"Afternoon, Mr. John." Winona moved to let him in.

He came in, hatless and stock askew, his coat shockingly draped over his arm. His tall form was backlit by the late afternoon sun that streamed across the kitchen courtyard and gilded the top of his head. He stopped and stared at Abigail for a long moment.

She touched her hair, then cursed herself for such a ridiculous, feminine instinct. She snatched her hand behind her back.

He shifted his attention to Winona, who had gone back to her preserves. "How is Tess?"

Winona looked around, amusement curving her lips. "I don't know, Mr. John. You better ask Miss Abigail here. I been so busy helping Miss Camilla with the children and tending to the laundry, I ain't had time to even look in on her. Miss Camilla say the lady's been in good hands." She smiled at Abigail.

"Tess is a little stronger." Warmed at Winona's praise, Abigail lifted her chin. "Even without the opium, she slept well last night and most of today."

"I'm glad to hear it." He gave her a curt nod and stalked off toward the clinic.

Abigail gave Winona a wry glance. "Is he always this charming?"

An inscrutable smile played around Winona's full mouth. "He can turn it on when he wants to."

Abigail didn't want to know what that meant. "When will Dr. Laniere be home?"

"Oh, right about—" The kitchen door rattled and opened—"now." The doctor came in whistling, with his hat under his arm, and Winona reached to take it from him. "Miss Camilla said to tell you she's up in the nursery when you get home. The two older boys're down with the pox now. It's a mess for sure."

The doctor's cheerful expression fell. "All five of them? Poor Camilla." He sighed. "All right. I'll just check on Miss Montgomery, then I'll see about the children. I'm sure Camilla's got things under control."

Abigail followed him into the clinic, where she was just in time to witness the unhorsing of Sir John the Terrible, who had leaned over to grasp Tess's wrist between thumb and two fingers.

Abigail slipped past Dr. Laniere when he halted just inside the ward, holding his hat behind his back with both hands. He rocked on his heels, watching his student with a sardonic expression that Abigail found impossible to interpret.

"Well, Mr. Braddock." Dr. Laniere's dry tone conveyed not a trace of the tenderness he'd shown in his ministrations to Tess. "I see that having skipped early rounds, you decided to compensate with a late-evening tour of duty. I trust you've recovered your customary blooming health."

Braddock dropped Tess's hand with a start and backed up a step. "Professor! I was just—"

"No, no, carry on, Braddock. You were doing quite well. Would you like to borrow my stethoscope?"

Braddock recovered his aplomb. "No, sir." He discreetly pulled back the sheet to examine Tess, who turned her head away, enduring the humiliation with her eyes closed.

Abigail anxiously watched her friend's face. She'd give anything to be a doctor herself, able to spare women the degradation of being handled familiarly by male strangers. It wasn't the first time she'd entertained this utterly hopeless dream. She clenched her hands, silently, fiercely repeating it, almost a prayer. All she wanted was a chance to study, to learn the things John Braddock took for granted.

Resentment gave her boldness. "I'll take Mr. Braddock's rounds tomorrow morning if he doesn't want to go."

John Braddock snorted. "Very funny." Straightening, he dropped the sheet back into place and folded his arms across his chest.

Abigail's bravado disappeared when Dr. Laniere turned. "What did you say?"

"I s-said I would like to assist you as nurse. I've quite a bit of experience." Abigail found her knees shaking. She put a hand against the wall behind her.

"I don't believe that's exactly what you said." Dr. Laniere tapped his lower lip with a finger. "But if you'd like to assist, you may meet me in the carriage house at seven in the morning. We'll see what you can do. So I suppose you should stay another night or two. Camilla could use an extra pair of hands, if you don't mind pitching in."

Abigail felt the blood rush from her head. "S-Sir! Do you mean it?"

"Professor!" Braddock's hazel eyes all but popped out of his head. "This woman is no nurse! She's a prostitute!"

Abigail came away from the wall, indignation overpowering her sense of unworthiness. "Tess and I are both respectable women who have fallen on difficult times. We are not prostitutes. Do not compound your idiocy by spouting such utter claptrap!"

"My *idiocy*—"

Dr. Laniere raised a hand. "The two of you may continue this discussion outside, if you please. I wish to examine my patient in peace and quiet." When Braddock looked about to argue, the professor's brow knit. "Now."

Braddock clamped his lips together and stalked toward the doorway into the kitchen. He paused beside Abigail and bowed with elaborate exaggeration. "After you, ma'am." He waited for her to precede him out of the ward.

She grasped her skirts as daintily as if they were finest silk and gave him the curtsy her mother had made her practice before a mirror when she was a little girl. Rising with gratifying grace, she turned to Dr. Laniere. "I shall meet you in the carriage house in the morning, sir." She smiled at her unexpected champion. "Thank you, sir."

Braddock followed her outside into the shadow-dappled courtyard, shutting the door sharply behind him. "What do you think you're up to?"

She whirled to face him. "Accepting an invitation."

"You invited yourself. What possible help do you think you'll be—you'll only get in the way of those of us who have paid tuition and earned a spot at the professor's side."

"What difference does it make to you whether I'm there or not? Do you think my brain will absorb all the information in the room, leaving you without any?" Closing her eyes, she placed her thumbs at her temples in imitation of a French Quarter spiritist. "Ooh, I think you're right. I definitely sense your intellect dissipating by the second." She looked at him in mock sympathy. "No wonder you seem so monumentally stupid."

"Don't be absurd." His mouth quirked a little in spite of the heavy frown. "It's a matter of what's fair."

"Fair?" She could feel her fingers curling into her skirt. "How does Dr. Laniere's generosity remove your benefit? Besides, even if I had the wherewithal to pay tuition, I wouldn't be allowed to take classes with you. So don't prate to me of fairness, Mr. Braddock."

His mouth opened, but he couldn't seem to articulate whatever was boiling behind those hot multihued eyes. "It's just not right," he finally muttered. "We keep women out of medicine to protect them."

"Well, I've been protected right out of my homeland and my family, thank you very much," she said. "Now that I've landed on my feet here, you're not going to convince me to go back."

"Miss Neal—Abigail," his voice softened, "I wouldn't send you back to the District. I merely want you to consider carefully before you force your way into a place where you won't be accepted, much less welcomed. The other fellows will be brutal if you show up tomorrow morning."

Abigail stared at him, chin raised. "Your warning is well taken. And I shall prepare myself accordingly." She dipped him another curtsy and turned for the door. "Good afternoon, Mr. Braddock."

She forced herself not to look over her shoulder as she reentered the kitchen, leaving her adversary fuming on the other side of the door. John Braddock had a thing or two to learn about women if he imagined he'd thwarted her desire to follow rounds in the morning.

Chapter Six

"Girard, if you want someone to crack your knuckles, I'll be happy to do it for you." John continued his circular route around the Charity Hospital entryway, almost hoping for an excuse to vent some of his pent-up restlessness.

John and Marcus, trailed by Weichmann, had arrived at Charity Hospital thirty minutes earlier than the time appointed for rounds with Dr. Laniere. None of them wanted to be accused of slacking, and John was determined to be the epitome of punctuality and dependability for the rest of his life.

Miss Charlemagne had let them in, her garments pristine as always, though John had noted a streak that looked suspiciously like a pillow crease on the elderly woman's round cheek. No one had ever seen her so much as yawn. She was the first person he saw in the morning and always seemed to be available for nighttime emergencies. He could only suppose she slept with her eyes open. She was not a nurse, but her genius for administration made her more valuable to the doctors who attended from the medical college than a hundred nurses.

After pocketing the brass key suspended from her belt with a copper chain, she had cautioned the three young men to be quiet, then whisked herself into the chapel to pray. John had considered asking her to pray for him, but the memory of Weichmann's response to yesterday's mention of God and burning bushes dissuaded him.

Weichmann, seated beside Marcus on the next-to-lowest step of the central staircase, pulled out an enormous pocket watch that he claimed had been given to him by an uncle descended from German royalty. "Braddock, there's probably time to send Crutch out for breakfast. I wish you wouldn't be so stubborn."

John took another turn across the tiled foyer. "If you'd seen Prof's face last night—"

"We *did* see it, when you didn't appear yesterday morning." Marcus grimaced. "If you have a death wish, Braddock, there are less painful ways to go about it. I had more to drink than you did and I still managed to get up on time."

Weichmann put away his watch. "Are the tests graded yet?"

Marcus avoided John's eyes. "I don't know."

John pounced. "You've seen the grades. Did I pass?"

"I told you I don't—" Marcus tried to pull John's hands away from his cravat. "Let go, you Neanderthal. I saw mine, but Pa caught me before I got any farther."

Releasing his friend, who indignantly tried to restore order to his mangled neck cloth, John shoved his hands into his trouser pockets. "So what was your score?"

"Let's just say I won't be starting my own pharmacy anytime soon. And don't say you told me so. I studied in my own way, it just didn't stick. All that Latin. Gads! Why can't we speak English?"

At that moment the front door opened, admitting Dr. Laniere, followed by a troop of medical students and a beautiful young woman.

John did a double take. He'd never imagined Abigail Neal would have the brass to show up this morning. She wore a different dress than the ugly black one she'd had on yesterday, this one a high-necked affair that quite incidentally duplicated the new-leaf color of her eyes. It was a bit short-waisted, and...his gaze traveled to the hem, which, judging by the deeper hue of the fabric, had been recently let out. He frowned, shaken by this reminder of Abigail's poverty.

"Mr. Braddock, if your breakfast disagreed with you this morning, I shall be happy to excuse you to return to your bed."

John looked up to find Dr. Laniere and the other students eyeing him with varying degrees of amusement, sympathy and gleeful malice. Abigail herself gazed over his shoulder, an expression of supreme indifference on her serene face. Except for the slight quirk at the corner of her mouth.

"Gads!" repeated Marcus. "You ain't bringing a *woman* into the hospital, are you, Prof?"

"Ah, I neglected to introduce Miss Neal, didn't I?" Dr. Laniere turned to smile at Abigail, sweeping an ironic hand toward John and his cohorts. "Miss Neal, I present to you Marcus Girard and Tanner Weichmann, both second-year students. Mr. Braddock you've already met, of course."

"Already *met* her?" blurted Marcus. "Is this your Amazon?"

John sent a scalding look over his shoulder, ignoring the guffaws of his fellow students. He regretted the pink that stained Abigail's sharp cheekbones.

Her lips tightened, but she looked down at Marcus as if he were a particularly nasty species of cockroach. "And you would be his…" She hesitated. "Harlequin?"

Marcus, red-faced and speechless, tugged the carnelian-and-saffron diamond-patterned waistcoat down over his trim stomach.

Laughter erupted among the other fellows and John struggled not to join them. She'd pegged Girard to the penny. Time to flank his troops and reconnoiter. "Nurse told us a new gall bladder case arrived last night, Professor. Second ward."

"Excellent," said Dr. Laniere, "but first I wish to make one thing clear to you gentlemen." The doctor's deep-set eyes bored directly into John's. "Miss Neal is here at my express invitation and I expect her to be treated with the utmost respect and courtesy." Prof tented his long, elegant fingers beneath his chin and scanned the faces of his students one by one. "Am I understood?"

Silence fell as everyone else looked at John. He swallowed hard. He had nothing against the woman, really. In fact, there had been a moment of connection at the baby's funeral—a connection he was at a loss to explain. Although she was odd as a three-legged duck, he had no objection to handing off nursing duties to her, as long as she kept her mouth shut and didn't challenge him at every—

Her lashes lifted; the magnificent green eyes slammed into his and he suddenly realized Abigail Neal's presence was going to be a very dangerous thing, indeed. This was no off-limits matron with a pillow crease on her cheek. Intelligence and humor and mockery and all sorts of mysterious elements were buried in those eyes. He was going to have to be very careful not to get left behind in his chosen profession—especially if Professor Laniere decided to take Abigail Neal under his wing.

Abigail lifted her chin and John bowed with as much irony as he could muster. "Quite," he said. Which didn't really answer the question, but seemed to satisfy Dr. Laniere.

Prof led the way up the stairs to ward two, John on his heels, with Weichmann and Marcus and the other students trailing.

John was acutely aware of Abigail Neal's quiet presence just to his left. She glided along, turning to look into the open door of the first ward as they passed. The moans of the patients within drifted toward them, creating a music John found soothing in a bizarre kind of way.

He was looking forward to the gall bladder examination. Taking tests on medicines was all well and good, but a fellow learned best by doing.

Professor Laniere breezed into the ward, a broad open room smelling of carbolic acid. Through a bank of four uncurtained windows, evenly spaced along the west wall, weak sunlight splashed across the bare plank floor and six white-painted iron beds.

A nurse was feeding something soupy to a patient in the middle bed. She looked up and smiled at the professor. "Dr. Laniere, you'll be happy to know Mrs. Catchot is feeling like eating her grits this morning."

"Capital." The professor approached the bed, inserting the earpieces of his binaural stethoscope into his ears.

Some time ago, John and the other students had been allowed to examine the auscultation instrument. He'd found it much more efficient and precise for diagnosing lung aberrations than those favored by older physicians. Dr. Girard, for example, still carried a short, tubular monaural steth carved out of ivory. The instrument had no earpiece at all, just a flat plate that allowed sound to dissipate into the air. John had been angling for his father to cave in and buy him a stethoscope like Professor Laniere's for his birthday.

Prof moved the bodice of the woman's gown aside and set the stainless steel listening bell against her chest.

She gasped. "That's cold!"

The doctor spared her a sympathetic glance, but held the trumpet of the stethoscope firmly in place. After a moment, he gestured for Abigail to approach. "What do you hear?"

She hesitated, then accepted the instrument from his hand. Brushing back wisps of hair escaped from the knot at the back of her head, she inserted the two rubber earpieces into her dainty ears. Ignoring the patient's objection, Abigail listened, eyes widening. She looked up at the professor with a grin. "That's amazing!"

He nodded. "Indeed. Now what do you *hear?*"

Abigail sobered, concentrating her gaze inward. "It's…off," she said slowly. "There's a sort of…bump, I don't know how to say it."

"Yes. Arrhythmia." Dr. Laniere gave her an approving glance. "We can tell a lot about a patient's body by listening. Remind me to loan you my extra stethoscope. You may get a sense of what a healthy body should sound like by practicing on any willing party." He looked down at the woman on the bed. "But I believe you came in complaining of abdominal pain?"

"No, sir." The patient's voice trembled. "My belly hurts. Especially right after I eat."

The professor nodded, a twinkle in his eyes. "I beg your pardon. Your belly, of course." He chose Weichmann to quiz. "Diagnosis and scientific name?"

"Cholecystitis, sir. Inflammation of the gallbladder."

"Correct." Another approving nod. "Show Miss Neal the correct procedure for palpation, Weichmann."

Weichmann's lips tightened. John knew the young Jew desperately wanted to be a doctor, though he was perhaps the least gifted in the class. The small Orthodox community from which he'd come provided little in the way of modern medical care and his mother's slow, painful death from a corrosive brain disease was a powerful impetus for Weichmann's educational pursuit.

He also detested being the center of attention.

But he straightened his shoulders and drew the sheet down, exposing the body with relative modesty from lower sternum to groin. He bent to observe the contour of the abdomen at eye level. "Breathe normally," he instructed the patient. After a moment he straightened. "Please cough."

John felt a light hand on his arm. He looked down to find Abigail intently watching the examination. "What's he looking for?" she whispered.

"He's observing the movement along the inguinal canal." John couldn't help feeling superior. She wouldn't know what the inguinal canal was.

"Ah. The Latin is *inguinalis,* which is the groin." She chewed the inside of her cheek. "So we want to see if there are abnormalities there?"

John stared at her. "That's right."

Weichmann laid his flattened palm against the patient's abdomen. The woman craned her head to see the professor. "Does everybody have to stare at me?"

Dr. Laniere's smile was kind. "Mrs. Catchot, this is a teaching hospital. My students can't learn if they don't watch."

"I know, but what is that *girl* doing here?" The woman's voice was petulant.

"Miss Neal is studying nursing. She may be the one to care for you later. The more she knows, the better she'll be able to attend you." Dr. Laniere gestured for Weichmann to continue the examination. "You should start light palpation farther away from the most tender point."

"She could flex her knees a bit to make that easier," Abigail murmured.

John glanced at her, annoyed at the distraction.

Dr. Laniere cleared his throat. "Weichmann. You're forgetting something else."

Weichmann reddened. "Mrs. Catchot, let's pull your knees up slightly to relax your abdominal muscles."

Groaning, the patient complied as John intercepted a triumphant look from Abigail. "How did you *know* that?" he demanded in an undertone.

She smiled. "Simple physics."

Dr. Laniere snapped his fingers. "Braddock, pay attention. You'll be next."

"Yes, sir." He scowled at Abigail, then turned his focus back to the examination.

Again laying his hand on the woman's belly, Weichmann gently flexed his fingers, progressing toward the spot where she'd reacted earlier. She began to whimper in pain and poor Weichmann looked like he wanted to run from the room. "Mrs. Catchot, I need you to relax. Can you take some deep breaths?"

The patient lifted her head. "It hurts. I'm going to die."

"I don't think so," said Weichmann. "It's just a—"

"You're doing a fine job," interrupted the professor, laying a hand on Weichmann's shoulder, "but I'll take over from here." He moved to the patient's right side and slid one hand behind her ribs, then placed the other flat on her anterior abdominal wall. "A deep breath through your mouth, please."

As John watched the firm, sure pressure of Dr. Laniere's hands, the woman's inspiration turned into a gasp of agony. "Students, note that when Weichmann released the pressure of his fingers, the pain increased. Rebound tenderness is an indication of organ infection. Deep palpation confirms the diagnosis. I want each of you to copy my movements and see if you can feel the sharp, smooth, flexible edge of the liver—which is normal—and the enlarged gallbladder. Mrs. Catchot, please bear with us. We are going to make you feel better soon."

One at a time the six students placed their hands on the patient's midsection. When John's turn came and the shape of the organs slid under his hand, the power of knowledge rushed through his entire body. The woman gasped as he pressed the infected gallbladder and he resisted the urge to flinch in sympathy. A physician must remain in control.

"My turn," said Abigail boldly.

John looked up frowning, but she stared him down. He grudgingly moved aside, giving her room. She had been standing with her arms crossed, fingers tucked under her armpits. Dropping them, she leaned over the patient, placing her hands in the correct position.

"Your hands are warm," mumbled Mrs. Catchot, visibly relaxing.

Abigail began the examination, her movements becoming more deft until she found the tender spot. "Hold on. Oh, I feel it." She looked down into the patient's eyes. "I'm so sorry. You must be in a lot of pain." She glanced at the professor. "Will you remove the infected organ?"

He'd been observing the procedure with a finger to his lips. "What do you know about surgery?"

She looked frightened. "Nothing." She backed toward the wall, head tucked against her chest.

"Humph." Professor Laniere, frowning, returned to the patient's side and replaced the woman's gown and bedclothes.

John took his life in his hands and stepped close. "Will you, sir? May we watch you take it out?"

The professor glanced at him, but addressed his patient. "Mrs. Catchot, your pain is caused by an inflammation of a tiny sac attached to your small intestine and liver. If we remove it, you'll have a good chance of recovering with no residual effects."

The woman's eyes widened. "*Remove* it? You're going to cut out part of my stomach?"

"Mr. Braddock, please give Mrs. Catchot a brief summary of what is involved in cholecystostomy." The professor's black eyes narrowed. "Gently."

John blinked, snatching for last week's lecture during dissection laboratory. "The surgeon—Dr. Laniere—will administer ether anesthesia. Then he'll make a small incision in your lower abdomen. The gallbladder will be removed with a quick cut and the intestine tightly sutured back together. A few stitches will repair the abdominal incision."

"But—if you cut it out, won't I die? The Good Lord put it in there for a reason!"

"This surgery has been successfully performed for about ten years now," John assured her. "You'll recover in about six weeks and never miss that little piece of flesh."

"Thank you, Mr. Braddock, that's quite enough," said Dr. Laniere drily. "I assure you, Mrs. Catchot, that if you *don't* have the surgery, you'll continue to experience excruciating pain, and the infection could poison your entire system, leading to an early demise." He patted the woman's rigid shoulder. "Try to rest. I'll send someone in to prepare you for surgery. Come with me, gentlemen."

The whole troupe hustled to keep up as the professor exited the room. John, the tallest, managed to edge out everyone except Abigail.

Dr. Laniere spoke without looking over his shoulder. "Girard, you will give Miss Neal the history of the cholecystostomy."

"Yes, sir!" Marcus all but ran to catch up with Abigail's long, gliding steps. "Dr. John Stough Bobbs from Indianapolis, Indiana, was operating on what he thought was an ovarian cyst and rather accidentally found some stones in an inflamed gallbladder. He took them out, stitched up the gallbladder and left it in the abdomen. But here's the funny part—" Marcus burst out laughing. "The patient recovered and outlived Dr. Bobbs!"

A wicked glint of humor lit Abigail's eyes. She looked at Marcus, eyebrows up. "Just think how many of your patients will outlive you and your drinking partners." She slid a glance at John.

The woman had a tongue sharper than any scalpel. "Alcohol is a fine preservative," he said, annoyed. "Girard didn't finish. Just last year, Marion Simms designed and performed the first cholecystostomy on a forty-five-year-old woman with obstructive jaundice. Unfortunately, she lasted only a few days because of internal hemorrhaging. But Dr. Laniere has been to Berlin to observe Carl Langenbuch, who perfected the procedure." He looked at his teacher. "Langenbuch is only twenty-seven years old and he's already director of Lazarus Hospital. Prof says we'll see astonishing things in our lifetime."

Abigail looked away. "I'm sure you will."

The history lesson was aborted as the class approached another ward. As they examined a young man whose foot had been amputated at Antietam, John made a deliberate effort to ignore Abigail's distracting presence. Before he knew it, they'd finished rounds and were given half an hour to themselves before afternoon lectures.

John met Marcus and Weichmann in front of the hospital for their daily run to the French Quarter for gumbo. He didn't care what happened to Abigail Neal. Weichmann caught him looking over his shoulder as the three of them dodged through the midday traffic on Rue Baronne.

"She stayed to talk to Professor." Weichmann grinned.

"Who?" John quickened his pace.

"The girl. The *pretty* girl. You'd better guard your spot as the favorite."

Marcus snorted. "Prof ain't the susceptible sort." He dug his elbow into John's ribs. "Unlike some people."

"Shut up, Girard," John muttered automatically. He glanced at Weichmann. "I've got more important things to worry about than a street tart with a penchant for voyeurism."

Weichmann shook his head. "Smartest street tart *I've* ever run across."

"Citing your broad experience," John said with a quelling frown. "Let's talk about something more interesting—ingrown toenails, for example."

Girard exchanged delighted glances with Weichmann. "Braddock's got his drawers in a twist because the lady's got better hands than he has. Fifty says she'll give him a private lesson in deep palpation before the end of the term."

John grabbed Marcus by the shoulder and whirled him around, heedless of the milling crowd on the street corner. "If I hear you speak of her that way again," he said through his teeth, "I'll take your head off."

Girard's mouth fell open. "You called her a street tart!"

"I was mistaken."

Girard swallowed. "Weichmann, Braddock just admitted he was wrong. Look for the four horses of the Apocalypse."

Suddenly aware of just how foolish he had made himself, John laughed and let go of Girard's shoulder. "Best hope not. By all accounts, I doubt any of the three of us are ready."

Chapter Seven

After the hospital rounds, Abigail was not allowed to accompany the men to the medical college for lectures; she was not a tuition-paying student, of course, and even if she were, women were not allowed into the hallowed halls of the medical college.

The decision to stay created complications. The fear of being found out never left for one moment, and of course she would be giving up the job in the sail loft. Although she would eventually have to go back for her few belongings, the opportunity to learn medicine under the tutelage of a man of Dr. Laniere's stature was too good to pass up.

So she agreed and presented herself to Camilla Laniere, who found other chores requiring Abigail's attention: trapping and disposing of a mouse determined to build a nest in the clinic medicine chest, folding piles of linens and alphabetically organizing the contents of the pharmacy. Every so often she would run upstairs or return to the clinic to check on her patients.

But by mid-afternoon, Tess, far from lying in bed

where she should be, insisted she was well enough to go home and back to work.

"You aren't well enough to go back." Abigail held Tess by the shoulders to keep her in her chair, looking to Camilla for support. "Besides, we need you here in the clinic."

"I'm glad you're feeling well enough to be up and around a bit." Camilla stood in the clinic doorway with Meg in her arms. "But I wish you wouldn't try to do too much too soon. Your fever only began to come down last night."

Tess looked down, pleating the black skirt Winona had lent her. "It's too hard. I can't watch the children…"

Abigail knelt and took her friend's restless hands. "Tess—"

"And I'm no good with nursing. Sewing is all I know how to do."

With a smile, Camilla glanced at the pile of darning in her workbasket on the table. "There's plenty of that around here. I could truly use your help."

Tess got up and moved to the window. Pressing her hands against the glass, she watched a fine carriage rattle down the brick side street. "You're very kind, Mrs. Laniere, but I simply don't belong here." She turned her head and met Abigail's eyes. "You don't either. You should go back with me."

Stung, Abigail got to her feet. "If you insist on leaving, I can't stop you, but I'm going to stay here as long as they'll let me. I'll go back to the District when I've learned enough to make a difference—"

"Make a difference?" Tess turned her back on the sunny window. "People are going to do what they're going to do. So what if you save a few lives? Save them for what? More poverty and prejudice and hopelessness?"

Camilla took a step toward her. "My dear—"

"And you—with your beautiful dresses and fine house and handsome husband. What do you know about where we came from? What do you care?" Tess's face was white. "I used to be just like you—" She pressed her fingers to her lips.

This was more than Abigail had learned about Tess in the six months she'd known her. She reached for her friend.

Tess shook her head hard. "Let me go, Abby." She looked at Camilla. "I'm sorry to have insulted you, ma'am. You didn't make my choices for me. But you can't undo the consequences, either." A small, bitter smile curved her lips. "There's much truth in what the Bible says about that."

"There's *all* truth in the Bible, although you're missing the healing parts." Camilla's deep sigh blew Meg's fine curls. "As Abigail said, we can't hold you here. But remember, you're always welcome to come back."

"Thank you, ma'am." Tess hesitated, then rushed to kiss Abigail's cheek. "Goodbye, Abigail. You've been a good friend."

Before Abigail could blink, Tess was gone. She stood there, tears escaping in a messy flood. Helplessly she looked at Camilla. "What can I do?"

Camilla's soft, heart-shaped face was tight with emotion. "Pray that God will deal with her."

"You heard what she said! God doesn't help those who don't believe in Him."

"Is that what you think?" Camilla's smile suddenly lit her face. "Oh, my dear. You do indeed have a lot to learn."

Later that night Abigail turned the page of the textbook she'd been studying, setting the candle flame aflutter. Camilla had firmly adjured her to get a good night's sleep, placed the candle in her hand, and sent her up to her new attic bedroom.

After Tess's departure, the day had been a long one. To keep her mind off worrying about her stubborn friend, she'd catalogued in her neat script the clinic's medicines in a book Camilla gave her, separately noting all the names she didn't recognize. After supper she presented the list to Dr. Laniere, who smiled and went to his library for the book now lying across her lap.

Resisting the urge to rub her stinging eyes, she adjusted the pillow behind her back. Sleep beckoned, but she had to know about the anesthesia to be used on that poor woman in the hospital. Maybe, armed with information, Abigail could return in the morning before the surgery and allay some of the woman's fear.

Here it was. Ether, a flammable gas with a distinctive, sticky-sweet odor. Side effects could include postanesthetic headaches, nausea and vomiting. But it had been found to be more effective than chloroform as an anesthetic during surgery.

Abigail frowned. The side effects sounded almost as unpleasant as the disease. She set the book aside, blew out the candle and settled under the fresh sheet with which she'd made up her bed. The Chinese women she'd tended who had died of internal infections—some of which she suspected were gallbladder related—could undoubtedly have been saved if this relatively simple surgery had been performed. If only she'd known how. If only she could watch and learn.

She pictured John Braddock's face that morning as he'd realized she could perform an examination every bit as thorough and skillful as he could. Smiling, she fell asleep.

Miss Charlemagne let John in without a cross word about the earliness of the hour and he took off his hat and stared at her in surprise. He'd left his curtain open so the rising sun would wake him early. Filching a biscuit from Clem's gigantic bread box, he'd let himself out, saddled Belladonna and made it to the hospital before the church bells chimed six.

Faintly smiling, Miss Charlemagne gestured toward the spartan little room off the entryway, furnished for the use of doctors in consultation with patients' families. "Miss Neal struck up a conversation with Crutch, so I sent them into the parlor to keep the noise down."

"Miss Neal?" He frowned. "She's here already?"

The smile slid perilously close to a smirk as she patted his arm. "You've quite the task to keep up, don't you? Call me if you need me."

Juggling a confusing mixture of irritation and anticipation, John headed for the parlor. He stopped in the doorway, trying to decide whether to laugh or call the watch.

Abigail and the hospital handyman faced each other in the two wing chairs, knee to knee. Crutch had removed his jacket and sat in his shirtsleeves, still and rapt, as Abigail listened to his chest with Professor Laniere's spare stethoscope.

John folded his arms and leaned against the doorframe. "How industrious of you, Miss Neal, I must say."

Abigail jumped, dropping the bell of the stethoscope, and turned. "John—Mr. Braddock! You frightened me."

"My sincere apologies." He bowed. "Perhaps in future I should announce my presence with a ram's horn."

"A simple knock on the door would suffice." Her hand fluttered to her hair as she removed the stethoscope from her ears, a self-conscious little gesture that softened his inclination to tweak her. "I thought I'd have time to look around and talk to any of the patients who might be awake." She hesitated. "Everyone's asleep, so I persuaded Mr. Crutch to let me practice auscultation upon him."

"I trust you found nothing out of order." John nodded at Crutch. He was a good man, if a bit simple.

The elderly handyman jumped to his feet, proudly thumping his chest. "Lady says I'm right healthy. The old ticker's strong as a mule."

"I'm very happy to hear that."

Abigail rose, clutching the bell of the stethoscope in one hand, her skirt in the other. "Mr. Crutch, I apologize for interrupting your morning routine," she said evenly. "Thank you for your assistance."

"Don't mention it, miss." Crutch shuffled into the entryway and looked over his shoulder at Abigail. "Mayhap you'll want to check the young doc here's chest. There's some say he ain't got no ticker at all." With a sly grin he disappeared in the direction of the kitchen.

Resisting the urge to protest such nonsense, John

turned the ladder-backed desk chair around and straddled it, folding his arms along its back. Abigail's patent discomfort at being alone in the small room with him was almost comical. She edged behind the wing chair she'd vacated, as if to place as much distance between them as possible.

He rested his chin on his forearms and looked up at her in amusement. "What do you think, Miss Neal? Is there a hole in my barbarian chest cavity?" When she gasped, he laughed. "Camilla told me what you said. Although how you can equate the desire to ease a patient's pain with lack of civilizing manners is beyond my understanding."

She fingered the modest frill of lace at her collar. "Of course there's nothing wrong with anesthetizing before surgery. I studied everything I could find on the subject last night."

He studied the purple shadows beneath her fine green eyes. "Perhaps *all* night?"

She moistened her lips. "I got plenty of rest, though I thank you for your concern."

He *was* concerned, although it galled him to admit it even to himself. "You must have arrived before the sun rose. Did you walk all the way here by yourself? Next time, let me know and I'll come round to get you."

"Thank you, but…as it happens, I rode in to the hospital this morning with Dr. Laniere."

"Where is Prof?" John looked over his shoulder. Wouldn't do to get caught sitting idle.

"He's upstairs with paperwork." There was a long moment's silence during which Abigail avoided John's gaze. Finally she huffed a little sigh. "Why are *you* here so early, Mr. Braddock? Making sure you don't fall out of favor again?"

"As a matter of fact, yes. But my rotation is with Dr. Girard today."

"Dr. Girard?"

"Marcus's father. Chemistry and clinical medicine. He's less exacting than Prof in some ways, but considerably more volatile of temperament."

"Indeed." Abigail grinned. "I should think that would make you friends."

He frowned. "I'm not volatile."

She tipped her head.

"I'm not. In fact, I'm going to be magnanimous to the point of offering my body on the altar of science." He thought of Marcus's remarks about palpation and felt his cheeks heat. "I mean, perhaps you'd like to listen to my chest and lungs to see if there's indeed anything missing."

"I'm not sure that's a good idea." She stayed behind the wing chair, looking as if she didn't quite trust him.

He could hardly blame her. But he shrugged out of his jacket and began to unbutton his vest. "Come, Abigail, missishness will get you nowhere in our profession." He leaned forward across the back of his chair. "You start by telling me to take a deep breath."

She glanced at the open doorway, biting her lips together. Then, squaring her shoulders, she put the stethoscope's earpieces in her ears and approached him. She hovered beside him, a foot or so away. Finally she laid her hand on his shoulder and pressed the steth bell between his shoulder blades. "Take a deep breath."

Involuntarily he sucked in a breath, jerking at her

touch, modest and impersonal but warm through the linen of his shirt.

"Thank you. Now out."

He forced himself to release his breath slowly. There was a very good reason women should not be allowed to treat men. She moved the bell to a position just above his left kidney. He breathed again, in and out.

"Your lungs are quite healthy," she said. "But I'm detecting an alarming acceleration of the pulse."

John looked up at her and found the green eyes brimming with laughter. He sat up straight as she stepped back, removing that warm hand from his shoulder. "Perhaps you'd like to listen to my chest."

"Some other time, Mr. Braddock. Your fellow students will arrive soon and I wouldn't want you to risk a reprimand from your irascible professor."

He regarded her narrowly as he reached for his outer clothing. "Will you be joining us for rounds?"

"I'm afraid not. Dr. Laniere wants others to train me in some of the less complicated nursing duties this morning. But he says I may watch the gallbladder surgery. So I'll see you in the operating theater at nine."

"Very well." He rose, buttoning his vest. "I wish you a successful morning, then. Until we meet again." He bowed and exited the room, resisting the urge to see if she followed. Abigail Neal was proving to be a most unsettling addition to the hospital staff. In the presence of such a lovely, off-limits young woman, no wonder his pulse rate refused to remain normal.

Even for such a relatively simple procedure as the removal of a gallbladder, the surgical amphitheater was crowded with students, doctors and interested citizenry—all men. Dr. Laniere had planted Abigail in a corner seat—she could still hardly comprehend his courtesy and generosity—and repaired to a scrub room to prepare himself for the operation. As the room filled, loud male conversation echoed off the vaulted ceiling and marble panels set between the huge windows, but the seat beside her remained empty. Apparently no one wanted to contaminate himself by proximity to the brazen hussy in the ugly dress.

Which was just as well. She wanted to observe without having to make conversation. It was a good thing God had seen fit to bless her with keen eyesight. She was so far up in the tiers of seats she was likely to suffer a nosebleed from the height. But no complaining. She was here. She was unmolested. The Toad would never think to look for her here.

Still, she couldn't help examining the backs of all those heads below her and to the right. None of them, thank God, had the lumpy, flattened shape she'd trained herself to watch for and run from.

"I'm going out on a limb to assume that the seat isn't taken. May I?"

Abigail looked up to find John Braddock, hat in hand, at the far end of the aisle. To reach the empty seat beside her, he would have to step over several gentlemen, all of whom were looking at her with various levels of curiosity and disdain.

She sighed. There went her solitary enjoyment of the experience. "I suppose."

"Pardon me. I beg your pardon," John repeated as he made his way down the aisle toward her. When he finally reached her, he sprawled in the seat, dropping his hat onto his knee. "Whew. That was a job." He looked at her. "It took me a few minutes to find you, stuck way up here in this treetop. I usually only sit here when I have a test to study for."

"I imagine Dr. Laniere was hoping to keep me from attracting too much attention. Which, thanks to you, seems to be a lost cause." Still, she couldn't help a surge of pleasure that he had sought her out. She folded her arms. "How were your rounds with the dyspeptic Dr. Girard?"

"As usual, he singled me out for acerbic asides about illiterate rich boys. As if he hasn't raised three of those himself. But, fortunately, I maintain perspective. The more he growls, the happier he is." He sent her a wry smile. "And what about you? Did you learn anything today?"

"Yes." Abigail nodded. "I was taught the proper way to lift a patient from one bed to another, and the science of bedpans."

A stir at the front of the theater caught Abigail's attention. A couple of orderlies trundled in a cart with the patient, lying on her back with her hands folded across her stomach. She seemed to be asleep.

As a hush fell across the observing audience, John sat forward. "I watched them put her under anesthesia," he whispered to Abigail. "She fought the ether like a wild woman."

"She must have been frightened to death." Busy with the nurses that morning, Abigail had not been allowed to see the patient as she'd hoped to do. She studied John's face and was relieved to find sympathy rather than the avid excitement she'd expected. "How would you do it differently?"

He frowned. "I'm not sure. I wonder if there's a way to prepare the patient—"

"Shh!" someone hissed from the other end of the row.

Abigail jerked her attention back to the operating theater. Dr. Laniere, assisted by a couple of students Abigail remembered from yesterday's rounds, was adjusting a row of gleaming instruments laid out on a nearby table. An older gentleman in beard and spectacles, whom she assumed to be another surgeon, busied himself with the lights and then stationed himself at the foot of the patient's bed. Abigail could hear the men murmuring to one another, and she'd have given anything to know what they said.

As if he'd read her mind, Dr. Laniere lifted a hand and addressed the audience. "Gentlemen, we are about to begin the procedure to remove an infected gallbladder, commonly referred to as cholecystostomy. Symptoms that indicate acute sepsis include enlarged gallbladder, persistent pain in the abdomen and a slight jaundice of the skin. Please observe that the patient is completely under the influence of ether-based anesthesia and will neither feel nor remember the incisions."

Absorbed in the surgeon's deft movements and clinical explanations, Abigail sat forward, clasping her fingers around her knees. The operation proceeded almost to the letter as Marcus Girard had described it yesterday. There was blood, yes, but far from swooning in disgust, Abigail found herself awed and fascinated that such a drastic action as invasion of the body with a knife could result in healing.

Incision. Removal of infected tissue. Suturing. Scarring. Regeneration.

As she watched, Abigail ran the words through her mind. Spiritual implications nudged her heart, but she pushed them away until later. Right now she needed to learn what she could from the physical experience.

She'd almost forgotten John's vital presence to her right when he drew in a sharp breath. "She's hemorrhaging."

The action on the theater floor suddenly quickened as sponges, clamps and needles flew, and every person in the audience leaned forward. Then, as quickly as it began, it was over. Dr. Laniere gained control, sutured the patient's internal incision and moved back to let one of his students close.

"You may relax now, Abigail—the danger is past." John's amused baritone broke into Abigail's concentration.

She looked down to find, to her utter horror, that she'd been clutching his hand. Releasing him, she brushed her palms together as if washing them. "I'm so sorry—"

"Never mind, I understand," he said with a surprising absence of teasing. "Prof is a dynamic surgeon, but I admire him most because he makes it look so easy." He looked around and lowered his voice. "Some of the surgeons with a deal less skill are much more apt to play up the theatrics of a situation. Flourishes, raised voices, all that nonsense. Prof teaches us to take care of business with thoroughness and precision."

Abigail nodded, distracted by the lingering sensation of John's large, fine-boned hand wrapped around hers. Helplessly she remembered the feeling of his broad shoulder under her hand as she'd stood in the hospital parlor, listening to him breathe. Strong, vital, male. Oh my, she was undone. "Will Mrs. Catchot recover now?" she said rather at random.

"Undoubtedly." John rose as the gentlemen around them began to stir, discussing the operation they'd collectively witnessed. He offered Abigail a friendly hand to assist her to her feet.

She stared at it for half a second, then jumped up on her own. "Oh, dear, it's nearly noon. I promised Camilla I'd come back to help—please excuse me, Mr. Braddock."

He stared at her, nonplussed, but moved to the end of the row and waited for her to hurry past. "Would you like to join me and the fellows for—"

"No, thank you, I really have to go." Dipping a curtsy, she fled down the theater steps, dodging doctors and laymen lingering in conversation.

Only when she was safely on her way back to Rue Gironde on foot did she realize what a ninny she'd been, allowing her ridiculous, unwanted interest in John Braddock to keep her from learning what she could.

Taking a breath and releasing it, she slowed her steps. She looked up at the sky, where weak sunlight filtered through a bank of soft gray clouds. Control had brought her this far. Persistence and willingness to face her fears. She'd finally maneuvered her way to safety and a possible means of attaining her desire to become a doctor. If she could only stay the course, who knew what she might accomplish?

Besides, she wasn't afraid of John Braddock. What nonsense.

Chapter Eight

The midweek French market was a jumbled discord of music, laughter and multiple languages, a gumbo of color, odor and movement. Inured to the crowd and noise, John effectively blocked out everything but his single-minded quest for the perfect orange. He was crouching to poke through a pile of fruit in a vendor's basket when a hand touched his shoulder.

He looked up to find Abigail Neal standing over him.

"Behold, the vassal on his knees." Eyebrows quirked in amusement, she swept a dramatic hand through the air.

"Abigail!" He lunged to his feet. "I thought you were going back to the Lanieres'."

"I did." She gestured vaguely in the direction of Rue Gironde, setting the empty canvas bag in her hand flapping. "Camilla sent me to buy a chicken for the evening meal and I saw you over here." She plucked the orange out of his hand. "I thought you medical people never stopped to eat."

"Citrus helps ward off colds and influenza."

"Indeed." She examined the orange as if she'd never seen one before. Perhaps she hadn't.

John chose another one and called to a dark-skinned woman seated on a three-legged stool at the booth's entrance. "I'll take both of these. How much?"

The woman, dressed in a multilayered gown and head rag, answered in the Acadian French mumble of the Quarter; John drew a penny from his pocket and tossed it to her. He looked at Abigail and jerked a thumb in the direction of a jambalaya vendor's stall. "Come on, I'll buy the rest of your dinner."

She hesitated, looking over her shoulder at a poultry farmer's noisy stall.

He handed her one of the oranges. "Camilla won't expect you back right away. I daresay she won't even know you're gone." He didn't know why he was insisting when she'd made it clear she didn't want his company. But then he'd never been able to resist a challenge. Smiling with gentle mockery, he backed toward the stall from which the aroma of crawfish, onions, peppers and tomatoes drifted like a siren song. "Come on, Abigail. You know you're hungry."

She looked down at the sack dangling from her wrist. "I suppose I could stay Chanticleer's execution for another hour." Tossing the orange over her shoulder and catching it behind her back, she picked up her skirts. "All right, then."

He glanced at her as they approached the jambalaya booth. "You've read Chaucer?"

She shrugged. "Where I grew up, there wasn't much to do but read."

"Considering your vocabulary, that doesn't surprise me. But *Canterbury Tales* is a fairly bawdy choice."

She slid him a sidelong look. "Make up your mind, John. Either I'm a lady or I'm not."

The conundrum had entered his mind more than once since her abrupt departure from the operating theater. Sometimes it seemed she understood the rules of society and other times she appeared to delight in flouting them. He stared for a moment without answering, then turned to the aged mulatto stirring a pot of something fragrant over an open cookfire. "Two bowls of jambalaya, if you please."

A few minutes later they were seated side-by-side on a low brick wall opposite the market, watching the foot traffic pass by as they ate. Abigail had already finished her orange, dropping the fragrant rind onto the ground for the seagulls, and was engaged in scooping jambalaya into her mouth with an oyster shell provided by the vendor. A cluster of dark-skinned women swayed past, one of them winking over her shoulder at John.

Abigail glanced at him. "Do you ever wonder where all these people come from? Where they live and what sorts of occupations they have?"

"I'm fairly certain what those particular women do," John said drily.

"You thought the same about me, but you were absolutely, unequivocally wrong."

"Unequivocally?" He'd have to admit he'd never met a prostitute with quite the vocabulary Abigail flaunted. "I stand corrected. Perhaps you could redirect my ignorance as to how you and Tess *did* manage to support yourselves in that squalid little room I found you in."

"We worked in the sail loft on Julia Street. I waxed twine and Tess hand-stitched grommets."

He gave her a skeptical look. "Where did you learn to do that?"

"Tess taught me. She was working there—she's quite a seamstress, you know—and put in a good word for me. The work isn't difficult to learn, just tiring and a bit hard on the hands." She rubbed her fingers together and he could hear the swishing of callus against callus. "Some days I thought my back would break from sitting in one place for ten or twelve hours straight."

John frowned. "That's inhumane."

Abigail looked down at the oyster shell in her empty bowl. "It kept us out of the brothels." Brushing off further questions with a wave of her hand, she smiled at him. "Thank you for my dinner. I was actually looking for you because I wanted to ask you something."

Wary, he searched her face. Her sharp cheekbones had filled out over the last few days, turning her from a gaunt Amazon into quite a striking young woman. Her hair glowed with healthy streaks of umber and gold and, loosened a bit from its severe brown bun, revealed a distinct wave. The green eyes, bright and rested, regarded him with frightening intelligence.

"You may ask," he said, "but I make no promises."

"I would expect no less from you, Mr. Braddock" she said tartly. "Yesterday I heard Professor Laniere reading a piece from a medical journal to Camilla. The subject was autopsy. The author seemed to think the practice a bit of, shall we say, overkill." Her lips twitched.

John chuckled. "The medical profession is divided over the issue, but Prof advocates autopsy as a method of preventing disease. The more one knows about what causes death, the better the chances of heading it off the next go-round."

"I gathered that." Abigail tipped her head. "Which is why I want you to teach me what you know about it."

John stared at her. "You can't be serious."

"Why not?" She set her bowl down on the wall. "I know the professor makes you fellows cut up and examine every charity case that comes through the hospital morgue. Surely you're capable of demonstrating the rudiments."

"Of course I'm *capable.*" John scowled at her. "But you'd not be allowed into the morgue. And—and even if you were, where would we get the body to examine? And why do you *want* to do this?" The idea of a woman willing to watch a human body cut from stem to stern, the organs lifted out, weighed and measured, prodded and poked…

Preposterous.

Abigail leaned forward. "The body is a mystery I've longed for some time to unlock. Tess, for example. I'd no idea how to help her baby get out safely because I didn't know the arrangement of the parts inside."

"I know the arrangement of parts, but that didn't help me," John pointed out. "Besides, I can draw that for you with pencil and paper. Any good anatomy textbook will show—"

"I've seen the textbooks. I want to examine the organs' texture and color, compare the sizes of male and female, see the physical arrangement inside the body. And I want to see anomalies. John, you of all people

must understand this…this craving I have to know."
Her eyes burned into his.

John had never met a woman like this one. His
mother and sister swooned at the sight of blood—or
at least pretended to. Camilla Laniere, somewhat more
down-to-earth, never shied away from her husband's
work or her children's needs. But John had never heard
her express a desire to observe an autopsy, much less
participate in one.

"I'll ask the professor," he said reluctantly. Prof would
put the hammer down on the idea.

"I already asked him. He said he didn't have time to
spare from his family and his students—"

"Then there you have it." John shrugged. "It's out of
the question—"

"—but he said if one of his students wanted extra
practice and was willing to go in after hours, he'd approve the release of the body."

John set down his bowl with a clatter. "I can't believe that!"

"It's true. Ask him."

"Why didn't you ask one of the other chaps? Weichmann or Girard would jump at the chance to show off."

"Because I want the best. If I can't have Dr. Laniere,
I want you."

John resisted her blatant flattery. "You don't know
what you're asking. Have you ever seen an adult cadaver?"

She nodded. "I assure you I can tolerate more than
you think. Look, I'll make it worth your while. I was
going to propose a trade."

"A trade?" Startled, he laughed, taking in her shabby

dress and broken shoes. "What could you possibly have that I would want?"

For a moment she regarded him with cold fury. "I was going to offer to tutor you in Latin and Greek—which I happen to be very good at."

Somehow he knew she wasn't making false claims. "What makes you think I need help with Latin and Greek?"

She reached into his jacket and plucked out his dictionary. Her thumb fanned the pages. "I saw you sneaking glances yesterday as we made rounds. And this morning in the surgery theater. You're afraid Girard will outgun you."

"Girard? You're mad. He can barely speak English."

"Then it's Weichmann. You're terrified of losing first place in the class." Her eyes dared him to deny it.

Pressing his lips together, he stared across the street, where the new Courtyard Hotel was undergoing construction, the masons calling to one another, singing over the slap of brick and mortar, scrape of trowel. Abigail had somehow hit on his Achilles' heel. Although he was acknowledged to be brilliant in maths and sciences, reading had never come easily, and Latin declensions gave him migraines.

But as she said, if he could somehow turn his problem around, his place would be secured. The professor had given him another chance to prove himself. Supervising an autopsy, even for the benefit of a woman, was a privilege.

"All right. I'll do it." He frowned at Abigail to squelch her obvious triumph. "But you'll do exactly as I say and don't tell any of the other fellows about it."

"But you said—"

"I don't want them to get any ideas. Are we agreed on the terms?"

She looked at him silently, then nodded, a brief jerk of her head. "Agreed. Can we begin tonight?"

"If there's a body available."

Her smile was grim. "In this city, right here by the waterfront, there's always a body available. Where and when shall I meet you?"

"You've no business walking anywhere alone after dark. I'll come for you at eleven." He thought for a moment. "I'll have to let Miss Charlemagne in on it, get the key from her. She won't tell anyone."

Abigail's smile broadened to a grin. *"Mors gaudet succurrere vitae."*

"You might start your tuition by translating that."

"Death rejoices to help those who live."

Abigail waited for John that evening in the clinic entryway. Winona had just gone to bed, leaving a small oil lamp on the table to spread orangey shadows into the kitchen.

The young housekeeper had stood in the doorway of her room, shaking her head over Abigail's insane desire to cut open dead bodies in the middle of the night. "It's all well and good for Mr. John and the other students hacking people apart, but you're a lady." When Abigail just shrugged, Winona snorted and disappeared, taking her disapproval with her.

Abigail slid back the small window panel in the door and peered out into the dense darkness. She wiped her sweaty palms down the sides of her skirt. She wasn't ready for this as she'd pretended. An adventure that had seemed like a good idea in the bright noonday sun of the French Quarter now loomed with nightmarish grimness.

She took a hard look at herself. Leaning against the door, she looked down at her hands. The nails had been trimmed to the quick, the cuticles and fingertips cracked from exposure to lye cleansers. Not the hands of a lady. But what had the title ever given her or any other woman she'd known? Protection? She pictured her mother, imprisoned in a Chinese missionary compound, unprepared for any work except maintaining her white skin and corresponding with herself in a journal.

There had to be more. Abigail would *make* more, gladly forfeiting her right to be called anything except a useful human being.

At a soft rap on the door at her back, she turned and released the latch. John Braddock stood there, shifting from one foot to the other. Dressed simply in white cotton shirt, loose breeches and boots, he held a lamp in one hand and the handle of a large wooden case in the other.

He moved back to allow her to pass. "Are you ready? I had trouble getting out of the house, so we're a bit late."

"I'm ready." She stepped into the carriageway and kept pace with him until they reached the street. The residential area was quiet at this time of night; only the sound of water dripping from leaves after a late-afternoon rain shower accompanied their footsteps. The scent of frangipani from someone's garden drifted on a sultry breeze. They'd walked two blocks before she broke the silence. "Why would you have trouble leaving the house?"

He glanced at her, lips curved. "My landlady's a bit of a dragon."

Abigail smiled. "Why don't you live at home? Winona says your family is wealthy and well-connected."

"I prefer that my mother not be aware of all my comings and goings."

She could understand that. "You're fortunate to have choices."

He looked down at her again, a gleam of curiosity in his eyes. "Do you not have a family who wonders where you are?"

"My mother left before I did."

"Left where?"

"The mission compound." There could be no harm in telling him that much.

"Your father is a missionary? I've been trying to place your accent. Where is he?"

Abigail knew she'd said enough. "In a sensitive area. It's best that I not divulge his location."

John swung the lamp high, throwing light across Abigail's face. She shielded her eyes.

"Who are you?" he demanded. "You speak like a lady, but comport yourself like...like no other woman I know."

"Perhaps your circle of acquaintance isn't as large as you seem to think." She walked on.

He quickly caught up to her, but maintained a stubborn silence until they reached the hospital entrance. The building loomed, white stucco gleaming in the light of the stars.

"John." Abigail touched his forearm: hard, corded

sinew and muscle, live and real. She needed the grounding of his company.

He kept walking, heading for the rear of the hospital. "What is it, Abigail?"

She trotted after him. "I'm sorry I keep offending you. Truly I know what a favor you're doing by bringing me here, especially because you probably need to study." She hesitated. "Can you accept that there are things I can't tell you without putting myself in danger?"

He wheeled. "There's a reason you're so determined to learn how to keep people alive. Who did you kill, Abigail? Was it your husband? This father of yours in the mission compound? Did he beat you? It happens all the time." He lowered his voice. "Who was it?"

After a stunned moment Abigail got her voice back. "You think I *killed* someone?" A hysterical giggle escaped. "You're willing to give a murderess an autopsy knife?"

He swung the lamp wildly, slashing light across the drive path. "What am I supposed to think? A handsome, educated young woman like you—living in a tenement, versant with medical terminology—refusing to talk about your family? It doesn't make one bit of sense!"

Abigail smothered her laughter. "I assure you my father is alive and well. And I've never been married."

"Then what? What are you running from?" John steadied the lamp, his expression troubled, but for once, not particularly threatening.

Abigail bit her lip and stared at the strong, tanned throat rising like a Greek column from the open collar of his shirt. For reasons she couldn't immediately put her finger on, she was reluctant to lie to him.

"Myself, I suppose," she murmured. "I didn't want to be that girl anymore. The one who did what they said, who watched bad things happen." She met his stormy hazel eyes. "My mother escaped and I knew I could, too. It just took some planning."

"And this is worth it?" He glanced around, slopping oily light onto the hospital's mildewed walls. "You're better off here?"

"As long as..." She folded her lips. "Yes. It's better. Now let's go inside. I want to know what you know."

He stared at her a moment longer, sighed, then turned to rap on the door.

It opened to reveal Miss Charlemagne, bearing a small lamp like a gnome in a children's picture book. She nodded as if she welcomed visitors into the morgue at midnight on a regular basis. "Come in, children. I've made tea if anyone cares for refreshment."

Shoving away the discomfort of John's questions, Abigail smiled at the woman as she stepped inside the shadowy anteroom. "Thank you, but we don't have much time. We won't keep you, if you have other duties."

The older woman gave John an uncertain look, as if confirming his authority.

He sighed, visibly restraining impatience. "Dr. Laniere instructed me to make sure we finish well before dawn."

"Then come with me. I've had Crutch move the body onto the table for you." She turned, skirts swishing, and led the way through an open doorway to the left, through which Abigail could see lights burning.

As they entered the room, the odor of formaldehyde

bombarded her senses, watering her eyes and stinging her nose.

"This is most extraordinary," said the woman, turning up several lamps in wall sconces to illuminate a white-shrouded body lying on a slanted marble table. The sides of the table were raised, portals in the lower corners providing drainage into a couple of metal buckets. "I've never heard of an autopsy at night."

"There's a lot about this that isn't normal." Gesturing for Abigail to stand beside him, John inclined his head to Miss Charlemagne. "We'll call you when we're finished."

Miss Charlemagne glanced at a bell pull suspended from the ceiling and stretching through an aperture in one wall. "Ring for me, then. I'll be in the kitchen, preparing for morning meals."

"She likes you," Abigail observed as John reached into his pocket for a pair of kid gloves.

"It's mutual." He handed them to her and produced a second pair for himself. "Put those on."

She slipped on the gloves, marveling at their tight fit. "Where did you get these?"

"Begged them from my sister's maid. She'll never miss them." He took a deep breath. "Are you ready?"

Abigail nodded, mentally bracing herself. "Is it a man or a woman?"

"Female." He stripped back the shroud, exposing dark hair and the gray, still face of a young woman.

Abigail swallowed. At least the eyes were closed. The cheeks were puffy, the mouth slack. She fought a feeling of invasion, as if she were the second-in-command of a conquering army. The upper torso came into view.

"Stop," she blurted. Blushing, she looked up at John, but found only sober and respectful interest in his expression as he continued to remove the shroud.

His eyes flicked to her face as he folded it and laid it on a nearby table. "There's no embarrassment in death, Abigail," he said with a certain amount of sympathy for her discomfort.

The embarrassment was that hundreds of women died daily in the tenements around the hospital, alone and unwanted by their families, abandoned to the indignities of the surgeon's knife. She could learn from this one.

She braced herself as John opened his case of implements. Out of their velvet bed they came, one at a time, shining sharp steel. He explained their uses as he laid them on the table.

Skull chisel. Rib cutters, looking like a small pair of pruning shears. Scalpel. Suture needles that reminded her of her job in the sail loft. Toothed forceps. Bone saw.

Abigail watched and listened, wholly absorbed. She was going to make a difference. Armed with knowledge, she *would* make a difference.

Chapter Nine

"Mortui vivos docent," Abigail murmured, staring down at the red-brown liver in her hands.

"The dead teach the living." John nodded at the stainless steel scales. "Lay it down there. We're going to weigh it first."

Abigail glanced at him as she laid the spongy organ in the scale. "You *can* translate when you try."

"I can do a lot of things when I try."

"What does that mean?"

His gaze dropped to her mouth. "Nothing."

She looked momentarily disconcerted, then shrugged and adjusted the balance weight. "Two and three-quarter pounds. That's light."

"Yes." He studied her a moment, puzzled by her reaction. Had she really not understood the subtext of his comment? "You've read Morgangni's pathology text?"

"Professor Laniere let me borrow it yesterday."

John grunted. She'd probably read the whole thing in a couple of hours. "You don't know how privileged you are, having access to that library." He moved back to the table. "All right. Now put the liver on the table and we'll dissect it." He handed her a scalpel. "Short incisions across each lobe, spaced one inch apart."

She bit her lip as she obeyed. "Like this?"

"That's it." He watched her competent movements. "Stop. What do you see inside the cuts?"

"Lobules. Veins." She bent to peer at the liver. "The color doesn't look right."

"How do you know?"

"The drawings from the textbook..." She hesitated. "The texture is brittle. It's supposed to be dense."

"That's right." He gently inserted his thumbs into a cut to spread it open. "Do you know what the liver does?"

"It's a...filter of sorts. Aids in digestion. A toxin would do this kind of damage, wouldn't it?" Abigail looked up at him, her green eyes intent.

He nodded. "This is similar to cirrhosis—diffuse fibrous content. Typical of patients from the District."

"Alcohol abuse," Abigail said sadly. "Or maybe opium."

John lifted his shoulders. "This woman was a prostitute, a known opium eater." He nodded at the clock on the wall. "We won't be able to stay much longer. Quickly, show me the left hepatic duct, the inferior vena cava and the hepatic artery."

As she did so, she explained the etymology of each word. John listened, absorbed, repeating back what she'd taught him. She was a good teacher, patient and thorough.

They finished with the liver, then removed and examined the reproductive organs. The uterus was scarred, indicative of multiple abortions. Abigail's eyes went glassy when dissection revealed a tiny embryo imbedded in its lining, but she blinked and correctly named the parts as John touched them.

He returned all the dissected organs carefully to the body's cavity. "Look in the case for my needle and sutures. We'll sew her up and be out of here."

Without speaking, Abigail complied with jerky movements.

John held the body together and watched her neat, evenly spaced stitches. "Very good."

She looked up at him briefly. "I worked in a sail shop for six months."

"So you've never…sold yourself in the District?" He couldn't contain his curiosity about this odd, brilliant, self-contained young woman. In his wildest imaginings he wouldn't have conjured a gently bred woman possessing the brass to enter a hospital morgue in the dead of night for the purpose of cutting open and examining a naked dead body.

Tugging on the final stitch, she fashioned a neat knot and clipped the thread. She backed away, her body taut, trembling, her eyes narrowed. "I'm going to tell you this one more time," she said, voice low and fierce, "and if you ask me again, I will happily demonstrate my finesse with a scalpel. I haven't to this point been forced to sell my body to survive, although I have lived among women who have. There's a thriving trade in this city of which you may not be aware—it is a vile form of slavery and it is to these women I wish to minister." She stepped closer to John then, fisting her gloved hands at her sides.

"And *that* wish makes it possible for me to endure your insults to learn what you know."

Odd she might be, John thought, and decidedly prickly, but she had a very fine pair of eyes and her refusal to buckle under his questions made him smile. He took her hand and gently pried her fingers apart, removing the needle and returning it to its case. "All right, Abigail," he said mildly. "Objection noted." He reached up to pull the bell cord. "Crutch will be here shortly, to dispose of the body. We'd best wash our hands." He gestured toward the basin and ewer sitting on a table across the room. "You first."

"Thank you." Abigail stalked around the table and lifted the ewer to splash water into the basin.

Watching her stiff back, John shook his head. "I truly meant no insult. I only wondered."

She looked over her shoulder. "Is that an apology?"

He considered for a moment. "Yes, I think it was."

"All right, then. You are forgiven. But the subject is closed." She moved aside to allow him access to the ewer.

As he washed, he studied Abigail from the corner of his eye. She stood head bowed beside the shroud-covered figure on the table, almost as if she were praying. An intriguing woman, perhaps more attractive than any lady he knew. His mother would be horrified at his assessment.

He smiled.

Abigail trailed behind as John supervised Crutch in the removal of the body.

"Careful, Crutch," said John, steadying the horse-drawn wagon waiting in an alley behind the hospital. "The poor woman led a hard enough life. Let's don't add to her embarrassments by dropping her into the sewer."

Shooting him a glowering grimace, Crutch slid the awkward, tarp-wrapped bundle onto the wagon bed. "The charity catacombs was full up last time I showed up with a body. Don't know what they're gonna do with this 'un." He raised the tailgate, secured it with a leather strap to the wagon's wooden side and wiped his hands on the seat of his filthy pants.

"That's not your problem." John slid a coin into the man's waiting hand and turned to Miss Charlemagne, who was in the doorway, arms folded inside her cloak. "Thank you for your help. We'll be back for rounds later. Come along, Abigail. I'll walk you back to the professor's."

As she and John rounded the front corner of the hospital, Abigail looked up at him. "Rounds are every day?"

"Yes. And lectures in the afternoons." He crossed the lawn toward the street, where carts were beginning to rattle toward the market, stirring the early morning quiet.

Abigail squinted at the rising sun, which radiated violet and gray streaks across the tops of the buildings. "You'll have a long day, then. Thank you for bringing me with you tonight."

He checked as a dray passed, then ducked across Common, heading for the dark green sward of the park. "Tell me how you came to learn a nearly dead language." Shortening his long stride, he pulled her hand through the crook of his elbow.

Wondering if he was aware of the courteous gesture,

she smiled at him. "My father taught me to read, translate and speak Greek and Latin. He was a schoolmaster as a young man, then became a minister."

"But you're—" He looked down at her, perhaps unwilling to state the obvious.

Abigail sighed. "Of course I'm a female. But that doesn't mean my brain doesn't work. I had little to otherwise occupy my time—until recently, that is. Not much time to study in the sail loft."

John stared at her, still clearly perplexed.

She smiled. "I'm grateful my father had no sense of propriety regarding the education of females. And that I am an only child. Otherwise he might have concentrated his considerable talents as a teacher on my hypothetical brother."

John chuckled. "I salute your unconventional sire." He walked on in silence, then after a moment gave her a sheepish look. "I beg your pardon again for my bumbling and embarrassing questions. I asked out of pure curiosity and had no intention of insulting you. It's just that—" He paused and she felt the sudden tension in his arm under her hand. "I'm sorry, but I've simply never encountered a woman who is both gently raised and entirely without qualms regarding the more grisly aspects of the medical profession. The scientific mind is not usually associated with femininity."

"That's ridiculous."

"I'm beginning to think you're right." He smiled at her. "But if you met my sister you might understand my point of view."

"Perhaps no one has yet made the effort to enlighten and educate her."

"Undoubtedly true. But my mother would be horrified at the idea of teaching Lisette anything beyond the ability to snag a socially acceptable husband. In fact—" John's lips tightened. "I had to fight for my own education beyond the basics. My father wishes for me to continue in the family business." He drew Abigail to a stop and looked up at the imposing brick facade of the building to their left.

Abigail looked up. They had walked down this block earlier, of course, in the dark. The sign above the front door was painted in enormous block letters: "Crescent City Shipping—Offices—Warehouses located on Commerce at Joseph." On either side of the sign was a large crescent moon—a symbol that had haunted her dreams since she'd left China nearly a year ago.

She stared for a moment, incapable of speech. "Your father is—this is your family's enterprise?"

Apparently he didn't notice the strain in her voice. "Yes." He started walking again. "I suppose, like you, I have rather mixed feelings about my father. His business acumen has enabled me to afford my medical college fees and books. But it has been a source of considerable contention between us that I refuse to follow him into the transportation industry." His voice took on a bitter edge. "China this, China that. One would think that nothing of value happens on this side of the world. You should count yourself fortunate that your own father was more interested in the classical languages than the exotic ones."

Abigail swallowed, suppressing the impulse to give John Braddock a shove and run as fast and hard as she could. "Indeed," she murmured. "I am very fortunate."

* * *

"Appleton, please tell my mother I've answered her summons." Handing his hat over to the Braddock family butler, John looked around. He hadn't been home in several weeks. Fleur, the housekeeper, had placed fresh chrysanthemums in the tall crystal vase on the mahogany side table; their spicy aroma filled the entryway.

"If you want me to put it in them terms, Mister Johnny, it ain't gonna be a pleasant visit," Appleton said cheerfully, dusting the hat off by whacking it against his thigh.

John shook his head, grinning a little. "I'll trust you to interpret." Although perhaps not the personification of the well-trained servant, Mick Appleton had served as first mate on John's father's maiden voyage thirty years ago. Upon his retirement from the sea when John was only nine years old, Appleton had landed in a position of household authority second only to Eliza Braddock. For all intents and purposes part of the family, he was in the nature of a favorite uncle to John.

Whistling, Appleton limped up the stairs while John wandered into the Chinese parlor situated just off the entryway. It was overwhelmingly red and black, the ebony furniture upholstered in crimson velvet with thick brass studs; tapestries woven of exotic silken designs hung between and on either side of the two wide French windows, clashing with a complex striped wallpaper pattern. John closed his eyes. Lack of sleep had engendered the beginnings of a migraine and his mother's hideous decor did nothing to help.

Still he couldn't regret last night's rendezvous in the morgue. Abigail Neal was easy to look at, if one overlooked the statuesque build and frequently sardonic expression. At least she didn't make fun of his struggle with Latin as the other fellows did. And she was teachable and appreciative of a fellow's talents.

He was standing at the window, smiling at the memory of Abigail's inventive imagination when he heard a rustle of skirts in the doorway. He turned. "Mother—it's good to see you."

Never one to release her self-control, Eliza Dreher Braddock extended both hands and offered John a smooth cheek to kiss. "John, my dear. It's been too long since we saw you."

"Seventeen days, I believe you mentioned in your note." He waited for her to seat herself upon a red slipper chair before he sprawled in the wing chair opposite. Her light brown hair was dressed as usual in a complicated mass of loops and curls, and her high-necked pink gown complemented her still-slim figure and unlined fair skin. "You're looking beautiful as usual. Where's Lisette?"

With a pleased smile, his mother accepted his compliment as her due and relaxed against the arm of the chair. "She is driving around the Commons with Dorothée Molyneux. They enjoy one another's company so, one would think they are already sisters."

"In this nasty weather?" John ignored the blatant insinuation in the word "already."

His mother gathered her shawl closer. "Yes, indeed, it is messy, but these young girls... Always after attracting the attention of the town beaus. Dorothée will be wed before the year is out, I am sure, and Lisette will be inconsolable to lose her best friend."

John suppressed a sigh. "Perhaps we could arrange

transportation for semiannual visits at least," he said lightly.

"John, you know what I mean." His mother pouted charmingly, although a firm edge lined her soft voice. "I don't understand why you put off courting Dorothée, now that she's had her debut season. Her parents are expecting you to call."

He crossed one knee over the other. The gloves were off. "Mother, I'm far too busy with my studies to waste time sipping tea and dancing attendance on a spoiled little girl with the vocabulary of a six-year-old."

Mother stiffened. "There is no need for insult."

"I'm sorry. I've tried to hint that your hopes for a match between me and Miss Molyneux aren't likely to come to fruition."

"But John—"

He held up a hand. "And don't try foisting some other equally boring debutante on me. If you could see the stack of textbooks waiting on my nightstand, the contents of which I must absorb before Christmas—"

"John." His mother frowned, her fine hazel eyes dampening. "I do not understand why you must be so obstinate about the one thing I ask of you. If *you* could see the times I have intervened when your father wanted to refuse the funds that pay your matriculation fees…" She bit her soft lips together and looked away. "I only want to see you settled with a nice girl."

He stared at her profile, his headache now raging. His mother had indeed provided a much-needed buffer between him and his sire. *Was* he being selfish? Would it be so terrible to find himself shackled to plump, dimpled Dorothée Molyneux? At least maybe then his parents would leave him alone. He could set up his own household, take on a titular role in the shipping business and pursue his studies unmolested by social obligations.

He rubbed his temple and sighed. "Perhaps I might call on her for a drive, after I finish my anatomy examination next week."

Mother spread her fan, looking at him over its lace-edged top. "Really, John?"

He had to smile at the hopeful flutter of her lashes. "No promises of courtship, but I'll make an effort to get to know her."

She dropped the fan and exhaled a happy sigh. "I'll give a party. A ball! We'll invite the Molyneux family and the Lanieres and perhaps the Girards, if you insist. I'm sure there are others I'm not recalling at the moment, but it will be a grand occasion. You'll have *such* a lovely time, John."

He thought of the cool dark recesses of the morgue, where he'd been challenged, amused, and touched by a tall young woman in a patched dress. He sighed. "I'm sure I shall, Mother."

Abigail had been struggling to stay awake all afternoon as she helped Camilla put up squash. The second time Abigail's eyes closed while she was pouring a pot of boiling water through a sieve in the sink, Camilla took the handle of the pot from her.

"Sit down, my dear, before you drop that and scald us both." Camilla finished straining the squash.

Abigail sat down, her knees buckling. "I'm fine. Really."

Camilla glanced over her shoulder as she set the pot

on the stove. "Certainly you are. Did you not sleep well last night?"

Abigail forced her eyes open again, then gave up and rubbed them with both fists. "Not particularly." She yawned. Professor Laniere had told her not to tell anyone about the autopsy. Presumably that meant his wife as well.

But Camilla was not easily deflected. She frowned as she dumped the next batch of squash into a fresh pot of water. "You stayed up all night studying, didn't you? I admire your persistence, but you can't function without sleep."

Abigail grinned at her. "Says the woman who stayed up three nights running with poxy children."

Camilla laughed as she sat down across from Abigail. "Well, I've caught up on sleep the last two nights. Thank goodness the children aren't itching so badly anymore."

"I remember when I had those. The blisters felt like fire ants crawling all over, me and every child in the village had them. It was the way my mother found out I'd been sneaking out of the compound—" She stopped herself too late.

"Compound?" Camilla's eyebrows were up. "You mean a missionary compound?"

Abigail stared at her, dismayed. If she hadn't been so tired... Finally she looked away. "Please, I don't like to talk about it."

Camilla was silent for a moment, then reached out to touch Abigail's hand. "I won't interrogate you, if you insist. But—Abigail, I confess I'm curious about your spiritual upbringing. There's nothing shameful about being the daughter of missionaries."

"It depends," Abigail said, endeavoring to keep her voice level. "There are missionaries and then there are missionaries." She risked a look at Camilla, whose lips were pursed thoughtfully.

"Are there, my dear?" Camilla said gently. "Tell me about it. Where were you?"

"China," Abigail blurted, unable to contain the burden any longer. "The Shandong Province. I was five when my parents moved there. For days on end it was just me and my mother in our little house, until I found a way to slip out." She swallowed. Her mother's depression had led to long bouts of sleeping, day and night. Abigail had found herself virtually alone while her father went into the village and taught the Chinese "heathen" about Jesus.

"And you caught chicken pox and your mother found out?" Camilla leaned her elbows on the table, her topaz eyes bright with interest. The pot of squash boiled merrily on the stove unheeded.

"Actually," Abigail said reluctantly, "it was my father who found me, scratching away, when he came home one evening." She touched her stomach. "I have scars to this day and it's miraculous the blisters hadn't yet infected my face. Papa woke my mother up and told her the infection was going around the village. Demanded to know why she'd taken me out of the compound."

"And of course she hadn't," Camilla guessed.

Abigail nodded. "Papa beat me with a strap, then Mama bathed me in some herbs the Chinese women had given her."

"He *beat* you? A seven-year-old who was ill with chicken pox?"

Abigail looked up, startled out of her memories. Camilla looked as ferocious as a gentle-eyed woman with tawny hair curling all over her head and spectacles on her nose could look. "I disobeyed him and left the compound. I suppose he thought it was dangerous." She shrugged. "After all, I did contract that infection."

"Where was your mother while you were out on your own?"

Abigail's instinctive response was to defend her mother. Mama had been fragile, physically and mentally—unlike Abigail, with her large hands and feet, her tough, boyish body, her insatiable curiosity. "She—she wasn't well. I made her nervous. So I learned to read and play by myself. Eventually I found an opening in the compound wall and kept going farther and farther until I saw the Chinese children. They laughed at me, but eventually they taught me to speak and sing in their language. That is, until Papa caught me."

"You speak Chinese?" Camilla gaped.

Abigail felt the old inner chant: *freak, freak, freak.* She had said too much. She shook her head. "Camilla, I confess, I'm exhausted. May I go to bed? Dr. Laniere promised I could join the class for early rounds in the morning, then I'll come back to help you finish the squash."

Camilla released Abigail's hands and glanced at the pot. "Of course. This is the last batch anyway." She rose, patting Abigail's shoulder as she moved to the stove. "Sleep well, my dear, and don't worry about what you've told me. I'm good at keeping secrets."

Abigail nodded. "Thank you, Camilla. Good night."

She rose and staggered toward the stairs. If knowledge was power, please God she had not revealed too much to Camilla Laniere.

Chapter Ten

Rounds. There was something in the word, John thought, that aptly described some parts of his chosen profession. Repetition. Procedure. Scientific experiment.

Early on Friday morning, he and Girard, Weichmann and a couple of other fellows, tagged behind Prof, with the ever-present Abigail Neal bringing up the rear. Unlike the rest of them, her eyes were bright and alert, taking in every detail of the professor's movements—the way he gripped a patient's wrist to check a pulse, the position of the stethoscope on the chest or back, the firm but careful flexing of a limb. When the men arrived, she'd been waiting inside the hospital, perched on the bottom entryway stair, hands clasped demurely atop her knees.

Prof stopped at the bedside of the woman with the gallbladder case, who was recovering nicely from her surgery. John glanced at Abigail over his shoulder; her cheeks reddened as she met his eyes. Maybe she was thinking of the way she'd grabbed his hand during the hemorrhage scare. At the time he'd been too startled to enjoy it, but the memory of the strength and delicacy in those beautiful, long fingers returned every time he looked at her.

"How are you feeling this morning, ma'am?" asked the professor.

The woman let out a theatrical moan. "I never had so much pain." She lifted the edge of her gown, revealing a neat white four-by-six-inch gauze bandage. A faint pink stain revealed the location of the wound, a minor indication after such serious surgery, in John's opinion. "Those nurses don't pay enough attention when a body needs to take care of certain…necessary functions."

The professor smiled. "The fact that you feel the urge for those necessary functions is a good sign indeed. I'll ask one of them to tend you." He looked around at his students. "Come, gentlemen."

Abigail cleared her throat. "I'll stay and help her, Professor."

Prof looked over his shoulder. "Very well, Miss Neal. You may catch up with us as soon as Mrs. Catchot is comfortable." He walked on.

"It's a wonder he trusts her not to break open the wound," muttered Marcus, catching up to John. "She's not a trained nurse."

As late as yesterday, John might have agreed, but last night's adventure in the morgue had forever altered his view of women in general and one in particular. He scowled at Marcus. "I've observed Miss Neal to comport herself with great common sense as well as compassion."

Girard's mouth fell open. "Hey, whose side are you on?"

Prof looked around with an amused glint in his eye. "Braddock, I want to speak with you." He lengthened his stride, leaving Marcus to fall back with the other students, and addressed John without slowing down. "How did your project proceed yesterday?"

John looked back to make sure the others were still occupied in arguing over the relative benefits of carbolic acid and iodine as a disinfectant. "Cause of death was liver failure, as far as I could tell." He lowered his voice. "And she performed very well, considering.... Well, she's a dashed odd woman," he burst out. "The first time I ever autopsied, I was sick all night."

Prof chuckled. "As we wend our way into the next decade, if the Lord tarries, I suspect we fellows are going to have to abandon all preconceived notions of womanhood."

"That's exactly what I mean, sir. It's not natural for a woman to show such interest in disease and death. Isn't there some biblical injunction about women maintaining modesty in public?"

The professor stopped, raising a hand to capture his students' attention. "Gentlemen, please proceed to the next ward. I'll want reports of pulse, temperature and other indications on each patient when I join you in a moment. Mr. Braddock, a word with you."

Mutiny built on Marcus's square face. "But Prof, wouldn't we all benefit from your instruction?"

Dr. Laniere frowned. "This is a matter of a personal nature, Girard. You may serve as clerk while the others do the examinations."

Giving John a puzzled look, Marcus regrouped and

hustled to the head of the line of students traversing the hallway.

With a jerk of his head the professor indicated that John should follow him, then wheeled into an open room which served as supply closet and office for the nurses. It was empty at the moment.

Prof shut the door. "What do you know about biblical instruction to women, Braddock?" The professor's tone was dry, but not unkind. "I was under the impression that you regard the spiritual implications of medical treatment rather by the way."

John scrambled for dignity. "I…confess the subject has piqued my interest of late, sir. I did a quick survey of the copy of Scripture my mother gave me when I reached my majority."

"A quick survey? May I ask what caused this sudden religious fervor?"

"Well, sir, there have been some rather peculiar events occurring lately." John tugged his cravat. "Your willingness to include a woman in our lessons here at the hospital being one. And—and I'm dreaming about things that never used to bother me."

Prof's rather flinty black eyes softened marginally. "What sorts of things are bothering you, Braddock?"

"The baby we buried on Sunday." John looked away. "I wake up, shaking it to make it cry. And the woman we autopsied, Abigail and I—she was pregnant. Did you know that, sir?"

The professor sighed. "She was a prostitute, Braddock. Are you truly surprised?"

"No. But I find myself wild to understand what it means. How to help these girls, so they won't slowly kill themselves and their babies with opium." To his horror, John's voice cracked. "Until Sunday, I never thought much about it. Medicine was a little like a—a large puzzle, but all of a sudden it's like some veil has come off my eyes, and—Professor, I really don't know if I can stand it." In his agitation he cracked his knuckles and stared at his mentor.

For a long moment the professor stood with his hands clasped behind his back, head bowed. The little room hummed on a dense silence. The odors of lye and disinfectant, the distant rattle of carts in one of the wards, reminded John that they were in a hospital.

Dr. Laniere looked up and gripped John's shoulder. "I remember the moment when something similar happened to me." The professor's deep voice was quiet, intent, his eyes searching. "I had partially finished my training as a doctor, but had given it up because—" he sighed "—a set of complicated circumstance demanded it. But I met a young woman whose faith challenged my cynicism and selfishness. It seemed everywhere I went I saw the hand of God moving in miraculous and loving ways in spite of dire and dangerous circumstances." He smiled, a slight curve of the lips. "Eventually it began to seem ridiculous to run."

"What does this have to do with allowing Abigail Neal to study medicine?" John squirmed internally at the personal twist the conversation had taken. He wasn't sure it was proper to know so much about one's teachers.

The professor lifted his brows. "Come, Braddock. Miss Neal's presence is a minor irritant. A symptom of the disease, if you will. Your real problem is spiritual."

John glowered at him. "You know the respect I have

for you, sir, but I have great difficulty reconciling science and faith. Part of me *wants* to believe. But then I slam up against the fact that one simply cannot prove God."

"And that is exactly the point. God is so big that one can never prove Him—at least with human measurements. But once I took off in a leap of faith He began to prove *Himself* to me. Over and over. Surrender came surprisingly easy, once I realized what I was missing."

John lifted his hands. "And what was it you were missing?" He felt unmanned, asking these kinds of questions. But one thing he'd learned in the laboratory, one never learned anything without questions.

"Love, my dear boy," said the professor simply. "The best kind of love—not the finite love of a woman, although that came later for me—but the kind of love that looks past every conceivable fault and receives a man on the basis of unearned favor. The kind that Christ exhibited by giving His life."

If those words had come from anyone other than his esteemed professor, John would have laughed and walked away. He stared at Prof, heart thundering as if he'd run all the way from the docks. "You know my father," he said in a strangled voice. "If he thinks I've become religious, he'll assume I've caved in about joining the family business. I cannot let him roll over me."

Prof was silent for a moment. "This is not entirely about your father, John, just as it only peripherally has to do with Miss Neal. And it's not about being 'religious,' as you put it. But if you're worried about how Phillip will react, you can leave him to me. I'll be the buffer." He squeezed John's shoulder. "Make your decision on your own."

"I'll—think about it," John said with difficulty.

"Professor? Mrs. Catchot is asleep now."

John looked at the doorway and found Abigail Neal standing there, hands clasped at her waist, expression perfectly bland. He wondered how much of the conversation she had overheard.

Flushing, he stepped out from under the professor's hand and turned toward Abigail. "I'm off to make sure the other fellows haven't set the ward on fire." He stepped past her, careful not to touch her.

She murmured something to the professor, then caught up to him while the professor followed at a more measured pace. "Is everything all right, John?"

He glanced at her. "Certainly. Did you read the paper this morning?"

She blinked at the sudden shift in topic. "No, I—you know I was here early, first thing. Was there something of particular interest?"

"There was a fire in the District this morning."

He shouldn't have been so blunt. Her eyes widened in horror. "A fire? Where?"

"Not on Tchapitoulas," he said quickly. "It relates to the hospital. The board of directors had set up an infectious diseases clinic and apparently some of the neighbors resented it. They decided to take matters into their own hands."

"People set a *clinic* on fire? To burn out sick people?" Abigail looked horrified. "Was anyone hurt?"

"Two dead, three burned terribly. And there were a couple of caretakers injured as well." John cracked his knuckles, wishing he could wrap his hands around the neck of the cretin who had set the fire. "Some of us are going over there later to see what we can do to help. Thought you might like to come."

"Of course I would! If Mrs. Camilla can do without me, that is." She turned. "Professor, did you know about this—the fire? Why are we not over there right now?"

"We'll go directly after we finish rounds," said the professor. "The rest of the available hospital staff and faculty are already there."

With the conversation safely deflected from the topic of his soul, John relaxed his shoulders and joined Prof and Abigail in planning strategy for treating second- and third-degree burns and outlining the supplies they would need.

He could think about God later, when there was not such pressing need for action.

The scene was chaos. Abigail scrambled out of the ambulance wagon behind John, then involuntarily halted to look up at the smoldering black remains of a tenement house not so different from her old home with Tess. The roof had caved in on one side; shards of glass blown out of the upper-story windows crunched underfoot as the students worked to transfer supplies from the wagons to the brick street, which had been blocked off from foot traffic. Horse-drawn fire wagons were rattling away from the scene. The air reeked of smoke and charred wood and other pungent but unidentifiable smells.

"Abigail! Come on!"

Startled, she looked around and found John standing on the sidewalk, medical bag in hand. When she caught his eye, he turned and hurried toward a huddle of fire victims in the middle of the street.

Drawing a clean handkerchief from her pocket, she folded it into a triangle and tied it over the lower half of her face, covering her nostrils. With her breathing now unhampered by contaminated air, she followed John. She had no medical instruments of her own but had managed to stuff bandages, antiseptic and rolls of cotton lint into a canvas knapsack one of the nurses had given her. She carried it by its drawstring, and it bumped against her legs as she ran.

By the time she caught up to John, he had knelt beside a man with a bleeding head wound and started rooting around in his leather case. Coughing, he looked up at Abigail. "I forgot iodine."

She flung herself onto her knees on the other side of the patient. "I brought it." She yanked open the drawstring of her bag and extracted the heavy brown bottle that had bruised her leg.

"Good. Swab this clamp, then hold the wound together while I stitch."

She wet a lint pad with the yellow-brown iodine, glad of her handkerchief which blocked its pungent odor. Capping the bottle, she took the clamp from John and used it to hold the patient's torn flesh in place. It looked like he'd been sliced by a jagged piece of wood; splinters still clung to the man's matted, bloody hair. Thank God he'd already fainted from the pain or he would undoubtedly have been writhing and therefore impossible to treat.

John plucked a pre-threaded needle from a small case inside the larger bag, swabbed it with the iodine-soaked pad, then took a breath and proceeded to sew. Because she had watched him tend to Tess, Abigail was not surprised at the neatness and thoroughness of his work. But the expression on his face made her stare at him in wonder. The cold detachment with which he generally operated had been replaced by a grim, almost feverish determination.

She wasn't sure it was a good thing. His hands shook.

"John, what's wrong?" she said quietly.

"What?" He glanced at her. A crash from inside the house accompanied the shouts of firemen and doctors, the dying crackle of the fire.

She raised her voice. "Are you all right?"

"Of course I'm all right. Don't let the clamp slide."

He was back to his normal curt self. Biting back a breath-wasting retort, she adjusted her grip and watched him sew. When he finished, he reached into the bag for a pair of scissors and cut the suture thread. He looked around. "We've got to move him to a wagon. He needs to go to the hospital."

The man began to stir. His eyelids fluttered. "Help me," he murmured. "Libby…the baby…"

"Be still." Abigail laid a hand on his shoulder. "We'll find—"

"Never mind, Abigail, get his feet." John stood up. "I'll take his shoulders." He seemed to realize she was all the help he was going to get. The other doctors and students were occupied with victims of the fire. With the rising of the sun, the stench of burned flesh had become so powerful that it was hard for Abigail to breathe, even through her handkerchief. She didn't know how John could stand it.

"Hold on," she told their patient. "We're going to carry you to the ambulance."

"No!" He tried to sit up as John grasped him under the armpits. "Where's my wife? Libby—"

"We'll find her," John grunted. "Abby—get his feet!"

It was a good thing she was a tall, sturdy woman, she thought as she and John hauled the heavy patient with as little jostling as possible toward the nearest ambulance wagon. He had fainted again before they got him there; they made him as comfortable as they could, leaving instructions for Crutch to keep him still if he should wake up and go looking for his wife.

For the next two hours Abigail accompanied John from patient to patient, soothing burns with aloe extract, bandaging or sewing up flesh wounds, once setting a broken leg with a splint made from a piece of doorpost. In an attempt to find their first patient's wife, Abigail addressed every woman they encountered as Libby. She was unsuccessful in that, but she learned more about medicine than by reading a stack of textbooks. John was swift, efficient, thorough—and she was increasingly impressed with his gentle touch.

It was nearly noon, with the sun straight overhead, when Professor Laniere called his students together. They clustered under a bare-limbed sugar maple across the street from the burned tenement, panting and sweating despite the clammy chill. The men had all removed coats and cravats and rolled up their shirtsleeves; Abigail would have given anything to be shed of her high-necked, full-skirted gown. As it was, she defied convention by unbuttoning her wristbands and rolling the sleeves as high as they would go on her forearms.

She had also unfastened her detachable collar, tossing it into her supply sack. Let them call her a strumpet: at least she wouldn't faint from heat exhaustion.

"Gentlemen—and lady," the professor added with a slight smile for Abigail, "the worst cases have been cared for and sent on to the hospital for the nuns to settle into quarantine. You've all acquitted yourselves well. Lectures for this afternoon will be suspended."

A general huzzah erupted from the students as they dispersed.

Abigail detained the doctor by touching his sleeve. "Professor, there was a man we treated—Mr. Braddock and I, that is. The man was looking for his wife and baby."

The professor's calm gaze went from Abigail to John, who had hesitated when she stopped. "Where is he now?"

"We put him on the ambulance," said John. "Told him we'd look for the woman—her name is Libby."

"But neither of us saw her. Or any babies either, for that matter." Abigail knitted her fingers together. She'd given a promise. "Do you suppose the firemen found her too late?"

"Several unrecognizable bodies were recovered and taken to the dead house before we got here," the professor conceded. "I'll inquire. The baby ought to be a giveaway."

John nodded. "Thank you, Prof. Will you let us know if you find them?"

Dr. Laniere agreed and took his leave to stride across the street, where the last of the ambulance wagons waited.

"Happy now?" John smiled at Abigail, the brilliance of his hazel eyes augmented by sweaty smudges of charcoal across his forehead and cheeks where he'd repeatedly wiped his face.

She nodded, thinking he looked like a particularly handsome and well-bred savage. Even though she'd never denied his physical beauty, for the first time she found herself attracted to the man, the doctor. She had watched him perform today like a hero in a penny novel.

Then his gaze shifted over her shoulder and he nearly crushed her hand. "Father. What are you doing in this part of town?"

Abigail turned to find a tall, heavily built gentleman bearing toward them. A stovepipe hat covered his dark, longish hair; muttonchop side-whiskers, a thick mustache and heavy eyebrows accented a pair of ice blue eyes.

Mr. Braddock reached John and laid a large hand on his son's shoulder. A broad smile revealed strong white teeth, although there was little real humor in his expression. "Seems a man has to attend a fire in the worst street of the District to have a conversation with his offspring these days. Your mother told me you were by the other day. Why did you not stay for supper, you ungrateful whelp?"

Abigail's instinct to run was forestalled by John's grip on her hand. He didn't look at her, but she knew somehow that her presence helped him. But oh, how she wanted to get away. She tried to shrink behind John's broad shoulder. *He doesn't know you. He's never seen you,* she reminded herself.

John tugged her hand through his arm. "I have afternoon rounds and examinations to study for, Father."

"Yes, we all know how busy you are these days. No time for the fellow who pays the bills." Braddock Sr.'s laughter boomed as he squeezed John's shoulder hard before releasing it. He looked around. "Just hell-bent on rescuing every pox-infected dock worker on the south side of town. Now when are you going to introduce me to your fair companion?"

Abigail wished she'd thought to roll down her sleeves and replace her collar. Desperate to evade the sneering inspection of those cunning blue eyes, she tried to pull her hand from John's elbow.

John visibly regained some of his customary aplomb. "Father, may I make you known to Miss Abigail Neal, who is a houseguest of Dr. and Mrs. Laniere? Miss Neal, I present my father, Phillip Braddock."

John's defiant gaze was on his father's face, but she detected a faint tuck in the corner of his mouth. Facing the senior Braddock, her chin went up a notch. Perhaps in her creased and stained gown, hair disheveled and falling down about her shoulders, she did look like one of the inhabitants of the red light district. But she literally was staying with the Lanieres. "How do you do, sir?" she said with all the demureness her mother had taught her when she was still a tiny child.

John's father studied her for another moment in patent disbelief, his eyes moving from her sunburnt nose to the open vee of her dress to her bare wrists. "You're a guest of Gabriel and Camilla?" He pursed his lips. "How very interesting." Dismissing her, he gave his son another jocular look. "In that case, you should invite Miss

Neal to your mother's party next week. I'm sure Doro-thée would delight in a new acquaintance."

If he expected John to back down, he was sorely mis-taken. John inclined his head with a marked absence of respect. "As you wish, Father. It will be my pleasure to introduce Miss Neal to the finest of New Orleans so-ciety. She'll make a glittering addition to my mother's company."

Phillip Braddock stared at his son's mocking face for one pulsing moment before he smiled without warmth. "I'll see that her name is added to the invitation list. Good day, my son." He turned on his heel and swung down the street toward the docks.

Abigail wheeled, jerking her hand out from under John's arm. "That was not funny, John."

"Oh, yes it was." Chuckling, he slung an arm across her shoulders. "Worth the price of admission. I see Weichmann hailing us. Let's go see what other mis-chief we can get into."

Chapter Eleven

As he tangled with a declension of the word *suppurare,* John sneaked a glance across the library table at Abigail Neal. Tongue between her white teeth, she was studying one of his pharmaceuticals texts. He couldn't wait to find out what his sister would think about her. Abigail had returned to the Lanieres' for a bath before meeting him in the school library to help him with his languages. While he pored over a Latin translation, she'd wandered around, poking at the shelves until she found something to interest her.

Now that he looked at her, he noticed that her sage green gown—white collar firmly attached and sleeves buttoned from elbow to wrist—turned her eyes to a velvet moss color. The sunburn lent her skin a glowing, Raphaelesque beauty that would have made his sister, famous for her magnolia-white complexion, scream with envy.

He'd introduced Abigail to his father mostly as an irritant—and as a buffer against some of the nonsense with which the old man liked to bully him. The more he thought about it, however, the more he liked the idea of pitting the acerbic tongue of the eccentric Miss Neal against his sister's sugary steel wool charm. As he watched Abigail's fine eyes flit down the page, appreciation for his own idea grew until he felt the urge to stand on his chair and crow his brilliance.

Abigail looked up and frowned. "That was very badly done of you, you know. You embarrassed me and your father, and now your mother will have uneven numbers at her dinner table."

"And the world will fall in upon itself if one's dinner numbers do not match." Very perceptive she was. How had she ascertained the direction of his thoughts? "Tell me, Miss Neal—how many formal occasions have you attended in your short life?"

"Five," she retorted. "One of them with an emperor. So do not, if you please, make fun of me."

He stared at her. "Put that book down and tell me how you know an emperor."

"You wouldn't believe me, so I shan't bother." She lifted the forty-pound translation of *Treatise of Elemental Chemistry.* "Lavoisier lists light as an element. How is that possible?"

"It's not. Light is electromagnetic radiation. Lavoisier was a genius, but he had some blind spots—which could explain why he ultimately lost his head."

Abigail laid her book down and regarded him with amused exasperation. "Braddock, you're horrible!"

Apparently she knew the great French scientist had been beheaded at the height of the French Revolution. John grinned. "Tomorrow I'll let you borrow Maxwell's *Treatise on Electricity and Magnetism,* which explains his theory of light as waves. Fascinating stuff." That a woman should be not only interested in scientific subjects like the properties of light, but also capable of comprehending them, was astonishing.

"I should love to read it. How are you coming with the translation?"

"Suppurare comes from *sub-,* meaning 'under,' and *pur* means pus." He squinted at her. "So any word that has those derivatives will have related meanings?"

She smiled. "Now you have it."

"It's beginning to make sense. I'd begun to think things were randomly named just to give us poor English-speaking fellows a hard time."

"You did not."

"Well, I suspected there must be some kind of code, but I couldn't break it. Mathematics I can understand. The rules don't change."

She sat quietly for a moment, her eyes on the book. "I didn't get the impression you like rules so much, John."

"I do when I see the reason for them."

Her gaze lifted. "What would you do if the rules said you couldn't study what you want to study because you were born male?"

"You *are* studying." He thumped the back of her book. "Nobody's stopping you."

"That's wrong on so many levels. First of all, perhaps I borrowed a couple of textbooks, but even if I learned everything Professor Laniere knows, I couldn't hold a license to practice medicine."

John frowned. "Are you going to be one of those man-eaters like that crazy Stanton woman?"

"Who?"

"Mrs. Stanton. The one who's trying to get women the vote."

"Why shouldn't women vote?"

Because Abigail's tone was inquiring rather than aggressive, John tried to explain. "I'm not saying they shouldn't. But my father says most know nothing about the political process. And they're going to vote with their husbands anyway."

"If we were allowed to gain higher education we wouldn't be ill-informed. And the only reason I'd never heard of this Stanton women is because I've been…out of the country. That doesn't make me ignorant." Abigail frowned. "I don't dislike men in general. But I resent being treated like a child—by anyone. Don't you?"

John thought about the way his father spoke to him. "I suppose," he said slowly, studying Abigail. There was nothing remotely childlike in her broad brow and wide, intelligent eyes. "But voting is a huge responsibility."

"Raising children is an even greater responsibility. Women do that all the time."

"But you're suited to that."

"*You?* Do you mean women in general or me in particular?" Abigail was smiling now. "I assure you I would make a terrible mother."

"No, you wouldn't." He suddenly knew that as well as he knew his own name. "I've seen you with the Laniere children and the children in the hospital. In fact," he added recklessly, "you would make a stellar doctor."

"You think I would make a good mother, a good doctor, but not a responsible citizen?" She laughed. "John, that's ludicrous."

"You're twisting my words. I was trying to give you a compliment."

Her eyes still twinkled. "I'm honored, I assure you. And I'll enjoy the Maxwell book, if you're serious about lending me it."

"I'll be happy to." John looked around the library. It was late afternoon and he and Abigail were the only ones left. "We should go. You must be exhausted after the morning we had."

Abigail slammed the Lavoisier textbook shut and rubbed her eyes. "Not really." She yawned, then laughed. "All right, I'm tired, but it's a good kind of tired. We helped people this morning."

"Yes, we did." He stood up and offered her a hand. "Come on, Doctor Abigail. I'll walk you home."

She looked away and sighed. "Home? I'm not sure where that is…" She laid her hand in his and rose.

But he stood looking into her face, her physical presence warming him like the gaslights that sent shadows flickering across her cheekbones. His gaze traced her sweetly curved lips and he laid his free hand at the back of her neck, just under the thick knot of brown hair. She flinched.

"What's wrong, Abigail?"

She took a sharp breath. "A lady doesn't allow familiarities."

"Make up your mind." He stared at her in frustration. "Are you a lady or a woman who wants to be a doctor?"

"Why can't I be both?" She stepped back, eyes clear. "I'm going to change the definition of a lady."

"Fine. Be a lady. And I'll be a gentleman…a gentleman who wants to kiss you." His lips curved as he moved to whisper in her ear. "Call it a gesture of friend-ship."

"Friendship," she scoffed, but this time she didn't step back. "You don't offer to kiss the other fellows you study with."

"Touché." Cupping his hand under her jaw to tilt her face, he bent his head. "You have no idea how beauti-ful you are."

Her lips parted and softened under his for a startled moment before she put her hands against his chest and pushed. "Don't, John."

He stared at her for a moment, then picked up the stack of textbooks he'd brought with him. "Friendship, Abigail, comes in several varieties." He tried not to show his triumph. She'd almost kissed him back.

On Saturday afternoon Abigail worked alone in the dispensary. Winona had gone home to visit her parents and Camilla had taken the children to the park.

She walked along the shelves, taking down jars of medicines one by one, dusting them, opening them to smell the contents and compare them to the list of ingre-dients the professor had given her. With the inventory alphabetized, it was a simple matter to memorize their efficacies and side effects. Maybe John didn't want to go to the bother—"I can always look 'em up," he'd told her brusquely—but she had to believe that an understanding of chemistry was essential to treatment. Even though she'd grounded herself in herbology as thoroughly as possible before leaving China, advances in pharmaceu-ticals had blossomed in both Europe and America, far outstripping her Chinese instructors. Why not prepare herself in both disciplines?

Coming to several little brown bottles of morphine and its derivative, laudanum, she hesitated before taking one down. Lying in her palm, it looked innocent enough, with its cork stopper and label printed neatly in her own fine hand. She unstoppered it and allowed the sickly sweet odor to evaporate into the narrow aisle between shelves. She squeezed it in her hand, resisting the urge to fling it down to smash against the tile floor. *Mama, oh Mama. The first taste is what destroyed you.*

Bitter truth that what could ease pain, even save a life, could also create untold heartache. Hurriedly she replaced the cork and set the bottle back on the shelf. No need to study this one. She knew it intimately.

She had reached the third row of shelves when the distant sound of the clinic door opening and closing caught her attention.

"Abigail?" Winona's voice came closer, rising in distress. "Abby, where are you?"

"In here." Abigail moved to the door of the dispensary and leaned out. "What's the matter?"

Winona, holding a small girl by the hand, stood in the kitchen doorway with her back to Abigail. She turned, an expression of relief breaking over her lovely dark face. "There you are! Thank goodness!" She tugged the sobbing child, who looked to be five or six years old, toward Abigail. "Would you mind taking a look at Essie's ears? She's in awful pain."

Abigail frowned. "You should take her to one of the doctors or a student at the very least. I'm not—"

"They're all in class or in surgery." Winona dropped

the child's hand and drew her close. "Besides, you've got more kindness and common sense than all those arrogant young men put together." She brushed her hand across the little girl's tightly braided black hair. "Please, Abigail."

Abigail could see nothing but the child's coffee-colored little ear peeking from the folds of Winona's apron. The heartrending sobs sounded both congested and painful. Abigail thought quickly. She'd been left in charge of the clinic, with instructions to refer any emergency patients to Dr. Lewis, Professor of Obstetrics and Diseases of Women and Children, whose home office was two blocks over.

She opened her mouth to say so, but Winona held up a hand. "And don't tell me to take her to that whiskery Dr. Lewis," she said. "He's so deaf he roars like a lion and scares the little ones."

Unable to suppress a smile, Abigail shook her head. "I don't have a license to prescribe medicines. But perhaps I could just look and see if there's something simple I could do to temporarily relieve the pain." She smiled at Essie, who had stopped wailing long enough to peep at Abigail. Cognizant that she was the center of attention, she promptly recommenced the concert.

Winona winced. "Thank you." She led Essie into the clinic, picked her up and set her on the examination table situated next to the window. "Here, lambie, be a big girl and stop crying."

As Abigail rooted through a storage cabinet in the corner, she did her best to ignore the child's cries because they had shifted in tone from real pain to a sort of self-conscious bleating. She extracted an otoscope, a cone-shaped metal tube which she had observed Dr. Laniere using to view the inside of a patient's ear. She'd studied drawings of the ear canal in the medical texts she'd read over the last weeks and had a fair notion of what she should expect to see. A real human ear, however, was quite different from the flat black-and-white page.

A little flurry of excitement rose in her stomach as she gently grasped Essie's small ear with her left hand to stretch the canal a bit, then inserted the narrow end of the tube. Even with the strong afternoon sunlight flooding through the window and illuminating the ear canal almost to the eardrum, Abigail wondered how she would know if there were anything behind the eardrum causing the child's pain.

Essie began to hiccup, and Abigail rubbed her back as she removed the otoscope. *Lord, I don't have a clue what's wrong. Please help me.*

The prayer had flitted through her mind without her conscious volition. She glanced at Winona, who was watching her anxiously. Winona believed in prayer as Abigail used to. A rusty gate creaked open in her heart. God had seemed to fade away during the months she'd been on that vile opium-bearing ship, then disappear altogether when she was living in abject poverty with Tess in the District. And she'd turned away from Him when Tess's baby had died.

God? She closed her eyes. *Are you there?*

Suddenly she had a vivid mental picture of watching Dr. Laniere demonstrate the otoscope in the hospital a couple of days ago. He'd peered inside an old man's ear, then taken another instrument from the case.

Abigail's eyes popped open. She hurried to open the cupboard again. "Look, Essie," she said with a smile, manipulating the long, flexible snakelike tube of a Siegel's otoscope. She showed the child the silver bell at one end and the small mouthpiece at the other. "Watch this." Putting the mouthpiece between her lips, she held the bell against Essie's neck and blew gently.

Essie giggled. "That tickles!"

Abigail smiled at Winona, who watched with approval. "I'm going to blow just a bit in your ear and see if you can feel it. Can you sit very still?"

Essie stared at her, brown eyes wide. "Yes, ma'am," she whispered.

"All right. Here we go." Abigail placed the bell into Essie's ear canal, peered into it and softly blew through the tube. The child jerked, but managed to stay quiet. Abigail realized, as she had suspected it might, that the membrane of the eardrum had remained rigid. Infection had packed mucus behind the ear, rendering it immobile.

Abigail removed the otoscope. "Does your ear feel stuffy? Like you've got cotton in your ears?"

The little girl nodded. "It hurts when I lay down."

"I'm sure it does." Abigail wiped off the earpiece with alcohol, then coiled the otoscope tube around her hand and tucked the instrument back into its space in the cupboard. "Have you had a cold?"

"Yes, ma'am. But it's better..."

"Well, your ear got swollen from the cold and trapped water inside your eardrum. That's why it feels all stopped up." She looked at Winona. "I know what the problem is, but there's not much to do about it. She needs to rest, drink lots of water, eat oranges."

Winona's brow wrinkled as she cupped her hands over Essie's ears. "She lives in a orphanage in the worst part of the city. Her mother died and her father is a stevedore at the docks, a former slave. He couldn't take care of her..."

For the first time Abigail noted the threadbare state of the little girl's rough-spun dress and the broken, too-small shoes. She frowned. "Clean water is a problem, then."

Winona nodded. "And fruit's out of the question. There's more'n thirty children in that orphanage." She pulled Essie close.

"With proper care she'd get well on her own." Abigail sighed. "All right then. Go to the market and find some witch hazel for the pain. If she can sleep with her head elevated, that will help. Tell the matron to do her best to keep her quiet until the stuffiness goes away. Within a week or so the fluid should have drained away."

Winona nodded and looked down at the child, who already seemed better for the attention. She was playing with the ribbons on Winona's skirt. "I knew you'd help."

"I haven't done anything," Abigail said helplessly. "I wish Dr. Laniere—"

"Hello! Anybody home?" The clinic's outer door slammed, rattling the windowpanes.

Winona smiled. "Lectures must be done for the day. We're in here, John," she called.

Abigail squelched an unexpected leap in her midsection when John stuck his handsome head into the clinic.

"Can a fellow get a chunk of bread and cheese?"

"As a matter of fact, we all can. Come along, Essie, let's feed the ravening hordes." Winona boosted her little charge off the table, took her by the hand and curtsyed to John on her way by. Essie dimpled and copied her.

John looked at Abigail. "Who was that?"

She avoided his eyes as she latched the cupboard doors. "A case of acute otitis media with effusion."

John's eyebrows rose. "And how do you know this?"

"The eardrum doesn't move. Don't worry," she added, "I didn't presume to prescribe anything but rest and elevated sleeping couch."

"I could look at her."

Abigail put her hands on her hips. "You could. But why upset her again? She's just stopped crying."

"And crying would increase the pressure and the pain." John stared at her for a moment. "All right. Come share a bite of cheese and I'll tell you about the surgery."

"Does your boarding house mistress not feed you?" She followed him into the kitchen.

"Her bread isn't nearly as fine as Winona's." He gave her a teasing grin. "And she's not nearly as pretty as you two." He flung himself onto one of the benches at the table and rubbed his eyes. "It's been a tedious afternoon. Stuck in an amphitheater with a lot of smelly fellows watching Prof sew some poor fellow's leg back together. He'd gotten it stuck in a cotton press and nearly mangled it to the bone."

Winona, slicing bread at the counter, looked over her shoulder. She looked pained. "John. Please."

"Oh, sorry." He laughed. "I knew Abigail the Ghoul here would want full details." He glanced at Abigail, hazel eyes twinkling. "I'll tell you later."

Abigail poured a cup of milk for Essie and sat down beside her. "I'd rather have been there. It's not the same secondhand." She stroked the child's thick braids and watched her gulp the milk. "Do you men ever go into the homes of the poor?"

John accepted a basket of bread and cheese from Winona with a smile of thanks. "As often as we can. But usually it's all we can do to care for the worst cases that come to us."

Abigail absently took a slice of the fragrant bread. "It seems you'd prevent some of those worst cases coming to be. If you could treat people early, I mean. Maybe even…" She glanced at John, who was munching contentedly, oblivious to Essie staring wide-eyed at his beautiful bottle-green coat. "Maybe you could teach principles of good health in those communities where disease spreads so quickly and easily."

"I've wondered that myself." John shrugged. "But it's not practical, Abigail. The doctors' energies are needed at the hospital. Besides, the nurses go into the parishes every day, with little accomplished. People live the way they want to live and they're skeptical about medical advances. You tell 'em sickness is caused by things you can't see and they look at you like you're crazy."

"But when they come to the hospital to see a doctor, don't they go along with whatever he says? That's why it's important for the medical community to be active in public health." Abigail leaned her elbows on the table. "People mistrust the nurses because they don't know any better. Education is—"

"I like the thought, Abigail." John looked uncomfortable. "But the professors are very busy. You've seen Prof's schedule." His eyes were intent on her face. At least he was taking her seriously.

Winona cleared her throat. "I'm going to take Essie back. It's my day off, remember. I'll be spending the night at home." She paused. "Abigail, would you like to come to church with me in the morning?"

Abigail blinked, jerking her gaze from John's. She'd nearly forgotten Winona and Essie's presence in the kitchen. "I suppose I could," she answered, rather at random. "Mercy! And I promised I'd start supper for Miss Camilla." She scrambled up from the bench. "Where should I meet you, Winona?"

Winona met her gaze with a knowing twinkle in her dark eyes. "I'll be at the corner of Philippa and Poydras at ten. If it's raining, wait under the balcony of the millinery shop." She backed out of the kitchen, tugging Essie along with her.

Abigail edged around to put the table between herself and John. She wasn't exactly afraid of him. It was herself she couldn't trust. She'd almost given in to kissing him yesterday. "I have to get supper started. Did you need something else?"

He sighed. "I suppose not. I wanted to talk to Prof about the surgery, but it can wait." He tipped his head. "So you're going to church in the morning?"

"Is that so odd?" Taking a pot off its hook over the stove, she set it in the sink and began to pump water into it.

He was silent for a moment. "I suppose you don't need an escort."

His tone was so odd that she looked over her shoulder. Their gazes held for a moment. Flustered, she shifted the pot and slopped water all down her front. "Oh my."

She looked down at herself. "I imagine you'd be quite out of place in Winona's church."

"And you wouldn't be?" He sounded amused.

"I'm invited." She didn't know where to look. "You'd best attend with your family. I'm sure they'd miss you."

"If I appeared for services at St. Domini's, my family would assume someone had died." His familiar sardonic expression appeared as he stood. "Never mind. Clearly my presence would make you and the lovely Winona just as uncomfortable as you seem to be now. I shall remove myself." He plopped his hat on his head and bowed. "Good day, Miss Neal."

The door shut gently behind him and Abigail fought the urge to call him back. He was gone and she was glad. What had possessed him to ask if she needed an escort? It was almost as if he wanted to come to Winona's church—but no, that wouldn't be like him at all. Still, she couldn't help imagining what it would be like to attend services in the company of a man like John Braddock.

Chapter Twelve

A damp chill enclosed in a messy fog drifted from the river to blanket the tumbledown buildings and twine around Abigail and Winona's ankles as they crossed Poydras Street the next morning. Abigail wished she'd brought a wrap. But that would presuppose she *had* one, which she didn't. Perhaps she could save a bit of what Camilla paid her in next week's wages and make something serviceable for the mild New Orleans winter—a cloak or even a shawl. The cold weather would come in fits and starts, then be gone by March. But when one needed a wrap, one needed a wrap.

She looked around. Nothing in the District had changed, of course. Same hovels with uncovered windows and broken doors, same pitted road, same reek of garbage in the gutters. Barely a week since she'd moved in with the Laniere family and already her life was so drastically different she hardly recognized herself. She'd gotten used to cleanliness and order, the fresh scents of baking bread, antiseptic and lye. As she walked along beside Winona, hugging herself, dodging mangy dogs and vacant-eyed beggars, she held her breath against the almost palpable odor of corrosion and fear.

She couldn't help thinking of the families who had been evicted from the burned tenement, particularly the man whose wife and baby had gone missing. They had never been found. *Oh, Lord, where are you when I come back here? Have you abandoned these people?*

She glanced at Winona, whose curly dark hair was twisted in a knot at the back of her head, the ends of a sober brown shawl blowing around her shoulders as she walked. Dressed in a brown-spotted cotton dress, a bit faded with washing but otherwise neat, Winona managed to look fresh and content with her circumstances. Well, and why not? Like Abigail, she had somehow escaped the clutches of the District, to hold a position with a prominent family who treated her with respect and paid her an adequate wage.

Abigail's thoughts leaped helplessly back to Friday afternoon in the library. After John had walked her home, maintaining an amused silence that set her teeth on edge, he'd bid her adieu in the clinic anteroom and sauntered into the kitchen to talk to Winona. Abigail had rushed up the stairs. Pausing at the landing, she'd listened shamelessly, but John and Winona's conversation was serious, their voices low and intense. An unexpected discomfort made Abigail hurry on to her room. She was *not* jealous. Positively not.

But why must her thoughts continually circle back to a pair of laughing hazel eyes?

To escape her circling thoughts she touched Winona's arm. "Have you lived here all your life?"

Winona glanced at her and smiled. "Since I was

small. My parents were slaves over in Mississippi. We escaped here after the Union took New Orleans."

"Oh my." During the American war between the states, Abigail's family had been in China, insulated from the conflict that tore apart her place of birth. In the short time since she'd returned, she found herself jarred again and again by the ramifications of the recent struggle.

Winona sighed. "Freedom's a blessing. But you know the lives of our people—it's far from easy." Her gesture took in the buildings jockeying for place along the street, the levee at its end, which held the Mississippi River at bay. "From day to day you never know if education is gonna be extended or withheld, what jobs will be available, whether housing and property will be taken without warning…" She looked down, lifting her skirts as she stepped over a pile of refuse in the bumpy, muddy street.

"Yet you seem to be content." Abigail couldn't put her finger on the source, but it was more than happiness. It was a sort of bone-deep assurance she was loved and protected. Abigail longed to possess that sort of peace, but had no idea how to pursue it.

"The Bible says to 'count it all joy when you encounter various trials and the testing of your faith.'" Winona's smile was inward. "My family's always full of joy."

Abigail hesitated. "I've had trials, too, but I don't know that they make me happy. In fact, I rather resent them."

Winona's eyes smiled. "That's natural, unless you understand the trials are making you stronger, increasing your faith, making you more like the Master."

"Do you really believe that?" Knowing the answer, Abigail hurried on. "My father wanted to preach the gospel to the heathen, so he took me and my mother into some awful places. Strange places where we were looked upon as outsiders. Always outsiders." She'd never told another person about it and didn't feel any better to air it. If anything, her chest burned with deeper bitterness.

Winona flicked a thoughtful look at Abigail. "I also knew about being an outsider."

Shame washed over Abigail. Maybe she *had* been a tall, gawky, light-haired stranger in an Asian nation full of tiny black-haired people, but at least she had never been enslaved. "I'm sorry—"

"No, no." Winona laid a gentle hand on Abigail's arm. "I only meant I understand. But, Abigail, any of us who follow Christ gonna be outsiders in this world. Because the world wants to go its own way. And the world can't understand what only spiritual eyes can see—that we're loved by God in an all encompassing way. And He wants to love others through us with the overflow of that love, so they'll be more likely to see Him."

Abigail walked a few more paces, hardly aware of the overcast sky, the fog blanketing tin-roofed shanties with half-rotten porches on either side of the road. A window seemed to have opened inside her—a window through which light poured on the paucity of her faith. How could a woman who had grown up in a missionary compound have managed to escape the glowing truth in the words of a former slave?

"Will I find it?" She fumbled over the words. "That love…in your church today?"

"For certain. But now's a good time, too. God listens to your heart all the time."

Perhaps He *had* been listening all along—all the way from China, through the poverty of the District and into the relative comfort of life in Professor Laniere's clinic. Maybe if she continued to seek Him He would lead her into her heart's desire.

A chance to study medicine, a chance to practice her gift of healing.

Maybe God would heal *her.*

By the time John, Weichmann and Marcus exited the High Hat saloon, the morning fog had burned off, leaving a bright winter day in its wake. As they crossed the street toward yet another drinking establishment, John exchanged disgusted glances with Weichmann. High noon on a Sunday morning and already Marcus was three sheets to the wind.

John himself couldn't bring himself to drink his beer, which had sat at his elbow while they played cards and listened to the singing drift from the churches in the Quarter and the Treme neighborhood nearby. He wasn't sure why he'd agreed to come. Funny how his taste for alcohol had dried up since that conversation with Prof. And without the haze of liquor clouding his mind, he found little enjoyment in Marcus's ribald jokes nor the suggestive conversation of the easy women who frequented the bars. Instead he and Weichmann wound up discussing Friday's surgery.

Now the three of them marched along the side of the street, John and Weichmann bracing Marcus on either side to keep him from lurching into the gutter.

"The yeller-haired one wanted me to come home wi' 'er, I swear." Marcus hiccupped.

John steadied him. "And you'd've come home with the pox, so it's a good thing you ran out of money."

"Well, but what're we goin'a do the rest of the day?" Marcus gave John a belligerent look. "Jus' because it's Sunday, nuffin' goin' on our side of town. Boringest day of the week."

Weichmann leaned around Marcus to speak to John. "Hey, that looks like your Amazon."

John followed Weichmann's gaze to a tall figure in a dark blue dress disappearing around the side of a blacksmith shop on the next corner. "She's not my Amazon," he said automatically but dropped Marcus's arm and hurried after Abigail. He rounded the corner just in time to see her enter the front door of a barnlike two-story building on the other side of the blacksmith.

He stopped, frowning. What was she doing in a colored orphanage?

"Braddock, what's got into you?" demanded Marcus from behind him.

John turned to Weichmann, who was supporting the weight of Marcus's shoulder against his arm. "She went in the orphanage. Want to come along?"

Weichmann moved away and looked around with a grin when Marcus sat abruptly in a mud puddle. "Good thing you're so close to the ground, old man." He caught up to John in two long strides, paying no attention to Marcus's yelps of indignation. "What do you suppose she's up to?"

"No idea. But I'm going to find out."

The orphanage yard was a weedy, soupy mess that

ruined his boots before he got to the door. The odor of rotting vegetation was indescribable, even to a man who had exhumed and preserved bodies for dissection. He tugged his handkerchief from his pocket to cover his nose and knocked on the door.

It was yanked open by a young girl dressed in the same rough brown fabric as the child Winona had had in the clinic yesterday. This one was older, perhaps twelve, her wiry hair braided neatly and coiled around her head. She looked up at John with huge near-black eyes.

Because she appeared to be dumbstruck, John lowered the handkerchief and smiled at her. "Good afternoon. I'm looking for Miss Neal."

"She's back in the baby room," the girl whispered and stood back for John to enter. "With Miss Winona and Mammy."

He looked around to make sure Weichmann followed and found an expression of extreme discomfort on his friend's thin features. "Buck up, Weichmann." John stepped into the dark interior of the orphanage. "We've seen worse."

"I doubt we've smelled worse," muttered Weichmann. But he followed John inside, closing the front door behind him.

John stopped, appalled. He'd seen some bad places, including tenements like the one in which Abigail and Tess had lived. But that had been a palace compared to this: scrubbed wooden floor with gaps so wide he could see the mud beneath, oiled paper windows, crumbling brick walls covered here and there with sailcloth. There was not a stick of furniture in the place except for a few crates upon which fifteen or twenty children of various sizes, genders, and shades of brown sat playing with bits of wood and metal, apparently scavenged from the docks.

John could hear babies crying through a closed door at the back of the room. He looked around at Weichmann, who stood near the front door, arms folded, lower lip between his teeth.

Weichmann shrugged and came off the door. "I didn't know this was here, did you?"

"No. Come on, Weichmann." Something had shifted in John, something irrevocable as a broken levee. While the girl who had let them in squatted to tend to a weeping toddler, John strode through the children, who looked up at him with wide, curious eyes. He lifted the latch of the interior door and it swung open with a loud creak of rusty hinges. "Abigail?"

She was sitting in a straight-backed chair facing the door with a colored infant in her arms. Winona sat on a crate nearby, holding two more in her lap, and a black woman leaned over a rickety crib in which four or five babies were tumbled together like a litter of puppies.

Abigail looked up at him, lips parted and eyes wide. "What are you doing here?"

"Following you." He stepped aside to admit Weichmann. "We saw you round the corner—"

"I told you not to—"

"We didn't come for church."

Winona laughed. "You boys out hunting up trouble on Sunday morning?"

"Who has to hunt?" John glanced at the babies gnawing on their fists in her lap. "Are they sick?"

Abigail jiggled the wailing infant. "We just got here. Did you speak to Essie on the way by?"

"Who? Oh, the little girl from yesterday. Is this where she came from?"

Winona nodded. "I suppose you should meet the matron, Mammy Jonas. Mammy, this is John Braddock, one of the students from the medical college."

Mammy, a thin, sharp-faced Creole woman, lifted one of the babies out of the crib and looked John up and down. "You the one took our cow and left her tied to the flagpole at the courthouse?"

That had been Marcus, and John had tried to talk him out of it, but explanation would be pointless. "No, ma'am," he said, mustering all the humility at his disposal.

"Humph." Mammy dismissed him with a regal turn of her head. "Young men ought to have better things to do."

John nodded absently as he walked to the crib. "Where'd these babies come from?"

"You've had advanced anatomy and you have to ask that?"

John shot Abigail a look. "You know what I mean." He leaned over to lay the back of his fingers against the cheek of one sleeping infant. "There are so many of them."

"They mamas left 'em to go wet nurse rich white mamas' babies." Mammy's voice shook. "They make good money and leave a bit in the church poor box— which we get some of."

John stared at Abigail in horror. Wet nursing was a common enough practice, but he'd never considered the implications for these abandoned babies. If anything, he'd assumed the nursing mothers had lost their infants to death. "Is this true?"

Abigail bowed her head, tracing the beautiful black wing of the baby's eyebrows with her finger.

"The practice has to be stopped." John said. "Wealthy women ought to be able to nurse their own babies."

"Of course they can. But they'd rather shop and take tea and drive around the Commons."

John could hardly blame Abigail for her cynical tone. His own mother and sister were at this moment driving home from church in a tooled leather carriage, dressed in fine cotton gauze, satin ribbons and Mechlin. They would have passed this orphanage without a second glance.

"Do they have enough to eat?" The one lying on his back with his thumb in his mouth looked wiry and tough, but there was a rattle to his breathing that John didn't like.

"Once we got our cow back," Mammy said with an undertone of humor.

"I'll get you another one." Weichmann's sudden deep voice startled them all. He plucked one of the babies out of Winona's lap and laid him against his shoulder, eliciting a loud burp. Laughter leavened the tension in the room.

John had no idea where Weichmann would get a milk cow, but had no doubt he'd manage somehow.

By mid-afternoon John and Weichmann, assisted by Mammy, Abigail and Winona, had examined every child in the orphanage, diagnosing two cases of pleurisy, a cleft palate—which John thought could be improved

with surgery—and rampant disorders of the lower in-
testines. He wanted to bring the little fellow with rattling breathing to the hospital for further examination.

On the way back to the Lanieres' the four of them
discussed the problem. "If it's pneumonia and we don't
treat it, he'll die," John argued.

Weichmann shook his head. "The nurses don't like
contagious cases brought in."

"There's got to be a place to take them," Abigail said.
"Those children deserve professional care." She looked
at Winona. "I know Mammy's doing the best she can,
but proper nutrition and hygiene would make all the
difference."

"If my mother could just see…" John muttered. "She
could make a difference." He stopped and grabbed Abigail's wrist. "That's it. We'll make her see."

"How are you going to do that?"

He looked around. Weichmann and Winona had
walked on, leaving John and Abigail behind. "My
mother is throwing a party to introduce my sister to
society. You remember, my father mentioned it. I want
you to come."

Her gaze flew to his. "You can't be serious. I'm no
society deb, John. I'd be completely out of place. I have
no pretty dresses—"

He cut her off with a slice of his hand. "I'm sure Camilla will find you something appropriate. You always
look neat."

She gave him a fulminating look. "Neat is one thing.
Evening dresses are quite another. Do you have any idea
how much silk costs?"

"Of course I know what silk costs." He waved away

the objection. "I've a bit left of my last quarter's allowance. I'll buy you a dress."

"You cannot!" she gasped. "Even I know a lady doesn't allow a man to buy her garments unless they are wed." To his astonishment, tears sprang to her eyes. "You're trying to shame me."

"And you're being unreasonable. You need a dress and I can help you get it. What's wrong with that? Nobody has to know. Abigail, please. I want you there. I..." He swallowed. Somehow the conversation had shifted from sick children to something more personal. "I need you there."

She stared at him. "What possible difference could my presence make at some family dinner party—or whatever it is."

"Dinner, drinks, dancing. You might actually enjoy it."

She turned her head, deliberately, though he could tell she was weakening. "John, I don't even know how to dance. I'd be humiliated."

He leaned close to her ear. "I'll teach you. I'm a good teacher, remember?"

She swayed toward him, then stiffened. "No. You've got some selfish motive behind this and I'm not falling for it. Ask someone else."

He sighed. "All right. I'll come clean." He slid his hands down to cup her elbows. She stared at the top button of his waistcoat. "It's not just the children. My mother has a girl picked out for me to court. She'll be there and I don't want to get stuck with her before I have a chance to look her over. I need you for a sort of...buffer."

Abigail's mouth dropped open. Then she began to laugh. "You're absolutely mad! Nobody in their right mind would take me as a rival for some finishing school debutante. Your mother will throw me out of the house the instant she lays eyes on me."

John's eyes kindled. "She most certainly will not. As my guest you'll be afforded all proper respect. Besides, my father already invited you."

"John, I could come in with a fistful of invitations and nobody's going to take me for anything but what I am—a misfit clinic attendant from the District."

He stared at her for a moment, his lips clipped together. "If you won't take my word for it, would you believe Camilla?"

Abigail shrugged. "Camilla has more common sense than you. She'll agree with me."

John grinned and leaned down to give Abigail a loud kiss on the forehead. "We'll see about that."

Chapter Thirteen

With a creak of leather and springs, the Laniere carriage stopped in front of the Braddock mansion on Chestnut Street. Abigail waited for Camilla to move, not sure what manners dictated in these circumstances. She had never in her life been delivered to the door of a mansion via any method but her own two feet. Even the dinner with the emperor had required no transportation, as she and her father had been housed within the palace.

Before she could do more than glance at Camilla, however, the carriage door was jerked open from the outside, and the Lanieres' man-of-all-jobs slid the steps in place.

"Go ahead, Abigail," said Camilla kindly. "I'll be right behind you."

Abigail took Willie's gloved hand and stepped down. As she waited for Camilla and the professor to alight, she smoothed a hand down the side of her dress. It was the most beautiful garment she had ever owned. Made of jade shantung silk and trimmed with pale green banding, it hugged her waist and hips, bunched in a smooth bustle in the back and fell in graceful folds to her dainty slippers. The Vandyke bodice was modest, its lace jabot tickling her chin, but the design accentuated the curves of her figure. Camilla had assured her it was appropriate for a formal occasion, so Abigail had to take her word for it.

Smiling, Professor Laniere was offering an arm each to Camilla and Abigail. "Ladies?"

Abigail slipped her hand in the crook of his elbow and looked up at the lights blazing from the enormous three-story brick house. The second level was ringed by a wrought iron balcony in the French style, supported by four tall, white columns. At least eight windows opened on each level, spilling gaslight halfway down the street.

Abigail wanted to stop and simply stare, but she meekly followed her hosts up the flaring front steps. Somehow John had managed to have her included in the invitation delivered to the Lanieres' front door by post a week ago. She'd tried to demur, but Camilla was a force to be reckoned with. Insisting on providing Abigail with a new dress, she'd accompanied her to the shops for silk, thread and trimmings. Then she provided slippers and a fan and the most luxurious silk-lined cloak.

The cloak was so soft and warm, Abigail was loath to part with it when the Braddocks' funny, Cockney-voiced butler tried to take it. Recollecting herself in the reflection of Camilla's amused eyes, she relaxed and let Appleton, as he called himself, bear it off in triumph along with the other guests' outer garments.

And then she was following the Lanieres into a ballroom dazzling with lights and music and laughter. She hung back, overwhelmed. She was going to embarrass her hosts, humiliate herself, say something in Chinese or Latin, spill something on that polished marble floor.

She'd actually picked up her skirts and turned to run when John stepped in front of her.

"Where are you going?" His eyes were bright, amused.

She'd barely seen him since the encounter in the orphanage nearly two weeks ago. And never had she seen him so elegantly and formally dressed in white shirt and stock, pristine against black dinner jacket and trousers. His hair was arranged to fall into his left eye, his side whiskers neatly trimmed to accent the strong jaw and humorous mouth. He belonged here in this beautiful home, with all these beautiful, glittering people.

"I'm going home." She tried to step around him.

He blocked her again. "Abigail, you can't cross the city by yourself at night."

"I'll take the streetcar. Let me pass." Panic surged through her stomach.

His smile faded. "It's not like you to run away. I want to introduce you to my parents." John stepped closer and took her gloved hand, letting his eyes caress her face. "You look lovely tonight. I want to dance with you."

"John!" came a sweet feminine voice behind Abigail. "There you are. Dorothée is asking for you."

"Lisette." He looked over Abigail's shoulder with a smile. "Come here and meet Miss Neal."

Abigail snatched her hand away and clutched her fan so hard she heard it crack. She turned and found a diminutive dark-haired young lady staring up at her with huge, myopic brown eyes.

"Oh! You're so very tall!" exclaimed Lisette Braddock. "I mean—How do you do?" She dropped a blushing curtsy.

"Miss Braddock," Abigail murmured, surveying the girl's sunny yellow gown, which displayed a thin, childish figure. Lisette couldn't be more than eighteen.

Lisette dimpled. "Please excuse my staring. I'm nearsighted, and Mama insists I may not wear my spectacles during a formal occasion. Isn't that silly?"

Abigail relaxed, charmed by her young hostess's ingenuous chatter. "I'll defer to your mama." She glanced at John. "Perhaps, because you're wanted elsewhere, your sister will consent to make the introductions to your parents."

Lisette beamed. "I'd be happy to—"

"That won't be necessary. I'm sure Miss Molyneux will find her dance card quite full without my monopolizing her time." John offered his arm to Lisette and took Abigail firmly by the elbow. "You're not getting away from me that easily," he murmured into her ear. "Speaking of dance cards," he said more loudly, "where is yours, Miss Neal?"

"I don't have—"

"Oh, I have an extra!" Lisette fumbled in a tiny beaded bag dangling from her wrist and produced a small square of cardboard connected to an equally wee pencil stub. She handed it to Abigail. "Be sure to make John—"

"Thank you, Lise," he said affectionately, "but I'm capable of contracting my own engagements." He commandeered the dance card, wrote Abigail's name at the top and scrawled his name on it three times. "There." He handed it to Abigail. "Now you can't run away."

"Run away?" Lisette looked bewildered. "Why would she run away?"

"Your brother is teasing us both." Abigail sighed. She would have to make the best of this awkward situation and use it to help the women of the District. She smiled down at John's sister. "Miss Braddock, I understand you've an interest in philanthropy."

Lisette looked uncertainly at her brother, who didn't even try to hide the twinkle in his eyes. She put up her small, pointed chin and smiled at Abigail. "Yes, of course I do."

Abigail ignored John's chuckle. "Then might I share with you a need that your brother and I have encountered in a neighborhood not far from here? There is much good that could be done with just a little effort." She linked arms with her young hostess, and the two of them began to stroll toward the stairs, which presumably led down to the ballroom on the ground floor.

As they walked, John accompanied them, mercifully containing his part in the conversation to murmurs of agreement as Abigail explained the need for education in maternity and nutrition in the poor areas of the city. Lisette was a quick study, her hero worship for her big brother patent, and plied Abigail with intelligent questions. By the time they had reached the head of the stairs, where a middle-aged couple stood receiving guests, Lisette and Abigail were in perfect charity.

Lisette eagerly tugged Abigail toward her mother, a brown-haired woman in dark blue satin, who had Lisette's fragility and John's fine good looks. Her husband Abigail had already met, of course. His evening clothes did little to hide the air of ruthlessness that hung about him like the cloud of smoke emanating from the cigar between his fingers.

"Mama!" Lisette rushed to take her mother's elbow. "You must meet John's Miss Neal. She has quite opened my eyes to a way we can help our neighbors. She's the one staying with the Lanieres, and she's from—" She turned to Abigail, confusion in her nearsighted eyes. "Oh dear, I forgot to ask where you came from!"

"Lisette," Mrs. Braddock sighed, clearly exasperated by her daughter's social ineptitudes. "*Try* for a little decorum." She smiled vaguely at Abigail. "Welcome to our home, Miss Neal. I hope you will find our little party invigorating. This is my husband—"

"Miss Neal and I are already acquainted, my dear," said Phillip Braddock heartily. "She was helping John and the other fellows haul bodies out of the tenement that burned in the District a couple of weeks ago. Wasn't that enterprising of her?"

Lips parted, Mrs. Braddock gave Abigail a blank stare. "Er—quite. John, I don't believe you mentioned that to me."

Wishing she could sink through the floor, Abigail felt the muscles of John's forearm cord under her hand.

His face remained bland, however, as he laid his hand on top of hers. "Miss Neal is one of the most heroic women I've ever met, Mother. Capable of saving lives—a much more useful talent than ruining reputations, wouldn't you say?"

"I—" Eliza Braddock helplessly looked at her husband.

He executed a brief bow, as if in touché, toward his son. "It appears our guests have all arrived, so if you'll excuse me, I'll speak to the orchestra director and start the dancing."

He was gone, leaving Abigail to stare at the floor while John gave his mother more unwanted details about the aftermath of the fire. Lisette, however, seemed enthralled with the story, gasping at appropriate intervals.

"I could never be so brave," she said, looking at Abigail with wide, admiring eyes. "I'm afraid the closest I've come to such adventure is in the pages of a book. Did you read *Uncle Tom's Cabin,* Miss Neal? I found it *most* instructive."

"Indeed, I did," Abigail said. "My father had it in a shipment of books from—" She paused, noting too late the frost in John's mother's eyes. Mrs. Stowe's antislavery novel would not be a popular title with the Southern gentry. "That is, I lost my copy some time ago. Oh! I hear the music. What fine string players..."

"Indeed, they are." John gestured toward the staircase where the strains of a waltz drifted from the ballroom. "And I believe this is our dance, Miss Neal."

"Is it?" She glanced at the little dance card, blind with embarrassment.

"It is. Mother, if you'll excuse us?"

Abigail found herself stumbling down the stairs beside him, hardly aware of her surroundings except for the fine texture of John's sleeve and the strength of his arm beneath her fingers. She didn't belong here and she was a fool to have agreed to come.

They descended into a glittering gaslit room—one wall lined with mirrors, two painted with a spectacular garden mural and the fourth a bank of French windows opening onto a well-lit brick terrace. As she and John twirled round the room Abigail felt as if she were in the center of a floral kaleidoscope, the dresses of the women like colorful stained-glass petals against the reflected greenery of the walls.

She hung on to John, staring up into his unsmiling face, feeling one of his gloved hands at her waist, the other clasped around hers. They had explored death together. This mindless shuffling of feet should not have been so exalting. But she found herself moved to the point of tears by the burn of his eyes on her face. His fingers gathered hers closer, threading through hers, palm to palm. And then his lips curved, a lazy droop to his eyes.

Oh, he knew what he was doing to her.

She stiffened, jerked her gaze to his shoulder. "Stop it," she whispered.

"Stop what?" His voice was slow, amused.

"I don't know what you want from me, but you don't have to look at me that way."

"Abigail. You're a beautiful woman. How else am I supposed to look at you?"

"Is this a show for Dorothée or whatever her name is?"

He chuckled. "It'll give my mother something to think about. Quit jerking at my hand. You're ruining the rhythm. *One* two three—Which reminds me. You told me you didn't know how to dance."

"I'm a fast learner." Trembling in the circle of his arms, she turned her head away, terrified that she might have revealed her feelings. And how had this happened, anyway? How could she have any sort of affection for a man she so mistrusted? A man who was so different from her in every way? He might *say* she was beautiful, he might pretend to look at her with that tender, amused gleam in his eyes, but why on earth would a man like *him* want *her*—tall, desperately gauche, without any sort of financial or social recommendation?

"Indeed, you are," John said quietly. "In fact, I think you could learn anything you set your mind to."

She looked up at him, mutinously silent. He wanted her to bat her lashes, simper, fall at his feet in adoration. This she could not afford to do. The hard-won measure of respectability she had regained was too fragile to withstand the kind of dalliance he clearly had in mind.

He chuckled, snatched her close for a breathtaking moment, then whirled her to a halt next to several young matrons. He bowed to Camilla Laniere. "Mrs. Laniere, I return your protégée healthy and whole."

Camilla tucked her arm through Abigail's. "My dear, are you having a good time? John, you must procure a glass of lemonade for Miss Neal. She's looking quite flushed."

"I'll be happy to." He bowed again, turned and disappeared into the crowd.

Abigail flipped open the fan she'd borrowed from Camilla for the evening. "I'm having a lovely time. It's just the heat…" She plied the fan vigorously.

Camilla laughed. "Indeed. I remember it well."

Abigail gave her a doubtful look, but judging by Camilla's sly expression, pursuing her cryptic remark would not be wise. "Your husband said there was a gentleman he wanted me to meet."

"Yes, I believe he—oh, there he comes with Dr. Girard—and Drs. Pitcock and Cannon and—Gabriel, what on earth is going on?" she demanded as her husband approached at the head of a line of well-dressed gentlemen. "You aren't planning to talk shop at Eliza's party?"

Dr. Laniere smiled and tucked his arm around his wife, a quite unfashionable public sign of affection. "Only for half an hour, my dear. If one invites a bunch of physicians to the same event, a certain amount of medical conversation is inevitable."

Camilla raised her brows. "You might have given us some warning that you planned to descend on us all at once," she teased. She caught Abigail's alarmed gaze. "Miss Neal, I beg leave to present the faculty of the medical college en masse—well, as near all as makes no matter. Here is Dr. Girard, professor of chemistry and clinical medicine. You've met his son, I believe." She nodded at a bald, roosterlike man, who bore a striking resemblance to Marcus.

Abigail dipped a curtsy. "Sir." His skeptical look made her wonder what wild tales Marcus had told his father about her.

"And this," Camilla continued, "is Dr. Lewis, professor of obstetrics."

The jowly gray-haired gentleman gave her a grumpy scowl and shouted, "How'd'ye do!"

Remembering Winona's characterization of the elderly doctor as a lion, Abigail smiled but didn't try to penetrate his obvious deafness with a reply.

Camilla nodded at a suave middle-aged man who surveyed Abigail with blatant curiosity. "Dr. Pitcock is professor of physiology and pathological anatomy."

"The rumors of the autopsy cannot be true," he murmured to Dr. Laniere.

"Wait and see," Dr. Laniere replied and smiled at Abigail. "One more in the lineup, Miss Neal. Dr. Cannon is our retiring professor of anatomy and clinical surgery. We've worn him out over the last twenty-five years, poor fellow."

Abigail's gaze went to a thin, wispy old gentleman notable for a pair of thick-lensed spectacles perched on a beak of a nose. Of the four doctor-professors, he was the only one who bowed to her as if she were as much a lady as Camilla Laniere. "Miss Neal, I look forward to discovering what has triggered your interest in the medical sciences."

She looked at Dr. Laniere in alarm. "But—is my interest general knowledge, sir?"

"No, no, my dear—only among us professors. I would never have your name bandied about in the general community." He sent a cautioning look at Dr. Cannon. "But I confess we're all fascinated by the idea of a female of such exceptional talent in a field previously reserved for the male sex. In fact—" he glanced at his wife "—I would be interested to see what would happen if your wits were pitted against those of some of our best students."

Abigail's lips parted. "You cannot be serious." She looked around the ring of teachers staring at her as if she were a specimen under a microscope.

Dr. Pitcock sniffed. "Women are entirely too weak-minded to compete with men in the scientific fields, Laniere. You're wasting our time."

Adjusting his glasses, Dr. Cannon leaned toward Abigail to peer into her ear. "She's very tall, but I confess I was expecting a larger head—if she were truly as bright as you say."

Caught completely off guard, Abigail laughed. "Why would the head of an intelligent woman be larger than a man's?"

"Never mind that," growled Dr. Girard. "Is it true you're fluent in Greek, Latin and Mandarin Chinese? What happened to ladylike languages like French and Italian?"

Dr. Laniere coughed. "Er, perhaps we should dispense with personal remarks and see if Miss Neal might be willing to stand for a few questions. I believe you gentlemen will find her quite well-spoken."

"I want to ask the girl some questions!" roared Dr. Lewis.

"Good idea," Cannon shouted into his ear.

Unfortunately, at that very moment the music halted, along with the conversation, and every guest in the vicinity turned to find the source of the commotion.

Abigail wanted to be allowed to quietly study medicine and she had begun to dream of one day holding a license to practice. Finding herself the center of a gawking crowd, however, was her idea of a nightmare. Her old instinct to run kicked in.

Then she happened to see John Braddock, standing just behind Dr. Laniere's shoulder, a glass of lemonade in each hand. His expression was frankly horrified, as if a pet bear had suddenly got loose.

His patent disapproval sent a steel rod up her spine. "I'll be happy to answer your questions," she said clearly. "I studied Latin and Greek with my father because the sciences were originally documented in those languages, and I was frankly interested. I learned Mandarin out of necessity." She paused, flicking a glance at Camilla for courage. "What else, professors?"

"You *used* me to get yourself into the school!" John shoved one of the glasses of lemonade at Abigail and dragged her behind a potted palm.

"Don't be ridiculous. How could I have possibly imagined they'd ever consider admitting a female?" She waved her hands, sloshing lemonade all over his mother's ballroom floor.

"You—you stood there and answered questions as cool as a cucumber!"

"What did you imagine I would do? Go up in hysterical flames?"

He almost wished she had. As she'd defended herself quite competently, he had experienced a revolting mixture of worry, embarrassment and suicidal pride in her utter self-possession under attack. And he hadn't been able to do a thing about it. She hadn't even needed his lemonade.

Now she seemed likely to pitch the contents of the glass in his face. To his surprise, she instead tipped it up and drained it in one long gulp. "Thank you," she said tight-lipped.

"You're welcome," he said coldly. "Do you think anything but disaster is going to come of the spectacle you made of yourself? And of me?"

"I was under the impression that you care very little what anyone else thinks, particularly your father. And what my behavior could possibly have to do with you, I fail to see."

"Everyone saw us dancing. Now they'll think—"

She uttered a short, hard laugh. "No one will suppose you anything but a benevolent host to the crazy woman who thinks she can compete intellectually with men. How Professor Laniere could do that to me in public—" She looked away, her throat working.

"Don't you see? He did it in public so that your abilities cannot be denied. Everyone saw you answer every question—brilliantly, I might add. You made Professor Pitcock look like a moron."

"Which will in no way endear me to him," she muttered.

"It doesn't matter. Now they'll be bound and determined to put you in there and prove you can't survive."

She looked at him, her green eyes burning with something that might have been rage, might have been humiliation, but was in no way tame or feminine. "And where do you stand on the issue, John? If Professor Laniere sponsors my application, do you think I can survive?"

He wanted to shout *yes!* He wanted to assure her again that she could do whatever she put her mind to. But the truth was, he was afraid for her. If she entered medical school, her reputation as a lady was gone and she would be forever lost to him.

Four bars of a minuet lilted before he shrugged. "I don't know."

For half a moment her eyes shone brilliant with unshed tears. Then she blinked and straightened her shoulders. "Well. Ultimately it doesn't matter what you think. Professor Laniere says I can do it. And he's willing to talk the others around." A hard smile pulled at her lush mouth. "Which will make me a rival for that first spot you want so badly. So you'd better learn to study, John Braddock."

Chapter Fourteen

In the quiet darkness of the enclosed carriage, Abigail huddled inside her cloak opposite Camilla, who was asleep on her husband's shoulder.

"I shouldn't keep her out so late." The professor tenderly adjusted the hood of Camilla's cloak. "The children wear her out, plus running the house and clinic... It's been good to have you for an extra pair of hands, Abigail. Winona's going to miss your help."

Abigail, who had been drowsing, head jarring against the seat's leather squabs, jerked awake. "Sir? Are you throwing me out?"

The professor chuckled. "Not at all. But when you start regular lectures and rounds you won't have time for tending babies and peeling potatoes and doing laundry. That's why you're the perfect candidate for our little experiment. No husband, no family, no other responsibilities."

"No money," she added drily and laughed with him. "I'm not naive enough to suppose the tickets to the lectures and matriculation fees come free. How can I expect the professors to teach me at no cost?"

"Hmm. That is a most excellent question." The professor's voice was smooth and quiet, but a hint of something else prickled the nerve cells along Abigail's neck. "I do have a proposition that I think might solve your dilemma…and be of some service to me at the same time."

Abigail's stomach clenched. The evening's social confrontations had worn her to the bone, rubbing all her defenses on the raw. As she tried to imagine what else would be expected of her, her mind leaped from one terrifying possibility to the next. The things she had seen in Shanghai…

But surely Dr. Laniere was the moral, upright gentleman he seemed to be. He had never said or done anything untoward; in fact, he had treated her with the utmost respect and kindness.

"What is it, sir?" she forced herself to ask. "I can't think of anything I'm qualified to do, other than the housework you've already said will be out of the question."

"No need to sound so terrified, my dear." The professor sounded amused. "Having observed your gift of observation and memory, I merely ask you to apply it in a more specific sense. However, before I divulge anything else, I require your promise to keep this conversation between the two of us."

Abigail hesitated. "Is Camilla aware of this…assignment?"

"She knows some, but not all. You are free to talk to her at any time, of course, but I should prefer that you come to me first."

The fact that the professor had not excluded his wife was reassuring. Abigail took a deep breath. "All right, then," she said recklessly. "I'll give you my promise of secrecy. And I'll help you with anything that is within the bounds of the law."

"Good." The professor nodded and settled back. "Then I should first explain a bit of my background. I don't make a practice of airing this information in our circle of acquaintance, but during the war between the states I served as an intelligence operative for Union naval forces."

"Did you, sir?" Abigail's political leanings were decidedly ambiguous due to her foreign rearing. She considered herself an American mainly because she had been born of American parents. "How very enterprising of you."

She could hear the smile in his voice. "Enterprising? Perhaps, though convincing my Southern-born bride to elope during the height of the conflict turned out to be a bit tricky. At all events, you can understand why I find it difficult to say no to serving my country when asked."

Abigail considered that. "I think I can. I still don't understand what this has to do with me."

"I'm getting there. My investigative duties after the war shifted back into the field of medicine, which, after all, was my first love. By then Camilla and I had married and started our family, so I needed a more stable and less dangerous way to earn a living. Research and teaching became my focus. But those of us on the forefront of the public health arena are increasingly convinced that regulation of licensing and control of addictive substances, at least at the state level, could be beneficial to the country as a whole. Our governor in particular is concerned about the unrestricted spread of opium use across the Deep South." He paused. "I have heard you discuss the issue with John Braddock on more than one occasion."

"We've disagreed on morphine's efficacy in pain control." She hesitated, unwilling to sound defensive, particularly with this learned and demonstrably broad-minded doctor. "American and European physicians are quite disparaging about Chinese acupuncture and herbology."

"We tend to discount what we do not understand," he agreed quietly. "Personally, I believe morphine and other opiates can be used safely and effectively when under the control of trained medical professionals. However, what concerns me is the widespread recreational misuse of these drugs."

Suddenly and quite unexpectedly Abigail was caught in knife-edged flashes of memory. She fought for breath, stuffing the shards away. "I…share your concern, sir."

After a moment, Dr. Laniere cleared his throat. "Would you care to share your story?"

"I cannot." She swallowed. "At least not now. Just… tell me what I can do. I can't imagine—"

"We think opium is being smuggled in through someone at the hospital, probably a student who needs the income to pay tuition. There are several in arrears and I've had my eye on them all, but so far have not been able to get close enough to obtain the information I need. I want to plant you inside as another set of eyes and ears."

"Me? But I'm a woman! The men will barely accept my presence, let alone talk in front of me."

"They will also view you with a certain amount of— let's face it—intellectual contempt. I'm hoping they'll be less likely to guard their tongues." He paused. "I also hope the novelty of having a women in lectures and demonstrations will distract from the questions you must ask."

"You know I'll do my best," Abigail said, trying to control her shaking voice. She assumed a man of Dr. Laniere's experience would have considered all the drawbacks, but she had to make sure. "What about one or two of the other students who...who do not seem to be in need of funds? John Braddock or Marcus Girard, for example. Wouldn't one of them be a better choice for this type of mission?"

The professor sighed. "For reasons I cannot go into, Braddock and Girard are both under suspicion themselves." He paused. "I hope you won't find it impossible to be objective where young Braddock is concerned."

Abigail's heart bounded into her throat. "I've no illusions about John Braddock's morals or lack thereof."

"It seems to me—in fact, one of the main reasons your participation in this little enterprise occurred to me—Braddock has demonstrated a rather marked affinity for you."

"You are mistaken, Professor," Abigail said in a suffocated voice.

"I rather think not," he said gently. "In any case, if you agree to the assignment, come by my office in the morning after rounds. I'll arrange to purchase your textbooks, equipment and supplies and meanwhile make you a loan of mine. You'll need to make appointments with each professor for tickets—which I'll pay for in advance—and be sure to see the dean for scheduling." He hesitated. "There's the formality of your application approval, but with myself and the four other faculty members who interviewed you tonight in your corner, you should have nothing to worry about." He laughed. "Except, of course, passing your courses! Do you think you can do that?"

"If Marcus Girard can do it, I can," Abigail said grimly. Or she would die trying.

Weichmann's breath wheezed in and out rhythmically as he and John followed Dr. Cannon around the pediatric ward Monday morning. Of course the rest of the group was back there as well, but Weichmann's debility hovered like a cloud, a reminder that there were some things even advanced medicine could not cure.

The thing about pediatrics, John reflected, wincing as Weichmann palpated the distended abdomen of a three-year-old little boy in bed four, was the noise. When children hurt, they screamed. Or whined. Or their mamas pestered the living daylights out of anybody who passed within a mile of the ward. Usually he could block it out, focus on the physical challenge. But this morning he found himself easily distracted. Wondering, for example, whether Abigail Neal had had the nerve to act on Prof's preposterous offer of admitting her into the medical college.

John hadn't minded helping her, loaning her books, teaching her to autopsy, accepting her help with the languages. There'd been no reason not to. After all, who was going to let a woman into medical college?

And then it happened. Dr. Laniere had lost his mind and decided it would be a good idea for *this* woman to invade the sacrosanct halls of medical academia.

Weichmann licked his lips and glanced at Dr. Cannon. "Professor, it feels like a lump—a ball of something—just under the skin."

"Really." Cannon brushed Weichmann aside and put his hands on the little boy's stomach. The child squealed. "Shush, bubba," said Cannon sternly, "the doctor's just checking on your tummy."

John exchanged glances with Weichmann. "The little guy's scared," John whispered.

"That knot's a bad one," Weichmann muttered. He looked at his hands, which were still trembling. Weichmann loved science, but was rather frightened of real people. "So, Braddock," he whispered with a sidelong look, "you run into any more burning bushes lately?"

John shrugged. "Breakfast was a bit lively this morning. Clem caught the toast on fire."

Weichmann laughed. "You know what I mean. I've been thinking about what you said. You think God cares what we do?" He glanced at the little boy, who suffered the professor's examination with tears leaking from the corners of his eyes. "Patients get well, patients die. We cut 'em up to find the cause, but by that time they're beyond help..." He sighed. "I'm losing focus, Braddock. I thought I knew why I wanted to do this, but sometimes it all seems...pointless."

Professor Laniere's words drifted through John's head. *Your real problem is spiritual, Braddock....Once I took off in a leap of faith, God began to prove Himself to me.*

It had been acceptable for John to discuss such matters with his professional mentor, a man of Prof's stature and experience. But a man did not admit confusion and weakness to his peers.

Evidently Weichmann hadn't the usual compunction. And Dr. Cannon had frowned over his shoulder at them. Twice.

John shook his head at Weichmann. "I know what you mean," he whispered, "but we'll talk about it later." He crowded closer to the attending doctor. "Will you operate, sir?"

Dr. Cannon pulled at his mustache, covering a pleased smile. "I most certainly will. This is a most unusual case, gentlemen, a malignant tumor rarely seen in a child of this age, probably a *fungus hematodes*. Notice the unusual size of the obstruction." He patted the child's thin shoulder. "Lie still, laddie, the doctors want to examine you. One at a time, gentlemen, slide your hands slowly, firmly across the abdomen, stopping at the tumor." He stepped back to allow the six students to gather closer. "Notice its firm, perfectly round contour. We will arrange for the surgical theater tomorrow morning and you may observe as I remove it."

John, who had waited with his hands warming against his body as he had seen Abigail do, took his turn to examine the presentation of the tumor's exterior. He gently pressed, expecting to feel something in the nature of a rock under muscle, but found less resistance—more of a jellylike texture. The little boy gave an involuntary yelp of pain, quickly swallowed when John smiled an apology at him. "Sir—" John looked around and found the professor engaged in making notes on a sheaf of papers. "If this is a tumor, shouldn't it come out now?"

Dr. Cannon looked up and frowned. "There is no immediate danger, Braddock. The thing's been growing for some time, and one more day won't matter. I wish to give my colleagues the opportunity to observe as I remove the mass—in the morning, when there are less distractions."

John made way for Girard to move in. Of course surgeries were in the nature of performances. The bigger the audience the better. If he were in Cannon's place he would have done the same thing.

He glanced at Weichmann. Or perhaps he wouldn't.

On Monday morning, due to unexpected complications in getting Abigail's supplies and textbooks settled, it was nearly nine o'clock before Dr. Laniere strode into the first ward with Abigail and six other first-year students in tow. Because the professor considered tardiness a sin punishable by hanging, his mood this morning was, in the words of young Ramage, a baby-faced cotton farmer's son from Booneville, Mississippi, "acid on persimmons."

The group finished its round of the ward in record time, and all would have been well had not a well-dressed woman of some thirty summers planted herself in Prof's path as they passed the pediatric ward. "Here, you!" She pointed, bosom heaving. "I've been waiting for someone to come for thirty minutes. I want you to look in on my son."

The doctor's countenance darkened at the woman's presumptuous tone, and Abigail tensed. She had discovered that the medical school's seven faculty members retained full attending privileges as physicians of Charity Hospital and divided the students among them for daily rounds, rotating them in and out of the various wards. The surgery wards were generally assigned to either Dr. Laniere or Dr. Cannon, depending on the severity of the injury or illness and Sister Charlemagne's mood at the time of admittance. The doctors' attitudes tended toward territorialism.

"This is Dr. Cannon's ward," Prof said reasonably enough. "Has his group not already completed rounds?"

"Yes, but I'm not satisfied with the diagnosis." The woman's face reddened. "What, if you please, is a *fungus hoematodes*?"

Abigail watched Dr. Laniere's expression go still. "How old is your son?"

"He is six." The woman swallowed. "He's in a great deal of pain and they won't operate until tomorrow morning."

"Hmm." Dr. Laniere's black eyes scanned his group of cowering first-years and fixed on Abigail, towering over the lot of them in the back. "Miss Neal. Is your Latin up to this one? *Fungus hoematodes*."

Terrified, Abigail cleared her throat. "*Fungus*—dating from 1529, parasitic spore-producing organism. *Hoematodes*—gathering of blood. It would be a cancerous growth which attaches to an organ and…" Faltering as the woman's face went ashen, she swiftly transferred her gaze to her teacher. "It can be removed with surgery."

Dr. Laniere nodded. "Yes, and those kinds of growths are exceedingly rare in small children. Perhaps it would be instructive for us to take a look. Mrs…?"

"DeFord," the woman supplied, looking relieved. "My boy's name is Roddy."

"All right, then. Gentlemen and lady—" he smiled at Abigail "—follow me."

At least she hadn't made a complete fool of herself, Abigail thought as she trailed behind the men into the pediatric ward. The sounds and smells here were unlike those in the adult wards or the Lanieres' home clinic. The nurses had done a good job of making the six little white iron beds clean and orderly, and straight-backed wooden chairs provided a place to rest for the few mothers in the room. But the fretful crying of the babies and the listlessness of the older children in all this spartan whiteness struck Abigail as nothing sort of depressing.

The professor seemed not to notice. He followed Mrs. DeFord to a bed in the center of the east wall, where a small blond-haired boy lay on his side. Tears slowly leaked from beneath his closed eyelids and dripped on the pillow.

"Roddy," said his mother, touching his hair gently, "this other doctor is going to look at you. Can you lie on your back?"

"It hurts, Mama." But he obeyed, drawing down the sheet himself to expose his midsection. There was a perfectly round egg-sized bulge on his right hip.

Dr. Laniere leaned over to palpate the affected area. "Did you injure yourself somehow, son?"

The little boy blinked. "I don't know. Me and my brother was playing in the hayloft one day, and the next this big bubble popped up."

The doctor glanced at his students. "Does anyone know what would be characteristic of a fungal mass? Texture, shape, color?"

The six male students looked at one another, avoiding the eyes of both the professor and Abigail. Several of them shrugged.

Abigail tipped her head, meeting the professor's eyes. "I don't know for sure, but common sense says such a mass would be lumpy, asymmetrical, hard to the touch."

Dr. Laniere nodded. "Correct. Touch this lump, Miss Neal." He moved aside to allow her space next to the bed.

Insecurity turned to curiosity as Abigail did a quick visual scan of the little boy's hip, then slid her hand over the protrusion. She looked at Dr. Laniere. "It has a jelly-like interior. That's pus—it's not lobulated like a fungus hematode would be." She paused, shaken by doubt. "Is that right, professor?"

His eyes lit briefly, although he did not smile—perhaps to avoid offending the boy's mother. "That's right," he said softly. "Good work."

A ridiculous burst of pride shot through Abigail, quickly squelched as she imagined the pain this poor little boy must be enduring. "So what will you do, Professor?"

"*You* tell me what we will do."

Her gaze went inward as she pulled up her meager store of information on abscesses. "Anesthetize him and open the hip. Depending on the location of the abscess, we'll lance and drain the affected area, then close him up, inserting a tube to release any remaining mucus that collects."

Dr. Laniere looked around at the young men listening to Abigail, mouths ajar. "Do you fellows see any reason to postpone the operation?"

"Actually, sir," said Ramage timidly, "if we wait, the abscess could burst and poison the boy within minutes."

"Then we'd better hurry," said Dr. Laniere. He touched Mrs. DeFord's elbow. "Do you understand the danger your son is in? I presume you have no objection to going through with the procedure."

"No—I mean, yes, I understand the danger, and of course you must proceed as you see fit." The woman bent to kiss her son's sweaty brow. "Mama will be right with you, Roddy, praying for you. Be a brave boy for the doctors." She backed away from the bed, glancing at Abigail with reluctant respect. "Thank you, miss."

Abigail nodded. "He'll be in very good hands."

"All right, then." Dr. Laniere patted Roddy's arm. "Miss Neal and Mr. Ramage, because you two have been brave enough to admit to having studied the affliction, you may both scrub up and attend me in the main operating theater." He turned to a nurse who had appeared in the doorway. "Our patient will need to be prepared for surgery. Be so good as to send Crutch to prepare the theater and then bring a wheelchair to transport young Mr. DeFord."

Abigail and Ramage stared at one another for a moment; then, galvanized, they rushed after Dr. Laniere, who was already halfway to the door.

Abigail could hardly restrain her exultation. She was going to assist in a surgery—because she had corrected the diagnosis of a tenured surgical and clinical professor. She had no notion how she had come into this situation—but suspected that it should be attributed to the intervention of the Almighty.

"Thank You, God, oh thank You," she whispered as she slipped into the washroom behind Ramage.

Chapter Fifteen

"What I want to know is how she managed this." John, lined up against the back wall of the peds ward with Girard and the other second-years, shot an envious look at Abigail. She stood quietly at Dr. Laniere's side as Dr. Cannon vented his feelings about his patient being co-opted by another professor.

"No explaining Prof's reasons for anything he does." Girard shook his head. "Thought old Loose Cannon was going to have an apoplexy right there in the ward. Still might." He glanced at Dr. Cannon's flushed cheeks, then Dr. Laniere's notably unrepentant countenance. "But Prof was right to go in immediately. Even *you* knew that lump didn't look or feel like a tumor."

"I'd have looked like an idiot, contradicting my professor. Still—glad the little boy's recovering, even if I didn't get to attend the surgery."

"You don't think they're really going to let her come to lectures, do you?" Girard's broad brow wrinkled. "I mean, a *woman* in the classroom—just ain't right. Might as well serve tea and put up curtains. She'll be fainting at the first sight of—"

"Girard, this is no maudlin wilting lily. You haven't seen her—" John stopped. He wasn't going to mention the autopsy. "—do an examination," he ended lamely.

Marcus made a rude noise. "Yes, I have. She's a pervert, if she can examine an unclothed body without losing countenance."

"It's not like that and you know it. After all, *we're* not perverts, are we?"

"Well, no, of course not. But it's different for women." Marcus was looking at him as if he'd gone round the bend.

Perhaps he had. Abigail Neal had turned John's life wrong-side out on so many levels there was no going back to normal. Whatever "normal" was. One minute she was all soft and feminine and confused—as she'd been when they danced together—the next she was taking over territory that had previously belonged to him. *You'd better study, Braddock.* What was a fellow to think about a woman like that?

The argument between the two professors sharpened into focus, with Abigail's serene face in the background. John looked at her more closely. There was a tiny crease between her eyebrows. And her knuckles were white where her fingers clasped one another at her waist.

John pushed away from the wall.

"Cannon told us to stay put, you moron," Girard whispered stringently.

Ignoring him, John moved next to Abigail, allowing his shoulder to briefly touch hers. She looked up at him, her expression shifting from that faint anxiety to annoyance. When he winked at her, her mouth pruned slightly.

Professor Laniere turned. "Ah, Braddock. Now that Dr. Cannon and I have gotten this situation sorted out, I believe we'll move on toward the schedule for the latter part of the day. You fellows may go for lunch, then report to my classroom for this afternoon's lectures." He turned to Dr. Cannon. "I trust this plan meets with your approval, Professor?"

Dr. Cannon visibly struggled not to argue. "Fine. But I insist on a faculty meeting no later than tomorrow. I wish to present my objections to the rest of the board."

Dr. Laniere bowed as John snagged Abigail's elbow and towed her along with him toward the door. "Come on," he muttered out of the side of his mouth. "Let's get out of here before you start something else."

"It wasn't my fault!" Abigail balked as he hustled her quickly down the stairs behind the rest of the students. "I could tell by Professor Laniere's face there was something wrong with that diagnosis."

"I'm sure you could. But Dr. Cannon is the *last* person you want on your list of enemies."

She shot him a look. "John, they're *all* my enemies— except Professor Laniere, of course. Nobody wants me here, not the doctors, not the students." Unexpectedly, her eyes glistened. "Don't pretend you like having a woman in the school."

"Of course I don't," he said, surprising her into a snort of laughter. "But Prof has made up his mind and until he boots you out I know what side my bread's buttered on." To his relief, her incipient tears had vanished.

"If you want to stay, you'd better not let the other fellows see any sign of weakness."

"Weakness?" She marched ahead of him down the stairs. "Is it a weakness to wish for one single friend?"

John clattered after her. "I'm your friend."

"Don't let the *other fellows* hear you say that."

"I think my reputation can stand it." They reached the landing and John moved to open the heavy front door. "Besides, it's time I quit spending all my free time cutting up with the boys."

"Indeed?" She gave him an amused glance as she passed him.

"Yes. My mother keeps telling me so, anyway." He looked up at the iron-colored clouds painting the afternoon sky. "It's going to rain. We'd better hurry."

She nodded, picking up her pace. "Supposing you suddenly reform—what are you going to do with this sudden massive quantity of free time?"

"I like experimenting. I thought I might invent something." It was the first thought out of his head, a random comment intended to make her laugh.

She rewarded him with her infectious chuckle. "That's a splendid idea. What are you going to invent?"

Clasping his hands behind his back as they crossed Common Street and headed toward Canal, John gave Abigail a sidelong look. She was taking him seriously. "A folding wheelchair," he blurted. "With an interior push wheel so the patient can push himself and not get his hands dirty."

"That's magnificent! You should really do it."

He hunched his shoulders, plowing his hands into the

pockets of his trousers. "It's absurd. I don't know anything about engineering."

"But you could find someone who does. You understand the needs of the sick and injured." She beamed up at him. "You're bright enough to figure it out—"

"John! Johnny! What are you doing here?"

John turned at the sound of his sister's voice and found her leaning out of the family carriage as it rolled down Canal Street. He waved.

"Stop, Appleton!" Lisette called to the driver. "I want to speak to my brother. Stop, I say."

As the carriage came to a halt with a creak of springs and rattle of harness, John leaned close to Abigail's ear. "Rescue me, I beg you."

She shook her head and smiled, but accompanied him across the muddy brick street.

Lisette's bonnet had disappeared inside the carriage, but the door suddenly popped open, exposing small slippered feet and a froth of petticoats. His sister beckoned imperiously. "Hurry, John! It's starting to rain and we want your company!"

"We?" He approached the carriage with no intention of obeying his sister's ridiculous commands. Making sure Abigail was behind him, he rested his forearm on the side of the carriage "Is Mother with you? Where are you going?"

"Not Mother!" Lisette bubbled with giggles. "It's Dorothée. We're on an expedition for new gloves and ribbons." She turned to speak to her companion. "Move to the other side of the carriage, Dorothée. We have to make room for John."

The carriage lurched as, presumably, Dorothée

shifted to the other seat. Sighing, John met Abigail's eyes. "I suppose we could ride with them as far as Bienville. I didn't bring an umbrella."

Abigail, clearly reluctant, stepped back. The rain was coming down in earnest now, soaking her hair and clothes. "Go ahead, I'll catch up to the others."

"Don't be ridiculous." He leaned into the carriage. "Move over, Lisette. Miss Neal will need space, too." As Abigail climbed in, he gave Appleton instructions to drive to Descartes's Oyster Bar, then got in after her.

If Dorothée Molyneux was less than enthused about sharing the carriage with a strange female—and an exceedingly damp one at that—she covered her chagrin by batting her eyelashes at John as he sank onto the leather seat beside her. He watched Abigail pull her skirts close, making herself as small as possible next to Lisette. Raindrops trembled at the ends of her black lashes, the long spikes accenting the green of her eyes, and her dress clung to her figure. John made himself look at his sister.

Despite Abigail's drenched aspect, Lisette seemed to have no trouble recognizing her. "Dorothée, I don't think you met Miss Neal at our party—it seemed every time I tried to introduce you, John whisked her off somewhere else. She is a fellow bibliophile and has done amazing and heroic things with John and his medical friends. And then of course, she answered the questions of the professors quite brilliantly. I promise I should have been absolutely *stricken* to have been so put on the spot."

Blond Dorothée, whose voice reminded John of a squeaky door, simpered. "What a positively ferocious brain you must have, Miss Neal."

Since Miss Molyneux's brain rarely contended with

anything more taxing than deciding which ribbon to add to a bonnet, John didn't waste time arguing with her. Besides, he thought, letting his gaze skate back to Abigail's amused face, Abigail did indeed possess a rather razor-like mind. It was one of the things he most admired and feared in her.

Abigail ignored the implied insult. "Thank you for taking us up, Miss Braddock. Your brother and I have to be back for a lecture in less than an hour."

Lisette's expression quickened. "What kind of lecture? John never tells me anything he's learning."

"Lise, you know you're ill at the sight or even the description of blood." John flicked a glance at Abigail. "Be careful what you tell her."

"I'd be faint at the very idea of touching sick people." Dorothée shuddered. "Indeed, Miss Neal, I can't comprehend how you can stand being with all those cadavers and…skeletons…and naked body parts!"

"I don't really think about it in those terms," said Abigail. "I'm interested in what makes people well. The body is so intricately put together that the slightest flaw sends it into imbalance. Yet most of us walk around healthy and whole. That's quite miraculous, I think."

John studied her. For a long time he'd denied the handiwork of Almighty God in designing the human body. Lately it had begun to seem only natural to believe.

"When John becomes a real doctor I suppose we shall hardly see him," Lisette sighed. "There are truly a great many sick and injured people in this city! Mama says she feels very sorry for Camilla Laniere because her husband is always at the hospital and bringing home one disease or another to the children. I could never marry a doctor!"

"If I married a doctor," said Dorothée with a thread of grit in her shrill little voice, "I should make him stay home in the evenings. How selfish—to endanger one's own family for the sake of strangers."

"That's quite a novel view of the responsibilities of the medical profession, Miss Molyneux," John drawled. "Not to mention those of a wife."

"My brother is the most unselfish person imaginable." Lisette frowned at her friend. "Why, he saved the lives of thousands and thousands of people after that fire."

John laughed. "That's a bit of an exaggeration."

Dorothée's blue eyes widened. "Of course I believe in charitable works," she said, flirting a look at John. "I only meant that the love between a husband and wife should take precedence over one's ideals."

"You are going to have quite a search to find a gentleman who will entertain such romantical notions, Miss Molyneux," said Abigail.

Though John agreed, the deep cynicism of her tone made him wonder. Her hands were clenched around her reticule, her lips tight.

But before he could question her, Lisette touched Abigail's hand. "I didn't say I agree with my mama. In fact, we had quite an argument with Papa last night." She looked at John. "That's why I'm so glad to see you today. I want you to ask him to allow me to go to college." Lisette set her little chin. "I want to learn how to do something that will help other people. If Miss Neal can do it, why can't I?"

"Because you're—" He stopped. *The daughter of a gentleman. My giddy little sister.* His gaze caught Abigail's, and the ironical look there shamed him. "What sorts of things would you do to help people?" he asked Lisette gently.

She shrugged. "I'm not smart enough for medical school, but I might like to be a teacher. I like children."

"You're going to have children of your own." Dorothée rolled her eyes. "You don't have to go to college for that."

Dorothée interference put John's back up. "I'll speak to Father next chance I get," he said but felt compelled to add, "just don't get your hopes up, Lise. You know how he feels about educating women." Just then the carriage drew to a stop in front of Descartes'. John looked out. The rain had dwindled to a fine sprinkle. "Here we are, Miss Neal," he said, opening the door. He stepped out and extended a hand to help Abigail alight. "Lisette, give my love to Mother. Miss Molyneux, your servant."

John and Abigail ducked into the oyster bar, a dark, smoky establishment patronized by law and medical students, as well as denizens of the docks. The decor was plain and rough, but the food cheap, hardy and freshly prepared. Abigail didn't seem to notice the overwhelmingly male company as she plunked herself on a stool beside John at the bar. In fact, she was so abstracted that John ordered two dozen oysters on the half shell and a couple of chicory coffees without her so much as opening her mouth.

He studied her tense profile for several moments after their drinks came—she simply held her cup in both hands, staring blankly at the mirror over the bar.

"Tell me, Abigail, why it is you don't subscribe to Miss Molyneux's penchant for romantic love between marriage partners."

She blinked and cut a glance at him. "What?"

"I'm curious to know if you're one of those women looking for all-consuming passion in a marriage partner."

"I shall never marry."

He laughed, assuming she was joking. But when she simply stared at him, his amusement faded. "You cannot be serious."

She shrugged. "Who would marry me?" A faint smile tipped her lips. "According to Dr. Pitcock, my head is too big."

"No—what he said is that you are surprisingly normal for such a bright woman. I suppose you think there isn't a man capable of keeping up with you."

She sipped her coffee, made a face, and pushed it away. "That's bitter." She shook her head. "I'm not so arrogant. But I've too much to accomplish to tie myself down to household and children." She gave him a wry smile. "Which generally accompanies marriage. Miss Molyneux is right in a sense—there are responsibilities that go along with committing to such a lifelong partnership. And when one party or the other is consumed with some outside passion, what you have is tantamount to adultery." Her lips tightened. "It's a difficult tightrope to walk and I will not place myself in the situation of making a choice between medicine and marriage."

"I think you're very cynical."

"No. I'm *realistic*." Her eyes glinted. "Don't tell me

you're actually thinking of marrying that little twit. She'd drive you mad inside a week."

"Of course I'm not thinking of... I'm not thinking of marrying anybody. It's just that I hate to see you cut yourself off from the possibility of... Never mind," he said hastily, catching the tray of oysters as the cook slid it down the bar. "Eat up and let's get back to class. I don't want to be late."

She picked up an oyster and slipped in a knife to expertly pop it open. "Your sister is surprisingly broadminded and educated. I like her."

John shrugged. "She's spoiled, of course, but she has a good heart. My father has several charitable enterprises that Lise dabbles in."

"Your father doesn't strike me as the charitable sort."

"He's been spending considerable political coin to bring better sewage to the poor sections of the city near the levees—which was largely his idea, by the way. He knows he's got to protect the homes of the dock workers for the benefit of his own livelihood." John rapidly put away his lunch as he tried to explain. "So his city improvements aren't entirely altruistic—but he's not as bad as some people paint him."

Abigail glanced at him, her expression unreadable. "How much of your father's business activity are you aware of?"

"Not much. Frankly, I'm not interested. As long as he pays my medical college expenses..." That sounded both selfish and ungrateful. "I mean, the old man's absolutely rabid about shipping, trading and building. At first he couldn't conceive that I was serious about studying medicine." John slid an oyster down his throat, remembering those months of icy silence between him and his family. "Went so far as to cut me off last summer."

Abigail's eyes flew to his face. "What about school? Did you have to drop out?"

John shook his head. "For a while I managed—I'd been putting aside my allowance, when I could. Finally swallowed my pride and asked Prof to see about having my tuition deferred."

"The faculty would do that?"

"Happens all the time. The professors are good about lending a hand to fellows who fall into arrears."

Abigail was silent for a moment. "I don't know how I'm going to manage," she said slowly. "I certainly have no money."

"It's an expensive education, Abigail." He wondered how far she'd actually go, what she'd give up to obtain her medical license. He'd never met a woman with more guts and determination.

"Yes. It is." She moistened her lips. "I hear there are ways of making money...under the table."

"Under the table? What do you mean?"

"This is a huge port, John, and smuggling opium is big business. Is that what you did?"

He stared at her open-mouthed. "I may not be the righteous specimen you think I ought to be, but I don't cheat or steal. Or smuggle drugs. And you'd better not try it either!" he added, for good measure.

"You know how I feel about opiates." Her expression was an odd combination of relief and curiosity. "I take it you eventually made up with your father."

He nodded. "Prof went to my father and talked him

around somehow. The Lanieres have influence with the governor, and the pater's got political ambitions."

"Your father sounds like a ruthless man."

"I suppose." He glanced at her half-empty plate. "We need to finish and get back to class. If you don't want those, hand 'em over."

Looking troubled, she shoved her plate toward him.

He ate the oysters, sliding them down one after the other in rapid succession. Yes, his father was ruthless, but how else would a man make his way from bayou fisherman's son to the owner of the largest shipping line on the Gulf Coast? Since when was John appointed to be his father's conscience? And what was Abigail implying anyway?

Over the next few days, Abigail kept her eyes and ears open as she followed Dr. Laniere around the hospital. Pending a meeting of the entire faculty, the other professors tolerated her presence in the lecture rooms, but only reluctantly answered her questions. Dr. Cannon in particular, as John had predicted, remained cold and contemptuous. The male students, except for John, treated her more or less as a joke.

One afternoon she arrived in dissection lab to find that her cadaver had a suggestive note attached with a string to the toe. Swallowing her furious embarrassment, she'd removed the note without comment, slid it into her pocket and proceeded with the lesson. At the first opportunity she'd given it to Professor Laniere. He seemed to think he'd be able to analyze the handwriting to discover the prankster's identity. Leaving it at that, she'd tried to dismiss her humiliation. If that was the best the "boys" could do in their desire to be rid of her, she had little to worry about.

But on the Monday of the second week of December, she sat at breakfast in the Lanieres' kitchen, reading with dismay—and mounting indignation—the morning edition of the *Times Picayune*. A second-page editorial wondered in derisive language what the medical school board members were thinking, to consider attempting the higher education of a woman, "thereby opening the doors to a most shameful liberality of morals which would ultimately result in the demeaning of pure femininity."

"What rubbish!" she muttered, folding the paper and handing it back to Camilla, who sat across from her feeding the baby. "Why must my morals always be called into question?"

Camilla slipped the spoon into Meg's mouth. "People attack when they feel threatened."

"Threatened? By what?"

"Some men worry that their control over their households will be upset. If you complete a professional degree, other upper-class women will follow suit." Camilla thumped the spoon comically against the table. "No more dependence on husbands and fathers. Complete anarchy will ensue!"

"But—I'm hardly upper-class." She thought about John's aborted response to Lisette's question in the carriage the day they had lunch at Descartes'.

"Perhaps that's the point. If women can give themselves independence with an education, social lines will inevitably blur. Think about it. One element of a man's power status is his ability to keep a wife in indolence."

Camilla shook her head. "Personally, I think the women of my class would benefit from greater mental and physical exercise. My husband agrees, which is why he has taken you on as a sort of project." Her smile was warm and a bit anxious. "Don't let him down, Abigail. He's risking his reputation to champion you."

"I have no intention of backing down, I assure you." Much more than Dr. Laniere's reputation was at stake here.

Chapter Sixteen

Friday evening John handed his hat and overcoat over to Appleton, who gave him a bluff "Family's in the Chinese parlor, mate" and waddled off toward the coat room like a cheery little tugboat.

John strode into the parlor to find his mother, dressed in plum-colored velvet, at the pianoforte twiddling over Mozart. His sister sat on the fainting couch yanking at the knots in a sampler held close to her eyes, her yellow skirts spread decoratively around her.

Looking relieved at the interruption, Lisette dropped the fabric and hoop. "Johnny! You're late."

"There was a jam-up on the street car line. A wagon full of cordwood spilled across the rails at Esplanade." He crossed to the fireplace and picked up the poker. "Where's Father?"

His mother turned on the piano stool, her mouth drawn into a moue. "He sent a note around an hour or so ago, saying not to wait dinner for him. Business delay."

Business. Nothing unusual about that, but John couldn't help thinking of Abigail's questions about his father's shipping enterprises—enterprises that had been the family income since John had been in short pants. There was no reason to think there was anything "under the table" involved. Smuggling opium, for instance.

John returned the poker to its stand with a clatter. "If you don't mind, Mother, there's a book I remember seeing in Father's study that I'd like to borrow. Perhaps we could delay the meal after all, while I look for it."

His mother rolled her eyes. "You men can't leave your pursuits and relax for more than ten minutes at a time." She sighed. "Very well. I'll tell Cook to keep everything in the warming oven for a bit. But don't get distracted and forget about us!"

Already at the door, he turned to wink at Lisette. "Me? Distracted?"

In the study he shut the door, then walked around the perimeter of the room, running his hand along the spines of hundreds of books his father had collected during his travels. Two of the walls were lined, floor to ceiling, with leatherbound copies of the classics as well as modern-day bestsellers. More than likely Father had actually read few of them. Phillip Braddock was a man of action, a man of business. Sitting for hours with his nose in a book would not have appealed.

Why, then, had he amassed this collection that would have made Abigail Neal stare with envy? Was it purely to make a gentlemanly impression on visitors?

John stopped at a long, narrow table on the inside wall upon which a teakwood humidor rested beside a tray containing a set of snifters and a corked bottle of fine brandy. Here were his father's true pleasures, tastes John used to associate with manhood and cosmopolitan polish. Because of the influence of a professor and a beautiful young woman, he now found more value in the knowledge contained in books.

And best of all, he'd come to know God in an intimate, life-changing way.

So what would his Lord expect him to do about his father's misdeeds—if indeed there were any?

He looked around, trying to pin down what it was that made him so sure Father was hiding something in here. Little things. The fact that, despite his father's complaints of his absence, John was never invited to spend time with him in this room. The odd comment about "concerns" in China. Nothing concrete enough to draw undue attention. But puzzling nonetheless.

John touched the humidor's latch and it swung open. He spun the carousel and let the dense odor of fine tobacco permeate the air. John had smoked his first cigar at the age of sixteen, but it wasn't a taste he'd cultivated for long. Conscious of his bodily health, he didn't like the way the smoke hampered his breathing, even though he knew many physicians who smoked. Tobacco wasn't for him.

Still, it was a minor vice, certainly not illegal and it didn't warrant any particular concern for his father.

No, there was something else. He was about to move to the big mahogany desk when the door jerked open.

His father stood in the doorway and stared at him for a moment, then advanced into the room, shutting the door gently behind him. "What are you doing in here?"

"Looking for this book." John pulled a copy of *The History of China* off the shelf. "Is Mother ready to serve dinner?"

"She sent me to find you." His father dropped awkwardly into his desk chair. His face was pasty, John noticed, except for the red veins in his nose. "But stay a moment—I want to talk to you without the women listening."

"What is it?" John tucked the book under his arm and sat down in front of the desk.

Maybe he could broach Lisette's desire to attend college. Abigail had already asked if he'd followed through, and a man should keep his word.

His father pulled a cheroot from his pocket and lit it. "It's that woman," he said. "The one stirring up trouble about the medical college."

John sat up straight. "You mean Miss Neal."

"Yes. As a trustee, I felt I should intervene before the reputation of the entire college is damaged."

"Wait. Father, you're not getting embroiled in that, are you? I assumed the faculty would be the ones making the decision whether to admit her or not."

"The faculty can be influenced. They should listen to reasonable minds, especially those of us with a financial investment in the college."

John stared at him. "What financial investment? Why, you've sabotaged my every ambition of graduating."

"Well, it's more in the nature of a loan." Father smiled sourly. "I'll have to credit you with determination, son. I decided that if my heir was going to be associated with the institution, I had best make sure it succeeds."

"Father, what have you done?"

"Only what was necessary." His father looked at the glowing tip of the cigar. "As you know, Gabriel Laniere's proposition to admit Miss Neal had found favor with some of the faculty. I have simply argued that the students whose diplomas will be affected should have some say in the matter."

"What do you mean?"

"Next week the matter will be taken to a vote of the student body. The faculty—even Dr. Laniere—agreed that if the students balk at Miss Neal's presence, she will be refused admittance." His father's shoulders lifted. "It's fair and reasonable."

If there was anything Phillip Braddock failed to control, John had yet to encounter it. He shouldn't be surprised at this interference. The students would vote Abigail down, of course. And having come so close to achieving her dream, she would be devastated.

"How much?" John asked quietly. "What did it take to buy that much influence?"

"There's no need to be crude." His father leaned forward to tip the ash into a granite tray on the corner of the desk. "But because you asked, I've loaned just under seven million dollars to the college."

All the air left John's lungs and his voice came out in a hoarse croak. "Seven million—Father, where did you get that kind of money?"

"Tea. Silk. And other necessary substances." His father's eyes narrowed. "I've worked hard to build my fortune and have something of value to pass on to you and your family. Which is why it's critical that you marry for political power."

John stared at him grimly, thinking of Abigail's questions about opium smuggling. Would his father consider the drug to be a "necessary substance"? "I thought I'd convinced you I want to make my own way. Neither your fortune nor your political advances mean anything to me."

His father slammed his big, meaty hands on the desk. "And I keep telling you, your precious medical college depends on it."

"We shall see." John rose and made his father a stiff bow. There was no possibility of him being open to Lisette's interest in college. "Mother and Lisette are waiting. Perhaps we'd better join them."

For a long moment they stared at one another. Finally, his father nodded and rose. The two of them left the room and walked side-by-side into the dining room as if they were casual acquaintances, rather than father and son. John didn't know how he was going to help Abigail, but he knew he had to do something.

And he was going to start with prayer.

Abigail had never heard such music in her life. Standing beside Winona in the third pew on the left-hand side of the little clapboard church building on Basin Street, she let it move her to tears and laughter. There were hymns, of course, like the ones she'd learned as a child at her mother's knee—like the one she'd heard Winona sing when she first came to live with the Laniere family. But the preaching was also interspersed with loud, emotional bursts of extemporaneous chants and choruses, echoes of an almost wordless energy that was foreign to her in every sense of the word. Still, she found herself stamping her feet, swaying and shouting "amen!" with the rest of the congregation. God seemed a real personality who hovered and yet infused, who was pleased and honored by His people's exuberant adulation.

When it was over and the congregation started filing out to shake the sweating preacher's hand, Abigail followed in the wake of Winona's family, almost in a stupor of joy. She felt electrified all over, as if she'd experienced the Scriptural text firsthand. *Enter into His gates with thanksgiving and unto his courts with praise.*

This was the fourth Sunday she'd attended church with Winona since that first time—the day they'd visited the Colored Orphans Asylum. The day she'd first seen real compassion in John Braddock. As she shook the pastor's hand, accepting his blessing on her week, she wondered if John had a place like this to belong to. Only recently had she become aware of the absolute necessity of surrounding oneself with likeminded believers. Faith without support became vulnerable to discouragement. She should have encouraged John to come with her when he asked. Selfish and self-protective of her to put him off.

Come to think of it, she thought as she walked home with the Caldwell family for lunch, she didn't know for sure the level of John's faith. He'd admitted never attending church with his family, but he'd solicited his mother's help with the orphans. The last time Abigail and Winona went back to check on them, they had found conditions much improved.

"Take care, Miss Abigail," cautioned Winona, dropping back from a conversation with her younger sister to hook arms with Abigail, "or you gonna be falling in one of these big old potholes and we'll never find you."

She steered Abigail around a rut in the road. "What's that weighing so heavy on your mind?"

Abigail hesitated. "I was thinking about John Braddock."

"Ohhhh." Winona's beautiful black brows went up. "Now there's a subject that'll keep a girl up all night. I told you he could charm the birds out of the trees if he halfway tried."

Abigail fought her embarrassment. "He seems to like you a lot—confide in you maybe—I was just wondering if you'd talked to him about—about God or church or—" She swallowed. "You know what I mean."

"He asks me questions sometimes, but I don't know that John Braddock opens up to anybody." Winona shook her head. "He's pretty sure of himself on most subjects." She slanted a look at Abigail. "Why don't you ask him yourself?"

"I rarely see him, now that I'm busy with classes. He's a year ahead of me, you know. It was just—being in church today, feeling so happy and accepted, I worry about John. He seems so lonely—well, except for those young men he runs around with. They hardly seem like elevating company."

"I dunno." Winona looked thoughtful. "That curly-haired boy seems all right. The one who came with him into the orphanage."

Abigail nodded. "Tanner Weichmann. He is nice, although he's a bit shy."

"Tanner," Winona repeated with a smile. "I didn't hear his name that day. They said they were going to get some help for the little ones, but they never did."

"I was just thinking about the orphanage. Mrs. Braddock has helped some, but perhaps she could think of some ways to get some more wealthy people interested in helping out down here in the District. Some of these folks work so hard in the cotton presses and sail lofts and at the docks." Abigail continued thinking out loud as she blindly followed Winona into her parents' home. "I worry about the children most. If we could just open up a free clinic for the women and children, maybe staff it with medical students under the supervision of a rotating doctor.... Not to compete with the hospital, but to bring the most basic care here where people live."

She looked up and found Winona grinning at her. "You sure are a dreamer, Abigail Neal. Wouldn't have known that about you at first."

As she passed the saloon on Franklin, Abigail scanned the row of horses and carriages tied to their hitching post. She hoped she wouldn't encounter anyone from either the medical school or the hospital here. Not that she had anything to be ashamed of, returning just to make sure Tess was all right. Still, explanations could be tedious.

She'd been planning to make the trip down to her old habitation eventually, but it was Winona who encouraged her to do it today. "You're a strong woman, Abigail," Winona had assured her as they parted ways at the corner of St. Louis and Marias. That big warm smile had lit the colored girl's dark eyes. "You don't got to be afraid of losing your place now. Besides," she added mischievously, "those Laniere children got so used to having their personal storyteller around, they'd send their daddy after you in a heartbeat if you decided not to come back."

Losing her place was the least of Abigail's worries now. She was more afraid of getting sidetracked by the desperate needs here in her old neighborhood. Certainly, she knew, there was immediate good she could do— even with the limited training she'd received so far. But she could best serve her friends by finishing.

Press on, she reminded herself as she knocked on the warped, peeling outer door of the tenement where she'd spent six months with Tess. *Don't look back.*

She was just about to give up and go home when the door opened under her hand. Tess stood there for a moment, her face a blank of surprise, before she flung her arms around Abigail with a glad shriek. "You came back! Oh, I missed you!"

Abigail returned the hug, strongly, laughing. "I missed you, too. But I've been so busy—"

"Come in, come in." Tess let go of her and backed up to admit Abigail into the little square entryway. The floor looked like it had recently been mopped, which was a good sign. Tess was a fanatical housekeeper when she wasn't plagued by depression. "I was just having a Sunday afternoon splurge, making tea." Tess bumped open the apartment door with her shoulder. "Have you had lunch?"

"Yes, do you remember the black girl we met in the Lanieres' kitchen? The housekeeper, Winona? I came down to attend her church and had a meal with her family." Abigail stopped just inside the door, taken off guard by an odd queasiness. It was almost as if the person she'd been when she lived here wanted to reinhabit her body. Which was nonsense.

"I remember. Sit down, sit down." Tess moved to the cookstove in a flurry of motion, waving at two wobbly chairs, new since Abigail had left. Other than that, Tess hadn't moved anything. Her old roommate might profess to be a rebel, but in practice, she didn't like change. "Della Tackwood has moved in. She's a singer at the Mermaid—she's gone to rehearsal and won't be back until late. You'd like her."

Tess continued to chatter as Abigail gingerly took a seat at the three-legged table and laced her fingers together in her lap. Apparently the loss of her baby hadn't affected Tess in the way Abigail had imagined it would. Abigail studied her friend as she poured tea into a couple of cracked mugs and stirred in a few grains of sugar. On second thought, maybe there was a brittle edge to her bright conversation.

When Tess set the mugs on the table and bounced into the other chair, Abigail laid her hand on Tess's wrist to still her frenetic motion. "Tess, this is me," she said quietly. "You don't have to pretend."

Tess's fingers tightened around the handle of her mug. Her eyes flashed to Abigail's face, stricken. "I don't know what you mean."

"It's been five weeks. Not a very long time for such a great loss."

"Oh. The baby, you mean." Tess sat back, looking away. "I didn't want a baby, remember? No husband. No way to feed an extra mouth. It's much better this way."

Abigail saw the start of tears. "I'm sorry, if you don't want to talk about it."

"No, I—it feels good to get it out." Tess pulled in a breath and held it a moment, clearly trying to gain control. "All right, I would've loved to have a baby, but I wasn't ready for the responsibility. And I learned my mother was right about men." She laughed. "You can't trust them to stick around, so it's best to avoid them."

Abigail thought of Dr. Laniere and John Braddock and other men she'd encountered in the last five weeks. Winona's father and brothers. There *were* good men, if one looked for them in the right place.

Then something in Tess's acerbic comment struck her. "Tess, where is your mother? Is she still alive?"

Tess's mouth tightened. "I don't know. I suspect she is. But she's got my sister and doesn't need me."

Abigail stared at her. "Why on earth would you say that?"

Tess shrugged. "I've been right here, half a day's train ride away and they've never come looking for me."

"Half a day in which direction? In Mobile?"

Tess's eyes widened—apparently Abigail's guess had been correct or close to the mark. "I'm not going back there. They didn't want me. Let's talk about something else. Tell me what you've been doing. You look so beautiful...so healthy and well-fed." With patent envy she examined Abigail's plain but neat dress of navy blue worsted. "The rich doctor's family must be treating you well."

Abigail smiled. "Tess, you won't believe it, but they've let me stay, and—and there's a possibility I may be allowed to study medicine. Maybe even earn a license to practice." She paused, then blurted, "God has been truly good to me."

Tess looked skeptical. "I hope you're not banking on that overmuch. You're the one who always said people will take advantage of you if you let them. There's got to be some catch."

"No, I was wrong." Abigail leaned forward, intent on making Tess listen. She'd always been so bullheaded, it was miraculous the two of them had stayed friends. "I've seen people who live their faith in Jesus—not like my father and that awful man he wanted me to marry."

Tess's gaze sharpened. "So that's it! I always wondered what you were running away from. Was it some missionary?"

Abigail almost laughed the question away. Once she'd gotten out of China, she'd refused to speak of Stephen Lawton. But if she expected Tess to trust her, perhaps she should return the favor.

She nodded reluctantly. "Mr. Lawton was my father's friend, a younger missionary from England." She spoke slowly, awkwardly. How strange to tell the story aloud after carrying it inside her head for so long. Once begun, the words poured out quickly. "After his wife died on the field, he and my father decided it would be convenient for me to marry him. Papa was terrified I'd meet and fall in love with a Chinese national and there were no other single white men within hundreds of miles."

Tess stared at her, lips parted. "I have to confess, my life as a spoiled rich girl doesn't seem so bad. How did you get away?"

This was the part that was so difficult to tell. Abigail swallowed. "There was another man who—who traded with the Chinese. Not a good man. He bought silk and tea in the bigger cities like Shanghai, but the villages like the one my family lived in were encouraged to become opium farms. My parents didn't see the harm because it seemed like a way for them to keep from starvation. But then my—my mother tried it and she…"

"Oh, Abby."

Wretchedly, Abigail met Tess's eyes. "She became addicted. Eventually she just…drifted off one day and never woke up. After she died, my father pressured me harder—" Tears overtook her, flooding down her cheeks and dripping from her chin to her bodice. "Papa wanted to be able to go out farther into remote areas and didn't want me to come, so he—he insisted Mr. Lawton would take care of me."

Tess jumped to her feet and flung her arms around Abigail's shaking shoulders. "The miserable villain! I told you men are no good! Especially religious men."

Abigail pressed her wet face into Tess's shoulder. "Tess, that's not always true—"

"Well, I haven't seen one. Anyway, what happened next? Obviously you're here and not in China."

Drawing back, Abigail wiped her face on her sleeve. "The opium trader came to the compound one day when my father had gone into the village. I'd thought and thought about what to do. You have to understand that by that point my faith in God had almost died. I had certain morals ingrained in me—I was not going to sell my body, not to Stephen Lawton, not even to buy passage on a ship back to America—but I had no compunction about lying. I told the trader I was an heiress. That my grandfather—my mother's father—would welcome me back to the States, if I could only find a way to get there, and that he'd reward the man who brought me."

"Abigail!" Tess's mouth fell open as she sat down again abruptly. "That's ingenious. But how did you convince him to believe you?"

"I'm such a liar," Abigail said, inwardly writhing in shame. "I don't know how God will forgive me. But I showed him my mother's journal. I had copied her handwriting and added enough details to make it sound like she was indeed a runaway heiress. I can be…very convincing when I try."

Tess laughed. "I'm sure you can. You talked that stuck-up doctor into making a house call on a girl he thought of as a prostitute." She shook her head. "So you sneaked away from the missionary compound and then what happened?"

"My protector took me to Shanghai and left me in a bordello for nearly a week while he transacted business. He was an agent for the same New Orleans company that had been transporting opium from China to the United States. He threatened to kill anyone who touched me, but Tess, you cannot comprehend the evil of the men who run those places. Even the places here in the District aren't…" She shuddered, remembering the dead eyes of the women who lived in that house in Shanghai—drugged, abused, hopeless. "Some of the younger ones, as young as ten or eleven, were brought to the States with the opium on the ship. I don't know where they went once we got here—I was too intent on saving my own skin." She paused, twisting her fingers. "I can't let the Toad find me. He'll find out I lied to him about the inheritance…and he knows I saw all the terrible dealings the company was into—the drugs, the prostitute trafficking. He'll kill me."

Tess gasped. "How did you get away?"

"When the ship docked, one of the sailors, a Creole, felt sorry for me and promised to help me. He hid me in a tea chest and delivered it to an out-of-the-way warehouse, but he just…left. I suppose he was afraid of the Toad. I got away from the docks and—"

"—and met me in front of the sail loft," Tess finished. "You've had enough adventures to last a lifetime, my friend." She shook her head. "What are the chances of this toad-man looking for you in the hospital?"

Abigail wet her lips. "Slim, I would have thought. Except for one thing. I'm almost sure it's John Braddock's father who owns the shipping line that brought me from China. He's the one who makes the Toad jump."

"Abigail! You're sitting right in the adder's nest!"

"I know. But I have the chance to earn a medical license! I can learn to treat the diseases and handle the injuries that affect so many helpless women and children. I've even thought about going back to China one day—"

"Are you crazy? After what it took to get out of there?"

"I know it sounds insane. But my life is so different now. *I'm* different. I have a gift for healing. There are so many people without hope…" She and Tess stared at one another, at an impasse, for several moments. Finally she sighed, gripped Tess's hands. She felt almost lightheaded. "I've told you all my sordid stories. You'll have to tell me yours."

"My little story is a nursery rhyme compared to that," Tess said drily.

Abigail smiled. "Well, one reason I came back today

was to retrieve my mother's journal. I left it in my hiding place in the bed."

Tess spread her hands. "Help yourself. I'm sure Della hasn't disturbed it."

While Tess cleared away the tea things, Abigail got up and knelt on the floor at the foot of her old pallet. From the beginning she and Tess had kept their meager store of valuables tucked away here. Her and Tess's ideas of what was valuable couldn't have been more different.

Reaching into the straw ticking, Abigail pushed aside Tess's little walnut box full of jewelry. Her fingers closed on the journal. Extracting it carefully, she sat back cross-legged and stroked the book's creased leather cover. Her thumb fanned the worn gilded edges, opening the book to a page near the front. She stared at her mother's lacy, feminine script.

It was Mama who had awakened Abigail's interest in Chinese herbs and acupuncture by recording what she learned from the village women early in their lonely isolation. Abigail had memorized the list long ago, the words as beautiful and strange as the plants they represented. Flipping another page, she studied the diagrams her mother had sketched, ink drawings of the supine human form, arrows and lines indicating acupuncture points. Tears blurred her eyes. Mama had willingly joined her husband in spreading the gospel. In the end her obsession with science had cost her her life and forced Abigail to run.

Now perhaps both those things—faith and medicine—would save Abigail's life.

Chapter Seventeen

Two major topics dominated conversation among faculty and students during Monday morning rounds. The medical professors were all in a tizzy over the proposed takeover of several classrooms in the east wing by the newly reestablished academic department of the University of Louisiana. The medical department claimed that, as they had invested significant personal funds in the medical school, they had a right to exclusive use of the buildings. There was to be a faculty meeting that afternoon to decide what course of action would best protect the interests of the medical school.

Normally such administrative controversies would not have been bandied about in front of the students. But the professors were distracted into indiscretion by a second issue of major debate, namely the admission of Miss Abigail Neal as a candidate for the MD degree.

After afternoon lectures, John sat in the back of the west wing auditorium, with Weichmann on one side and Girard on the other, occupying himself with his notes from Dr. Harrison's morning lecture and demonstration on ophthalmic diseases. Admittedly, however, his concentration was broken by the general buzz of humorous conversation which blanketed the room. The students had been summoned for a special convocation regarding Miss Neal's application. They were, in short, to vote yea or nay.

By the time Professor Pitcock, dean of the school, banged his gavel on the lectern at the front of the room to call the meeting to order, John's conscience was letting out a full-blown wolf howl. His fellow students were never going to vote for Abigail's admission. A similar situation had faced Dr. Elizabeth Blackwell, the first woman to be admitted to Geneva Medical College in New York, but she had only prevailed because someone had convinced the students Mrs. Blackwell's application was a joke and they all voted yea. No such prank would intervene here. John's classmates were, to a man, adamantly opposed to a woman in their midst.

For most of his life John had been encouraged to take the morally easy way out. If you wanted something, you either turned on your charm or used whatever stratagems or influence was at your disposal. Competition, however, was something else. In John's personal code of behavior, whatever was most difficult to obtain was the very thing he was determined to win. And the stronger his opponent, the sweeter the victory.

Therefore when Abigail Neal entered his life, with her rigid sense of justice and lockjaw determination to learn, he instantly recognized in her exactly what he needed to make him the man he ought to be. The only problem: her sex. On so many levels. She was his intellectual equal, but she was unqualified to compete as a student. She was beautiful and unbendably upright, and he wanted her as more than a classmate: he wanted her for his wife. But she was off-limits not only because of her class—his parents would never accept a bluestocking from the District as a suitable bride for the Braddock heir—but also because she would never give up her education to become a society matron. And beyond that, she deserved a man who would stand up to his friends on her behalf.

He wanted Abigail to have the chance to study and earn a license to practice medicine. But he was not at all sure he was capable of setting sail in a one-man boat bound to crash on the rocks of humiliation.

So while Dr. Pitcock opened the meeting with prayer and presented the agenda, John found himself literally sweating with conflicting desires. Thank goodness Abigail herself was not in attendance. He wouldn't be forced to watch her face as the male students ripped her character to shreds, laughing at her as a roaring good joke.

Weichmann nudged him. "Braddock, you all right?"

John opened his eyes, realizing he'd had them squeezed shut in prayer. "Yes, I'm—good night, it's hot in here." He yanked out his handkerchief and wiped his face.

"You look awful. Clem have one of her dinner parties yesterday?"

John seized the excuse. "You should have seen the gravy." He shuddered. "You think this vote on Miss Neal's application is on the up-and-up?"

Weichmann shook his curly head. "Dunno. Pitcock's not much for practical jokes, though Dr. Laniere might—" He straightened, elbowing John again. "Heads up. Prof's up to speak."

John realized Pitcock had taken a seat in the row of professors behind the lectern, clearing the way for Professor Laniere to step forward.

With his calm smile Prof surveyed the student body scattered around the amphitheater like ants on a hill. "Gentlemen," he began, "I trust you've all had a successful day in rounds and lectures. As Dr. Pitcock mentioned, the faculty has decided to broach the groundbreaking issue of allowing a female to enter the hallowed halls of medical education by bringing it to you, the student body, for a vote. We all recognize that the value of your own diplomas hinges directly and indirectly upon the standards to which the entire college is held. In previous years it has been deemed wise to restrict medical licenses in the State of Louisiana to those who are able to meet a rigid course of scientific requirements. Because those requirements are of a necessarily graphic and sometimes violent nature, the courses and practice of medicine have been assumed to be inappropriate for the gentle female constitution."

The rattling and whispering of the students had ceased the moment Prof took the dais. When he paused to scan the first two rows of students, face by face, John could have heard a pin drop in the silence. Someone coughed and received a scalding look from every pair of eyes in the room.

"But having lived with a particularly strong-minded woman myself for some fifteen years—" Prof smiled faintly when several people snickered— "I find myself perhaps more open to the idea of women in medical practice than others. Then, when I met Miss Neal and witnessed her intellectual capabilities, coupled with a gift for mercy and an unusually strong stomach for the harsher realities of the healing arts, I began to suspect we have found the first appropriate test case for admitting a woman to our college."

John's stomach had been sinking as the professor talked. He looked around at his fellow students and found on their faces a variety of expressions from outright contempt to amusement to rage. These young men might respect their favorite professor, but they were not going to allow a woman into their medical school.

He stood up. "Professor, I'd like to speak to the subject before we vote."

Prof stared at him, eyebrows aloft. "Braddock, I don't remember asking for comments. This is a very straightforward yes or no."

"I know, sir." John could feel a hundred twenty or so pairs of eyes scorching his face, but he kept his own gaze on the professor. *Dear Lord, help me, please.* "But there are some things my classmates don't know about Miss Neal—things *you* might not have thought of, in defense of her application." He took a deep breath. "I'll admit that at first I was resentful that you'd invited her to attend rounds with us who'd properly undergone the application process, paid tuition, met the qualifications. Maybe this was because, as you said, I'd yet to meet a female with the analytical turn of mind necessary for absorbing and processing scientific information."

An audible rustle of tension passed through the student body, all of whom were craning their necks to see the fool willing to admit the possibility of equality of intellect between the sexes. Several started to mumble to one another, an undertone that gradually became a muted roar.

Professor Laniere lifted his hand to call the meeting back to order, but John wasn't about to lose this chance to finish what he'd started.

"Gentlemen!" he shouted, and the roar reluctantly faded. "I beg your indulgence for just a few more moments. This may be the most significant decision you will be privileged to make in your lifetime. Because I fear that if we make the wrong choice now, we may not only forfeit our right to make medical history—we may become as a body the laughingstock of future generations."

A startled silence fell as he paused. Prof gave him a faint smile. "Go ahead, Braddock. But keep it short."

"Yes, sir. I only want to say that if we fail to give Abigail Neal the chance she deserves—indeed that she has earned—we'll be missing out on association with one of the finest medical talents to come along in our lifetime. Most of you have not known her as I have—" He endured a general snicker in icy silence, then continued with all the dignity he could muster. "I have watched her teach principles of good health to the underprivileged, with a clarity and simplicity only available to the truly learned. She routinely displays creative insight as to cause and effect and the ability to apply what she knows in diagnosis and treatment. Assuredly she has much to learn about the makeup and function of the human body, but I have observed an almost palpable craving to replace ignorance with wisdom. Such a tenacious and truly teachable nature, whether it be male or female, can only be an example and inspiration to the rest of us."

He looked down at Girard, whose embarrassed posture had begun to straighten as John barreled on. Weichmann gave him a soft "Hear, hear, old man."

Encouraged, he boldly looked around at the rest of his visibly confused and intrigued fellow students. "So I, for one, will be voting to allow—no, to *invite*—Miss Neal to become one of us. And I encourage you all to consider the fact that, because women will inevitably make their way into professional realms, we would be well-advised to choose to make the transition as smooth and painless as possible for all. Thank you, Professor. I return the floor to you."

John sat down amidst crashing silence, withdrew his handkerchief and mopped his face. In obedience he'd done all he could do. The results were up to God Almighty.

Abigail had stayed away from the medical college grounds all day, knowing that her fate would be decided late that afternoon. She had arrived at the fork in the road: Either she would be permitted to stay as a full-time student, officially allowed to matriculate with the men, or she would never go back.

It was an odd feeling, this abandonment to whatever might happen. For most of her life she had either run from threats or scrapped for what she felt she deserved. Not by chance, she knew, had her morning devotions included the beautiful reminder from Isaiah: "They that wait upon the Lord shall renew their strength; they shall mount up with wings as eagles. They shall run and not be weary, they shall walk and not faint."

Wait, wait, she reminded herself again as she helped change bed linens in the "unrespectable" women's ward. "The least of these" was what these women were, at least according to the people who funded the hospital. Not the nurses. They served each one, providing food and bandages and a listening ear to prostitutes and bar maids, exactly as they did in the other women's ward.

Abigail tried to follow their example, patiently ministering when she was so tired she could have fallen asleep on her feet. She had stayed awake until the wee hours, rereading her mother's journal. Parts of it made more sense now that she had a rudimentary knowledge of chemistry and bodily makeup. Mama had possessed an amazing knack for absorbing and analyzing the properties of plants and herbs. Abigail was longing to ask questions of short-tempered Dr. Girard to confirm or refute some of her guesswork.

But she knew she'd never be allowed to do so, should the students in that amphitheater vote to exclude her.

"Please, Father," she whispered as she struggled to change the sheets of a heavily pregnant woman with a gash on her forehead from falling down a set of stairs. The woman was not cooperating. "Please let them say yes."

"What's that, dearie?" asked Nurse Wilhelmina, who was expertly slipping a bedpan beneath a woman ill with syphilis.

Abigail dodged her patient's attempts to whack her on the arm. "Nothing, ma'am. I'm just praying as I go."

"A lovely habit to practice." She placidly went on with

her task. But at a commotion in the hallway she looked up frowning. "Those boys don't know how to approach a ward quietly."

"Abigail!" John Braddock skidded into view, panting, cheeks ruddy from the cold. His overcoat hung open, his stock was askew and his hat had apparently fallen off somewhere along the way. The longish wavy hair fell into his wide, sparkling eyes. "Drop that right now and come with me!"

"For goodness sake." She stood between the huge exposed belly of her patient and the door. "Can't you wait just a minute or two?"

"Abigail, this is important."

Abigail shook her head. "Wait for me in the hallway. I'll be with you in a moment." She turned to finish her task—and the woman's fist hit her in the side of the head.

Sighing, John hurried over to help her. "Here now, settle down." On the opposite side of the bed from Abigail, he reached over the patient and grabbed the loosened sheet, neatly lifting her toward him. Trussed in the sheet, she couldn't wave her arms. "Abigail, spread the clean sheet on that side. Then we'll swap sides."

To Abigail's astonishment, the woman relaxed at the sound of John's deep, calm voice. Perhaps having a doctor perform such a menial task had stunned her into submission. Whatever the case, the bed was clean, fresh and unwrinkled, the patient tucked in asleep, in half the time it would have take Abigail to do it alone.

She looked up at John as he whisked her out to the hallway. "Thank you—"

"You're welcome." He snatched her up in a hug and

whirled her around and around. "You're in! It was close, but they voted yes!"

Laughing, Abigail caught his shoulders for balance. "Are you sure? Put me down!"

"No. I mean—yes, I'm sure, but I'm not putting you down until you kiss me." He whirled her around again until she was dizzy, dancing her down the hall.

Her heart was pumping like a locomotive engine and she felt a ridiculous smile taking over her face. "When did it happen? How?" Her arms involuntarily slid behind his neck to keep from being slung into the wall with his wild waltz. "I don't think I believe you."

"I'm to bring you back to meet with the faculty. They'll tell you." He finally stopped spinning, staggering to a halt at the end of the hall. He dipped his knees to reach the doorknob without letting go of her and opened the door. Ducking inside, he backed against the door and shut it. "Here we go."

Abigail found herself locked in a most improper embrace in an empty room with a tall, strong, overexcited young man. A small frisson of...something shook her. Anxiety? Excitement? She looked him in the eyes and halfheartedly pushed at his chest. "John, we shouldn't be here like this. People will think—"

"They'll think I'm going to kiss you. Which I am." He grinned at her.

Her fear dissipated. "You're incorrigible," she said, squelching laughter. "I suppose you think you had something to do with my happy news."

"Of course I did," he boasted. "Prof was about to ruin the whole thing, being all truth, justice and the American way in his presentation of your case. Those boys weren't going to fall for that—they're entirely too selfish." He laughed and shoved a stack of papers out of the way, then set Abigail on the desk. He planted his hands on either side of her hips and leaned in close to her ear. "But I," he whispered, "convinced them of the *benefits* of having a woman in our class."

"Oh, really?" She turned her head and found his mouth half an inch from hers. "And what would those benefits be?"

"I'll tell you…" He kissed her cheek. "After…" He kissed her nose. "You kiss me." He kissed her chin.

Abigail felt like a puddle of warm butter. She had never been this close to a man who was not her father, particularly one with gold-flecked hazel eyes and golden skin and a gravelly whispered voice. She knew she was in deep trouble because her reputation was paper thin as it was. He could walk out of here and tell everyone that the stories about women brazen enough to apply for medical college were absolutely true. They were women who could be coaxed into kissing men they weren't married to, in closets.

"John." She swallowed, looking at his chin instead of his warm, inviting mouth. There was a small shaving cut in its shallow cleft. "Please think of my reputation."

Slowly he straightened. He sighed as he put his hands in his pockets. "Double drat. I keep forgetting."

Ashamed that she was sorry he'd backed off, Abigail twisted her hands together in her lap. "Thank you. What do you keep forgetting?"

"That it's no longer I who live but Christ who lives in me, and the life I now live, I live by faith in the son of God who loved me and gave Himself for me." He sounded so glum that Abigail laughed. "It's not funny." He wheeled to look at the door. "It's going to be dashed hard to keep my hands to myself when you're at school and the hospital every day."

"John, are you telling me you've given your heart to the Lord?"

Joy soared inside her breast again when he nodded and looked over his shoulder. "I suppose it was inevitable, with Prof preaching at me all the time and you looking so beautiful and passionate and prim." He turned toward her again, his gaze fixed on her face. "Just look at you! Who could see that and not believe in God?"

Tears suddenly blinded Abigail. No one had ever, in her entire life, called her beautiful. "Come here," she said huskily, holding out her hands.

He stared at her for a moment. "What about your reputation?"

"I won't tell if you won't." She tipped her head. "Will you kiss me, John?"

A slow grin took over his face. He bent his head, smiling lips capturing hers softly. A moment later he jerked away and backed against the door. "That's enough," he said hurriedly. "I have to take you back to the college and I don't want there to be any question—" He picked her up by the waist and lifted her to her feet. "You're right. No more sliding into offices until—Never mind." He yanked open the door. "I have to take you back."

Abigail suffered herself to be hustled down the hallway toward the stairs and then unceremoniously bundled into the carriage he'd left waiting on the street. She kept staring at John as he drove them the two blocks over to the college. He seemed preoccupied and a little embarrassed and wholly unlike himself. Changes in him—changes in her. She could hardly comprehend the magnitude.

She'd made it into medical school, an amazing feat by any standards. An answer from God bigger than she'd dared to dream. But...she had to keep reminding herself that the last hurdle had not been passed.

She still had to deal with the consequences of her flight from China.

Chapter Eighteen

Freedom. John was as happy as he'd been in his life. But he still had to deal with his father. He'd considered asking Abigail to come with him or Professor Laniere. A bit of moral support would have made the coming confrontation easier to contemplate.

But something about hiding behind a woman's skirts, or even asking his mentor to step in to speak for him, seemed cowardly. So he'd dropped Abigail off at the college, leaving the carriage he'd borrowed from one of the professors, and walked the three blocks to his father's office. Alone.

But not alone, he remembered as he waited for the street car to rattle pass, then crossed Common. The Lord had promised to be with him. He smiled to himself, turning north toward Rampart Street.

He said the word to himself again, relishing its new meaning. *Freedom.* Freedom from that restless feeling of always reaching for something beyond his grasp. Freedom from the pressure to perform. Freedom from looking over his shoulder to see who was catching up.

He slowed as the row of offices where his father leased space came into view, well-kept brick buildings with the trademark French wrought iron gracing their balconies.

John had heard the story a thousand times, how the old man built Crescent City Shipping from the ground up, starting as barely more than a teenager with a couple of dray carts and three mules. He'd delivered supplies for storekeepers and bricklayers, iron foundries and printing companies, running back and forth between the docks and the business district until he'd earned enough to invest in a couple of small boats which could make the run out to ships at the mouth of the Gulf of Mexico. Eventually the boats had turned into ships of his own and Phillip Braddock opened the office on Common near Basin.

John had spent hours here as a child, climbing under and around the big mahogany sea chest that served as his father's desk; picking up the spyglass on the table under the window to look out over the city; begging exotic treats from the businessmen who came to visit. As a teenager he'd lost interest in the shipping side of the family income, preferring to experiment with his chemistry set. Unaware of the obsession he was about to release, his father had given the apparatus to John for his fourteenth birthday and had a workshop built for him off the kitchen.

He opened the front door, setting its bell jingling. Nowadays he and the old man were as different as night and day—except, perhaps, for that characteristic streak of obstinacy. He smiled at old Mr. Starkey, who sat on his stool with a ledger open on the counter in front of him, his spectacles propped on top of his shiny head.

The lack of hair on top was more than made up for by the luxuriant gray side whiskers framing his full face.

"Johnny-boy!" The Scotsman slammed the ledger shut and came from around the counter to shake John's hand. "Hain't seen ye in a coon's age. How goes yer experimenting these days? Blown up yer ma's kitchen lately?"

John shook his head. "The last time I did that, she told me she'd put me out to sleep in the stable if I ever brought chemicals into the house again."

The old man cackled. "You was always an enterprising young pup. Hear yer growing up to be a fine medical man, top of yer class, right? Yer da talks about you all the time."

It was the first John had heard of any interest of his father in his studies. "Well, I'm working hard. I like what I'm doing." He looked around the otherwise empty office. "Is my father here? I wanted to speak to him."

Starkey's smile faded as he glanced at the stairs leading to the upper floor—his father's lair. "Crapaud's in with him. I was just about to leave for the day, but you can wait if you want, they should be done soon. They been locked in there for nearly two hours."

John frowned. He'd met his father's new agent, a nondescript roustabout with an ugly, smashed-in face, once or twice over the last couple of years and was not impressed. A man of little education and no refinement, he was not a man one wanted to engage in conversation. John supposed Crapaud must serve some redeeming purpose in his father's business.

"I'll wait." No sense putting off a bad job.

Fifteen minutes later he was still cooling his heels

staring out the window at foot traffic, battling rising impatience. A clatter of boots on the stairs brought his head around. It was the agent, followed closely by John's father.

"Follow up on the problem," Father was saying. He stopped two steps from the bottom when he saw John. "Johnny! Why didn't you let me know you were here?"

Distracted by Crapaud's quickly masked expression of contempt, John yanked his thoughts back to the subject at hand. "I needed to speak to you about something that has just come up." He wiped a sweaty hand down the side of his trousers. "Something important."

A frown darkened his father's heavy brow. "It must be important to interrupt your studies on a Monday afternoon." He reached the foot of the stairs and turned to Crapaud, who hovered, clearly interested in the exchange. "Crapaud, I'll release you to take care of your errand." He paused, a peculiar weight lending force to his words. "To this point you've not failed me. I rely on your discretion—understand?"

Crapaud dipped his squashed chin, a sardonic acknowledgment of authority. "I understand more than you think."

Dismissing his underling with a curt nod, John's father beckoned him toward the stairs. "Let's have this burning conversation, then."

John followed his father to the upstairs office, noting the fine wainscoting of the walls, the new carpet on the stairs. How could Father afford upgrades to the office and a seven million-dollar donation to the medical college as well? The business must be going very well. He trailed his hand along a fine ebony side table in the upstairs landing, new since he'd last been here nearly three months ago.

Their last conversation had been that head-on confrontation over Abigail's admission into medical school.

Breaking free wasn't going to be easy. He might resent his old man, but there was a deeply seated respect that had always kept him from permanently severing their relationship. And then, there was the need for his money, even though he'd insisted he wanted to make his own way. Praying for wisdom, John firmed his backbone. With God's help he'd stood up to his fellow students on Abigail's behalf. He could buck his father as well.

Freedom.

Leaving the door open behind him, symbolic of his intentions, he ignored the chair in front of his father's desk. Looking down at him might give him an advantage.

Father sat down heavily behind the desk. "Where are your manners, boy?"

"I'm not going to be here long." John tapped his hat against his leg. "Considering your unusual interest in the results of the vote regarding Miss Neal's application to the medical college, I thought I should be the first to inform you of its outcome. The students voted to endorse her application."

There was a frozen pause as his father stared at him. "And how did *you* vote, may I ask?"

John shrugged. "I may as well tell you—you'll hear it eventually—that I felt compelled to come to Miss Neal's public defense. I'm proud to say—I hope, I mean, that the results of the vote can be directly attributed to my remarks to the student body."

"Are you telling me," John's father's voice was ominously quiet, "that you publicly flouted my wishes?"

"Father, your interference has gone too far. Abigail Neal is more than qualified to pursue a medical degree, whatever the inconvenience to myself and my fellow students. And what is more, it's because of her influence that I've come to my senses and realized my need to surrender my life to Christ. I probably don't deserve her—and I have no idea how this is going to work out in practicality—but I plan to ask her to be my wife."

He'd almost said that out loud to Abigail, barely restraining himself with the realization that his proposal would be better offered somewhere besides an empty office. But articulating his desires to his father seemed necessary. His personal declaration of independence.

He had no idea how he was going to fund the remainder of his education. But if he had to give up his room at Clem's, move into the hospital and eat off the dole from the Church so be it. He braced himself for the explosion.

He should have known his father would never play by the rules of normal human discourse. His father began to chuckle. "Well, well, well. My own fire-breathing preacher, taking the pulpit under my very nose. I suppose I have Gabriel Laniere to thank for this. He's been trying to convert me for years. Now he's got hold of my boy."

"I made my own decision," John said with dignity. "But I wish you'd helped steer me toward God a little sooner."

The laughter on his father's face disappeared. He had

that *look* in his eyes. The one that had taken him from a straw-tick bed in a boilermaker's shed to a desk at the helm of the wealthiest shipping empire on the Gulf Coast. "All right, you hardheaded young whelp. Propose to her if you insist. But you'll end by thanking me for my *interference*." He stood, leaning over the desk, knuckles planted. "Now get out. I'm busy."

John opened his mouth to argue, but his gaze fell on the shipping manifest beneath his father's hand. It contained some odd items, which he promptly memorized. Abigail was right, but the answers had been here, rather than in the office at home.

Cold apprehension settled in his gut. Clearly his father was in no mood to listen to reason and threats would do no good. He'd said what he came to say and broken with his father. There was nothing else to be gained by staying. He clapped his hat on his head and wheeled for the door.

Abigail's skirts blew around her legs as she walked along the darkening levee toward Tess's room. The street was deserted, as businesses had closed for the day and most folk were inside preparing for supper. They were smart enough to get out of the cold.

She pulled the shawl Camilla had loaned her tighter around her shoulders. The erratic December climate had finally tilted toward winter, replacing the damp chill of November with a bone-deep icy wind that blew off the river and shoved its way into every pore of a person's skin. Abigail was remembering with something akin to fondness the suffocating heat of summer. When she got to Tess's, they'd pull close to the little cookstove for a bit of warmth. She couldn't wait to tell Tess what had happened. Maybe this enormous miracle would be the tipping point to convince Tess that God did indeed have good plans for His daughters.

The meeting with the medical college faculty had been awkward in the extreme. By the time she'd arrived, the eight professors had been apprised of the outcome of the vote. Judging by the generally acidic expressions, there had ensued some kind of battle over their promise to honor the students' wishes. When she'd taken her seat at the table in the first-floor conference room, only Professor Laniere had greeted her with his usual smile. Girard, Pitcock and Cannon clearly wished her at the devil.

"What's she doing here?" Dr. Lewis had demanded in his trumpeting voice.

"The students voted her in," explained Dr. Harrison, looking as if he'd swallowed embalming fluid.

"Nonsense." Dr. Lewis looked confused. "We don't have girls in medical school."

"We do now," said Dr. Harrison glumly.

In the end, they'd made her acceptance official—perhaps only because Dr. Laniere reminded them all of their word as gentlemen. In any case, Abigail was presented with a stack of matriculation tickets permitting her to finish out the remainder of the term with six courses of lectures, and including the right to accompany any of the eight attending physicians on their daily rounds at the hospital. She was to have full privileges in the chemistry and dissection laboratories. All eight professors agreed that if she refused to fully participate in what was expected of any student, she would be expelled.

Dr. Laniere had looked at her apologetically when

that pronouncement was made by Dr. Girard. "I'm afraid that's a nonnegotiable, my dear."

Putting up her chin, she'd stared them down. "And it's a reasonable rule. I see no reason I cannot comply with all requirements of the degree."

Afterward, when they'd dismissed her, so they might continue arguing over the particulars of the practical dilemmas created by their new student, she'd rushed outside and cast up her lunch in the bushes.

Now, attacked by doubts, she wondered if she hadn't been overly ambitious. How on earth was she going to anticipate every stumbling block put in her way by a hundred fifty resentful male students? And though Dr. Laniere had assured her that fellowships for worthy students were already in place, the financial aspect of the venture was frightening.

Lost in her tumbling thoughts, she barely had time to register the scuffling step behind her before a hand was clapped over her mouth, jerking her against a rough woolen coat and scarf. The impulse to scream burst against her throat, but the callused hand tightened, forcing her to gag instead. Before she could do more than awkwardly jerk her heel backward into her attacker's shin, she was hauled into a waiting closed carriage and thrown onto the seat.

"If you say a word I will kill you," growled her attacker and slammed the door.

Immediately she lunged for the door. It was locked from the outside, a cloth covering the window. The carriage lurched into motion, throwing her to the floor.

Her throat was so constricted with fear she couldn't

have screamed if she'd wanted to. Shuddering like a boat in a hurricane, she hugged herself. Her worst nightmare had just caught up with her.

Chapter Nineteen

John ran all the way from his father's office and found the Lanieres' house lit from top to bottom. He pelted up the front steps and pounded on the door.

Winona yanked it open. "John! What you doing at the front door?"

"I'm in a hurry. Where's Abigail?" He peered over Winona's shoulder. He could hear the sounds of the children playing somewhere upstairs. It was nearly nine o'clock. He'd have thought they would already be abed.

Winona stepped back, eyes wide. "You haven't see her? Doc Laniere hoped—"

"No—she said she was coming here after her interview with the faculty. I wanted to know what happened."

Winona bit her lip, then pulled him into the foyer. "Come in. Miss Camilla will want to talk to you."

"Why?" He didn't want to talk to Camilla Laniere. He wanted to talk to Abigail. He wanted to tell her she was right about his father. That shipping manifest on his father's desk had contained more than cotton and tea and silk.

Winona just shook her head. "I've got to help with the children. They're wild and it's time to get 'em in bed." She gestured down the central breezeway toward the back of the house. "Wait here. I'll go get her." She turned and darted upstairs.

John shifted from one foot to the other, turning his hat in his hands, wondering what was going on. He could hear Camilla's low, husky voice underneath a child crying and Winona shushing somebody. He wondered what had happened to Prof.

And where was Abigail?

It seemed like an eternity, although it was probably only two or three minutes, before Camilla hurried down the stairs. "John!" She grabbed his hand. "Are you sure you haven't seen Abigail?"

"No. Where do you suppose she is? When's the last time you saw her?" His stomach started to knot.

"I haven't seen her since she left the house this morning." Camilla went to the window beside the front door and twitched aside the curtain. "It's been dark for an hour. I don't like her walking by herself this late, I told her—" She wheeled to face John, her gentle face tight with worry. "Gabriel went back to the hospital to see if someone there knows where she went."

"But—wasn't he with her? There was a faculty meeting. They were to sanction the student vote, provide her tickets—"

Camilla was shaking her head. "Gabriel was going to bring her back home, but she wanted to talk to someone first, said she'd walk to the hospital, then take the street car home. John, when did you see her last?"

"Just before the faculty meeting. I picked her up from

the hospital and…and…" He swallowed, thinking about their delirious dance down the hall to the supply closet, where he'd kissed her. "And then took her to the college. I've been at my father's shipping office." He and Camilla stared at one another in mutual dismay. "I'm going to the hospital. Prof may not know where to look."

"If she's there, he'll find her, John. Be patient and let's see if—"

The door opened. Professor Laniere came in, sweeping off his hat. He stopped abruptly when his startled gaze met John's. He looked at his wife. "Has she returned?"

Camilla's face crumpled. "No. Oh, Gabriel, John hasn't seen her either!"

John crushed his hat between his hands. "Prof, we've got to find her. Do you suppose she went back to the District? She's awfully fond of those orphans."

Dr. Laniere frowned. "I suppose we could look there. What about her friend Tess? Would she have gone there?"

"That's possible." Relief lifted the weight off John's chest. "I've been there—when I delivered the baby. It's beside the saloon on—Look, Prof, let's split up to make this faster. You go to the orphanage and I'll try Tess. We'll meet back here when one of us finds her."

The professor nodded. "That's a logical plan." He addressed his wife. "Camilla, I'm afraid I'll have to leave you here with Winona and the children. But Willie's here if you need anything. I'll be back as soon as I can." He leaned down to kiss her briefly, then gripped John's shoulder. "Be careful, son."

John nodded. A toxic combination of fear and anger

fought for control of his gut. Abigail Neal had no business endangering herself and worrying all the people who cared about her. When he found her he was going to shake her—right after he kissed her senseless.

Sitting on a straw pallet in a warehouse storeroom, tied hand and foot with her back against a wall, Abigail stared at the Toad. He sat in a stout wooden chair cocked back against the wall, picking his teeth with his knife.

She hadn't seen many physically uglier men, but it was not his squashed-in face or the thin scar that ran from his right eyebrow across his cheek to his jaw that repelled her. It was the knowledge that he had contributed to her mother's death and her father's abandonment.

Then she reminded herself that Phillip Braddock was behind this despicable man. John's father. Impossible to reconcile. If his behavior earlier that day was any indicator, John loved her. How could he not know what his father had done? Dealing in thousands of dollars worth of illegal narcotics was one thing, but trading little innocent girls into prostitution.... Her mind recoiled.

And why had it taken her eight months to take action? Perhaps, at first she had been too numbed, too traumatized, to do more than change her name and bury herself in the District—until Tess's crisis jolted her to life again.

Now it appeared her fears had been justified. Phillip Braddock had finally connected her to Abigail Nieland. She'd waited too long to take the notes in her mother's journal about Crescent City Enterprises, not to mention her own experiences, to Dr. Laniere. She couldn't imagine why the Toad hadn't already killed her. Perhaps he thought she'd already talked. Perhaps they wanted to know what she'd told the authorities before they got rid of her.

She swallowed the nasty taste of fear that coated her tongue and froze her throat. She'd cut open a dead body and examined its inward parts. *Through Christ who strengthens you, you can do all things.*

The fear did not instantly go away, but remembering what God had already brought her through and remembering the lives she had touched, whose lives had touched hers, gave her courage. She forced herself to look at her captor, who sat flipping and playing with the knife. What had caused that awful scar? The eye that it crossed was white and dead.

Perhaps sensing her regard, the Toad grunted. "He'll be here soon." His accent was Cajun, the timbre deep and thick.

"Who?"

He didn't bother to answer the question, just flipped the knife again, a thick, brutal blade without shine. The steel haft came down in his palm. "You been here before."

"No, I—"

"Yes. Courrégé say so." The Toad suddenly smiled. "He be very dead now."

Abigail had no idea who Courrégé was, but the name made her think of courage. She looked away from the Toad's dark, smiling face. *He* was coming. Did that mean John's father? What would he do to her? Involuntarily her eyes closed. Her imagination, fueled by a week in a Shanghai brothel and eight months in the District, took her places she didn't want to revisit. *Oh, God. Are You with me now? You must be.*

At the sharp creak of hinges Abigail opened her eyes. The door slid open to reveal a well-dressed gentleman in a dark green overcoat and elegant hat which made him seem taller. John had towered over his father at Lisette's party. Now she could hardly believe she'd stood in the same room with Phillip Braddock, knowing the evil dormant under that polished exterior. She'd been completely brazen to breach the wall around John's privileged world.

Having never seen her himself, Braddock hadn't known who she was then. He'd stared right at her, contemptuous of her poverty and the lack of gentility that led her to seek an equal place in a man's world.

She should have screamed his corruption to the rooftops, but fear had strangled her. As it did now.

He spoke first to the Toad. "Well done, Crapaud. You've taken care of the sailor's body?"

"Aye." The front legs of the chair crashed to the floor and the Toad bent to slide the knife into a scabbard on his boot.

"Then you may go. But hold," Braddock added as Crapaud lurched to his feet. "What about the woman from the sail loft? Does she know what her friend knows?"

Crapaud shrugged his massive shoulders as he glanced at Abigail. "Mebbe. Don't know what our girl told her."

Braddock turned to Abigail, walked toward her with his hands behind his back. "So, Miss Nieland. What exactly *have* you said to your former roommate?"

All the blood seemed to leech from Abigail's head, and a strange buzzing infected her ears. Tess was in danger because she'd told her too much. She shook her head, unable to speak past the sudden thickness of her tongue.

"Now why do I not believe you?" Braddock sighed. "Women. Always lying to manipulate us poor fellows. Fabricating that story about your mother. Did you spin the same web for my son?"

"Of c-course not," Abigail managed to stammer. "I would never—it was the only way I could think of to get out of China."

Braddock sat down, crossing his legs as if he were in someone's parlor, rather than a warehouse stuffed with bales of cotton. He addressed Crapaud over his shoulder. "Perhaps you should take care of the Montgomery woman, just to be safe. Miss Nieland seems to have trouble remembering what she said to whom."

The four-block square area just north of the hospital and medical college, generally referred to as the District, had been one of John's favored haunts since he was old enough to slip out of the house without getting caught. But with his stomach in a knot over Abigail's disappearance, carousing was the last thing on his mind.

It took him fifteen minutes to run the short distance to Tess's apartment. He arrived out of breath, his heart hammering in his chest. He banged on the rickety door, hardly aware of the blazing lights and jangling music emanating from the saloon next door. *Dear God, please let her be here. Please let her be safe.* A desperate, perhaps childish prayer. But he meant it with all his heart.

He'd set his shoulder against the door to force it, when it opened suddenly, revealing Tess's irritated face. Staggering, John righted himself. "Is Abigail here?"

Her expression shifted to surprise. "Dr. Braddock? What are you doing here?"

"Didn't you hear me? I'm looking for Abigail."

"She isn't—" His dismay must have registered. She looked around, then yanked him inside the tiny entryway. "What's the matter?"

He just stared at her. He'd been so sure he would find Abigail here. "We can't find her. I was with her around six, left her at the college. She never went home. Dr. Laniere's gone to look there and the orphanage. I thought she might have come here to tell you—"

"It's that man! He's found her."

John took Tess by the shoulders. "What man? If you know where she is—"

She jerked away from him. "*You* should know. He works for your father."

"*Who?* I don't know what you're talking about."

"Some man she called 'the Toad.'" Tess wrung her hands. "I should have convinced her to go to Dr. Laniere immediately." Tears began to pour down her cheeks.

John was even more bewildered than ever. "I don't know of anyone my father employs called 'the Toad.' And why would he be looking for her? Is she in danger?"

Tess backed away from him. "I don't trust you. I shouldn't have said anything. Get out of here."

John wanted to shake her, but instead plowed his hands into his hair. He forced his voice to remain steady. "Listen to me. I *love* Abigail. I'm going to ask her to marry me. But I've known all along there was something about her past she wasn't telling me. If you know something about it, perhaps between the two of us we can find her."

"You're not listening to *me!* Your father has something to do with her disappearance, I know it. She was afraid of him. Even if I knew anything, I wouldn't tell you—"

"Tess!" he roared, frustrated beyond control. "I saved your life! I broke with my father this very day. I've known for some time his business transactions aren't always aboveboard, but as of today I'm willing to do something about it. And if he's behind Abigail's troubles, I swear to you I'll make him pay." He lowered his voice, aware that he sounded like a madman. "Please, Tess." He reached for her hands, gripped them. "Please, if you know where she is...."

She stared up at him, clearly torn between belief and fear. "All right," she said at last, returning the pressure of his hands. "All right, I've got to trust somebody. But I think we're going to need more than just me and you. Take me to Dr. Laniere and I'll tell you Abigail's story on the way. Maybe you'll pick up on something that will shed some light on what happened to her."

Relief weakened John's knees. "Good. Get your cloak, it's cold outside."

She shook her head. "I don't have one."

John shrugged out of his overcoat and dropped it around Tess's slender shoulders. "Come on, then. It's a long walk."

All Abigail could do was pray that Tess would be able to get away. *Father, it's not her fault she befriended such a dangerous woman as me.*

"So you used my agent for your own purposes," Braddock continued silkily as Crapaud slipped through the door into the night without a sound, "then disappeared the moment you landed in New Orleans. Crapaud investigated and found that there was no such family as Neiland in New Orleans. When he informed me of how he'd been duped—and exposed our company's unsanctioned enterprises in the process—my first impulse was to do away with him." Braddock sighed. "But my anger cooled as I realized he'd been acting in my best interests. Besides, why should I cheat myself out of a valuable employee?"

Abigail just stared at him.

Braddock uncrossed his legs and leaned forward, elbows on his knees. He steepled his fingers under his chin. "We have been looking for you for six months, Miss Nieland," he said softly. "And here you have been all along, right under my nose, seducing my hardheaded son. I wonder that he thinks you so brilliant. Appearing at a party in my home, exposing yourself to public ridicule by seeking a medical degree? These are not the actions of a smart woman."

"I did not seduce John," she repeated doggedly.

"But he is completely enamored with you." Braddock shook his head. "Which is why I have brought you here for this little chat. Despite what you may think, I am not a murderer. I simply have a proposition to make."

"You'd best let me go," Abigail said in a suffocated voice. "The Lanieres will be looking for me. John will be looking for me."

Braddock raised his heavy brows. "I suppose he will. My son has never listened to wisdom. But if you'll listen to reason, he'll forget about you soon enough."

"He's going to destroy you," she said with certainty.

She would have to enlist the help of Dr. Laniere to keep volatile, possessive John Braddock from sabotaging his career by exacting premature and violent justice against his father.

"No. No, I think not." Braddock tapped his fingertips against his lips. "Because you are going to accept my generous offer and disappear. I don't care where you go, as long as you keep your mouth shut and never again approach my son."

"Why on earth would I do that?" Abigail hissed. "You're insane."

"Oh, no, I'm in perfect command of my faculties." He smiled again. "And you'd best consider your response. As I told John, I've recently made a rather large loan to the medical school which would be jeopardized by any hint of scandal attached to my name."

"Your money is foul!" Abigail spat. "You made it in the course of farming and trading a narcotic that destroys people's lives. It ruined my mother! And you're shipping little girls overseas like cattle, trading them to brothels where they're exploited as prostitutes." She struggled against the ropes that bound her hands behind her back.

"There is no need to insult me." He sat back. "I made my money to take care of my family. I don't want them to endure the privations I did as a young man. And I certainly don't want my daughter soiling herself by associating with the likes of you. Which is another reason you must leave New Orleans. Lisette has become entirely too strong-minded since she met you."

"You cannot seriously expect me to just walk away from John and my chance to graduate from medical school." Abigail stared at him, panting. Should she tell him Dr. Laniere was onto him? Her skin felt like it was on fire. "No amount of money is worth—"

"I certainly do expect it. I cannot afford to lose such a valuable source of income as my opium trade." His voice had hardened, as if he'd suddenly tired of playing the paternal game. "And if you feel you cannot comply, you'll be sorry. I know where to find your father, and Crapaud would be most happy to bring his pathetic missionary efforts to a merciful close."

Chapter Twenty

John's body shook as he and Tess turned onto Canal Street, but he couldn't have said whether his tremors resulted from the cold wind whistling down the narrow deserted street or rather from his internal shock and anxiety for Abigail. Tess walked beside him, head bent, swallowed in John's greatcoat. She'd been silent for several minutes, letting him absorb the story of Abigail's escape from China.

Escape? A violent shudder gripped him as he imagined the degradation, the privation his love had endured since she'd landed in the great United States of America. Forced to lie to a criminal, she'd buried herself in the seamy underbelly of New Orleans to escape whatever vengeance he would exact when he discovered she had no rich grandfather. Six months of ten-to twelve-hour workdays, six days a week, to keep body and soul together, barely able to afford the paper-thin walls of a tenement room.

He glanced at Tess. God had indeed blessed Abigail with such a friend. There was something oddly refined in Tess's carriage; even her speech sometimes slipped into a cultured drawl not unlike John's own mother and sister. He'd paid little attention to these details when she'd been a patient in the Laniere clinic; now he wondered that he'd managed to miss her beautiful white teeth—indicative of a healthy diet for most of her life— and the luxuriant reddish hair expertly twisted into a fashionable knot. The typical lifelong prostitute who worked in the District rarely took such pains with her appearance.

No wonder the two young women had been drawn to one another. When it came down to it, they were peas in a pod: resourceful, strong, loyal. It crossed his mind to wonder about Tess's faith in God. Had it survived hardship and persecution as had Abigail's? What about the father of her baby? Who was he and why had he abandoned her?

The questions flitted across his mind, but bled away in his concern for the woman he'd come to love more than life.

"Tess, do you think Doc Laniere will know what to do with this information? He knows my father about as well as anyone. Why do you suppose he hasn't noticed or confronted him about it?"

She shrugged without looking up. "You know the great doctor, John. Rich people like him—like you— don't always react the way you'd think they would."

What did she mean by that? He grabbed the sleeve of the coat dangling past her hands. "You said Abigail had come back for a journal that day. Did she take it home with her?"

"I don't remember—" Tess's gaze flicked over his

shoulder, her eyes widened. "Look out! Run!" She took off.

A heavy body shoved John from behind and hurtled after Tess. Recovering his balance, John ran after the man, dove and tackled him. They fell heavily, John landing painfully on his left shoulder, but the other man quickly lurched to his feet. Rolling, John dodged a kick aimed at his kidney and jackknifed upright. He whirled to find his attacker plowing his round, bullfrog-shaped head straight for John's midsection. His father's agent, Crapaud.

John danced out of the way just in time. Too late to stop his forward momentum, the man staggered to his knees. John shoved him hard with a foot to the backside, but his opponent was more lithe than his stocky build would indicate. Grunting with pain, Crapaud flipped to his back, grabbed John's foot and threw him to the ground.

The breath knocked out of him, John lay unable to move, absorbing kick after kick aimed at ribs, face, groin. He could feel the warmth of blood pouring from his nose and mouth, pain taking over his body. The man was a bull, relentless.

But at least Tess was out of the way. Suddenly the beating stopped. John heard Crapaud's heaving breaths, even louder than his own, and a moment later, the snick of a knife coming out of a sheath. John was going to die here on the street, within blocks of the hospital. And Abigail was still in his father's hands.

He could not let that happen. Groaning, he tried to rise and protect himself. But before he could do more than shove himself to his knees, a blood-curdling rebel yell echoed along the street and running footsteps pounded toward him. He saw Crapaud's one good eye widen as he turned to look. Crapaud lunged with the knife, managing a swipe at John's upper arm before the new arrivals tackled him. John was crushed beneath the pile.

There was a confusing tangle of limbs and fists, cries of "Kill him!" "My turn!" and grunts of pain before John finally felt the melee roll off him into the gutter. Ears ringing, absorbed in pain, steadily losing blood, he simply let the battle rage. His vision went black around the edges until it overtook him, and still his thoughts, when he could grasp them, were on Abigail.

The blackness won.

She should have known John's father would be no weak pushover. Abigail had stared at Phillip Braddock long and hard, considering the consequences of each possible decision. She couldn't simply leave and overlook the things she knew about John's father. Besides, she had dropped enough hints to John about his father that there was every likelihood he'd already begun investigating. Once he discovered the truth, he would not keep quiet. On top of that, there were Dr. Laniere's suspicions to consider. He was not a man one could easily deceive.

On the other hand, telling what she knew would result in her father's execution. Papa might have been a less-than-stellar example of fatherhood; still she loved him too much to sign his death warrant.

The only thing left to do was to simply wait for rescue. So she remained stoically silent in the face of Phillip Braddock's blatant sneer.

Wait. The word now seemed to be the mantra of her life, when everything in her screamed for action. But the kind of waiting Scripture mandated involved the action of prayer: *Wait upon the Lord.* This she could do even while being gagged, rolled into a rug and unceremoniously hauled onto a man's shoulder. She could wait upon the Lord while being bundled into the frightening darkness of a closed carriage, tied hand and foot and barely able to breathe. While being tossed into a cart and transported, blinded and bruised, bumping along what smelled like the river levee, up and up a ramp onto the deck of a ship.

To be left utterly alone.

"Abigail," John muttered as a white canopy swam into his blurry vision. He blinked. The canopy shifted to reveal the creased forehead and crooked eyebrows of Miss Charlemagne. "I mean, Miss C."

She smiled and patted his shoulder. "Shush now." She dabbed a gauze pad soaked in iodine against his cheek. It stung like crazy and stank.

As he pushed to his elbows, pain radiated from his ribs throughout the length of his body. He looked around at the emergency ward at the back of the hospital. "How'd I get here?" Beyond the closed door, male voices clashed against the moderated tones of a nurse. That sounded like Weichmann and Girard.

Before she could answer, the door burst open and Girard's sandy head poked through the opening.

"Braddock—you're alive!" Girard, apparently wrestling with someone trying to restrain his entrance, spoke over his shoulder. "I'll be quiet. Mercy, what a fidget! We've got to find out what that rough-and-tumble was all about." He pushed into the room and shut the door behind him, obliterating nurse Wilhelmina's irate face. He hurried over to John and lifted his eyelid to examine the pupil. "Concussion. Lie down, old man, before you barf on my new waistcoat."

John ignored him, though he did indeed feel queasy. "I've got to go find Prof. Can you send Crutch to bring around a carriage? It'll be faster."

The nurse tsked. "I've already sent him after Dr. Laniere. Someone responsible needs to know what's going on around here."

Girard shook his head. "You're not going anywhere with cracked ribs and your mouth split like the Grand Canyon. I had to stitch you back together once already. I'm not doing it again." He studied John's face critically. "Neat job, if I say so myself—fixed your pretty mug good as new. Maybe I'll start a whole practice, re-doing people's faces."

John touched the stitches on his aching upper lip. He didn't care what he looked like as long as he found Abigail. "What happened to Crapaud—the man who attacked me?"

"With a name like that, no wonder he's so ugly. His ancestors must've worked long and hard to come up with a handle that means 'toad' and begins with—"

"What did you say?"

"I said it begins with—"

"No, the part about what it means."

Girard looked gleeful at the idea of one-upping John.

"You and your languages. *Crapaud* is French for 'toad,' moron."

"No wonder—" More pieces fell into place. John's head reeled and not just from getting beaten to a bloody pulp. "My father's agent was Abigail's liaison getting out of China. Tess must have known that. That's why he went after her and beat me when I got in the way."

Girard planted a hand on John's chest and pushed him flat on the examining table. "You're raving. What's your father's agent got to do with Abigail? She hasn't been in China, she's been right here shoving her way into medical school. And who's Tess?"

"Never mind that." John knocked Girard's hand away and rolled to the side. Panting, he sat up. The room spun like a whirligig. "I've got to get to the professor and tell him…" The rest of his sentence split into shards of pain exploding through his head.

Girard grabbed his shoulders and kept him from falling off the table. "Idiot—"

"I'm here." The professor's authoritative voice cut through John's agony. "Tess said she and John were set upon." A pair of strong hands cupped John's head gently. "Let's get him back down, Girard. We've got to keep him awake."

John felt himself eased to his back again. "No, Professor, we have to look for Abigail," he mumbled. "I think my father took her somewhere. Crapaud will know where—"

"Crapaud's the scum who beat him up," said Girard. "Locked in the storage shed off the stable. Didn't know what else to do with him."

"All right, you boys get him, bring him here. We can't

move John yet and I need to talk to both of them," Prof said. "Charlemagne, I've got the situation under control. Will you keep the other nurses out of the room and deal with any emergencies that arise?"

"Of course, sir."

A confusing series of footsteps ensued, the door opened and closed a couple of times and then John was alone with the professor.

"Braddock, are you lucid enough to listen to me for a moment?"

Thankfully, John's head had stopped its gyrations. He cracked one eye open and found Dr. Laniere staring at him, concern in every line of his face. "Yes, sir. What's going on, sir? I'm worried about Abigail. We can't wait around any longer—"

"Of course you're right. I had just gone home to tell you Abigail was nowhere to be found, when Tess barreled in, raving about an attacker. She's waiting outside the room in case we need her. Having heard her part of the tale, I think I understand what's going on. But you'll be more helpful to me if you know a few more details of my part in this mess." Prof paused. "If you can follow me. Are you all right?"

John swallowed his nausea. "Yes, sir," he said through his teeth. "I'm fine."

"Good. Keep your eyes open and listen. My background is a little more complex than the typical medical professional. Since my youth I've been...assigned to government service. Although semiretired, I'd recently agreed to assist the governor with uncovering the source of shiploads of opium entering New Orleans illegally.

You'll probably not be surprised to know your father was under suspicion—"

"No, sir. I'm not surprised."

"—which made you suspect as well. I'd set Abigail the task of watching for signs that you were involved." The professor sighed. "I didn't anticipate such violent results because I was not aware Abigail already had ties to your father's Chinese enterprises."

"I hope you know, Professor, I have nothing to do with my father's criminal activities." John anxiously surveyed his mentor's face.

Prof smiled faintly. "No, I don't suppose you'd be lying here on this table if you did. But I need to know anything that will help us find Abigail and stop your father's determined efforts to spread the scourge of drug addiction in America. It's already destroying China, and the empress is ready to declare war on anyone involved."

John pulled his whirling thoughts together. Prof was a government agent. Abigail had been set to spy on him. He let out the breath he had been holding. "My father has a fleet of six ships that ply back and forth between New Orleans, Asia and Europe. I know he doesn't always report what he imports, which is how he avoids some of the heavier taxes. Until recently, I never saw the reason to report any of this—it really seemed to have nothing to do with me." He met Prof's eyes. "But now that I know the Lord, I seem to have a new set of eyes...or something. I can't just stand by and let him steamroll over everyone. I can't let him ruin innocent people's lives." Painful, embarrassing tears warmed his eyes, and he blinked hard. "I'm sorry he's my father."

Prof laid a hand on his shoulder. "We'll sort out all

those feelings later, son. Right now, I'm grateful for your corroboration of what I'd suspected but couldn't prove."

The door opened, admitting Girard and Ramage, one on either side of Crapaud. The agent's hands were bound with a length of rope, his puffy face nearly unrecognizable. He had clearly been patched back together with less than the students' usual precision. The bandage which covered the top half of his head appeared to have been fashioned from his cravat and he winced every time one of his captors jerked on his arms. There was a large rip in the knee of his pants and most of his shirt buttons were missing.

John suddenly felt much better. This time he sat up slowly to avoid upsetting his head or his stomach. He still felt as if his brains might explode at any moment, but at least the room no longer spun. "What have you done with Abigail Neal?" He stared at Crapaud with loathing as John's friends shoved the man into a chair.

"You mean the Nieland girl?" The man sneered. "Ask your pa."

John glanced at Professor Laniere. "Do you know what he's talking about?"

Prof's expression stilled. "I hadn't considered that she might be under an assumed name." He walked around to stand behind Crapaud. "Is there something going on here besides smuggling?"

"I ain't telling you anything else until I know what's in it for me."

John had always thought of Crapaud as inarticulate and therefore not quite bright. Now he realized his father would never hire an agent who didn't possess a certain amount of diabolical cunning. "I'll make sure you're rewarded," he said, trying to prevent his tension from bleeding into his voice. One had to maintain a position of strength to influence this sort of man.

Crapaud didn't look impressed. "I happen to know every dime you possess depends on your pa's income. If he goes down, you go down." He shrugged. "You'll have to do better than that."

Professor Laniere suddenly clamped the muscle at the side of Crapaud's neck, near the collar bone. Crapaud yelped and Prof said silkily, "*You'll* have to do better than that if you want to avoid life in prison for kidnapping, extortion and slave trading. I imagine we can unearth a conviction for murder as well, if we look a little harder."

"Ow! Let go—All right, I'll talk. But I don't know where the girl is by now. When I left, Braddock—the elder one," he added with a contemptuous glance at John "—was trying to get out of her what she'd said to the red-headed gal."

Prof sent a warning look at John, who was getting ready to launch himself off the table at the scoundrel. "The red-headed girl would be Tess?"

"Yeah."

"Where were you having this fascinating conversation?" Prof wandered around to Crapaud's side, his hands clasped behind his back as if they had all day. But John could see the tension tightening the corners of the doctor's mouth.

"The company owns a warehouse on the New Levee. We took her there."

"I see. I'm sure they're gone by now, but—Girard, take Ramage with you and see what you can find. Come back here to report." The two young men rushed out, leaving Weichmann protesting that he "wanted in on the fun," but Prof gestured for him to be quiet. "I may need you here. Patience. Crapaud, I want to know where Braddock is likely to have taken Miss Neal—Nieland."

Crapaud's ugly face scrunched. He paused. "Maybe a pardon?"

There was a thick, waiting silence in the examination room. John could literally feel every beat of his heart in the pulse of blood through his battered face. He watched Crapaud's still, crafty expression. *Please, Lord, give the professor wisdom. I want Abigail back. I want her safe.* He didn't give a flip whether she was an heiress or a seamstress in a sail loft. He just wanted another chance to tell her he loved her and wanted to spend his life with her.

"I don't have the authority to issue pardons," Prof said finally.

"I know where she is, Prof!" John slid off the table, heedless of bruised ribs and aching head. The mental picture of Abigail seated at a window overlooking the New Orleans harbor, stitching grommets into a sail across her lap, had lit up his brain with sudden insight into his father's likely actions. When Phillip Braddock was cornered, he'd take to the sea. Appleton had told him tale after tale of his father as a young man, sailing off to the far corners of the world whenever the responsibilities of being husband and father got to be too much.

There were signs of it all over the house. John's chemistry set brought from Paris. The furniture from Egypt. The dining room chandelier from Germany. The Chinese silks for Lisette's dresses and the teas his mother loved so much. Only recently had he begun to slow down, when he'd taken on Crapaud as his agent.

John stalked toward the prisoner. "He took her to one of the ships, didn't he? That's the only place he could put her where no one could find her. We'd have searched all over the city and she'd be halfway to China." He snatched Crapaud by the front of his shirt and hauled him to his feet, heedless of his own screaming muscles. "Which one? Which ship is she on?"

"Hey!" Crapaud tried to wriggle free. "That's no way to treat a man who's just trying to help."

"I'll help you!" John shook him.

"Braddock." Prof set a hand on his shoulder. "Gently. I don't want you to hurt yourself."

Through a red haze John looked up at the professor, blinked and slowly released Crapaud, who sank back into his chair. Clenching his fists John scowled at the prisoner. "Where is she?"

"All right." Crapaud gulped. "The *China Doll*. That's the one he had ready to sail in the morning."

John looked at the professor, triumphant. "Can we send Weichmann and the Sears boys to search the others in port? Just in case he's lying?"

Prof nodded. "That's an excellent suggestion."

John looked at the other three students. "That would be the *White Pearl* and the *Dancing Dutchman*." He jerked his head toward the door. "Go."

Weichmann ran, leaving John and Dr. Laniere to haul Crapaud back to his storage room prison. They locked him in, instructed Crutch to guard the door, and headed for the levee. John limped along beside the professor, thinking it was high time he started carrying a gun or at least a walking stick. A man never knew when he was going have to play knight-errant.

Chapter Twenty-One

Abigail had no idea how long she had been left bound and gagged in the hold of the ship as it rocked gently at its moorings. Perhaps hours. She slept for a while and woke up astonished at her body's ability to relax when fear had her mind in a vise. She lay encased in the warmth of the rug—at least she could be grateful not to be cold and wet. She had managed to wriggle to the edge, so that the top of her head was in the open and she could breathe freely through her nose, but could go no farther. The buckle of her shoe had caught on a strand of the rug and because her hands were tied, she could not free herself.

Realizing the discomfort of her stomach was actually hunger, she listened for activity in other parts of the ship. She hoped someone would bring her something to eat soon. Random screeches of chains and the bangs of hatches opening and closing alternated with the voices of sailors preparing to set sail. The growl of hunger turned to the acid of terror. Phillip Braddock wasn't going to be interested in feeding a woman who refused to cave in to his demands. He was more likely to make shark bait out of her.

But the fact that he'd stuffed her down here, hiding her even from the sailors, told her he had some use for her. Where was he planning to take her? His ships went all over the world. Once they sailed into the Gulf of Mexico, John would never find her.

Sudden despair overcame the optimism with which she'd forced herself to pray since the Toad had thrown her into that carriage. Had God abandoned her after all?

A few minutes of helpless and perfectly useless tears, which served only to clog her head and make her eyes puffy, left her spent. And determined not to give up. The ship's hold was darker than she'd imagined a place could be, but she closed her eyes anyway. She might be alone, but in her helplessness she knew God's presence in a powerful and sustaining way.

She didn't know how much longer she lay there before a shaft of light pierced the darkness. Her eyes flew open, and she tried to scream against the gag but only succeeded in straining her throat muscles. Ineffectually she struggled in the suffocating binding of the rug. Footsteps descended the ladder behind her head. Was someone coming to release her? Or was it one of Braddock's men?

Oh, Lord Jesus, please, please, please. I'm here…

"Abigail?"

John! she screamed inside her head. *I'm here!*

"I can't see anything below the stairs, Prof. I'm going on down."

"I'll take the other deck," answered Professor Laniere.

"She could be anywhere. Look inside every barrel, every chest. There's no telling where he put her."

"Maybe we should've looked for him first. Made him tell us what he did with her." John sounded anxious, frustrated.

The very fact that he'd come looking for her sent waves of joy coursing through Abigail in spite of her discomfort. Again she screamed against the rag between her teeth. Maybe a slight sound had issued from her sore throat.

Facing upward, Abigail couldn't see John, but his footsteps had stopped near the bottom of the ladder. The lamplight swayed wildly back and forth across Abigail's forehead, making her eyes water.

"Abigail? Are you down here somewhere? Sweetheart, can you make some kind of noise so I'll know where you are?"

Sobbing silently, she gave a great sniff through her nose.

And the light poured across her face as John lunged toward her. "The rug! Oh, God, thank You!" He set the lamp down and laid his hands on the top of her head, petting her hair and laying his cheek against her forehead. "Be still, beloved, I'm going to get you out of here. Hold on, I love you, don't cry…"

It seemed to take him forever to untie the ropes around the rug—his hands shook so he couldn't manage the knots at first—and unroll her from her soft, warm prison. When she finally saw his face, her eyes widened in horror. He looked as if he'd been in a bar brawl. His nose was swollen and slightly off-center, and a series of stitches held his upper lip together. But as he regained his composure, he managed to unknot the gag.

"Are you hurt?" He worked on the ropes around her wrists. "What did he do to you?"

"I'm all right, just scared and hungry." The cotton texture of her lips and tongue made the words awkward. "John, I love you." She began to cry again. The tears seemed to proceed from a bottomless well of relief and terror. "I love you so much."

"Shh. Shh." He kissed her gently in deference to his broken mouth, and some of his natural humor asserted itself. "Jiminy, you're salty." When she laughed, he kissed her again and went back to work on her wrists. "Never mind, I'll have you free in just a minute."

"I'm already free." She threw her arms around his neck. "Praise God, we're both free."

"I think you should definitely go home to Mobile." Abigail held Tess's eyes steadily across the Lanieres' breakfast table. "You've waited far too long."

It was Tuesday morning, and the two of them lingered over coffee while Camilla hustled the children together for school. Baby Meg sat in Abigail's lap, sucking her thumb and shaking a rattle made of spools strung on a length of yarn.

Tess looked away from the baby's sweet face. She had only consented to stay overnight because John had convinced her Abigail shouldn't sleep alone last night— trauma and all that. But Abigail suspected that deep down, Tess wanted someone to convince her that she was done with life in the District, as Abigail was. It had just taken her a little longer to come to the sticking point.

"Abby, not everybody deserves a happy ending like you." Tess's voice was low, embarrassed. "They're not going to welcome me with open arms, you know. I was a selfish brat and took everything my father would give me before I left. I offended everybody who loved me, and—and I'd had another baby before the one who died in October. He's growing up with another family."

Abigail brushed her hand across the top of the baby's soft head. "Well, you won't know unless you go find out. You start by apologizing and asking forgiveness."

Tess's eyes flashed to Abigail's face. "Who forgives like that? It's too much to ask!"

"God forgives like that!" Abigail insisted. "You remind me a lot of the prodigal in Jesus's story. His father was waiting for him to come back. Saw him from a long way off and *ran* to get him!" She smiled. "That's you and me. We were both a long way off and needed to come home."

Tess didn't look convinced. "You never did what I've done. People did evil things to you, and you stayed pure."

Abigail sighed. "Oh, Tess. If you just knew how bitter and angry I was for so long. How I hated John Braddock for having everything I wanted."

"That didn't last long," Tess said wryly. "You were drooling over him the minute he took off that fancy coat and flexed his muscles."

"I was not!" Abigail hid her face in Meg's neck, blowing against her skin to make the baby giggle. She peeked and met Tess's laughing eyes. "But I admit he makes my knees weak now. Even with ten stitches holding his face together."

Tess laughed. "Looks like the stitches got him the day off from school. I see a couple of black-and-blue eyes peering through the window." She rose and went through the clinic to open the back door. "Come in, Sir Lancelot. Guinevere's dying to see you."

John followed Tess back into the kitchen. He pulled off his hat and coat and tossed them at a coat rack in the corner. His bruised eyes were on Abigail. "Tess, Meg looks like she needs her nappy changed."

Tess rolled her eyes. "I've never seen two people more in need of a chaperone than you. But I won't tell if you won't." She took the baby from Abigail's lap. "Come on, sweetums, let's go see what your mama's doing." She sashayed toward the hallway leading to the stairs, calling over her shoulder, "I'll be back in five minutes!"

Abigail smiled but instantly lost track of anything but John, who lifted her to her feet and gathered her close. She nestled her cheek against his wool coat, relishing the feel of his arms around her, the masculine smell of outdoors and strong soap. "Good morning," she murmured. "I was hoping you would come by."

"Prof told me I could sleep in this morning—in fact, he told me he'd suspend me if I showed my face before Wednesday—said I'd scare the patients if I came in the wards looking like this." He tipped up her chin and studied her face as if she were a rare and precious treasure. "Do I scare you?"

She couldn't help laughing. Besides the stitched lip and the shiner, his handsome nose now had a distinct sideways bend at the arch. "You make me want to stand on the table and dance."

"The dignified Miss Neal? I'd like to see it."

"Miss Nieland," she reminded him, sobering. She looked down at the waistcoat button she was twisting. "I'm sorry I lied to you."

John stilled her hand, covering it with his. "I understand why you did. And I'm sorry for all the tragedy my father's actions caused you." He hesitated. "In a lot of ways, we're going to have to start over getting to know one another."

Abigail pressed closer to him. "What's going to happen to your father?"

"He's been arrested and charged with trafficking in illegal narcotics. There's no telling what else they'll find in the investigation. My mother—" He swallowed. "My mother's taking it very hard. No matter what, she loves him. Abigail, I hate this for her and for Lisette."

"I know," Abigail whispered. "I'm so sorry."

"And I don't know how I'm going to finish school, with this hanging over my head. I suppose I shouldn't worry, but I…"

When he didn't finish, she looked up at him. "What?"

He looked a bit sheepish. "I don't have any business even thinking about it. But there's this beautiful woman I would like to court…and I'm afraid she won't even look at the penniless son of a convicted felon."

"Well…" Abigail's already-racing heart began to gallop. "Perhaps if you reminded her that you have a most outstanding academic record at the most prestigious medical college in the South, and that you stand to become a very rich and sought-after surgeon, she might consent to listen to your suit."

"Perhaps." A smile tugged at John's ruined mouth. "Do you think it would help to offer my services as a dissection lab assistant? I mean, supposing she decides to continue with her own medical degree?"

"I can think of nothing more romantic than a midnight tryst in the morgue." Abigail giggled. "And I'm fairly positive she means to continue her medical school adventure. What a waste to throw away all that effort!"

John pounced and kissed her, letting out a small yelp of pain at the pressure on his lip. He let her go reluctantly. "Drat." He fingered the cut. "How long does it take for these things to heal?"

"Probably longer if you keep opening it like that." She pushed at his chest. "Tess will be back in a minute. You sit there—" she pointed at the bench on the opposite side of the table—"and I'll sit here." Slipping out of his arms, she seated herself, primly clasping her hands in her lap.

For a moment he stared at her, smiling, eyes on fire. "Oh, all right. If you're going to be all proper." He reached across the table, palms up, and she laid her hands in his. "What about your father? Are you going to try to contact him?"

Abigail looked away. "I don't know. He wounded me terribly. I don't know that I need a father anymore."

"Abigail." John's voice was tender. "Family matters."

She stared at him fiercely. "*You'll* be my family. Tess is my family. Even Camilla and Prof. Not a man who tried to get rid of me for his own convenience."

"We're both going to have to practice forgiveness." John kissed her hand. "I will if you will."

She smiled at him, a fresh wave of tenderness and gratitude washing over her. "That's a bargain, Dr. Braddock."

Epilogue

"Dr. Braddock, you're wanted in the children's ward."

Abigail, seated at the desk in the second-floor nurse's office, looked up from her task of recording the injuries and subsequent treatment of a young woman admitted to the hospital this morning after a riding accident. John's handsome head peered around the half-open door. She gave her husband a vague smile. "Is it an emergency? I need to finish this report while it's fresh in my mind."

John slipped inside and shut the door behind him. "Of sorts. The McLachlin boy hid my otoscope and won't tell where he put it unless the *pretty doctor* comes to listen in his ears." He shoved her papers aside and sat on the corner of the desk near her elbow. "And I can hardly blame him," he whispered, leaning down to kiss the corner of her mouth.

"John! Anybody could come in here!" But she briefly yielded to his warm mouth, thrilled all over again at the knowledge she and John belonged to each other in every sense of the word. She pulled back and touched her thumb to the white scar across his upper lip, a testament to his devotion. "Oh, Dr. Braddock. You are a serious distraction."

Six months of marriage had not erased her wonder at God's provision for their every need. Even after John's graduation last May, which made him a fully licensed surgeon, they'd both had to work and sacrifice to afford Abigail's tuition. But somehow they'd made it, and Abigail herself would graduate tonight.

"I love you, Abigail," he murmured, cupping her face, "and I don't care if the whole world knows." He grinned. "But would you please come help me find my otoscope?"

* * * * *

Author's Note

This book required extensive research into the history of medical education in the latter half of the nineteenth century, particularly that of the Tulane University Medical Center, which in 1879 was the medical department of the University of Louisiana. I wanted to take advantage of the exciting advances being made in the medical profession during that year, so for the purposes of the story I veered from actual history by predating the entrance of the first woman into the medical school in New Orleans by sixteen years. Mrs. Elizabeth Rudolph was the first woman conferred the degree of Master of Pharmacy from Tulane University in 1895 (she had actually completed the two-year course in 1890 but was not allowed to graduate). Not until the 1915-16 school year were women admitted to all classes on an equal basis with men. Linda Hill Coleman of Houston, Texas, was the first woman to graduate from Tulane with a medical degree (John Duffy, *The Tulane University Medical Center*, Baton Rouge: LSU Press, 1984. 84-85, 136).

The New Orleans red light district was a real place

known simply as "the District." Early in the next century, it temporarily became a legally sanctioned region of prostitution known as "Storyville" (Duffy). I have tried to stay true to historic names of streets and streetcar lines. Because maps from that era are a bit blurry, it's possible that I've misspelled some names. For that I apologize in advance. On another note: to avoid defamation-of-character issues, I changed the names of all the professors at the medical college and created my own. There are no real historical figures used as characters, except those mentioned in the context of medical backstory (for example, when the students recount the development of surgical techniques and disease theory, and the mention of Elizabeth Blackwell's admission to medical school in New York). Charity Hospital was the university's teaching hospital and was fully staffed by Catholic nuns.

With regard to historical details, besides the Duffy book, I relied heavily on *New Orleans' Charity Hospital* by John Salvaggio, M.D. (Baton Rouge: LSU Press, 1993); *Antique Medical Instruments* by C. Keith Wilbur, M.D. (Atglen, PA: Schiffer Publishing Ltd., 1987); and *Bring Us a Lady Physician*, by Ruth Abram (New York: W. W. Norton & Co., 1985). I am also indebted to a December 2000 interview with Dr. Sam Eichold of Mobile. Dr. Eichold founded the medical museum associated with the University of South Alabama Medical School. He was most generous with his time, experience and resources.

For early critique help I would like to thank my usual partners in crime, Tammy T. and Sheri. Because it was the thesis for my creative writing master's program, this book also underwent the rigors of a most talented group of fellow graduate students. Alyson, Marylyn, Jeannie and Tammy S—you challenged and encouraged me, and I'm looking forward to seeing your work in print one day. I'd also like to mention my University of South Alabama thesis committee, whose feedback strengthened the manuscript immeasurably: Dr. Sue Walker, Dr. James Aucoin and the inimitable Carolyn Haines, thesis director extraordinaire. Finally, kudos to my editor, Emily Rodmell. You're the best!

Eva Kendall slowed her pace as she approached the training facility where she worked training guide dogs.

Using her key, she entered the training center, thinking about the male chocolate Lab named Cocoa that she would work with this morning. Cocoa was a ten-week-old puppy born to Stella, a gift from the Czech Republic to the NYC K-9 Command Unit located in Queens. Most of Stella's pups were being trained as police dogs, but not Cocoa. In less than a month after basic puppy training, Cocoa would be able to go home with Eva to be fostered during his initial first-year training to become a full-fledged guide dog. Once that year passed, guide dogs like Cocoa would return to the center to train with their new owners.

A few steps into the building, Eva frowned at the loud thumps interspersed between a cacophony of barking. The raucous noise from the various canines contained a level of panic and fear rather than excitement.

Concerned, she moved quickly through the dimly lit training center to the back hallway, where the kennels were located. Normally she was the first one in every morning, but maybe one of the other trainers had gotten an early start.

Rounding the corner, she paused in the doorway when she saw a tall, heavyset stranger scooping Cocoa out of his kennel. Panic squeezed her chest. "Hey! What are you doing?"

The ferocious barking increased in volume, echoing off the walls and ceiling. The stranger must have heard her. He turned to look at her, then roughly tucked Cocoa under his arm like a football.

"No! Stop!" Panicked, Eva charged toward the man, desperately wishing she had a weapon of some sort.

"Get out of my way," he said in a guttural voice.

"No. Put that puppy down right now!" Eva stopped and stood her ground.

"Last chance," he taunted, coming closer.

Don't miss
Blind Trust *by Laura Scott,*
available June 2019 wherever
Love Inspired® Suspense books and ebooks are sold.

www.LoveInspired.com

WE HOPE YOU
ENJOYED THIS

LOVE INSPIRED®
SUSPENSE
BOOK.

Discover more **heart-pounding**

romances of **danger** and **faith** from the

Love Inspired Suspense series.

Be sure to look for all six Love Inspired

Suspense books every month.

Love Inspired. SUSPENSE

www.LoveInspired.com

Looking for inspiration in tales
of hope, faith and heartfelt romance?

Check out **Love Inspired**® and
Love Inspired® **Suspense** books!

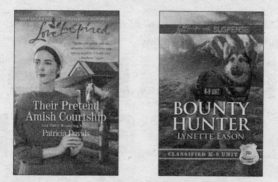

New books available every month!

CONNECT WITH US AT:

Facebook.com/groups/HarlequinConnection

 Facebook.com/HarlequinBooks

 Twitter.com/HarlequinBooks

 Instagram.com/HarlequinBooks

 Pinterest.com/HarlequinBooks

ReaderService.com

LIGENRE2018R2

When a young Amish man needs help finding a wife, his beautiful matchmaker agrees to give him dating lessons…

Read on for a sneak preview of
A Perfect Amish Match *by Vannetta Chapman,*
available May 2019 from Love Inspired!

"Dating is so complicated."

"People are complicated, Noah. Every single person you meet is dealing with something."

He asked, "How did you get so wise?"

"Never said I was."

"I'm being serious. How did you learn to navigate so seamlessly through these kinds of interactions, and why aren't you married?"

Olivia Mae thought her eyes were going to pop out of her head. "Did you really just ask me that?"

"I did."

"A little intrusive."

"Meaning you don't want to answer?"

"Meaning it's none of your business."

"Fair enough, though it's like asking a horse salesman why he doesn't own a horse."

"My family situation is…unique."

"You mean with your grandparents?"

She nodded instead of answering.

"I've got it." Noah resettled his hat, looking quite pleased with himself.

"Got what?"

"The solution to my dating disasters."

He leaned forward, close enough that she could smell the shampoo he'd used that morning.

"You need to give me dating lessons."

"What do you mean?"

"You and me. We'll go on a few dates…say, three. You can learn how to do anything if you do it three times."

"That's a ridiculous suggestion."

"Why? I learn better from doing."

"Do you?"

"I've already learned not to take a girl to a gas station, but who knows how many more dating traps are waiting for me."

"So this would be…a learning experience."

"It's a perfect solution." He tugged on her *kapp* string, something no one had done to her since she'd been a young teen.

"I can tell by the shock on your face that I've made you uncomfortable. It's a *gut* idea, though. We'd keep it businesslike—nothing personal."

Olivia Mae had no idea why the thought of sitting through three dates with Noah Graber made her stomach twirl like she'd been on a merry-go-round. Maybe she was catching a stomach bug.

"Wait a minute. Are you trying to get out of your third date? Because you promised your *mamm* that you would give this thing three solid attempts."

"And I'll keep my word on that," Noah assured her. "After you've tutored me, you can throw another poor unsuspecting girl my way."

Olivia Mae stood, brushed off the back of her dress and pointed a finger at Noah, who still sat in the grass as if he didn't have a care in the world.

"All right. I'll do it."

Don't miss
A Perfect Amish Match *by Vannetta Chapman,*
available May 2019 wherever
Love Inspired® *books and ebooks are sold.*

www.LoveInspired.com

LIEXP0419

Love Inspired®

Inspirational Romance to Warm Your Heart and Soul

Join our social communities to connect with other readers who share your love!

Sign up for the Love Inspired newsletter at **www.LoveInspired.com** to be the first to find out about upcoming titles, special promotions and exclusive content.

CONNECT WITH US AT:

Facebook.com/groups/HarlequinConnection

 Facebook.com/LoveInspiredBooks

Twitter.com/LoveInspiredBks

LISOCIAL2018